DEALING WITH THE DEVIL

VICKI THARP

JPC
Publishing

Dealing with the Devil is a work of fiction. Names, characters, places and incidents either are the product of the author's imagination or are used fictitiously, and any resemblance to actual persons, living or dead, business establishments, events, or locals, is entirely coincidental.

Original Cover Design by Designs EE

ISBN 978-948798-49-5

Cover Photography by: CJC Photography

Cover Model: Alex Sparrow

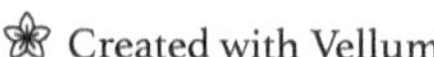 Created with Vellum

1

Run and never look back.

Jericho Saint gave all of his clients the same sage advice. Most heeded his hard-won words, though there were always some who didn't. But even the vast majority of those got away with one last trip back to their house or apartment. For some, like Nadia Bates, it was the last mistake they ever made.

His friends always told him that he couldn't save every person from their abuser. He knew that. He didn't need to save them all.

He just needed to save the ones brave enough to walk through his door.

It's not your fault. It's not your failure.

Maybe. But it sure as hell felt like it was.

Jericho sat in the parking lot of the Big Butte Casino, staring up at the massive lighted sign, his hands shaking even though it had been hours since he'd read the three short lines in the Murdock Daily News' online newsfeed.

If Jerome hadn't told him that Nadia had never made it off the bus, he never would have known that she'd been strangled to death in her apartment the night before. Strangled when she should have been on a bus to Cleveland, where a safe house waited for her and her unborn child.

But nobody knew she was dead.

Well, almost nobody.

What should have been front-page news in a small town newspaper had been reduced to three lines in the online police blotter because that same night, controversial shock jockey, Nathan Quest, had been mowed down on the streets of that same small town.

Murdered in Murdock, Wyoming.

The quiet little town nestled in the Rockies not thirty minutes from Alpine. The town almost no one had heard of was now on the front page of every newspaper in the US and trending on all the social media sites.

Were the police even looking for Nadia's killer?

Or would she be relegated to the back pages and internet rabbit holes, forever an unsolved crime because all eyes were looking for the killer of a man who probably deserved what he'd got?

Go home. Go home. Go home.

A casino was the last place a person with a history of compulsive gambling should go.

After reading the tragic news, Jericho couldn't stare at the four walls of his rented cabin any longer. Climbing into the truck, he should have known that he'd end up at the Butte, but fuck if he could think of anywhere else to go.

He didn't have to sit at a poker table and trade a stack of cash for chips. Instead, he could have a drink, or two, or more and take the elevator up to a room if the drinking got out of hand.

At least that's what he told himself as he hopped out of his truck and walked through the Butte's big double doors.

He didn't look right or left as he tuned out the all too

familiar sounds of the slot machines and the whoops, hollers, and laughter of the people trying their luck.

Instead, he kept his head down and followed the red and gold carpet winding its way through the casino. Where the carpet ended, he stared down at the polished concrete floor at the bar's entrance. Not much had changed in the years since he'd promised himself he'd never step through the Butte's doors again.

And as he fought that familiar pull of the poker tables, he realized that maybe he hadn't changed much either.

THE THING ABOUT THE PAST... IT ALWAYS HAD A WAY OF COMING back and biting you on the ass.

But what the past didn't know was that Cassie Kemp wasn't afraid to bite back.

And on the tenth anniversary of her estranged father's death, as she tossed his lucky poker chip into the air and caught it, she vowed to find a way to put the past down like a dirty, rabid dog.

She just didn't know if walking through the doors of the Big Butte Casino was the best way to do it.

The blast of forced heat hit her in the face and burned the evening chill off her exposed skin. That early in March, she hadn't expected so much of the winter snow to have melted, especially so close to the mountains, but Cassie would take her paltry wins where she could.

It might have been fifteen years since she'd last walked through the Butte's doors, but it felt like fifteen days—about as long as her father had ever managed to stay away from the casinos back then.

The same neon lights flashed *Winner Winner* above the floor overcrowded with slot machines. The same electro-techno sounds of the slots assaulted her ears. The same rumble-mumble of voices carried through the air. The same booze-imbibed cheers when someone's number came up on the roulette wheel. The same round of regretful groans when someone at the craps table rolled snake eyes.

And the same incessant pull of the roped-off room next to the cashier.

There were two men on a scaffold fixing the 'e' in the word 'poker' that had been burned out since her dad had first started sneaking her into the room when she was in kindergarten.

Probably couldn't get away with sneaking a kid in now, but her father had been on good enough terms with the dealers that Cassie had become their mascot.

She glanced around the casino and realized not everything had remained the same. As it turns out, the men repairing the burned out 'e' were not the only indication that improvements were coming to the Butte.

"Well, I'll be a monkey's uncle," came an all too familiar voice behind her.

She spun and launched herself into the arms of the burly man behind her. "Jimmy!"

The man caught and spun her around as easily as he'd had when she'd been a kid. He put her down and kissed the side of her head. At least he didn't give her the usual noogie and messed up her hair.

"Look who's all grown up and breaking hearts," he said.

Jimmy looked good. Really good. One of those guys who looked better with gray at the temples and creases at the corners of their eyes when they smiled. With his big, meaty hands and barrel chest, he looked like he should have been walking off the set of *Scarface* rather than haunting the carpeted floor of a Wyoming casino. All he lacked was a discernible accent.

"I don't know about breaking hearts." Cassie would probably

have to go beyond her typical one-night stands and get to know someone well enough to break their heart.

"Hey, Jimmy," a dealer in the Butte's signature uniform of black slacks, black vest, and shiny, ruffled red shirt called out from behind one of the Blackjack tables. "Whitehawk's looking for you."

"Mister Whitehawk still runs the Butte?" Nathan Whitehawk had seemed ancient when she'd been a kid, and for some reason, had always looked the other way the few times he'd caught her father sneaking her into the poker room on school nights.

"No. His son is running the place. He just started. That's why all the..." Jimmy waved his hands around, indicating the work to spruce up the place. Cassie was all for aging gracefully, but the old girl could use the facelift.

Jimmy's eye roll wasn't lost on her. "You don't like him?"

"He's a rule follower. He would never have turned his head and looked the other way when your father sneaked you in the way his father did, and that would have been a real shame."

"I don't know. Maybe that's not such a bad thing."

"*Psht.*" Jimmy waved her off. He looked her up and down from her high heels, to her mid-thigh sequined blue dress, to the sparkly bangles on her wrist, to the cascade of cubic zirconia dangling from her ears.

At least she'd grown out of the faded jeans and sports T-shirt phase of her life. Mostly.

"It doesn't look like it harmed you none."

Yeah, well, the emotional baggage didn't always come packed in a Hermes bag to throw over her shoulder for all the world to see. Not that she could afford a Hermes bag on an ex-EMS dispatcher's salary.

Jimmy leaned in and kissed her temple. "I've got to go before

Whitehawk comes looking for me. Great seeing you, kid. You going to be around?"

If she didn't chicken out on her hair-brained idea and run back home. But Jimmy had dealt cards long enough to spot someone who was bluffing, so instead of saying 'of course,' she said, "We'll see."

Jimmy's name was called over the loudspeaker, asking him to go to the manager's office before he could press her further. She watched him go, the sights and sounds of the casino slamming back into her consciousness. She rolled the poker chip across her knuckles the way Jimmy had taught her all those years ago and eyed the exit.

If she were going to do this, she didn't want to do it sober.

The last time she'd been at the Butte, she'd been too young to drink legally. So she commandeered a bar stool in a nearly empty bar and ordered a whiskey. She knocked it back with practice and ordered another, taking more time with the second.

When she ordered the third, the curvy bartender raised a dark brow and adjusted the pins holding her long black hair in a messy bun. Her tongue toyed with her thin, gold lip ring as she assessed Cassie. "Man trouble?"

The bartender had a kind face and a knowing smile that said she asked that question often.

Cassie's smile slipped a fraction, remembering what had brought her there. "Yeah, but not the fun kind."

The bartender fixed her drink and set it on a fresh cocktail napkin. "Not my business, but maybe you should pace yourself. The night is still young."

Even though the bartender couldn't be older than her mid-thirties, she had that combo momma/big sister thing going on that almost made Cassie want to tell her everything.

"You don't have to worry about me." Cassie glanced at the woman's name tag and appreciated that Kelly K. *did* worry about her. "There's a two hundred pound, booze-guzzling frat boy inside me trying to get out. I can handle my alcohol better than most men twice my size."

A man slid onto the barstool next to her even though every other stool was available. He leaned in and said, "Is that a challenge?"

Cassie spun in her seat to face him. He had bags under his red-rimmed eyes and that sexy bedhead look, but the natural kind, not the kind that takes hours in the mirror and a whole bottle of gel to materialize. He had an enticing curve to his lips Cassie wanted to kiss until the sadness left his eyes.

But she was here to exorcise her demons, not drag an unsuspecting man to her bed.

"Just an observation," Cassie said.

She looked him up and down. He wasn't twice her size, but the fir-green Henley he wore couldn't hide the bulge of his biceps. His hair fell over his collar, and it was hard to tell if that's how he normally wore it or if he'd been too absorbed in whatever he did to remember to get it cut.

From her time as a dispatcher at the Bison County Sheriff's office, she'd been around enough of the LEO and first responder types to pick up on his vibe. If he wasn't law enforcement, then maybe former military at the very least. One of those guys uncomfortable with their backs to the door and their head always on a swivel.

The bartender wandered over to take his order. He glanced at Cassie and asked, "Can I buy you a drink?"

2

Jericho wanted to slap some sense into himself as he looked at the nearly full drink in front of the beautiful blond beside him. Dumbest opening line in the history of ever. Plus, he didn't come to the Butte to hook up. He'd come here to drink up.

Though a woman like her with the short dress and the intelligent eyes could be just the distraction he needed on inarguably one of the worst days of his life.

Her lips twitched, and amusement lit her eyes. She took a long, pointed sip of her drink. "I have one."

He laughed. How could he laugh on a day like today? "Fair enough."

She ducked her head, though he had the feeling this woman in the shiny dress and the fuck-me green eyes was anything but shy. His stomach settled for the first time since he'd heard the horrific news.

"But I'm not opposed to a little conversation if that's what you're looking for."

He smiled, and it felt like an eternity since he'd had much of a reason to. "I'd like that. What's your name?"

"Are names really necessary?"

That made his smile grow wider. A woman of mystery. "No. Not at all."

The bartender delivered his drink and left them to their conversation to take the order of two men who'd walked into the bar holding hands.

Jericho took a sip, enjoying the burn of whiskey as he swallowed. The poker tables still called, but the woman beside him decreased their volume. At least for now.

He made a mental note to take his drinking up to a room if the draw of the poker tables became impossible to ignore. Bobbing his chin at her dress, he said, "Is this a celebration?"

"Of sorts."

"You play things close to the vest, don't you."

"Isn't that what gamblers are supposed to do?"

"You're not gambling."

Her wide, amused smile dove straight to his dick. He tried to ignore it as she leaned over and bumped her shoulder to his, her voice low when she said, "But life's a gamble, is it not?"

He clinked his glass to hers. "Touché. No names. No confessions. Got it."

"What brings you here?" she asked.

"Problems at work," he answered truthfully, though, with keeping with the theme of the night, he didn't feel the need to elaborate on his failures. Not that he'd want to in this instance.

And there came that devastating smile of hers. The one that stupidly made him want to wake up to a woman every day who smiled down on him like that.

You had that. And you ruined that. You don't deserve another chance at love.

"What was that?" she asked.

"What was what?"

She pointed at his face and made a small circular motion with her finger. "You lost your smile, and now you've got a crease between your brows. Did I say something wrong?"

"No. You're fine." He worked up a smile for her that didn't feel as fraudulent as he'd expected it would. "You're perfect, actually."

She chuckled. Deep. Derisive. And sexy as fuck.

You're not going to sleep with her. You're not going to sleep with her.

No. Definitely not.

"I'm far from perfect. But I'm okay with that. I think perfection would be exhausting." She took a long swallow, draining her drink to nearly nothing, and set it down. "Watch this while I visit the ladies' room?"

"Sure." Though if he were smart, he'd order a bottle and take it and his misery up to a room. After all, he had to get up early the next morning to get back to Elk Creek if he wanted to make it to his new job on time. He'd thought about calling out, but that wouldn't fly on his first day, especially when he couldn't explain why. And he needed the job if he wanted to continue helping people.

If his clients had the means to escape their abusers, they could usually do that without his help. It was the ones with nowhere else to turn that ended up at his door. And those documents didn't forge themselves, and those bus tickets didn't buy themselves.

But, like always, he didn't always make the best decisions when it came to his personal life.

He watched his mystery woman walk toward the restrooms. How she stayed steady on those high heels after a few drinks, he'd never know, but he appreciated what those shoes did for her calves and ass.

Cassie returned from the ladies' room, barely feeling the buzz rolling through her veins, noticing that Mr. Biceps had nearly finished his drink. She stumbled into him, and he caught her, not even noticing that she'd palmed his wallet.

Not that she intended to steal from him, but it was always good to keep her childhood skills current. While most kids had been learning how to play hopscotch or kick a ball down the field, she'd been perfecting card tricks, sleight of hand, and the prodigious use of sticky fingers.

She wasn't ashamed of her pickpocket skills. They'd come in handy more than a few times when her father had gambled himself into a rough corner, or he'd lost his paycheck. Keeping her fingers to herself would have meant going hungry that night or maybe for the rest of the week.

These days though, she only used her skills for a bit of good fun.

"Is it always this slow on a Wednesday night?" she asked the bartender, who was cutting up a bunch of limes. A few more people had wandered into the bar. On those occasions her father had sneaked her by, the nearly empty bar was nothing like she'd remembered.

"Wednesdays. And every other day of the week that ends in a 'y.'" She flashed Cassie a *what can I say* kind of smile, her lip-ring catching the light. "Most people these days usually go ahead and make the drive to the new casino."

"The one on the north side of the reservation?"

Cassie vaguely remembered reading something about the new casino opening in the Murdock News, but she'd been working double shifts in dispatch at the Sheriff's Office back then and had barely had time to eat and sleep, much less keep up with current affairs.

But now that she was unemployed thanks to a new job that hadn't panned out, she found herself with a lot more free time on her hands.

She sipped her drink and swallowed it down along with all of the self-recriminations that she couldn't stop heaping on herself. Her mom called her impulsive, imprudent, and always looking for the next shiny thing, just like her father.

And she was there at the Butte to prove to herself that she wasn't.

She bobbed her chin at the dregs of Mr. Biceps' drink. "How about I buy the next round?"

When he said yes, the smile that grew on his face almost made her feel bad when she produced his wallet and pulled a twenty out of it.

"Hey, wait..." he said as the realization dawned on him. Even though he recognized his wallet, he had to reach a hand to his back pocket to confirm it wasn't there. He eyed her, but instead of his face flushing with anger, he broke out another rusty laugh.

The bartender laughed as well, the tension easing out of the woman's shoulders as if she'd been ready to diffuse a bad situation. He pushed the bill across the bar, tucked his wallet between his muscular thighs for safekeeping, and said, "You have a light touch and amazing hands."

She dropped her voice to that sultry Lauren Bacall level that drove all the men nuts. "You'd be amazed what these hands can do."

Cassie rolled her eyes and smacked herself in the forehead. "Scratch that. I'm not trying to get you into bed. I'm just..." For the first time since the man sat down, she dropped her guard a fraction. But only a fraction. She didn't want him to see what a real mess she was. "It's been a day."

Whatever hurt that had caused the red to rim his eyes when

he'd walked into the bar returned, and she felt responsible even though his mood wasn't hers to protect.

"Tell me about it," he said as if he had his own demons to deal with. "What can I call you if you won't give me your real name?"

He reached up and fingered one of her dangling earrings. "How about Crystal?"

"They're cubic zirconia, but Crystal rolls off the tongue better. So, Crystal, it is."

He looked her up and down. "You don't look like a Crystal."

"That's because I'm not. What about you? I can't keep referring to you as Mr. Biceps. That's kind of a mouthful."

His eyes went to her mouth—as if he had very specific things he wanted her to do with it—before returning to her eyes. And damn if she didn't want to forget her troubles and oblige. "You noticed my biceps?"

"Among other things." Like his muscular thighs and his bulge, but divulging that information would only go to his head. "Are you going to pick a name?"

"You can call me Chad."

"*Oof*," she said, her lip curling up with an involuntary sneer. "I have an ex named Chad. And that's not a name I want rolling off my lips again, especially when I come."

He choked on his drink, and she had to pat him on the back until he managed to catch his breath again. And despite what she'd thought moments earlier, maybe what this day needed more than anything was a good fuck. If he were game.

Clearing his throat, he said, "You are direct."

"Is that a problem?" She'd never been ashamed of her sex drive. Sex made the world turn. And if a man expected her to be timid and demure, he'd better move on to another woman because that woman wasn't her.

When he smiled at her that way, with equal parts devilment and amusement in his eyes, it eased the tension in her chest and quieted the self-recriminating voices in her head. "Not from where I'm sitting. But since you shot down my choice of names, you're going to have to choose what you want to call me."

"Hmm... how about Steve."

"Steve?"

"Yeah. It's dependable. Who do you call when your computer gets a virus or your air conditioner needs repair? You call Steve. Steve gets the job done."

"I can't argue with that. Steve, it is then."

"Want to get out of here, Steve?"

He had a moment's hesitation before he said, "I do."

Cassie tossed the rest of her drink down and set her empty glass on the bar.

"Drink up." She stood, and when he finished his drink, she took his hand. "Come on. Let's make the best of a shitty night."

Jericho let Crystal drag him out of the bar. She didn't let go of his hand as they wound their way through the slot machines to the blackjack tables. She went from one to the other until she found the cheap ones.

"This okay?" she asked.

It wasn't a poker table, so he felt only minimal temptation. He had a gambling issue, but poker was his game. "It's fine," he said, declining to exchange his money for chips when he sat down at the table.

"You're not playing?"

"I'll have just as much fun watching you." All while avoiding breaking that promise he'd made to himself.

But you've already broken one promise you made just by walking through those doors. What's it going to hurt to break another?

Jericho ignored the destructive voice that had controlled his life for too many years. It had already cost him so much. A job. A woman he loved. Hell, he'd been inches from losing himself.

It had been a woman needing his help who'd stolen his focus when all he'd wanted to do was take the last few dollars in his pocket and find a poker game at the casinos or some illegal backroom.

His new obsession helping people escape abusive relationships had at times proved to be a bigger gamble than poker. Only with his new obsession, he stood to lose more than money. He stood to lose his freedom. Though considering the women—and some men—he'd helped escape horrible situations over the past few years, it had been worth the risk.

But he was very careful to keep his document forgery business on the down-low. The law considered it illegal. Black and white. But somewhere in it all, his moral compass had found the gray area.

After all, if the law couldn't keep these people safe, and he could, were the forgeries really all that terrible?

He'd been unable to save his mother from his father. And now, he could never say no when someone needed his help disappearing. He just hoped his illegal activity wouldn't catch up with him.

He often thought he should feel bad for breaking the law, but law enforcement could only do so much to help these people, and a restraining order never stopped someone intent on causing harm.

Not even his father.

With it being a slow night, the dealer allowed Jericho to sit in the chair at the end next to Crystal. It was a seven-person table, and even with him there, two seats were open.

"I'll have to ask you to move if more people want to join," the dealer said.

"Yeah, sure."

There was another woman at the table sandwiched between two men. The man beside Crystal leaned in, his hand going to her thigh as he whispered something in her ear. Jericho expected her to stiffen, for her smile to drop, or for her to look to Jericho to jump in and help.

As it was, it was all he could do not to take the guy by the collar and drag him into a back alley. She caught Jericho's nearly subconscious move in the man's direction and gave him a slight shake of her head.

Maybe she knew this asshole. An old lover, boyfriend, hookup?

The dealer started dealing the first hand. Crystal glanced over at the short man beside her with the balding head and deep wrinkles around his eyes.

She said, "Jimmy, could you kindly tell the gentleman on my right that I have trained with the best sous chefs in Paris and if he doesn't get his clammy hand off my thigh, I will fillet his nuts and serve them up to him in a rarefied truffle sauce?"

Jericho choked on an astonished laugh. The dealer's eyes shot to the man beside her. The man in question snatched his hand back. The woman on the other side of him shoved out of her seat. "You're a fucking pig, Blaine. I should have known better than to give you a second chance."

She stormed off, leaving about twenty dollars worth of chips on the table. The other man just looked at his friend with a reproachful shake of his head and said, "*Dude.*"

"Want me to get security," Jimmy, the dealer asked.

"I don't think that will be necessary." Then with a pointed stare at Blaine, Crystal said, "Do you?"

The man shifted in his seat, his hand subconsciously covering his balls. "No, ma'am."

In the time it took for the two men to run out of money and several sets of players to come and go, Jericho watched Crystal's original stack of chips double. As expected, she didn't win every hand, but she knew the rules and the odds. She split her hand when she should, doubled down when she could, and bet the minimum when she must.

Jericho kept his mouth shut because she clearly knew her way around a blackjack table, and he liked his balls intact and between his legs.

She kept checking her watch and glancing over her shoulder as if expecting someone. Jericho deflated. He should have known this dynamic woman was too good to be true. Of course, she would be with someone.

"Hot date?" Jericho leaned in and asked after she won another hand and checked the time.

"I'm not passing the time with you until something better comes along if that's what you're asking." That simple statement made the tension brewing in his gut dissipate, which was stupid. He hadn't come here to meet women.

But you did come here to forget.

"There it is again," Crystal said as she generously tipped the dealer and cashed out. He guessed that meant they were done. At least at that table.

"I don't know what you're talking about." He stood and helped her to her feet.

The lie came quickly and easily, even as he wondered how she read him so well. His ability to shutter his emotions was part of what had made him so good at poker. Luckily, he wasn't playing poker with her. He had a feeling he would lose every hand.

He thought she'd let the question drop, but they passed a

short, empty hall leading to the employee break room, and Crystal pushed him into it. Her hand landed in the center of his chest and shoved him against the wall. She was stronger than she looked, and that fucking turned him on.

Stepping in close, almost eye to eye in her heels, she said, "You going to tell me the real reason you're here tonight?"

3

IT WASN'T CASSIE'S DUTY TO CHASE THE DARKNESS OUT OF Steve's eyes, but damn if she didn't want to anyway. It seemed that both of them had something that had driven them to the Butte besides a little harmless entertainment.

And just when she thought he might let the smallest of details slip, when she thought he might tell her what had brought him there, he said, "Hard pass. You?"

At least that's what his words said. His tortured expression relayed the opposite. That he wanted to talk, but something prevented him from doing so.

And turning the question back on her wouldn't distract her. "I didn't push you into this hall to talk about me."

"I don't even know your real name."

"Would that make telling me any easier, because if it will—"

"No. Today's just not a good day. I'm here for a distraction. A break from a shitty reality that's hard to fathom."

Cassie knew she couldn't fix him. But distract him? *That* she could do. She stepped closer, one of her legs straddling his as she leaned up against him, loving how his pupils dilated and his hand automatically came up and rested on her hip. She pressed her lips to his, expecting him to take over the kiss.

What she hadn't expected was the soft *umpf* that escaped his throat, the sexy, needy sigh, the way his eyes closed, and his grip on her hip tightened as if he never wanted to let the moment go.

She pulled back to check on him. "Is this okay?"

"More than okay."

He leaned in and kissed her. This time, she tasted the whiskey on his tongue. And maybe a hint of regret as well. With her thigh between his legs, she knew the moment he got hard. And fuck if she didn't want to forget about the real reason she was there and drag him up to her room where they could be each other's distraction.

A voice came over the loudspeaker announcing the poker game she'd been waiting for. She broke the kiss and rested her forehead on his, her breath coming fast, hating she had to stop.

"As much as I'd like to take you upstairs and see where this might go, I came here tonight to do something, and I'll be mad at myself if I let you divert me from it. That game. That poker game they just announced… I need to be in that game."

He didn't groan. He didn't call her a tease or tell her she was killing him or made her feel bad in any way that she'd made it clear that even though she'd been the one to drag him into the hall, that she had to end it.

He just wrapped his arms around her waist, brought her in for a hug, and pressed a kiss to the side of her head. "Then let's go find that poker table."

With a protective hand on her lower back, he led her through the maze of gaming tables, straight to the poker tables as if he'd found them many times before. She bought into the game, the table filling up quickly.

"You're not playing, are you?" It wasn't really a question. She could tell he would sit the game out by the white-knuckled grip he had on the back of a chair and the way his eyes darted around as if he expected external repercussions just for standing inside the roped-off area around the table.

It could have been the lights, but he looked as if he'd lost two shades off his complexion.

"No."

"Not a gambler?" The Butte would have been a weird choice to go just to get a drink, but it wasn't the oddest thing either.

Cassie had liked the anonymity when the night started. But there was so much more she wanted to know about this man. His sweet gentleness in conflict with the darkness beneath the surface intrigued her.

Not dark in the way she thought he was a danger to her, but dark in a way that he'd seen too much. Working in dispatch all those years and getting to know the officers, she recognized haunted eyes when she saw them.

He pointed to a chair outside the ropes. "I'll be waiting over there."

"You don't have to stay."

"I'm not going anywhere."

That he planned to stay shouldn't have mattered, but it somehow, it did. When was the last time she'd felt like she had a man in her corner? Before she could come up with an answer, the dealer said, "First ace bets."

Cassie glanced around the nine-player table and felt the edge of her father's poker chip that she'd stuffed into her bra for safekeeping. Three of the chairs remained empty. There were two women, including Cassie. The other woman was older, not like *grandma come to try her luck* old, but like a woman who'd spent more nights at a poker table than at home cooking meals for her husband.

There were a couple of younger guys with backward base-ball caps and an old man with a beer gut that kept him from sitting too close to the table. Then there was the guy she considered would probably be her strongest competitor. He had to be around her age, though the dark sunglasses and hoodie nearly obscured his face.

Considering who she was up against, Cassie liked her odds.

In the way that poker games go, the first hour quickly turned into the second, which blurred into the third. The kids with the backward hats left with their tails between their legs within their first hour.

The guy with the gut made it into the second hour and might have made it into the third if he didn't have the nasty habit of sucking his teeth when he had a good hand. The woman hung on until nearly the end, but her tendency to bluff by betting more than she should sealed her eventual doom.

Then it was down to Cassie and Sunglasses. The chips were split nearly evenly between them, though it looked like she had a slight advantage. And even though Sunglasses looked around more, clocking the security cameras, guards, and management-level employees more than he paid attention to the cards, he was a damn good opponent. The young woman with him on Jericho's side of the ropes kept to herself.

What little buzz Cassie'd had from the booze at the start of the night had long since dissipated, and the only buzz she got was when she glanced back at Steve waiting patiently. Still there after all this time like he'd promised he would.

The dealer dealt the next round of cards. She placed her bet and glanced over at Steve. He looked dead on his feet, but when he winked at her, she wanted was to ditch the cards and take him up to her room. Even if it were only to hold him all night. He looked like a man who could use that right about then.

But she had a good hand. A *really* good hand. She and Sunglasses both upped their bets, and when the dealer dealt the flop, turning all three cards over. Sunglasses gave no tells that he was bluffing his way through the hand.

Theoretically, Sunglasses could beat her hand, but Cassie didn't think he had the cards.

"Look, I've got a hot guy waiting who's likely to make my night much more interesting. What do you say we speed this up a bit?" She pushed her remaining chips into the middle of the table, going all in. "What do you have?"

For the first time that night, the man smiled, pushed his chips to the center, and laid down his cards. A straight flush. Good cards, but not good enough to beat her royal flush. But instead of taking what she'd rightly won, she laid her cards face down on the table, reached into her bra, and tossed her father's lucky chip on top of the pile. "Congratulations."

Under her breath, for only herself and the dead to hear, she said, "You lose, Daddy."

This game... It had never been about winning. It had been about proving to herself that she could walk away.

CRYSTAL STOOD FROM THE POKER TABLE. JERICHO COULDN'T TAKE his eyes off the cards she'd laid on the table, dying to know what had been in her hand. The dealer flipped the cards over, and... *holy shit...*

Crystal's hand had won.

"But... I don't..." Jericho's words failed him. He'd never seen anything like it in his life. Why would anyone walk away from a winning hand and what had to be thousands of dollars? Not life-changing money, but it wasn't nothing either.

Taking his hand, Crystal dragged him toward a bank of elevators.

"Where are we going, and why the hell did you leave all that money on the table?"

"To my room." She pressed the button for the elevator. The confidence in her smile shifted, becoming less sure. He didn't like being the one responsible for dimming her light. "Unless you've changed your mind?"

"No, I haven't changed my mind, but that still doesn't answer my question. Don't you need the money?"

She laughed. It came out rough and raw and reedy. The elevator chimed, and the doors swooshed open. Inside, she pressed the button for the seventeenth—and top—floor.

"It's not that I don't need the money. I definitely need it." She leaned against the back mirrored wall of the elevator, her hand still holding Jericho's. "It's that I don't *want* the money. Not that money. Or what it represents. I had something to prove to myself."

"Well, did you? Prove it that is?"

That grin came roaring back. It had lost some of its luster after the long night, but it still had the power to light up something in Jericho that had gone dark for way too long. "Yeah, I think I did."

He leaned in and pressed a kiss to her lips, swiping a blond bang out of her eyes. "I'm glad to hear that."

The elevator came to a stop, and the doors slid open.

"That's us," she said.

He followed her down the hall, wondering if he should kiss her good night at the door and head home. Somehow, she'd managed to dull the overwhelming urge he'd had to hit the poker tables, and he'd be stupid if he didn't take the opportunity to get back to his cabin—and his real-life—before his willpower flagged. He settled a shoulder against the doorjamb while she dug into her tiny purse and pulled out her keycard.

Standing that close, he smelled her subtle, understated jasmine perfume.

The light on her lock turned green, and she opened the door. She stepped into the room, but when he didn't make a move to follow, she turned back. "What's wrong?"

"So many things," he said, too guarded, too weary, to elaborate. "But none of them have anything to do with this. With you."

"Yet you're still on the wrong side of the threshold. We don't have to have sex if you don't want to. It's okay. I just..." She shrugged. "It would be nice to have some company."

And fuck if those soft, vulnerable words didn't have his feet walking into that hotel room without his brain giving the order. As he stepped into the living area of the hotel suite and did a turn around the expansive room, he was damn glad that he didn't have Crystal's real name. And damn glad he didn't have her number because she had a way of getting to him that no woman in a very long time had.

He loved and hated it at the same time.

What did that say about him that someone that he'd just met could have that kind of effect on him?

Or maybe, like her, today was just one of those days when you needed something more than the words in your head and your own fucking company.

"I can't stay long," he said. "I've got to be at work early tomorrow, and it's a long drive back."

He sat on the couch. She kicked off her heels and straddled him. Her short dress rode higher, convincing him she wasn't wearing any panties. "For a woman who needs money, you certainly managed to spend a lot on this—" He cut himself off. "Scratch that. That was an asshole thing to say. What you do with your money is your business."

But damn… the number of bus tickets he could have bought with the money she'd paid for a luxury suite…

"It's a celebration, remember? The dress. The shoes. I won. Demons, zero. Ca—Crystal, one."

Had she almost said her real name?

Why, when he'd been content not knowing her real name the whole night, did he suddenly feel the need to know it now? He'd had anonymous hookups before. Not many, but enough to know that he didn't have to know a person's name before having sex.

But the woman on his lap, kissing her way down his neck, was different.

Maybe it was just the fact that as a gambler, he couldn't reconcile leaving your winnings on the table.

She'd walked away from a winning hand.

Like it was nothing.

And maybe it was that gambler who needed to know the kind of person who did that.

But then Crystal ground against his straining erection, and all higher thought vacated his brain. All he could think about was letting this woman do whatever the hell she wanted to with his willing body.

Her short skirt rode up, and he ran his hands over that sexy ass, and he groaned. "You're not wearing any underwear."

Fuck. Good thing he hadn't known that before. Otherwise, he would have spent the entire evening with a raging hard-on, much like the one he sported now.

She chuckled, the rich, warm sound going straight to his dick as she kissed her way to the other side of his neck. She raked his earlobe with her tongue and whispered in his ear. "This dress is too tight to hide any pantie lines. Plus, it's one less thing to have to take off."

Swallowing hard, he reached down between them and

adjusted himself. His head fell back. "Fuck. I thought I was going to break in half."

He ran his hands back up her thighs and cupped her bare ass. She ground against him even as she unbuttoned his jeans and raked his zipper down.

For an unknown and inexplicable reason, the headline he'd read that morning popped into his head.

Letting go of her ass, he gripped her forearms and stopped her from going any further even though his cock strained at the confines of his boxer briefs.

"Is there a problem?"

4

Cassie sat there on Steve's lap. Even though they'd agreed on a name to call him, her brain had an increasingly harder time reconciling the man with the name. She wanted to ask his real name, but with the shadow that just passed behind his eyes, she doubted he'd give it to her.

She let go of his fly and scooted back a couple of inches. Her girly bits called her a traitor, but whatever was going on in this guy's head was more important than her getting off. "This isn't going to happen tonight, is it?"

He scrubbed a hand down his face, his short stubble making a scratching sound beneath his fingernails. She understood. She could be a little too... too *Cassie* sometimes. How many times have men told her she needed to tone it down, to not be so damn *much*?

"I'm sorry," he said. "It's not you. It's me."

Usually, when men told her that, they flat-out lied. But considering how they'd met at the bar and whatever it was that had brought him to the Butte, she believed him.

"I got some bad news this morning," he said as if he had to explain himself. Which, since they hadn't even exchanged names, he absolutely didn't need to. "It's really fucking with my head."

"I'm sorry." She leaned in and pressed a kiss to his forehead. His eyes closed, and his deep sigh had her wrapping her arms around his neck and pulling him in for a hug. "I wish I could make it better."

He held on tight as if she were a lifeline keeping him from being dragged out to a fathomless sea. He buried his face into her neck, his breath unsteady before it eventually evened out again. Finally, after a long while, he released her, and she sat back.

Red crept up his neck, and he wouldn't meet her eye. "I should go."

The last thing he needed was to be alone. Cassie stood and wrangled her dress back into place. "You should stay." He made a face, and she added, "Do you trust me?"

He didn't answer right away, but after a deep breath and an assessing look, he put his hand in hers and allowed her to assist him to his feet. She led him into the bedroom, turning on the bedside table lamp.

She tossed the decorative pillows onto the floor on the far side of the bed and turned to him. "Strip. Then get in."

"Are you tucking me in?" He raised an amused brow at her.

Cassie rolled her eyes. "Just lose the clothes."

First went his shirt, and Cassie's subconscious growl of approval brought a cocky smile to his lips. "Like what you see?"

This wasn't going anywhere, so Cassie didn't bother to hide the note of petulance. "You know I do."

She made an impatient get-on-with-it motion with her hand. He dropped his jeans on the floor. Keeping his boxer briefs on, he laid on his side facing her.

Picking his clothes off the floor, she felt his wallet through the folds of cloth. Curiosity got the best of her. She palmed his wallet for the second time that night and placed his clothes on the crushed velvet bench at the foot of the bed. "I'm just going to freshen up."

And see who you really are.

She ran the water in the sink, quickly opening his wallet and pulling out his ID. *Jericho Saint,* the name read.

More like a fallen angel with a body made for sin.

Pushing that thought out of her head, she washed the makeup off her face, left her jewelry on the counter, and stripped out of her dress.

She hadn't thought this whole thing through when she'd dressed up and hopped into her car, telling herself that she could buy whatever she needed at the casino if she decided to stay the night. She never considered she'd need something in the middle of the night after the gift shops had closed.

But there was no way she was sleeping in that dress.

She wasn't shy, and modesty had never been one of her finest qualities. And walking out completely naked fueled her wide exhibitionist streak that she often had to wrestle into submission.

Hiding Jericho's wallet in the folds of the dress in her hands, she opened the bathroom door and turned off the light, nearly bumping into him. He caught one look at her and sputtered, the water he'd been drinking spilling down his chest.

"Jesus Christ." He swiped water off his chin with the back of his hand.

"You're supposed to be in bed."

"You're supposed to be clothed."

Her eyes darted to the front room where she'd left her purse and driver's license. Did his lips twist up, hinting at a smile, or was that just a play of the light?

She couldn't get a read on him, and if he'd sneaked into the other room to find out who she was, then she couldn't exactly call him out on it, considering she had his wallet balled up in the dress in her hands.

As casually as she could, she walked to the end of the bed and picked up his Henley, drawing it over her head and down her body. It skimmed the top of her thighs. She wasn't the shortest woman, so it didn't hang on her like a dress, but it covered the basics—boobs and booty.

He held out the glass of water to her, and she stepped over and took a sip, his tight boxer briefs unable to hide his erection. She set the glass down on the table. He closed the distance between them, brushing her blond hair out of her eyes and tucking it behind her ear. Since she'd cut it to chin length, it was just long enough to stay put.

With the soft look in his eyes, the breath wooshed out of her. No one had ever looked at her, *really* looked at her as if she'd righted someone's world and stabilized their orbit.

Or maybe she wasn't as sober as she'd thought.

He ran the pad of his thumb over her brow and the swell of her lip. "You were beautiful before, but all I can say is *wow*. Fuck, you're stunning like this, standing in my shirt in your bare feet, your face scrubbed clean. I can't get enough of looking at you."

Holding her chin between his thumb and forefinger, he pressed a kiss to her lips.

It didn't deepen.

It didn't demand.

It only cherished.

Jericho ended the kiss that somehow had the power to break him apart and put him back together.

How could one woman do that to him when he'd only known her a handful of hours. He wanted to know more.

Wanted to lay in bed and hear her every thought, every triumph, every flaw, every secret.

Especially now that he knew her name.

He'd found it when he'd wandered into the suite's kitchenette looking for water and discovered her tiny purse laying on the counter. A purse barely large enough to carry her cell phone, her driver's license, and—good for her, he liked an optimistic woman—a short strip of condoms.

He loved that while she hadn't thought far enough ahead to bring a change of clothes with her to the casino, she'd at least brought protection.

But they'd moved beyond the sex now, and he was okay with that.

She took his hand and crawled into bed. He watched the shirt ride up her thighs, and as he took the spot beside her, a wave of exhaustion rolled into him and knocked him for a loop. He hadn't realized how hard he'd fought the tide of emotions that had battered him all day. He appreciated how she'd shielded him from the onslaught with effortless ease.

Rolling to his back, he turned off the bedside lamp. When he went to roll back to her, she said, "Turn the other way."

He chuckled, unsure where she was going with this, but he turned on his side, facing away from her. She pulled the covers over them and snuggled in behind him, her front to his back. It took all of his willpower to talk his dick down as her full breasts flattened against his back.

As big as he was, never in his life had he been the little spoon, and as her arms came around his waist and snugged his ass against her lap, he realized he quite liked it.

A protector by nature, it had taken this woman to show him that he could put that aside long enough to allow someone else to be that for him. Her breath came warm on the space between his shoulder blades, her fingers drawing small circles in the fine hair beneath his belly button.

Soothing, not arousing.

As his breathing slowed and sleep began pulling him under, he said, "Thank you."

She kissed his shoulder and held him tighter. "Get some sleep."

For a very private man, for the first time since he could remember, there was more that he wanted to say, but she was right. It was time to get some rest. Maybe in the morning, he could convince Cassie Kemp that she could trust him with her name.

At least they'd ended up in her room and he didn't have to worry about her ditching him in the middle of the night.

JERICHO WOKE TO A LIGHT TAPPING ON THE SUITE'S DOOR. HE buried his head under the pillow and groaned. With the shades drawn, he had no clue what time it was, but the alarm on his phone hadn't chimed, and it felt like he'd only slept an hour or so.

Cassie no longer pressed against his back, and he reached an arm over to her side of the bed. Instead of finding a warm body, he found a cold spot where she should have been. *What the...*

He sat up in bed and spun around. He slapped on the bedside light and stood, his morning wood heavy between his thighs. From the bedroom doorway, someone let out a squeak of surprise.

"I'm so sorry," a woman in a black and red Butte uniform said. "I was told the guest had already checked out."

Red rushed up her face as Jericho scrambled to pull on his pants. "The woman who reserved the room... she checked out?"

"Yes, sir," the woman said, even as Jericho popped his head into the bathroom then searched the rest of the suite for Cassie, the maid following him. Cassie wasn't there. And neither were her clothes, or purse... or his shirt for that matter.

"For fuck's sake." He stood in the middle of the suite and scrubbed a hand down his face. "I can't believe she left."

The woman shifted from foot to foot and hitched a thumb over her shoulder toward her cart holding open the suite's door. "I'll just come back later."

She started backing out of the room, but not before her eyes snagged on the crotch of his still unbuttoned pants.

"Yeah, fine, great." He tried hiding his annoyance. It wasn't the cleaning lady's fault that Cassie had run out on him. It was *her* fucking room. He tamped down the disappointment. He shouldn't have expected any different. She didn't owe him anything.

Before the cleaning lady could leave, he asked, "Do you know what time it is?" Maybe he could lay down for thirty minutes or so before he had to hit the road.

The woman checked the time on her phone. "Eight-thirty."

"*Eight-thirty?*" Jericho made a beeline for the window.

He threw back the heavy blackout drapes back, and the bright sun blasted his eyes. From somewhere behind him, the door to the suite closed, and the cleaning lady left him to the realization that he was already thirty minutes late on the first day of his new job, and he was a good three hours away.

He plopped onto the sofa and scrubbed his hands through his hair, his forearms resting on his knees as he wrapped his mind around what had happened and decided what he'd do next.

A call to his new boss, Wyatt Wolfe, was in order.

Returning to the bedroom, he found his phone and wallet on the bench at the foot of the bed. As he waited for his call to go through, he checked the contents of his wallet, prepared to find it empty.

But it wasn't. She was a pickpocket, not a thief.

"Wolfe," the man said on the other end of the line.

"Oh, yeah, hey, it's Saint."

"Let me guess. You're going to be a little bit late getting in."

Considering he was already past *a little bit late*, Jericho said, "It's looking like it will be closer to noon by the time I get there."

Jericho thought about what he should tell Wyatt. He didn't want to make any excuses. In the heavy, drawn-out silence, he said, "This won't happen again."

"See that it doesn't."

Wolfe hung up. And Jericho finished dressing. Cassie had left him with his cash, cards, and keys, but taking his shirt...

Instead of being mad, he thought about how sexy she'd looked in it. If circumstances had been any different the night before, he would have had her out of it faster than she'd gotten into it.

And a smug part of him liked the idea of her walking around in his shirt. Unfortunately, he couldn't show up to work without a shirt, and as late as he was, he didn't have time to drive out of the way to his cabin and get another shirt. He called down to the front desk, gave them his credit card number, and asked if someone could buy him a shirt at the gift shop and have it brought up.

He was in and out of the shower in the short time it took for a bellhop to bring up a shirt. Jericho tipped him with a twenty and pulled on the shirt. The extra-large ran small, but it would have to do.

As he grabbed his wallet and keys, he caught a glimpse of himself in the mirror. The Butte's iconic *Winner Winner* sign plastered across his chest.

He jogged out of the elevator towards his truck, thinking

about how badly the night before could have ended. The T-shirt's slogan was right on.

By staying away from the poker tables, he'd won.

And he had a certain, light-fingered blond he wished he could thank for that.

5

Cassie in front of her best friend's houseboat. She'd driven there straight from the casino needing to talk to Geneva about the night before, but now that she'd arrived, she had second thoughts.

What was there to talk about? It wasn't like she'd ever see the guy again.

The guy. *You act like you still don't know his name.*

"Jericho Saint," she whispered even though no one could hear. Another time, another life, she might have pressed him for more, but she had a job to find and a derailed life to put back on track.

She didn't want to leave Murdock and all of her friends, who were more like family, behind. But a girl's got to eat.

Staring out at the houseboat on the pond in the foothills of the Wyoming Rockies, the incongruous sight still gave her pause, but her friend loved it and, more importantly, loved the man who loved living on the water so much, he'd found a way to make it happen.

It all looked so peaceful. The quiet boat, the calm water without even a ripple, the—

Mmmooooo.

Cassie jumped in her seat and slammed a hand down over her racing heart. Who would have thought that twelve hundred pounds of bones and beef could sneak up on you like a ninja?

A cow licked a long path up her window with her thick, slobbery tongue. Cassie buzzed down her window. "You scared the hell out of me, That-a-way."

That-a-way ran the tip of her pointed tongue up one nostril and then the other, her nose working, sniffing for the alfalfa cubes that Wyatt, her best friend's husband, kept on hand. "I don't have anything for you."

That-a-way tried to stick her head through the open window to smell Cassie's pockets for treats, but her crazy messed up horns, the ones that pointed in the same direction as if to say 'go that-a-way' brought her up short.

Cassie patted the cow's cheek. "I don't have any pockets. I don't even have any underwear."

"Why don't you have any underwear?"

Cassie closed her eyes and half-laughed, half-groaned at Massey, the grandson of the woman who owned the ranch that the cow, boat, and pond were on. He was also Wyatt's go-to computer guru.

He shooed the cow away with the rubber end of one of his crutches. When he leaned down to look at her, she said, "It's a long story."

"Sounds like a good one, though. Is that why you're here? To see Geneva?"

"Yeah, but maybe I should just head home and—"

"Nope." He popped the car door and, after adjusting his crutches, opened it for her. "She'll be mad if she knew you were here and didn't stop in. We haven't seen much of you lately."

She climbed out of her car and smoothed down her dress and Jericho's Henley she still wore over it, making sure they covered the necessities. It might have been a rotten move to steal his shirt, but if she couldn't have him, she could at least have *something*.

It smelled like him. An intoxicating blend of heat and sweetness that was all his own.

Massey reached out, the cuff of his crutch catching on his forearm as he tugged on the sleeve of the shirt, his smile teasing when he said, "I take it this is part of the reason you don't have any underwear?"

"Well, to be honest," she said as they followed That-a-way down to the newly constructed dock. "I started the night without any, but I would have lost them to this guy anyway."

The dock boards sounded hollow beneath her bare feet. Muddy hoof prints led the way down the short side of the 'L' shaped dock. The houseboat was tied along the long side, and at the end lay a pile of old blankets that That-a-way bedded down in. The contented cow closed her eyes and started chewing her cud.

Massey glanced up at Cassie through his disheveled bangs that always looked like they needed a trim. He couldn't suppress his grin. "You liked this guy."

"Of course, I liked him. I don't make it a habit of sleeping with guys I don't like."

Cassie didn't bother to correct her language that 'sleeping' hadn't been a euphemism for sex, at least where Jericho had been concerned. But for some reason, what they'd shared seemed more intimate than sex. And she preferred to keep that to herself for now.

She didn't know what it said about her that she preferred Massey thought she'd had sex with Jericho rather than that she hadn't. The latter would have raised too many questions that she wasn't ready to answer.

"I meant *like* like."

It felt wrong to deny it, as if it would somehow be a betrayal, which didn't make any damn sense, so she said, "I just met him." She'd let Massey assume the rest.

They stood at the edge of the dock, the door in the gunwale of the houseboat open. Massey bumped her shoulder with his. "Sometimes, you don't have to know someone for a long time for them to make an impact on you."

His sweet smile faltered at the corners, and Cassie wondered if Massey were talking from experience. Before she could ask him about it, he levered his smile back into place and called out in Johnny Depp's pirate voice, "Ahoy, Captain, permission to come aboard."

The rear sliding doors opened, and Wyatt stood there in a white T-shirt and jeans, his feet bare and hair wet from a shower. He looked positively disheveled as if Geneva had just had her wicked way with him. Of course, if Cassie had a man like Wyatt warming her bed every night, she would take advantage of it as well.

Not that Wyatt seemed in the least bit put out.

Massey grinned as he crutched his way across the rear deck and to Wyatt said, "Someone's getting a late start this morning."

Disappearing inside, Massey was no doubt heading for the coffee pot. Cassie figured it would suit Massey better if he just mainlined the whole pot.

Steam rose out of the coffee mug in Wyatt's hand, his dark, thick brow going up when he caught a good look at her. "And someone else is *still* up. I'd call it the walk of shame, but we both know you have none."

She grinned up at him. "Which is what you love about me."

Slipping past Wyatt, she met Massey at the coffee pot. He filled a cup for her before screwing the top on an extra-large tumbler. Having ditched the crutches in favor of his precious coffee, he used the counter for support until he made it to the table. He sat heavily and shoved his crutches out of the way."

Wyatt filled another mug that Cassie assumed was for Geneva. "If I had known that the *Lone Wolf* would become coffee central, I would have bought the industrial coffee maker."

Massey took a sip of his coffee, his eyes closing in bliss as he swallowed. "It's never too late to buy a bigger coffee maker."

"I'll get one for the new office. How does that sound to you?"

The new office, meaning the office and training facility for his newly formed Steele-Wolfe Securities firm. The new building, complete with offices, a conference area, and dorm-style rooms for the occasional all-nighters they would likely have to pull, wouldn't be finished for a week or two, the last Cassie had heard.

"And a small one for my desk?"

Wyatt rolled his eyes. "Fine. A small one for your desk."

"I'll leave you boys to it," Cassie said as she took the extra mug from Wyatt's hand and headed toward the master cabin at the bow of the boat, searching for her friend and a change of clothes.

"Knock, knock." She approached the partially open door. "I brought coffee."

Geneva opened the door, a smile on her face until she spotted the faltering smile on Cassie's. She took the offered mug with one hand, Cassie's wrist with the other, and dragged her into the room, closing the door behind them.

Dressed in a pair of jeans and a cozy sweatshirt, Geneva sipped her coffee and waved her hand in front of Cassie. "There's got to be a story here. Spill."

Moving one of Wyatt's shirts off the corner chair, Cassie sat and told Geneva mostly everything.

When she finished, Geneva handed her a pair of panties out of a new pack she had and gave her a pair of sweatpants to borrow. Cassie removed the dress but kept the Henley. She'd have to deal with going bra-less since she and Geneva were nowhere near the same size.

Geneva put her coffee on the bedside table and sat cross-legged on top of the rumpled covers, her insightful gaze assessing. "First, do you think you've put this thing with your dad behind you?"

"I think so." A bellyful of insecurity escaped with a laugh. "If not, I wasted a lot of money I didn't have paying for that suite and leaving all that money on the table."

Scrunching up her face, Geneva said, "Yeah, blowing that kind of money on the suite probably wasn't the smartest thing you've ever done."

"I know. If I could find a job, everything would be fine. I mean, I didn't make bank as a dispatcher, but it paid the bills."

"Have you thought about asking for your old job back? It's not like you left on bad terms. Sheriff—"

"Sheriff Day said he'd be happy to have me back, but they don't have any openings. Good for them that the new guy is working out. Bad for me, though. I should have known better than to quit before officially signing on with the new company. But I believed the HR guy when he said the offer was coming and that they wanted me to start right away."

"If you need money—"

"I don't need money. I need a job."

"Maybe Wyatt has something."

"The firm is barely off the ground. I refuse to be a drain on his finances because I was stupid."

Geneva made a sound in the back of her throat that came out as more of a *we'll see*. But neither one of them wanted to argue about it.

"Okay," Cassie said, knowing Geneva hadn't finished with

her. "You'd said '*first.*' What's second?" Though really, Cassie knew the answer to that one. *Jericho.*

"Second, I think you should talk to Wyatt. Maybe he and Massey can find this guy. He sounds special."

Cassie didn't tell her that she had a name. That she'd violated the man's privacy and sneaked a peek at his driver's license. If she did, Geneva wouldn't stop until she tracked Jericho down and learned every one of his deepest and darkest secrets.

"He was special. But sometimes people come into your life and boost you up, but they were never meant to stay. I think this is one of those times."

"Awh, honey." Geneva had one of those sad, empathetic smiles on her face. "That's so beautiful." Then her demeanor completely changed, and the all-knowing, determined Geneva replaced the empathetic one. "It's complete bullshit. But it's beautiful."

From the other room came the ringing of the boat's landline. Cell service around the ranch was hit or miss, mostly miss, so landlines were a must. Wyatt answered, his voice pitched upward, and the aggravated, "Let me guess. You're going to be a little bit late getting in," could be heard all the way into the master cabin.

"Come on," Geneva said, "I could use another coffee."

Cassie eyed Geneva. "Why did you give up so easily? That's not like you."

"Because I know how stubborn you are when you've made up your mind even if you're clearly wrong. Living with Wyatt has taught me to pick my battles. This is me waving the white flag."

Cassie would believe it when she saw it but followed Geneva back into the living area. The galley, dining table, and living area comprised one big space. It probably could have held ten to fifteen people comfortably. A big improvement over the smaller boat Wyatt had before Geneva bought the bigger one. That Sea-Celia had been crowded with only three people.

Wyatt paced the living area, which didn't seem quite so spacious, when a big man's strides ate up the tile floor.

"What's wrong?" Geneva stopped him mid-pace, wrapping her arms around his waist.

He blew out a breath and kissed her forehead, but before he could say anything, Massey said, "The new guy just called and said he's running late."

"So he's a little late."

"He was supposed to be here this morning at eight. Now he said he won't be here until noon."

"What happened?" Geneva stepped out of Wyatt's arms.

"He didn't explain." Wyatt paced back to the door, opened the slider, and tossed a couple of alfalfa cubes onto the dock to the waiting bovine. "Maybe I should have done a lot more than taken Brant's recommendation on this guy. If I can't even count on him to show up on time on his first day of work, how can I trust him when things get mission-critical?"

"Do you trust Brant?" Geneva asked.

Gil Brant was a former undercover ATF—Alcohol, Tobacco, and Firearms—agent. A man who'd cheated death one too many times and had retired to try life in the private security sector. He and Wyatt had only recently completed the partnership paperwork.

"I do."

"Then trust that his recommendation of this guy is solid."

Wyatt wrapped an arm around Geneva's neck and pulled her into his side. "You're right. I also wanted to show him around before Brant and Finn showed up."

"Ooh," Cassie said, she'd met Oscar Finn on a couple of occasions. He was the FBI agent in charge of a local joint task force. "What's Finn got going on?"

"I think it has something to do with the Nathan Quest murder," Massey said. "It's got to be."

Cassie poured herself another cup of coffee and sat down beside Massey at the table, plucking an apple out of the bowl of fruit in the middle. It wasn't a donut, but she was hungry, and it would have to do. She'd heard about the murder on the radio on the drive up to the Butte. "This may make me an uncaring bitch because no one deserves to die in a hail of bullets, but if someone had to, I'm glad it was him."

"I know some people who would have paid good money for it to happen," Geneva said. "I don't know how the network justified keeping such a bigoted, racist, sexist piece of shit on the air."

"Ratings," Wyatt and Massey deadpanned at the same time.

"And someone *did* pay. Or a lot of someones," Massey said. "Quite a bit, too."

"You still believe that crowd-sourced hit man conspiracy stuff?" Cassie bit into the apple. Her lip curled. It tasted like... an apple. "You don't strike me as the tinfoil-hat-wearing, mother's basement-dwelling, kind of conspiracy theorist."

"All I'm saying is that there was a seven hundred CoinIt bounty on that guy's head after it got out that he'd had sex with underage girls. And now he's dead, and the CoinIt is now out of that wallet. The bet paid out."

Wyatt whistled. "Seven hundred CoinIt? What's that, like a hundred grand, US?"

"Closer to one-twenty-five in today's market."

"That's a lot of cash," Geneva said, taking the apple out of Cassie's hand and taking a bite of the fruit she knew Cassie wouldn't finish.

"Well, sure, the money is gone. DeadMoney is a betting site, right? Although a morbid one. People bet on the date someone famous or infamous is going to die, and if they happen to get lucky, they get the payout. Like picking a baby's sex and weight only with bullets and blood," Cassie said.

"Is it?" Massey said. Cassie would have to have him fitted for his tin-foil hat if he didn't make one himself. "Jacoby Wilson was killed last month. Though it only paid out about two hundred CoinIt."

"That was an accident on set."

Massey raised a maddening brow. "Was it?"

"On that note," Cassie said, "I'm going home to shower and change into my own clothes." She turned her attention to Geneva. "What time do I need to be back for the lunch thing?"

Geneva grimaced. "Lunch with my sister is at one. But you don't have to run interference with my sister. She moved to the area. You aren't always going to be around as a buffer."

"Those other times you're on your own, but *this* time, the first time you've met with her in years? I'm going to be there."

Geneva bumped her with a shoulder. "Thanks." Then her mischievous grin grew on her face, and she waggled her eyebrows. "Maybe the new guy will be here by then. Tessa says he's hot."

Tessa was Gil Brant's new wife, a helicopter pilot for the local law enforcement agencies when she wasn't busy growing the baby in her belly.

"May I remind you that both you and Tessa are married?" Wyatt mock glared at her, which only made Geneva's mischievous smile wider. "We're married, dear husband. Not dead. And if he'll help Cassie get over her one-night-stand, then good on him."

"There's nothing to get over," Cassie insisted, even though it felt like a lie.

Jericho climbed out of his truck. He hadn't known what to expect out of a new security firm just getting on their feet, but a cow on a dock next to a houseboat wasn't it.

He thought about saying *fuck it* and turning his truck around and finding other work. But on the drive, he'd already received texts from Jerome, his contact in Ohio, who temporarily placed some of the people Jericho helped. Another woman had contacted him in need of fresh, untraceable documents so she could disappear.

And that brief thought about ditching his forgery business for good went where he knew it would—on the back burner where in reality, he knew it would probably stay for the rest of his life.

He didn't forge documents to make money.

He forged them to save lives.

And that took capital. Capital he needed from a decent-paying job.

Jericho stepped out of his truck, prepared to grovel for his job.

The cow with twisted horns stared at him as he walked down the dock. He'd never seen a cow who looked so judgmental, but then again, he wasn't normally on the side of the cow that didn't involve a fork and knife.

"You the top-notch security around this place?" Jericho said as he came eye to eye with the bovine blocking the open railing at the boat.

The cow belched, the scent of hot hay wafting over him, making his nose scrunch. He reached out and scratched her behind the ears and watched her eyes roll up into her head.

"Looks like you made a friend," came a woman's voice from somewhere behind the cow.

He wiped the dirt off his hands, and the cow ambled off. An inarguably beautiful woman met him, but she was nothing like the woman who'd wrapped herself around him when he had been ready to fall apart.

"You must be Jericho Saint," she said, offering her hand. Only briefly did her eyes drift down to the *Winner Winner* emblazoned on his shirt.

It took everything he had to prevent the heat from rushing up his face. Not only did he look like a tourist with his couple of days worth of stubble, he certainly didn't look like the professional he was.

All he could do was show up to work every day and prove that today was the aberration, not the norm.

He stuck out his hand, her grip firm, her expression amused.

"Geneva Wolfe," she said. "Come on in, Wyatt, Gil, and Massey are already inside."

Jericho boarded and followed his boss's wife inside. Three men sat at the table with their laptops open. Gil was the first to stand and greet him with a firm handshake and a one-armed hug.

"Good seeing you, man," Gil said. Gil was about as big as a bear, his hug nearly as crushing.

They'd gone through the police academy together back in the day but had never worked at the same station.

"Good seeing you, too."

Gil stepped aside. Wyatt's stood. Jericho recognized him from his internet research into the new company. Wyatt's grip didn't crush—it meant business. Jericho could respect that. Wyatt raised a brow at Jericho's shirt but didn't ask about his wardrobe choices. Probably for the best.

He reached across the table and shook the other man's hand. "You must be Massey."

"Guilty," the young man said.

"Any trouble finding the place?" Wyatt gestured toward the table, and they all took a seat.

"No. GPS took me straight here."

Geneva put her hands on Wyatt's shoulders. "I can't wait until Boomer finishes your office, and I can have my kitchen table back."

Wyatt squeezed her hand. "Boomer says it won't be much longer. We have the run-through for the punch-out list scheduled for next week."

"Can't wait." She kissed him on the cheek and started walking off toward the hall. "I'm going to leave you boys to save the world. I've got to get ready for my lunch date."

Jericho wanted to address his tardiness first thing to get it behind him. Wyatt hadn't fired him when he'd called earlier that morning, so it gave him hope that they would be able to move past it easily.

"About this morning," Jericho said, looking first at Gil and then Wyatt. "Anything I say is going to sound like an excuse when there is no excuse for showing up this late on my first day of work. All I can do is put my head down, get to work, and assure you that nothing like this will ever happen again."

Wyatt leaned back and considered him before he said, "Gil vouched for you. I trust his judgment, and I trust that you'll be a man of your word. Let's put this behind us. We've got work to do."

Jericho nodded. "Thank you."

Jericho rubbed his hands together, ready to start. He'd quit law enforcement before Gil had, working with various security firms over the years. But none of them promised to be as interesting as the new start-up, Steele-Wolfe Securities. With ties to local law enforcement and their stated mandate of looking for the people who refused to be found, he was ready to prove himself.

After all, if he was good at helping decent people disappear, he ought to excel at finding the bad ones that didn't want to be found.

"What's on the agenda?" Jericho asked.

"Got called last night. We have a meeting scheduled with Oscar Finn. He's FBI and in charge of the local joint task force." Wyatt checked his watch. "But he's running late. It's the theme of the day."

Jericho chuckled. It came out dry, but he appreciated that Wyatt didn't pull any punches and gave him shit about his inauspicious start. He liked the guy already.

"I'm surprised he's coming at all," Gil said, "Didn't Sheriff Day call the task force in to help with that shock jock's murder?"

"Jed doesn't have the manpower for the type of murder investigation this kind of national attention requires. I can't remember the last time there was a murder in Murdock. And now he's got two in one night."

"Two?" Gil sat back. "I only heard about Quest getting killed in that drive-by."

Jericho felt the blood drain from his face, and he got up and helped himself to the nearly full pot of coffee and one of the mugs hanging below the nearby cabinet. For a little bit, he'd allowed himself to push Nadia's murder to the back of his mind.

Now it came rushing back, along with the thought that he needed to find a way into her apartment to make sure he found her documents before the sheriff and his investigators did.

Fuck. He'd been so disturbed about Nadia's death that he'd forgotten that if she'd been killed at her apartment, there was a good likelihood that her forged documents were still there.

And if she hadn't followed his instructions about not returning to her apartment, would she have followed his instructions on eliminating any electronic or paper trail that might lead back to him?

Jesus Christ. He needed to get into that apartment. Would

the scene have been cleared and released yet? Or would the overloaded sheriff's department still be processing the scene?

He wouldn't risk going back before the sheriff's department released the crime scene. Not only did he not want to get caught, but he also didn't want to take the chance that he might inadvertently contaminate any evidence still needing to be collected. As much as he didn't want to be found out, he wanted Nadia's killer to be brought to justice even more.

"No. There was a pregnant woman murdered the same night," Massey said. "It just didn't get the coverage that Quest got."

Jericho returned to his seat, and Wyatt's eyes widened. Jericho almost broke out into a sweat until he realized that Wyatt was staring over his shoulder.

"Wow." Wyatt stood, pulling his wife in for a kiss. "You look beautiful. Kind of dressed up for a lunch date, aren't you?"

"I want to make a good impression."

"You don't have to impress Becca."

"I feel like I have a lot to make up for." The tears welling in her eyes had Jericho and Gil looking away.

"You don't," Massey said before her husband could, though Massey hadn't taken his eyes off his screen.

Geneva's phone pinged, and she glanced at the screen. "My ride's here. Wish me luck."

Wyatt walked her out to the rear deck. Jericho heard additional voices, and when Wyatt returned, he had another man and a woman with him.

Introductions were made all around. Gil had worked with Oscar Finn on the task force before leaving the ATF, but apparently, neither man had met his ex-wife, Shondra.

The tall, elegant Black woman dressed as expensive and sophisticated as her ex in clothes that would be hard to find outside of Jackson Hole, the place where all the celebrities liked to congregate. Either the FBI paid a hell of a lot better than Jericho had thought, or Finn came from family money.

"We'll get right to it," Finn said, "I've got a meeting with Sheriff Day later this afternoon. And I still need to make it back to my place for a quick shower."

Finn's suit might have been expensive, but by the rumples and creases, it looked like he'd been wearing it since news dropped that Quest had been mowed down.

"My friend Nadia was brutally killed," Shondra said. And then she said the words that Jericho feared she would say. "And I'm hoping you guys help find the bastard who did it."

6

AT THE BREAD SPREAD, THE TRENDY SANDWICH SHOP IN Murdock, Cassie sat in the booth next to Geneva, looking worse for wear while Geneva could have walked down the red carpet. Okay, maybe not the red carpet, even if there were one in Murdock, Wyoming, which, lord knew there wasn't and never would be. But Geneva still rocked the elegant blue knee-length dress.

Geneva's sister, Becca, sat across from them in her uniform. She'd recently been hired at a neighboring county's sheriff's department. Even though they'd been at the restaurant long enough for their mains to arrive, Geneva's leg still bounced. Conversation hadn't exactly flowed, which explained why Geneva had wanted Cassie as a buffer.

Cassie didn't quite understand Geneva's nervousness. It was highly unlikely that Becca would jump right into all the family drama. And who knew, maybe they'd both matured enough over the years that they could reconnect and get along. Cassie hoped so. She knew what it was like not to have a lot of family around for her to count on.

She'd take a sister, even an estranged one reaching out to reconnect if she'd had that option.

"Are you settling in okay?" Cassie asked.

"Nearly unpacked," Becca said. "Things at the department have been busy, especially since the Quest murder. They're swamped over there, and we're pulling extra shifts to fill in for some of their people pulled off their normal patrol duties."

Becca glanced at her new Sweetwater County Sheriff's uniform. "Sorry I had to come in uniform. I was supposed to have today off. I was lucky that Sheriff St. John didn't make me cancel."

"You're fine," Geneva said, finding her voice as her leg stopped bouncing. "I'm glad you came."

"Though the unpacking is going well, I'll have to find a trainer for that new mare I bought right before I moved. She's a lot greener than I thought, and I don't have as much time to train as I thought I would."

"I know a great trainer at the Lazy S ranch," Geneva said. "Sydney Wilcox. Though she's pretty busy training her mustangs. If she can't help, she might be able to refer you to someone who can."

"Thanks, I'll give her a call."

"Any new men in your life?" Cassie asked, wanting to get down to the good stuff. If she didn't have a love life, she might as well live vicariously through someone else.

And Jericho didn't count as a part of her love life since they hadn't had sex. Though by the way he'd kissed her, like he'd possessed her soul and never intended on giving it back, made her wish they'd had.

Becca rolled her eyes. She had Geneva's dark hair, but that was where the half-sisters' similarities ended. Geneva had at least six inches in height on her sister. Becca seemed slight beneath her body armor and uniform, though Cassie knew full well not to underestimate her if she was anything like her older sister.

"If I don't have time to train my mare, I definitely don't have time to train a man," Becca said.

Cassie and Geneva laughed, and the strain on Geneva's face relaxed. She'd been so stressed, wanting this meeting to go well. To prove it, Cassie had the string of late-night texts from Geneva ever since Becca had called to set up the lunch date.

Geneva held out her fist for Becca to bump. "Preach it, sister."

Tears welled in Becca's eyes.

"Whoa, whoa." Geneva got out of her seat and sat on the other side, her arm around her sister.

Becca laughed and sniffed. "Sorry. I knew you didn't mean *sister* as in literal sister, but it's been a long time since you called me that and—"

Geneva pulled her into her side, her voice thick when she said, "I've missed this. I've missed *you*, too." She let her sister go and waved at their passing waitress, pointing to Becca's nearly empty iced tea as if it were whiskey. "We're going to need another."

Becca wiped away her tears, and Cassie pushed Geneva's food across the table to her. Geneva picked up her fork and pointed it at Cassie. "Speaking of men, wait until you hear about Cassie's night, last night."

"*Geneva!*" Cassie said. "You weren't supposed to tell anyone."

"I didn't tell anyone anything. *You're* going to tell her. Since when have you been shy about sharing your sexcapades?"

"We would have had to have had sex for it to qualify as a *sexcapade*. And it's kind of embarrassing to be turned down at the point that I was grinding up against him. I mean, who does that?"

Becca laughed, the redness from tearing up clearing from

her face. "This should be good." Becca leaned forward. "Tell me everything."

Geneva began eating as Cassie launched into her story for the second time that day. By the time she'd finished, they'd devoured their meal.

"And you don't have any idea who this guy is?" Becca asked.

Cassie hesitated a moment too long before answering. Becca narrowed her eyes at her. "Oh, my god. You know who he is."

"*What?*" Geneva said.

"I do."

"Why didn't you tell me?" Geneva looked ready to come across the table and wring Cassie's neck.

Cassie wasn't proud about how she'd found out his name. "I swiped his wallet when I went in the bathroom to change. I had to know his name, but we were past the point of asking."

Geneva's bottom lip got all pouty. "That still doesn't explain why you didn't tell me."

"Because I knew you'd hound me until I told you his name, just like you're doing now. And if I had told you, you wouldn't have let it drop until Wyatt developed a complete dossier on him."

"Wyatt was a damn fine detective," Geneva said, not even denying it. "And an even better PI. Now that Massey has signed on with the firm. With his computer skills—"

"I'm not giving you his name."

Geneva deflated. "But..."

Becca leaned in, a cute, conspiratorial smile. "But you're going to Google him and stalk him on social media. Right? And if you need help with that, I'm your gal."

Cassie had to laugh. "You two are impossible. And I can see that the nosy gene runs strong in you both. You two don't look too much alike, but now I can definitely see you two are related."

Geneva and Becca smiled at each other, and at the same time, said, "We got it from our Dad."

"Well, I'm still not telling, and I'm not stalking and—"

Geneva reached across the table and held her hand on Cassie's forehead. "You don't feel like you have a fever. But if you were losing your mind, I'm not sure if you would have one."

"Funny," Cassie said, but she couldn't hold in the laugh. To see Geneva and her sister bonding over giving her hell was totally worth it. "As great as I thought the guy was, I don't think he's relationship material. At least not at this stage in his life."

She didn't elaborate, and Becca and Geneva didn't press for more, but only because Becca's radio went off and the dispatcher called her back in off her lunch break for a traffic accident not too far away.

"Sorry," Becca said as Geneva scooted out of the seat to allow Becca to leave. "I've got to run."

She started to pull money out of her purse, but Geneva waved her off. "I've got it. Go save the world."

Becca rolled her eyes. "I'm the new hire. I'm sure my saving the world will look a hell of a lot like directing traffic."

They waved their goodbyes and promised to get together again soon.

Geneva plopped down across from Cassie and blew out a breath. "Thank you so much for coming."

"I thought it went well, except for the part where the two of you ganged up on me."

Geneva knew Cassie was teasing. Cassie was fluent in sarcasm, and any friend of hers would have to be also.

"For a little bit there," Geneva said, "it felt like old times before our dad split from her mom and took me with him."

"She had to have understood that his leaving her behind wasn't about loving her less than you, right?"

Geneva shrugged. "Try explaining that to a ten-year-old.

Hell, I was four years older, and I didn't understand it either. Her mother was a hot mess."

The waitress came by, and Geneva handed over her credit card to cover all three meals.

"You don't have to do that. I still have some savings left."

"Not for long if you keep paying for suites and literally leaving money on the table."

"I deserved that room. I'm not even a little bit sorry about that."

"You deserve the world, Cass," Geneva said.

Tears stung the backs of Cassie's eyes. "All I want now is a job. I don't want to have to move away, but I will if I have to."

"Maybe your not-so-mystery man will sweep you off your feet and lock you away in his castle, and you'll never have to work again."

"I don't need a man to save me," Cassie said, "and as much as I liked this guy, seeing him again isn't in the cards."

MASSEY GLANCED UP FROM HIS COMPUTER, HIS FINGERS STOPPING their typing as he waited for Shondra to fill them in on Nadia.

Jericho didn't ask questions, afraid he'd sound too eager for information. Instead, he took one of the paper pads off the center of the table and started taking notes.

"How well did you know Nadia?" Wyatt asked as he tapped the end of his pen on the thick legal pad in front of him.

"I didn't know her long. My firm had hired her a few months back, and I kind of took her under my wing. She seemed like she needed a friend. And now..." Tears filled Shondra's eyes, and Finn squeezed the hand she had on the table.

For being exes, they seemed to be pretty close. Jericho

thought that said a lot about the two of them, that they'd been able to forge a friendship in the wake of a divorce.

"I don't understand what you think we can do," Massey said over the open lid of his laptop, "isn't this a Bison County case? It's an open investigation and—"

"Open. Technically." Shondra's mouth set in a firm line, and Jericho could tell she wasn't the kind of woman who liked to hear all the reasons why someone *couldn't* do something and preferred to focus on how they *could* do something. "But with Quest's murder, there are exactly zero people working on her case. They've all been pulled into the Quest fiasco. These first few days are crucial, and I don't want to miss valuable information that could help find her killer."

"This isn't exactly what we do." Wyatt dropped his pen and leaned forward as if he had bad news to break to a good friend. From Jericho's telephone interview with Wyatt, he knew that he'd been a detective when he'd been with the sheriff's office. The investigation would probably be right up his alley. You know, if Wyatt were still a sworn officer.

If *all* of them were still sworn officers.

But this was a security firm, not a sheriff's office.

"I know this isn't your firm's purpose," Finn allowed. "But this murder investigation needs people like you if we don't want the killer getting away."

"I wish we could help. But we have no authority here."

"Not officially. I can..." Finn glanced over at his ex, and though it looked like it pained him, said, "roll you into the task force as consultants. You'll have no law enforcement authority, of course. Only investigative. Information that you can come by lawfully."

That lawful statement had been pointedly directed at Massey. He blushed under the scrutiny but didn't argue.

"Can you do that?" Jericho asked. Was that even allowed?

Sure, victims' families have hired PIs to find the truth about their loved one's cases. It happened every day all around the world. But he'd never heard of law enforcement directing the request.

One of Finn's shoulders lifted and then fell. "I'm doing it. So I guess the answer to that question is yes. But as far as my supervisors go, I'm working on the assumption that forgiveness is easier granted than permission.

Beside him, Shondra sniffed, her eyes red as she tried to rein in her emotions. Finn squeezed her hand. "It's okay. We—*they* —are going to find this guy. And—"

"It's not that." Shondra shook her head, and a tumultuous smile quivered her lips. "I've never known you to break the rules before."

"I'm not breaking the rules." But it sounded like Finn was trying harder to convince himself of that than her. "I'm bending them."

"You don't bend rules either." Shondra's smile fell, and there seemed to be more personal pain beneath that comment than everyone else at the table was privy to.

"People change, Shondra."

The smile she sent Finn made Jericho want to look away. It seemed too private, too personal to witness.

"That's nice to hear. Truly."

Finn looked like he was about to lose his lunch. He swallowed that down and turned his attention back to Wyatt. "Do what you need to do to find this guy, yeah?"

Finn's phone rang, and he stood and took the call outside. Jericho retrieved the coffee pot and refilled everyone's cups. It didn't take long before Finn stuck his head through the open sliding door. "I've got to head back to Murdock."

Shondra's face fell, but it didn't look as if that kind of news was anything new to her. She turned to Finn and said, "I can fill them in on what I know. Thanks for doing this for me. And for Nadia."

He stepped back in and placed a platonic kiss on her cheek. "I'm glad to help." Straightening, he turned his attention to Wyatt. "Draw up a scope of work contract and email it to me. I'll try to approve it tonight."

Wyatt stood and shook his hand. "Will do."

Finn nodded to Massey, Jericho, and Gil. "Gentlemen."

Wyatt had barely sat down in his seat before Jericho said, "What can you tell us about Nadia?"

He wanted to know all he could, determined that if he couldn't help Nadia in life, he would help find her killer. He wanted to tell the group what little he knew about her, but there was no way he could jeopardize his operation. Not only could doing so endanger his freedom but there was the new woman Jerome had told him about who needed his help escaping her abuser.

And the sad thing was, there would be another one after her. And another.

And another.

What was it about men, about society, that men became so enraged at the thought of losing a girlfriend or significant other that drove them to kill the ones they were supposed to love?

Jericho didn't have the answer.

All he could do was do his utmost to keep people safe.

If that meant breaking a few laws to do it. Well, then he could live with that.

What he couldn't live with was another death like Nadia's.

"Did she have a husband? Boyfriend?" Wyatt asked. "We should start there."

"A significant other would be the most likely suspect," Jericho agreed. This wasn't anything anyone in law enforcement didn't already know.

"Or father of the baby," Massey added in. When all three sets of eyes landed on him, he said, "The boyfriend/husband isn't necessarily the father of the baby."

"Fair point," Wyatt said.

And if Jericho were honest, not something he'd considered himself. It was rare that his clients spilled their life stories to him. He didn't know the details of their lives. He just saw the bruises, the broken arms, the black eyes and knew they needed a way out.

No one came to him if they weren't desperate.

"I knew that she was involved with someone." Shondra rotated her untouched mug of coffee in her hands. "I'd tried to get her to confide in me, but she never told me who'd fathered the baby. Or who she'd been seeing at the time."

"That's... going to make things more difficult," Gil said.

Up to that point, he'd remained nearly silent, and despite his imposing presence that made him hard to ignore, Jericho had almost forgotten he was there. "And it's going to be tricky investigating this without stepping on law enforcement's toes."

"I called the detective assigned to the case this morning. Nadia's murder seems like nothing more than a footnote to his day. That's why I called Oscar for help."

It took a second for Jericho to realize that she was referring to Finn since everyone at the table always referred to him by his last name.

"Nadia was a sweet woman looking forward to the birth of her first child. She doesn't deserve to wind up a cold case shoved into the bottom drawer of some detective's desk because she had the misfortune to be killed the same night as someone famous —or infamous—depending on how you look at Quest. She deserves justice."

Massey clacked away on his keyboard, some mechanical

thing he'd plugged into his laptop even though the microphone he'd set up recorded everything she said.

"Who discovered her body?" Maybe that person had more information.

Shondra's eyes reddened again, and Wyatt pushed a box of tissues toward her. She dabbed at the tear-smeared mascara under her eyes. "I—I did."

After a moment, she cleared her throat and, with a more steady voice, said, "I had gone out to dinner with a ... *friend,* and Nadia had taken a file home to work on that I needed to review for a client meeting the next day."

"She couldn't have emailed it to you?" Massey asked.

"It's a sensitive case. We kept it on a thumb drive. Our office servers have been hacked in the past. I believe our issue has been resolved, but I couldn't take a chance with this client."

Now that they were getting into more details, Gil leaned forward, resting his forearms on the table. "Could her murder have anything to do with this case? Is it something that someone would be willing to kill to get that sensitive information?"

Shondra shook her head. "It wasn't that kind of case." She didn't elaborate, but they all took her at her word. Wyatt made a note as if he might revisit that point if the investigation faltered and needed a new direction to pursue. "And Nadia's laptop was still there, the thumb drive still attached. I didn't want to touch anything, so I left it there."

Jericho appreciated Gil's line of questioning because it paved the way for his more self-serving one without raising any eyebrows. "Anything else disturbed? Was the house ransacked as if someone were looking for papers or other documents?"

"A lamp had been knocked over, and a corner of the couch pushed out of position from the struggle, I'm assuming, but everything else looked untouched. Though I didn't go any farther than the den."

Which meant if the killer hadn't taken her forged documents, they could still be at the apartment.

Why had Nadia gone home with the file instead of catching the bus and leaving the way she'd planned?"

Jericho couldn't let it drop. "Is it usual for Nadia to take work home?"

"It's not common. But not unusual either. This was a last-minute thing that popped up, and..." Shondra pulled apart the tissue in her hand until she'd shredded it. She blew out a long breath and drew in another before meeting Jericho's gaze head-on. "I feel responsible for her death. She had plans that night, but they weren't until later, and she thought she could get the work done in time. I offered to do it myself and cancel my date..."

Gil plucked another tissue from the box in the center of the table and handed it to her.

"Thanks," she managed. "B—But she said that was her job and that she'd do it."

Wyatt rolled his pen over his knuckles, practiced and seemingly subconscious. "I don't get why you feel responsible."

"If she had been doing what she'd planned on doing instead of home working on the file, then maybe she'd be alive today."

Or if she'd been sitting at the bus station like Jericho had told her to.

"Maybe," Wyatt allowed. Shondra was a smart woman, and Wyatt didn't seem like the kind of guy to blow smoke up anyone's ass. He would be the guy who told his clients how it was. "But if this were a case of domestic violence instead of something work-related or a random home invasion, then this guy would have found her another night."

Not if Nadia had waited at the bus station for her red-eye the way Jericho had told her to do. She would already be in Ohio starting to put the pieces of her life back together.

"So you think it was her boyfriend or husband or whoever he was to her that killed her?" Shondra asked.

Jericho, Gil, Massey, and Wyatt all exchanged glances. Wyatt said, "That's the most likely of the scenarios. Especially considering the condition of her apartment. Though we'll investigate all leads. We don't want to miss something because we narrowed our focus too soon."

"Is that it?" Shondra asked. "Can I go now?"

"If you could give us Nadia's emergency contact information, we might start with that and see if she told her family members more of what was going on with her life."

"I'll get that to you as soon as I get back to the office."

"Anyone have any pressing questions?" Wyatt asked the group.

The three of them shook their heads. Jericho made a mental note to run by Nadia's apartment when he could to see if the police had released the apartment back to the complex.

"I guess that'll be all for now." Wyatt stood, and the rest of them did as well. Massey braced his hands on the table to stabilize himself. "We'll be in touch if we have any more questions."

"Sounds good. Thank you so much for agreeing to take the case. I couldn't sit back and hope that the sheriff's office didn't ignore it."

7

"ALL I'M SAYING," GENEVA ARGUED, BESIDE HER AS CASSIE DROVE them into Murdock for lunch. "is that you should look this guy up and see if maybe he's interested in dating."

"He's not. He's not even interested in sex. At least not with me."

"That's bullshit, and you know it. You're the one that said he was obviously going through something last night."

"I don't know if I'm the right person to build someone up. I wasted money I didn't have to prove a point to a dead man. I need a job, and my best friend thinks she knows what's best for me." Cassie added that last one with a smile, but Geneva would have known Cassie was only giving her shit even without it.

"Nothing you shared made me think he was broken. A little battered, perhaps, but none of us get through this life without battle scars."

If anyone knew the truth to that, it was Geneva. She'd lost her husband in the line of duty. It had taken time, but she'd come out on the other side of the tragedy stronger and wiser and now, with Wyatt, happier.

"Besides," Geneva said. "I know you really like the guy."

"What makes you say that?"

Geneva laughed. It was the kind of laugh that told you she was laughing with you and at you at the same time. "You went home to change, and you're still wearing the guy's shirt."

She rubbed at the fabric covering her arms. "It's really soft."

Geneva leaned in.

"You *did not* just sniff me."

"I sniffed the shirt. And it still smells like him. You want to try denying you don't like this guy one more time?"

"Okay, okay. Fine. Maybe you're right."

"I know I'm right." There was no hesitation in Geneva's response. "Promise me you'll look this guy up, or give me his name, and I'll have Wyatt—"

"*Absolutely* not. I'll try to find him. On my own time. I don't need your husband banging on this guy's door and scaring him away."

"I'm sure with Massey's help, Wyatt can check the guy out without banging on his door. Everyone has a digital footprint."

"At least his name isn't Joe Smith. I would be searching for the rest of my life and never find him."

Cassie gripped the steering wheel tighter as the nervous knots coiled in her belly. It could have been the chicken salad not sitting well with her, but deep down, she knew that those knots had more to do with the thought of facing the man that she'd sneaked out on again than food that might have gone off temperature.

She slowed at the entrance to the Yates ranch where Geneva and Wyatt kept their houseboat and drove over the cattle guard at the gate. Massey and his grandmother, Evie, lived in the brick ranch house near the front of the property, while Geneva and Wyatt lived on the pond. They were building their new office, shooting range, and training facilities on the part of the ranch that Evie had gifted to them.

The land had been a gift and a win-win all around. Massey and Evie had a place to stay for as long as they needed, and Geneva and Wyatt took care of the rest of the ranch. Evie had gotten too old to manage the property, and Massey's cerebral palsy made it difficult for him to do much of the physical work it required.

Cassie parked beside Gil's truck as a woman she didn't recognize walked up the dock and returned to her car. The truck on the other side of Gil's must belong to the new guy that Wyatt had hired.

Geneva popped her door. "You coming in?"

"I hate to barge in on the guys when they're trying to work."

"*Please*. It's my home, too, and you're more than welcome to hang out. If it's a problem for the boys, they can take their little meeting over to the new office. They're functional. It just doesn't have all the final touches on it yet."

"Okay. I'll come in for a bit."

"We can take my laptop up to the sun deck and see if we can find your mystery man."

Cassie rolled her eyes and didn't even bother admonishing Geneva again. It wouldn't do her any good. Once Geneva got something into her head, she didn't let it go. An admirable quality except when that extreme focus lasered in on her love life.

They hurried down to the dock because when That-a-way saw them pull up, she stopped munching the pond weeds and started heading their way. Which normally wasn't a bad thing except when she ate them while belly deep in the water.

The cow made it to shore, the water rushing off her like a submarine surfacing after a deep dive.

They ran down the dock ahead of the cow, laughing and

giggling and stumbling until they slammed the railing door closed behind them.

That-a-way let out a baleful moo, the water still draining off her chest and onto the side of the boat.

"Oh, my." Cassie laughed. "Who knew the old gal was so fast?"

Geneva clutched at her sides, out of breath as she scratched behind the cow's ears. "There you go, baby."

"This is seriously the weirdest thing," Cassie said. "Most people just have a dog."

"I can't help it if she has this thing for my husband."

"I think it's more of a thing for the alfalfa cubes he throws to her like beads at a Mardi Gras parade."

"No lie." Geneva wiped her hand on a hand towel laying over the railing they left there for that purpose. When That-a-way realized she wasn't getting any more pats or alfalfa, she ambled over to her bed at the end of the dock and laid down.

Cassie followed Geneva inside and waved at the table of men, her attention going from Wyatt to Massey to Gil to—

Ohmyfuckniggaaawd.

Jericho stood abruptly, his chair tipping over and clattering to the floor behind him. "Cassie."

"Jericho."

Geneva slapped a hand over her mouth, but she wasn't fast enough to stifle the laughter. "It's him, isn't it."

"That's my shirt," Jericho said at the same time.

"Who's him?" Massey asked as he glanced between Cassie, Jericho, and Geneva, trying to figure out what the hell was going on.

What Jericho had said must have filtered into his head because he grinned and, into the silent awkwardness, said, "This isn't awkward at all."

"Gil," Wyatt said, making a quick assessment while Cassie's

brain still struggled to catch up with the fact that her nearly one-night-stand stood in her friend's kitchen. "Come help me put up those bales of hay before they get rained on. Massey, come show me where you want them."

Massey looked at Wyatt with incredulity, not bothering to stand. "There's only one place in the barn to put the hay. The same place you've put it for—"

"*Massey.*"

"Okay, fine. But that won't be near as fun as this."

Gil had already headed toward the back deck. Wyatt handed Massey his crutches and herded him out. Not that Massey needed his help, but Cassie was positive it was because Wyatt wanted to make sure Massey didn't find a reason to stay behind and watch all the fireworks.

Not that there would be any fireworks. It's not like she was mad at him or anything.

No fireworks? What's that swirling going on in your belly? Why is your blood rushing, your skin heating?

By the time she came back to herself, Geneva had left as well. The traitor must have sneaked out with her husband.

"Um..." Cassie gave Jericho a little wave. "Hey."

"Hey, yourself."

She glanced at his too-tight *Winner Winner* shirt and couldn't keep the giggle from erupting out of her throat. "Sorry about the shirt thing."

He came around the table and leaned against it. "I'm not. My shirt looks good on you."

"You're not mad?"

He rested his hands on the tabletop on either side of him, his knuckles white. Whether that was to keep him from strangling her or pulling her in for a kiss, she couldn't tell. But from his heated gaze, she thought it was the latter.

"I'm only disappointed that you left without saying goodbye."

"I didn't want to make it awkward." They both chuckled since things were decidedly awkward. She glanced around the houseboat. "This was your thing you had to get up early for?"

"First day at the new job."

"How's that going for you?" Cassie asked inanely when all she wanted was for him to pull her into his arms and kiss her the way he had the night before.

"Wyatt didn't fire me on the spot when I showed up almost four hours late. So, I'd say pretty damn good. And considering I ran into you again, I'd say it's gotten even better."

"How long have you known my name?" Cassie asked.

He raised a brow, his self-satisfied smile crinkling his eyes. Did he have to look so damn adorable when he smiled? "Since you swiped my wallet and ran into the bathroom to change last night."

"I wasn't going to stalk you or anything," Cassie said. "At least not until Geneva convinced me to see if I could find you."

He stood and took a step toward her, his voice low and heated when he said, "And why did you want to find me, Cassie Kemp?"

He stepped close enough to touch her hands. He lightly dragged a finger up each arm until his hands rested on her shoulders. Instead of answering, she said, "Were you going to try to find me?"

"No." The answer came too fast, too dismissive for it not to be the truth. That lightness in her belly dropped, and before she could back up, could step away from his touch, he added, "I was too afraid that it was a dream. Not you. But how you'd made me feel. I was afraid to find out that I had imagined our connection. That it was the alcohol or the events of the evening that had warped my perception. In my mind, you were perfect, and I just didn't want to ruin that."

"I'm far from perfect. I told you that already. And now? Now, what do you think?"

"That I didn't remember anything right. That my mind had certainly played tricks on me."

Before his words could register, he pressed his lips to hers. A soft sigh escaped her. Instead of taking the kiss deeper, he pulled back and touched his forehead to hers. "That connection I felt last night is even more intoxicating, more compelling than memory could ever serve."

"So you feel it, too. The pull. The sizzle. The spark."

"Yes, to all three. It's insane, but it's there."

"Not to burst any bubbles, but I burp and fart and can't keep my mind out of the gutter. My friends have learned to go with it. It's easier than trying to fight it."

His smile only brightened the more she talked. That was a good sign. Right? Maybe she hadn't completely scared him off.

"I appreciate the... insight? Warning?"

"Definitely a warning." Cassie's cheeks hurt, her smile as wide as his.

"I should probably be getting back to work. I don't want to make an even worse impression on my first day than I already have."

"Oh, right, sure."

"Give me your phone."

What did it say about Cassie that she didn't hesitate to unlock her phone and pass it over? Was it that she wasn't into head-games and bullshit? Not that she was desperate.

Desperate is sooo not sexy.

He did a quick scan of her contacts, then added himself and put it in her list of favorites. "Call me. If you decide you're still interested."

Kissing her cheek, he left her standing in Geneva's kitchen with goosebumps on her skin and a grin on her face. Was it too soon to call him? It was, wasn't it?

She glanced down at her phone and pulled up his information. In the brief time that he'd scanned her contacts, he'd figured out her system. First name: Jericho. Usually, instead of the last name, she put how she knew someone because otherwise, she'd have no clue how she knew the person who was calling unless, of course, they were friends or family.

In the 'last name' slot, Jericho had put: *Little Spoon*.

That silly grin on her face only went wider. Like all of her previous relationships, she didn't expect this one to go far, but holy hell, she planned on having a good time until it ended.

As Jericho approached the hay barn, Gil and Wyatt had nearly finished loading the square bales inside. Even as he'd put his number into Cassie's phone, he wondered if that had been a wise move.

Part of the reason he'd been so successful at helping the people he helped was because he used extreme caution in making sure his private and professional lives remained far apart. He needed as much anonymity as he could maintain if he were to not only protect his clients but also protect himself.

After all, no way around the reality that forging documents was illegal, even for a good reason. One day, he may walk away from it all, but with the steady stream of clients needing his help, how could he do that and still sleep at night?

He helped carry in the last few bales, passing them to Gil, who passed them up to Wyatt at the top of the stack. When finished, Wyatt jumped down and brushed the hay off his shirt and jeans.

"Where's Massey?" Jericho asked.

"He's up at the facility. The delivery came for the new computers, and he's supervising the setup. I'd take you up now, but—"

"I'd rather get started on the case if it's all the same to you." The sooner they got started, the sooner they could take that asshole down. Jericho's only regret? That he was no longer law enforcement and wouldn't have the privilege of slapping the cuffs on a murderer.

But as long as *someone* did that, he'd be happy.

"I'm going to pair you and Gil up," Wyatt said. "I'll have Massey see what he can find online. Social media, etc., I'll call Nadia's emergency contact. Maybe between us, we can get a clue as to who the men in her life were."

Jericho didn't have the heart to tell him that there wouldn't be much to find on Nadia. Along with the forgery services he offered, he also helped people disappear. Which included helping them erase or at least minimize their digital footprint. Along with that, he'd helped Nadia close down her social media pages. But if police issued a warrant to the companies, the information could be found. However, for the casual user of the platforms, there wouldn't be anything there.

Too bad he hadn't known at the time how important that information would be.

Had the killer followed her on social media? Was the killer in a photo? In her DM's?

"Works for me," Gil said. "I'll drive."

He started heading toward his truck, and Jericho called after him. "I'll be right there."

When Gil ranged out of earshot, Jericho turned to Wyatt. "I didn't sleep with her if that's what you're thinking."

Wyatt rocked back on his heels. "I didn't ask you if you had."

"I just..." He didn't know what he wanted to say. He'd

expected Wyatt to come down on him. Wyatt's detached reaction wasn't what he'd expected. "If there's a problem with me seeing her, I need to know now because—"

"She's a grown woman. I'm not her keeper," Wyatt said. "I'm only her friend. Even if I had an objection, she wouldn't be the type to listen to me."

"Good to know." Jericho hitched a thumb over his shoulder and took a step back. "Better not keep Gil waiting."

Wyatt nodded, and it wasn't until Jericho had stepped out of the barn that Wyatt added, "Of all the reasons to be late on your first day of work, finding a good woman has to be one of the best ones."

Jericho chuckled, relieved that Wyatt wasn't going to make a big deal out of how inauspiciously his first day on the job had started. "I'll have to agree."

Gil had backed his truck out by the time Jericho caught up with him. Climbing into the passenger seat, he buckled up. Gil drove off, steering around the cow in the middle of the yard and bouncing over the cattle guard before heading toward Murdock.

They had about a thirty-minute drive ahead of them. It wasn't all that far, but the roads had some twists and turns and elevations that made it harder for the big trucks to climb, so if you got stuck behind a tractor or a big rig for a bit, it could slow you down.

Gil raised two fingers at a passing truck, the way people did out there even if they didn't know the person. Gil cleared his throat, and Jericho had that *here we go* feeling in the pit of his stomach. He might have gotten off light with his boss, but Gil *knew* him, and any thoughts that Gil would treat him the same as Wyatt had came down to wishful thinking.

"About Cassie," he started.

"What about her?" Jericho could have kept the defensiveness and the irritation out of his tone, but this was Gil, and he didn't have to keep his cool to impress him. His tone also held a note of warning. He would allow the subject to be broached, but he'd only allow Gil a certain amount of leeway.

Gil glanced over at him, then turned his attention back to the road, but Jericho read the *are you kidding me* expression on Gil's face even in that brief exchange. "I understand your interest in Cassie. But have you thought that maybe you're not the right person to be dating her?"

"One, we aren't dating. At least not yet." And despite thinking that getting involved with her would be a bad idea, he added, "And two, why the fuck *not* me?"

"Look," Gil's voice dipped, and he sounded more like the friend that Jericho remembered than the asshole who thought he had any say in Jericho's love life. "I *know* you. You're a good man. I wouldn't have recommended you for the job if I didn't think that. But not including your ex-wife, you've always been more of the love them and leave them type."

"Correction. You *knew* me. And what the fuck makes you think that you have any clue what I want or what I'm looking for? Or what Cassie wants, or what she's looking for? We could be on the same page, and unless you were in that hotel room with us, you know nothing."

"I just don't want to see anyone get hurt."

"I can appreciate that." Jericho didn't bother to add that in this instance, he felt quite certain that if anyone were likely to get hurt, it would be him.

He'd never had that type of immediate connection with a woman before, not even with his ex. The kind of connection that made you wonder what you'd been doing, how you'd existed all those years without that person's light in your life. "I gave her my number. What she does with that is strictly up to her."

"If you do start dating and it doesn't work out, as Geneva's friend, she's going to be around all the time. You wouldn't be able to avoid her."

"I can be professional," Jericho said as his phone buzzed with an incoming text. It was rare that his phone went off. He'd be lying if he said that his heart didn't rush a couple of beats, excited that Cassie had contacted him so soon.

8

"JERICHO SAINT IS A GHOST," GENEVA SAID. "ARE YOU SURE THAT'S his real name?"

The sun cast a glare on Geneva's laptop screen as she and Cassie sat on the houseboat's roof deck, cyber-stalking Jericho. From that height, the view over the ranch with the Rockies in the distance stole your breath away, but Cassie wasn't taking in the view.

She hunched closer to the screen and blocked the screen's glare with her hand. "It has to be his real name. You said Gil had recommended him to Wyatt. That they've known each other since their police academy days."

Leaning back, Geneva said, "You're right. But it still doesn't make sense that there is almost nothing about him online. No social media. Not even a LinkedIn account. And even when his name popped up on the Lincoln Police Department's website, the links to his photo all come up as that stupid *404 Not Found.*"

"But he doesn't work there anymore. Is that unusual that the link wouldn't be active?"

Geneva had even texted Wyatt to find out which security firm Jericho had worked for before coming to work for Steele-

Wolf. "It's just weird. His previous firm still has him listed on their website, but the photo of him is that generic placeholder. And who doesn't have *any* social media?"

Cassie struggled to find reasons to explain why they couldn't find anything. And she couldn't help the twist in her belly cautioning her that maybe Jericho wasn't who he said he was. On the other hand, Gil had vouched for him, so she knew Jericho was real. She just didn't know what to think and couldn't get past the feeling that Jericho had more depth to him than anyone she'd ever dated.

She didn't know if that was a good thing or a bad thing. "And not everyone is into social media," she reasoned. "Maybe he's like Massey and more security conscious. It would make sense with the type of work he does."

"Massey has a low profile on the internet, but even he has a dating profile on a couple of the dating apps."

That twist turned even tighter. "Dating apps are a meat market, a time sink, and shredding to your self-esteem. I don't blame Jericho if he doesn't want to be a part of that."

And yeah, Cassie heard all the excuses she was making for him even as she wondered if maybe she should delete his number and just remember their night together as an incredible, unexpected connection.

Don't be an idiot. Don't let your doubts about him ruin something before it even starts. If you have questions, you need to take them up with him.

"Oooh," Geneva said, her eyes lighting with an idea. "We never checked HotDix to see if he has a profile there."

"That's a gay dating site."

"Yeah, but—"

"If Jericho is gay, no one told his dick that when he had his hands on my ass and his tongue down my throat."

That comment wasn't lost on Geneva, nor did it deter her. She punched in the site's name. "He could be bi."

The grin Geneva shot her out-shined the sun. "If he's bi, you could have that MMF three-way you've always wanted."

"Don't get my hopes up."

They made a quick fake profile to scope out the site with a seven-day free trial, but... no luck.

Cassie huffed out a hot breath. "I'm kind of disappointed we didn't find him. You kind of got my hopes up for that three-way."

"Sorry." Geneva closed the lid on her laptop. "If not finding any history on him bothers you, you don't have to contact him. You'll see him here from time to time, but if he's the type of guy to give you his number instead of pressuring you for yours, then I think he's mature enough not to be an ass if you decide you don't want to see him again. Or I can get Wyatt to—"

"No. *Do not* get your husband involved in my sex life."

"You still want to see him, though, don't you?"

"Am I an idiot if I say yes?"

"Not at all. Just take it slow. Get to know him before you get too wrapped up in everything."

"I'm not the type to get wrapped up in guys. I'm the one voted *Most Likely to Remain Single* my senior year in high school, remember."

"Yeah, but you want to see him again, and this is the first time you're willing to overlook a potential red flag—"

"I don't think not being able to Google him is a red flag."

Geneva leaned back, the sun highlighting her dark hair. "Then what would you call it?"

"More of an orange flag. Or a yellow one. More yellow-green. Olive maybe."

Geneva wrapped an arm around her and squeezed her. "Oh, man. You have it bad for this guy."

Jericho retrieved his phone from his pocket, about to show Gil that Cassie was interested when he realized the incoming text came from a number he didn't recognize.

Unknown number: *This is Rhonda. When can we meet?*

Rhonda. His newest referral. A woman who needed his help escaping a physically abusive husband. Would it ever end?

Would he ever find himself without any people in need of his help?

Jericho: *I'm working today. I can meet tonight.*

Rhonda: *My husband is home tonight. I might be able to sneak out tomorrow night. He's supposed to go out with some friends.*

Jericho: *Name the time and the place, and I'll be there.*

A minute, then two passed with no reply text. The three little moving dots finally appeared, indicating Ronda was typing a response, but then Gil rolled into a dead zone, and Jericho lost signal on his phone.

"Fuck," he muttered. "How do you guys live without cell service? It's driving me mad."

"Not much we can do about it. No use trying to fight it. Was that Cassie? Does she want to go out with you?"

"It wasn't her."

And fuck if Jericho couldn't hide the disappointment in his voice. Maybe he should shut things down with Cassie before they got started.

He didn't have the time for a relationship, and having one would make it infinitely harder to help the women who needed him if he couldn't be available at unreasonable times. Because let's face it, trouble didn't keep a nine to five schedule.

"Sorry, man," Gil said.

"I thought you didn't want me seeing her."

"I just don't want anyone getting hurt. Not the same thing."

Because they wanted to hit Nadia's apartment complex at a time when more people might be there after work, they headed into the heart of Murdock, where Shondra had her law firm. Maybe one of her other employees had been closer to Nadia and might have some relevant information to share.

If things got off track, Jericho might have to direct the investigation more toward Nadia's boyfriend, but since the boyfriend/significant other would be a natural place to start looking for Nadia's killer, he'd rather insert himself into the investigation that way than expose himself and his operation if he could avoid it.

On arrival, Shondra set them up in her conference room. It had a view of the parking lot out back and enough chairs to seat six. As a single lawyer firm, Shondra had a staff of four—well, three now. It wouldn't take Jericho and Gil long to get through their interviews.

The first two employees each came and went in under ten minutes. They had little to add to the information Shondra had shared with them earlier that day—Nadia had been excited about the baby. She kept her head down, did her job, and promptly left at the end of the day, always turning down offers to grab dinner and drinks after work. She kept her personal life to herself.

And always had bumps and bruises that she explained away with transparent lies.

Knowing the controlling nature of the type of person who isolated and abused others, it came as a little bit of a surprise that Nadia's boyfriend even allowed her out of the house to work. Then again, Nadia hadn't had any money or other resources of her own, so the asshole had probably taken control of her money as well.

Predictable.

It made Jericho sick.

Did her boyfriend and all the abusers like him run the same psychological playbook? Was there an app? Some dark corner of the web where people like them hung out and learned that shit?

Demean.

Isolate.

Abuse.

Apologize.

Rinse. Lather. Repeat.

The last person they needed to speak with strode into the conference room with the confidence of a well-seasoned paralegal. They had short black hair tucked behind their ears and a *They/Them* pin on the lapel of their baby blue blazer.

Gil and Jericho introduced themselves, and they all shook hands.

"You can call me Jazz," they said. They leveled Jericho and Gil with a pointed look as if they were the one running the interview and not the other way around. *Damn.* If Wyatt needed a kick-ass assistant, Jericho knew who to recommend. "Tell me you guys are going to catch this motherfucker."

"That's what we're trying to do." Gil leaned forward. "We're hoping you might have some information that could help."

"If it's not her shit-bag of a baby-daddy, I don't know who else it could be. Her apartment wasn't broken into. Nothing was taken. At least that's what it said in that tiny paragraph on the back page of the Daily News. Is the sheriff even trying to track this guy down?"

Jericho didn't hold back. "I think they have their hands full with the Quest murder at the moment."

"Yeah, well, they should be looking to give whoever killed Quest a medal, not put him behind bars. He did the world a favor if you ask me."

"About Ms. Bates." Gil steered the conversation back to the

murder they all cared about. "Did she ever say anything to you about a husband or boyfriend?"

"Boyfriend," Jazz said, their lip curling as f they'd rip the guy's throat out with their teeth if given a chance. "And before you ask, no, I don't have a name. I wouldn't have even known that much if I hadn't gone into the supply room the morning she was killed and found Nadia crying into the paper products. I kind of stood in front of the door and wouldn't let her leave until she told me what the hell was wrong."

Jericho thought back. Two days ago. That had been the day he'd texted Nadia to tell her he had her ticket to Cleveland and a temporary safe location. But why had she been crying?

"What was wrong," Gil asked.

"They were tears of relief." Jazz glanced out the window, shaking their head as if the whole thing were too unbelievable for them to comprehend. Jericho understood. He dealt with this situation all the time, and he still couldn't understand it. "At least I think they were. As usual, she gave very little away. Just said that she didn't have to worry about her boyfriend anymore. That it was over. And that for once, she'd had good news.

"Whatever she'd meant by that. I don't know if she'd been referring to the abuse or the relationship. After that, Nadia wiped her eyes, squared her shoulders, and lifted her chin. I wasn't getting any more information after that, so I stepped out of her way. She turned back to me before she disappeared down the hall and thanked me for being a friend."

Jazz quit staring out at the parking lot and met both of their gazes. "It sounded like another end of something rather than the beginning."

"You think she had plans to leave?" Jericho wanted to get the idea out there and maneuver the conversation in that direction. Gil was a smart guy. If he hadn't already been thinking along those lines, he would be now.

A phone rang outside the conference room, and a red light blinked on the phone in the center of the table before someone answered.

"The most dangerous time in a victim's life is when they're about to leave their abuser," Gil said.

"That's what I've heard." Jazz glanced down at the recorder in the center of the table. The color drained from their face until Jazz's complexion became paler than their blazer. "Do you think that's what happened? Do you think he killed her before she could get away?"

Jericho reached over and cut off the recorder. "That would be my guess."

"I think it has to be our working theory," Gil said, "at least until evidence tells us otherwise."

Thinking of one more question, Jericho turned the recorder on again. "Did Nadia have a car, or did her boyfriend drive her to work?"

"She was saving up for a car. Mostly, she took the bus. A few times, I think she might have gotten a ride—from her boyfriend, I'm guessing—but on those days, she arrived at work first. We don't open until eight, but most of us arrive before seven-thirty."

Jazz stood. "Is that all? I really should be getting back to work if you don't have any more questions."

Gil and Jericho stood and exchanged a glance. Neither one of them had a follow-up question.

Gil shut off the recorder and stuffed it into the back pocket of his pants. "I think that will be all for now. Thank you for your time."

Writing his name and number on the back of a business card with the Steele-Wolfe Securities crest on the front, Jericho said, "Call us if you think of anything else."

Jazz pocketed the card. "I will."

Closing the door behind Jazz, Jericho and Gil fell back into their seats.

"We've got nothing," Gil said. He didn't sound defeated. It was too early in the investigation for that, but the disappointment that they didn't have one solid lead turned the edges of Gil's lips downward.

"Basically. I'm hoping a neighbor might have heard or seen something. Whoever her boyfriend was, he'd done a number on her even before that night. She'd learned to keep her mouth shut where he was concerned."

"It's going to feel so damn good when we find this guy." Gil glanced at his watch. "If we hurry, we can catch Nadia's neighbors as they're getting home from work."

They both stood, and Jericho said, "Let's do this."

9

Nadia's apartment complex consisted of a series of eight-plexes with four apartments on the ground floor and four up above. The entire complex only had six buildings around a grassy courtyard with the requisite communal grill, picnic tables, and a half-court basketball court.

A stiff breeze blew off the nearby mountains, swirling old decaying leaves into miniature tornadoes behind the staircase of Nadia's building. Jericho and Gil stopped at the apartment below Nadia's and knocked.

An older woman with curly gray hair and wearing a floral housecoat. She answered the door without asking who was on the other side as if someone hadn't been killed above her two days before.

"Evening, ma'am," Gil said in that charming country way he had that made old women melt. "I'm Gil Brant, and this is my partner, Jericho Saint. We're with Steele-Wolfe Securities, and we wanted to ask you some questions about your upstairs neighbor."

"That poor girl," the woman said. "I already talked to the

sheriff's deputy. I don't know what I can tell you that I didn't tell them."

Relief washed through Jericho. At least the sheriff's department had gotten that far in their investigation. Maybe the department had more going on behind the scenes than they'd thought. Jericho sure as hell hoped so.

"Who sent ya?"

The breeze kicked up again, and Jericho wished he had something else to wear instead of the cheap-ass casino T-shirt. "Friends of Nadia hired us to help find her killer."

"Could you tell us what you told the deputy, ma'am?" Gil asked. "Anything would be helpful."

"Aren't you the polite one," the woman said. "And please, call me Betty."

She opened her door wide and motioned for them to come inside. They declined drinks when she offered, and the three of them settled in her den overlooking the parking lot. It would be the same view that Nadia had from above.

Betty spun her recliner around and, instead of facing the parking lot, faced him and Gil on the pink chintz sofa. "I don't know what I can tell you. I had my bridge club that night. A tournament night. I didn't get home until nearly eleven. I went straight to bed."

Gil sat forward on the couch, his forearms resting on his knees. "You didn't hear any arguments from above? No one calling out for help. Nothing like that?"

"I would have called the sheriff if I had. I almost called them so many times before. Now I wish I had."

Now they were getting somewhere. Even though Gil had the recorder on the coffee table in front of them, Jericho pulled out his notepad. "Why? What happened before?"

"That man of hers was bad news from the start. I tried to tell her, but kids these days don't listen to their elders. I'd seen the way he'd lay his hands on her when he thought no one was watching." She nodded toward her front window. "But I was always watching."

"Can you tell us what he looked like?" Gil's words came out calm, but Jericho knew from their training days that the more calm Gil sounded, the more amped up he'd become on the inside. "Height, hair color, race. Anything you can tell us would be helpful."

Betty pursed her lips. Her eyes narrowed as if pulling the man's image up in her mind. After a few long moments, she said, "Average."

"Excuse me?" The words fell out of Jericho's mouth, his incredulity tripping out with his words. What the fuck did *average* mean?

"Average. Unremarkable. Not worth noting. Forgettable. I'd be happy to drag out my thesaurus if you'd like me to find a more fitting synonym."

Gil jumped to Jericho's rescue. "I don't think that will be necessary, ma'am. What we mean—"

"I know what you boys mean. The man wasn't big like you," she said, looking at Gil. "Or so handsome, like him." She pointed to Jericho with her bony-fingered hand. "No offense," she added for Gil.

Gil chuckled. "None taken."

Gil wasn't what people would consider conventionally attractive, but Jericho didn't remember Gil ever having problems finding dates back in the day.

"The man was white with medium brown hair and a medium build. About the most memorable thing about him was his eyes."

"What do you mean?" Maybe he had a rare eye color, or he had heterochromia—two different colored irises. Something that might make him stand out to someone else.

"They were dead." Betty caught a shiver talking about it. "If there had ever been any good in that boy, it had long ago been stomped out. I'm sorry that Nadia's dead. I'm not sorry that we won't see that man around anymore."

Jericho hoped that would be the case. More than likely, the man had disappeared and wouldn't show his face around Murdock or the apartments ever again, but sometimes these assholes didn't do what you expected them to, and Jericho counted on that.

Betty described the man's truck as blue and loud, but the make, model, and year posed a mystery to her.

"Did you hear his truck that night?" Gil asked.

"No. But he could have come and gone before I got home."

Without much more to add, Jericho and Gil gave her their card, thanked her, and went to talk to the other neighbors. They knocked on the other downstairs apartments. They had no answer on two of them. And the neighbor across from Betty had been out of town when the murder occurred. The occupant had been relieved that she was unlikely to run into Nadia's boyfriend again but described the boyfriend's truck as black. She shrugged when asked the make and model.

Climbing the stairs, they came to Nadia's apartment at the top. The first door on the right. Shondra had given them Nadia's apartment number from her employee records, but that proved unnecessary since the fragments of the yellow and black crime scene tape fluttered at the top and the bottom of the door where someone had ripped the tape away. The sheriff must have released the scene back to the apartment complex.

That was good for Jericho.

Jericho eyed the locks on the door. Like the other apartments, there was a locking door handle and a steel plate that he assumed marked the spot where the interior-locking deadbolt would be. Which, if he had to break in, it would make it that much easier since he would only have to get past the one door lock.

The man in the apartment next to Nadia's had heard some shouting, but because it had been something that he'd grown accustomed to, he hadn't paid much attention when it had started or stopped. Likewise, the couple across from him had dinner out that night and didn't know anything bad had happened until the crime scene tape had gone up.

Jericho and Gil tried the apartment across from Nadia's. If anyone had seen the killer coming and going, that person would be their best bet because of their view. She even had the same view out of the front that looked out over the parking lot.

Gil glanced around at the ceiling of the breezeway. "Shame there are no security cameras."

"I spotted one that pointed at the entrance to the complex, mounted on the side of the office, but nothing else."

"Same." Gil raised his hand, and before he could knock, the door swung open.

"Who are you, and what do you want?" The woman who answered appeared to be in her mid-twenties wearing a Teton's sweatshirt, dark leggings, and a skeptical expression. She eyed them up and down before she said, "You're here about Nadia, aren't you?"

They introduced themselves, and some of the wariness cleared from her eyes. "At first, I thought you two might be reporters, but then I realized with what happened to that asshole Quest that no news agency would spare two people for Nadia while that circus is going on."

"All we're doing is looking for some answers," Jericho said. "We want to catch this guy for what he did to Nadia and her baby. Anything you can tell us would be a big help."

Though she'd answered the door, she didn't go so far as to invite them in. Jericho could respect that.

"They kept to themselves. I didn't know Nadia more than someone I waved or nodded to when passing on the stairs. The one time I tried to talk to her, her asshole of a boyfriend opened the door and berated her and made her go inside."

"Do you have a description you could give us?"

"Medium build. Mousy brown hair. Always in jeans and a hoodie. Completely unremarkable. I could never figure out why she was with him. She was way out of his league. But I know relationship dynamics can be complicated, and how abusers can make someone feel they are unworthy of anything better.

"They fought all the time. I guess a better way to say it is he yelled at her all the time."

"You didn't call the sheriff on them?" Jericho asked. How could this guy have not ended up on law enforcement's radar?

"They were loud, but I never saw him hitting her or anything like that if that's what you're asking. And I live right across from them. I was afraid that if I called, he'd know it was me. I didn't want to worry about him coming after me."

Gil's expression softened. "That's completely understandable."

"I wish I had gotten one of those doorbell cameras now. A part of me had thought that if he ever had a reason to come after me, I would have it on video, but then I told myself that if I minded my own business, I wouldn't have anything to worry about. Now I wish I'd done it. Maybe then there would be definitive proof that he was the one who killed her. I'm a little freaked out. I still might buy one, but then I think that's like closing the gate after all the horses have already escaped."

"Do you know what he drove?"

"Blue Chevy pickup. I don't know the year. Loud as fuck, though."

Jericho jotted that down, though there was little likelihood that he would forget that detail. "Do you remember seeing or hearing it that night?"

The woman thought back. "Come to think of it... no?" It came out more of a question as if she weren't completely sure. "I had a pizza delivered around nine, I think it was, and I don't remember seeing it parked outside then, and I would have heard his truck if he'd pulled in after that. I was taking one of my online classes, and his truck drowns out the video when he pulls up."

Without much more to add, she accepted the business card they offered and agreed to call them if she thought of anything else that might be helpful. They thanked her and headed down the stairs and back to Gil's truck.

"We should run by the leasing office and see if they'll give us a copy of the security footage," Jericho said. "Maybe we spot this guy on the tape."

"Maybe it wasn't him."

Jericho stopped on the bottom step and had to crane his neck to meet Gil's eyes, where Gil stood a couple of steps above him. "You seriously think it could be someone else."

"We have to leave that possibility open. No one we talked to saw his truck in the parking lot that night."

They continued down the stairs and climbed into Gil's truck. Jericho didn't bother to buckle since they planned on stopping by the complex's office. "If you were going to kill your girlfriend, would you park in front of her apartment the night you did it, or would you park down the street or around the corner and hike in?"

"That's assuming he planned on killing her that night and that it wasn't an argument that got out of hand." Gil cut him a look, a mixture of disappointment and something else that Jericho couldn't quite read.

"What?" Jericho didn't bother keeping the irritation out of his voice."

"I expected you would approach this investigation with more neutrality. Yeah, we want to catch the guy who did this, but we want to catch the *right* guy."

"You don't think I fucking know that?"

Gil's eyes narrowed. "You're taking this pretty personally. What aren't you telling me?"

"Nothing." Jericho held Gil's gaze.

"Fine, keep it to yourself then." Gil harrumphed, unconvinced. He started the truck and backed out. "Remember, I vouched for you. Whatever's going on with you, you'd better not let it fuck up the investigation."

CASSIE STARED DOWN AT JERICHO'S CONTACT INFORMATION IN HER phone.

At nearly eight at night, and after being unable to find anything about him online, she questioned whether or not she should pursue him further. It seemed sketchy that there was almost no trace of him, but then again, she trusted Gil and Wyatt implicitly. If they'd been willing to hire him, how bad could he be?

And, though she didn't *know* him, she usually read people well and could trust her instincts. Nothing about him tripped any concerns, and that twist in her gut had more to do with the anticipation of seeing him again than concern for her safety.

If she'd thought she couldn't trust him, she never would have invited him up to her hotel room.

She considered calling, but in their area, calls didn't always go through, so she thought about texting instead and told herself she hadn't taken the chicken way out.

He wouldn't have given you his number if he didn't want you to call.

She tried to keep that in mind. Her stomach grumbled. She'd been out all afternoon putting in job applications and hadn't had a chance to eat.

Cassie: *Have you eaten?*

She set her phone aside to take out a load of laundry, not knowing how long it would take him to respond. She refused to sit there with the phone in her hand, waiting for three little running dots to appear.

Her phone pinged before she'd taken three steps. She grabbed for her phone.

Jericho: *I just started dinner.*

Cassie's thumb hovered over the keyboard. Should she invite herself over? If he'd wanted her to come over, wouldn't he have said so?

Before she could decide how to respond, a photo came through. Spaghetti sauce bubbling in a pot.

Jericho: *Come over.*

The next text that came through had directions to his cabin.

Should she?

She gave it about three seconds of thought, remembering how she'd felt in his arms, how his kisses had left her wanting more.

How his hands had lit a fire in her that refused to lay banked.

Cassie: *Twenty minutes.*

She didn't wait for a response. Quickly, she brushed her teeth and stuffed a strip of condoms into her purse, just in case.

Not that a dinner invitation meant anything more than that, but a girl could always hope, and she wasn't one to leave her sexual health in someone else's hands.

She still wore his shirt from that morning and didn't bother changing out of it. He'd already seen her in it—and had to buy himself another shirt. It wasn't like she had to hide that she'd taken it.

Within a few minutes, she ran out the door and rolled her engine over. She plugged his address into her phone but studied the turns closely before she left in case she lost signal in the mountains.

The twenty minutes took closer to thirty when she missed the driveway for his cabin and had to drive several miles out of the way until she found a safe spot where she could stop and turn around.

The more remote mountain roads made everything more difficult sometimes.

She pulled up to his cabin, her stomach rolling over again with a complaint.

The cabin sat in a small clearing. Not a massive monstrosity, but it probably had been built as someone's weekend place. It had a porch out front, and a shed on one side, with a stack of wood at the ready for those cold nights.

With nightfall at the higher elevation, the temperature had dropped enough that Cassie saw her breath upon exiting her car. She should have brought a jacket, but she'd been in too much of a hurry to bother.

And hopefully, she'd have Jericho to keep her warm.

The front door opened, and he stood in the doorway, his feet bare, his sweatpants slung low around his waist. He'd ditched the casino T-shirt in favor of another long-sleeved Henley, this one in a pale gray.

She liked that he hadn't felt the need to change out of his comfortable clothes. After he'd broken down in her arms, she figured they were beyond trying to impress each other with superficial things.

"Hey, there." His low, warm voice wrapped around her like a

hug. He took her hand and pulled her in for a quick kiss. He let her go way too soon and stood back to let her in.

She would have stayed on the porch all night as the temperature dropped if only he'd kept kissing her. Hopefully, there'd be more of that to come later.

"Smells amazing."

Cassie made her way to the kitchen along the back wall. It had a window over the sink that overlooked a thickly wooded area behind the cabin. The kitchen and den encompassed an open area with a fireplace as the focal point on one sidewall. A small island held the stove and had enough extra counter space to allow for two bar stools.

The pan of sauce bubbled on the burner, and she stirred it with the wooden spoon laying on the counter next to it. She sneaked a taste. "This is amazing."

Jericho chuckled, taking the spoon from her hand and setting it down on the spoon rest. "I have to confess. It's from a jar. I did add some ground beef and fresh garlic, and mushrooms. But that's all I can take credit for."

"That works for me."

"All I need to do is pop the garlic bread into the oven, and we'll be ready to eat in a few minutes."

The cabin had a two-top table by a corner window. He'd already set the table. "Anything I can do to help?"

"Just relax and tell me about your day. Any luck on the job hunt front?"

Cassie hooked a foot over one of the rungs of a bar stool, slid it out, and sat. "Total bust. None of the agencies within an hour's drive of here need a dispatcher. Emergency services in Cheyenne have openings, but I don't want to have to move. This is home. All my friends are here."

And Jericho is here.

Cassie tried not to let that cloud her judgment. Sure, it

would suck to move right when she started dating someone new, but her savings would only last her so long. And after that spending spree stunt she pulled at the casino, her savings had taken a monumental hit.

Though in hindsight, she couldn't say she regretted it.

"What about something other than dispatch that could tide you over until you find something you want?"

"I might have to do that. However, I'm not qualified for much else if you don't count tending bar. I did that for a bit while training for dispatch."

Jericho opened the upper cabinet beside the refrigerator and took out two wine glasses. He held them up. "Would you like a glass of red?"

'Yes' could be the only correct answer to that question, but the twists and turns she'd taken driving up the narrow mountain road had her thinking twice. "Am I driving home tonight?"

She expected some kind of grin. A shy one, maybe. Though if she'd been placing bets, she'd have put money down on a wide, enthusiastic grin. Instead, the flash of ambivalence that crossed his face had her rethinking accepting his invitation in the first place.

"I think this was a mistake." Heat crept into Cassie's cheeks and the temperature in the cabin rose about ten degrees. She stood and picked up her purse off the bar beside her. "If you don't want me to stay, maybe I should go now."

He rushed around the island, stripped the purse out of her hands, and set it out of her reach. "No. I want you to stay."

Eyeing him, Cassie judged his sincerity. He took her hands in his and threaded her arms around his waist, closing the gap between them. "Stay. *Please.*"

"We don't have to do anything you don't want to," she said. And why was she now trying to make her staying okay? "We can Netflix and chill, but *really* chill and not use that as a euphemism for burning through the ribbon of rubbers I brought."

He laughed, and the spark that lit in his eyes chased away whatever darkness had passed behind them moments before. "You brought condoms with you?"

"I'm a Boy Scout at heart," she said, though she had a hard time not grinning along with him. "Is that a problem?"

Tugging her closer, Jericho's erection pressed into her belly. He leaned in, kissed his way up her neck in a slow, methodical way that made her want to direct him to other places on her body that would enjoy that concentrated attention.

He whispered in her ear. "Not a problem. I fucking love the way you think."

The timer on the oven chimed. He stopped the kisses and pressed his forehead to hers. "Hold that thought."

After eating her fill, Cassie pushed her plate away and swallowed down the wine at the bottom of her glass. Jericho raised the bottle, with half of the contents remaining. "More?"

She covered her glass with her hand. "No. That'll do me. I want to remember every vivid detail, every last thing you do to me."

"No pressure." By his lazy smile, he didn't appear to be sweating the prospect.

"I don't want to forget anything I do to you either. Not one thing. How you feel in my hands. How you smell. How you taste. Nothing."

Jericho swallowed hard, and Cassie laughed. "Trust me, Saint, we're going to have a good time."

The wicked smile he gifted her made her nipples hard, and her breath catch. "I have no doubt."

She bussed her plate, prepared to help clean up the dinner mess, when Jericho stole the plate out of her hand and set it on top of his. "The dishes can wait."

"We should at least put the leftovers away."

"They're not going anywhere."

Though he'd given her no reason not to believe he was who he said he was, and she had complete confidence that Wyatt had done his due diligence before hiring him, she still couldn't get past the whole idea that Google had almost no idea who the hell he was.

Before she crawled into bed with him, she needed a few answers.

You didn't want any answers last night. You didn't even want any names.

Maybe, but an anonymous hookup was completely different than what she wanted to know before starting a relationship. Not that this was a relationship. It was just—

Fuck. She didn't know what the hell to call it, but she didn't need a label. She only required a satisfactory explanation.

"Why are you so hard to Google? It's like you're a ghost."

He sat back, the amusement disappearing from his face, replaced by something that looked a whole lot more like the inevitable that he hadn't expected to catch up with him so fast.

"You checked me out?"

"And you didn't check me out?"

His eyes flicked to the wrought iron and wood coffee table, and a smile toyed with the corners of his lips. "Cassie—no middle name—Kemp. Mother, Cecelia. Father, Charles. He rattled off her birth date, and the year she'd graduated high school. Worked at Joe's Bar and Grill before moving on to The Gin Joint while you trained for dispatch. On social media, you go by @sexy—"

"Okay. That's enough." She should've been annoyed, but she'd tried to do the same thing to him, only she couldn't get as far. "Why couldn't I find anything about you?"

"Ask me any question. I'm an open book. But I'm a private

guy when it comes to the internet. You can't be too careful, and I go out of my way to make my digital footprint as minuscule as possible. If you ask me, more people should do the same." He held his hands out to his sides and let them drop. "What do you want to know?"

"Is your real name Jericho Saint?"

"Yes. That's my real name. Ask Gil. He's known me for a lot of years. Way back to our academy days. I wouldn't have even made it that far if I hadn't passed the background checks required to get in."

"I checked everywhere I could think. The only thing I found was an old web page from the Lincoln Police Department. Your name was there, but no photo. No social media. No property records. I even checked the most popular dating sites."

He laughed at that. "Dating sites?"

"I was desperate." After being reminded of the dating sites, she recalled her conversation with Geneva and their escapades on the app. "We even made up a fake profile and signed up for HotDix."

"HotDix? You thought I was gay?"

"Not gay, but I thought you could be bi or somewhere else along the Kensey scale."

He didn't appear upset about what she'd considered, which got her hopes up about that MMF three-way fantasy possibly coming to life. She leaned in. "Are you? Bi that is?"

He had the cutest, sexiest grin on his face. "Why do I feel like you'd be disappointed if I said I wasn't?"

"A girl's got to have her fantasies. You know, me, you, another guy…"

She let the sentence trail off as the heat colonized her cheeks. Did she really say that out loud? But, fuck, how were you supposed to get what you wanted in life if you didn't put it out there."

"Sorry." He said it in such a way that he seemed sincere. "I'm straight."

Cassie moped for a moment, then let it pass. "Not everyone is perfect."

"That's not to say I wouldn't be up for making that little fantasy come true if that's what you wanted."

No telling what the expression on her face said. Some combination of shock with a heavy mix of surprise and *holy fuck is this guy real?* thrown in.

Jericho laughed. "I wish I had a picture of that face. I could insert it into the dictionary under *flabbergasted*."

"You would seriously consider that?"

He shrugged, apparently completely at ease with the idea. "What's life without a little adventure?"

"Every guy I've been with wouldn't even consider it."

Leaning forward, he pitched his voice low and picked up her hand, kissing his way across her knuckles. Who would have thought knuckles could be an erogenous zone? "I'm not *every* guy."

"You wouldn't be afraid someone would find out?"

He stopped kissing her hand and used his thumb to rub at the pulse point on her wrist. "I don't know how they would. But if they did, if they're so narrow-minded that knowing that about me changes what they think of me, then that's not the kind of person I want in my life. Plus, it's nobody's fucking business."

Standing, he helped Cassie to her feet and pulled her in close enough that no doubt crept into her mind that he'd be up for a little sexual exploration, which only turned her on more. This man was full of delightful surprises.

"What about your fantasies?" Cassie asked as she put her hands on his ass and tilted her head back, allowing him unfettered access to her neck. He didn't hesitate to take advantage of the offer. He kissed his way from the corner of her jaw down her neck.

She'd almost forgot that she'd even asked him a question when he came up for air, his eyes heavy-lidded and mischievous when he said, "Right now, my biggest fantasy is getting you naked and on or against any surface that suits. I'm not picky."

The table height seemed promising. Letting go of the hold she had on his ass, she placed her hand on the table and tested its stability. It could work, except they'd have to clear the dishes first.

"I love that deviant, devilish little mind of yours, but I don't want to take the time to clear the table."

He hitched his hands under her ass and lifted, wrapping her legs around his waist. "I've got an idea."

Gripping with her legs, she held on tight, his cock pressing into her crotch. She had no idea what he had planned. "Do I need to grab my condoms?"

"Eventually." He carried her to the couch in front of the stone fireplace. With the modest-sized cabin, he accomplished that in about four or five long strides. Instead of dropping her on the cushions the way she thought he would, he set her on her feet next to the padded arm. "But I'm going to make you come first."

"You really are perfect," Cassie teased after Jericho had told her that he planned on making her come.

"Hardly," he said as he cupped the back of her neck and kissed her. She tasted like red wine and with an undercurrent of florals and spice that belonged only to her. "But for a little while, I'm going to make you think I am."

She laughed, and the way her eyes sparked, they had a way of warming his heart and hardening his dick at the same time. His hand went to the button of her jeans.

"Uh, uh, uh." With a waggle of her hand, indicated his clothes. "You first."

"You don't strike me as the shy type."

"I'm not. I just really want to see you naked." She reached for the hem of his shirt, and he let her rip it off over his head.

"*Oooh, baby*," she ran her warm hands up his chest and down over the rounded muscles capping his shoulders. "I like."

He reached for her. He'd backed her against the couch. She sat on the arm and tugged the tie string on his sweatpants. "Now, these."

Fuck if she wasn't adorable with that sexy, hungry, unapologetic smile on her face. The gray sweatpants didn't hide *anything*, especially since he hadn't bothered to put on underwear after his shower. He hooked his thumbs into the waistband and dropped his sweatpants, kicking them off to the side.

His cock jutted out from his body, the slit already slick with precum. She took her damn sweet time taking her fill of him. A long slow perusal of his body, settling in for more than a few seconds on his junk, his balls heavy as he reached a hand down to stroke himself.

That devilish smile on her face inched higher, all sparkling teeth and hungry eyes, a starving woman bellying up to a feast. Her eyes skimmed up his abs to the hair on his chest and finally met his eyes. "I think we're going to have a lot of fun."

This time, when he reached for her shirt, she let him take it off. She reached back and popped the hooks on her bra. She tossed it to the side, where it landed on top of his sweats. She shimmied out of her jeans and panties and sat on the arm of the couch again.

Holy hell. He'd seen her naked before, but damn. "Yeah, definitely a lot of fun to be had here. Lay back."

That curious brow of her raised, but she did as he asked, reaching across to the other side of the couch for a throw pillow to put under her head. Jericho stepped between her legs and ran his hands up her thighs, his thumbs sliding into the crease where her legs joined her body and brushing through the short crop of hair.

He didn't stop there. His hands continued their exploration up her body, cupping her breasts and rolling her nipples between his thumb and forefinger. Leaning over her, he braced his weight on his hands, his cock nestling in her curls as he kissed his way up her lithe, curvaceous body.

She bucked up into him, the smile slipping from her lips as the heat rose to her cheeks. Her hand went to the back of his head and pushed down, directing him where she wanted him most. Jericho never pegged her for a woman who begged for what she wanted. She was the type of woman who demanded it.

And that fucking turned him the hell on even more. Kneading her breasts, he sucked first one nipple into his mouth and then the other, teasing the stiff peaks with the tip of his tongue. The needy, greedy sounds she made in the back of her throat brought a groan to his.

His dick strained, the precum leaking freely onto her lower abdomen. He wanted to be buried balls deep in her wet warmth, but not yet. First, he wanted to watch her lose control.

Wanted to push her over the edge.

Wanted to place the light in her eyes, the song in her ears, the beat in her chest.

She pushed down on the top of his head, sending him down where he'd already been headed. He kissed and nibbled on that sensitive crease where her legs joined her body as she arched up, seeking that friction and sweet, sensual release.

He chuckled when she lifted her legs and put them over his shoulders, right where he wanted them. Brushing a thumb through her folds, he found her already slick. He found her clit, and her saucy, sexy grin returned, though her eyes remained heavy-lidded and half-mast as if they wanted to roll back into her head and just... *feel.*

Sinking to his knees, he could no longer deny her what they both wanted. The first taste of her made his cock jump and her fingers fist in his hair, stinging his roots in the best way. He found her sensitive nub with his tongue and laved and sucked and kissed. She ground against his face, holding him there though he had no intentions of going anywhere anytime soon.

He buried his nose in her curls, wanting to breathe in her intoxicating scent. A combination of musk and wanton sex. Her heels dug into his back, and her head tossed side to side, her breathing turning into soft pants and strangled sighs.

"Fuck me," she groaned, equal parts curse and command. He stiffened his tongue and fucked her with it.

When her thrusts grew more frantic as she neared her peak, he replaced his tongue with two fingers and brought his lips down on her clit. Her legs clamped around him, a warm, wet vise. One he never wanted to escape. Then he curled his fingers and found that spot. She stiffened beneath him, the grip on his hair fierce as the climax ripped through her.

Finally, she released him, and Jericho wiped his face on his discarded shirt before returning to her with his hand outstretched and his cock harder than he could ever remember it being. Out of breath, she brushed the long bangs out of her face. Light from the kitchen kissed all the high points of her skin, the silky sheen of sweat glistening in the glow.

Blowing out a breath, she reached for his hand, her legs a bit wobbly when she stood. She locked her arms around his neck and kissed him, the strokes of her tongue languid. "Fucking amazing."

No lie. Eating her out hadn't been a hardship. "There's more where that came from."

"I like the sound of that." She reached down and, with little warning, wrapped her hand around his cock. For a moment, his brain waves flat-lined. She stroked from base to tip, an appreciative moan falling from her lips. "Now I know how Goldilocks felt."

He laughed, having no clue where she planned on going with that, but damn if he couldn't wait to find out. "Goldilocks?"

Cassie kept up the mind-numbing, thought stealing strokes as she explained. "Yeah, you know when she found the penis that was just right."

"I think that was porridge."

"I prefer what I found. Care to take this into the bedroom and show me what this bad boy can do?"

In answer, he lifted her, and she wrapped her legs around his waist, his hard cock caught between their bodies. He walked down the short hall to the only bedroom and dropped her on the bed.

Because of the cabin's limited square footage, the builder hadn't wasted valuable real estate on the bedroom. The queen-sized bed had enough room to walk around and have a bedside table on either side. The dresser sat on the wall opposite the foot of the bed. Nothing else. And since he rented, the walls remained bare, and the log-like bedside tables constituted all of his decoration. Even the window didn't have a covering. But this far up the mountain, he didn't have any close neighbors that would make not having them a problem.

Besides, he liked being woken up by the sun and seeing the glitter and glow of the stars and moon streaming through his window at night. The way it did right then.

"Wait," she said. "I forgot my purse." Which had the ribbon of condoms she so conveniently and thoughtfully brought.

Before she could stand, he pulled open the bedside drawer and retrieved an unopened box of condoms. "These should do. If we run out, we can always go get yours."

She picked up the box and held it up to the moonlight. A twenty-four count box. "This should do us for now."

11

CASSIE TOSSED THE BOX OF CONDOMS AT JERICHO. HE OPENED THE box and tore one of the packets open with his teeth. She almost stopped him and asked to put it on him herself, but she just rolled to her side and enjoyed the play of the sultry moonlight on the peaks and valleys of his chest and abdomen.

She loved the way he stroked himself—without an ounce of reservation or embarrassment—as he gazed down at her. He smeared precum over the head of his cock, and she licked her lips, wanting a taste of him. Despite coming a few minutes before, she wanted him inside her more, and she didn't want to do anything that might slow that down.

She could always go down on him later.

He rolled on the condom and crawled over the top of her. Straddling her hips, he braced his hands on either side of her head. She ran her fingers down the long length of the muscles on either side of his spine. Down to that muscular ass that she couldn't wait to get her hands on.

Shifting between her legs, his cock aligned with her. She ground into him, his erection teasing her each time it slid past her entrance. By the cocky, self-satisfied grin on his face, he knew damn well the effect he had on her.

She reached down and lined him up, tilting her hips to get the best angle. He sunk in slowly until balls deep, the stretch, the fill, the sensations stole her breath away. Definitely, Goldilocks hitting the cock jackpot. "You feel so fucking good."

He chuckled, the deep rumble rolled through her body. "Isn't that supposed to be my line?"

Slowly, he pulled almost all the way out before stroking in again. She knew he'd asked a question, but her brain lost the train of thought, and all that she could think about was the pleasure coursing through her expertly primed body. That first orgasm had wound her up, driving her desire to find the next.

His pace accelerated, his breathing amping up along with it. His grunts and groans egging her on. Leaning in, he covered her mouth with his, their tongues dueling. He broke free, the pace too relentless to allow them to kiss and breath at the same time.

Still, she wanted more.

Wanted that deep pounding that only another position would give her. Putting a hand on his sweat-slicked chest, she said, "Hang on a minute."

He stopped instantly. "You okay?"

"I want to turn over."

His eyes flashed. The light came from the inside and had nothing to do with the ambient shine from the moon. He pulled out, and she rolled over, going to her hands and knees. She smiled at him over her shoulder and wiggled her ass at him. He slid inside without hesitation, falling forward and hugging her back to his chest.

Vertebrae by vertebrae, he kissed his way down her spine between her shoulder blades, one of his hands snaking down to rub her clit. She ground against his hand and thrust back, taking him deep, but it wasn't enough. Going down to her elbows, she stuck her ass into the air.

"More." One word. A command, but it came out on a ragged breath.

Jericho groaned, his hands trailing up her body and kneading her ass. "You're fucking lethal, Cass."

That brought a smile to her face, though he couldn't see it. She loved knowing that she had the power to unravel him. Loved knowing that she could tear him apart the way he did to her. His big hands grasped her hips, using her as leverage for those long deep thrusts she craved, the angle just right that she didn't need her hands on her clit to come.

Reaching a hand back, she caught the back of his thigh, encouraging him to go faster. She had to hand it to him. He took instruction well.

He pounded into her. The sounds of his heavy balls slapping her filled the air, the musk growing thick, his breathing ragged and jagged.

The pressure built. Intense. Exquisite. Cataclysmic. She climbed ever higher. At the peak, she didn't wait for him before she fell. She cried out, the waves washing over her. He pumped into her again and again before his strokes became erratic, and he stiffened behind her.

She collapsed onto the bed, and he went with her, snaking his arms under her torso holding her tight. He buried his face into the crook of her neck, his breath hot, his kisses soft.

The tenderness undid her more than the double orgasms had.

He pulled out way before she was ready for him to. Normally, once a guy finished, she was ready to leave. But for the first time in recent memory, that urge to run didn't overwhelm her.

Maybe because you're finally with a man who sees you for more than a pretty face, a great ass, and a mind-blowing fuck.

She didn't know that. How could she? She hardly knew the man.

But that wasn't true either. He'd allowed her to see him at his most vulnerable. Allowed her to hold him and give him what strength and comfort she could. That spoke to her heart. She didn't know what had brought him so low, but that wasn't important right then. If he wanted her to know, he'd tell her.

He ran his hand over her hip and gave it a light squeeze. "I'll be right back."

Returning after disposing of the condom, he stretched out on the rumpled covers beside her, his breathing still elevated. Well, he had worked damn hard. She had to give him that. She snuggled up against his side and threw a leg over his.

He brushed a hand up and down her spine. "Give me a minute, and I'll be ready to go again if you want."

Those were words she loved to hear, but even as he said them, she couldn't deny the exhaustion running through his words. They'd been up very late the night before, and even though she'd had a chance to catch a nap before lunch with Geneva and her sister, he'd gone straight to work and had been going and going all damn day.

She crawled over the top of him and got out of bed, knowing she should ask if he wanted her to leave but was too afraid what his answer would be to ask.

As best she could, she cleaned up with a wet washcloth in the bathroom, too tired to take a shower. When she returned to the bedroom, she found him with his phone in hand. He must have retrieved it while she'd been away. She propped a shoulder on the door jamb. "What are you up to?"

He startled as if he had something to hide. Just a flash.

Maybe he hadn't heard her come out of the bathroom, even though she hadn't made an effort to be quiet.

Jericho set the phone on the nightstand. "Checking the time."

"It's late."

He had work tomorrow. The only thing she had was another list of places to apply for jobs. "Do you want me to go?"

The hesitation wouldn't have been noticeable if she didn't want to stay and wasn't hyper-aware of what his answer would be. "Stay."

She flicked her eyes to the phone. "If you have somewhere else you need to be. A date. A hookup. A—"

"No." He rose on an elbow, his soft cock laying on his thigh. Fuck if he didn't have the nicest cock. "It's nothing like that."

Normal Cassie would have said, 'then what is it like?' But this unrecognizable, unreasonably needy woman standing naked in front of him let it go.

He patted the spot on the bed beside him. "Come here."

And because she wanted nothing more than to stay, she did.

JERICHO LAY AWAKE LONG AFTER CASSIE HAD FALLEN ASLEEP CURLED up against his chest. He feared that if he closed his eyes, he'd fall asleep and miss his opportunity to go to Nadia's apartment and make sure nothing there might lead the authorities to him.

The sheriff hadn't come knocking on his door yet, but he couldn't take the chance that even though the scene had already been processed and released back to the apartment complex, that a detective might return to see if they'd missed anything.

Slowly and carefully, he extricated himself from Cassie's arms and gave her his pillow to hug. She shifted but never opened her eyes. By feel and starlight, he rummaged through the bottom drawer of his dresser and pulled out his black sweats, and pulled his black hoodie from the top of his stacking washer and dryer stuffed into the tiny hall closet.

Dressing quietly, he slipped out the front door. If he were quick, he could be back in an hour, tops. As heavy as Cassie had been sleeping when he'd left, the chances he'd get back before she ever realized he'd left were high. As a recovering gambler, even he could see that as a safe bet.

When she'd arrived earlier, she'd parked in the spot beside his truck. He only had to shift his truck into neutral and coast down the hill until he was far enough away that his engine wouldn't wake her and his headlights wouldn't fill the bedroom with light.

Once in Murdock, he made one pass by Nadia's apartment complex. After midnight in a medium-sized town, not a whole lot went on. A few cars on the road, but basically quiet, and more importantly, no sheriff's vehicles anywhere around.

He parked in the back lot of a local bar. Even if the bar closed before he returned to his truck, it wouldn't raise any suspicions because people would think that whoever owned it had gotten too drunk to drive and had found a ride home.

The bar's parking lot backed up to a natural drainage ditch that ran along one side of the complex. Jericho dug his lock pick set out of the hidden compartment at the bottom of his center console before exiting and blending in with the trees and over-grown brush.

In a matter of minutes, he stood in the shadowed treeline abutting the complex and watched Nadia's building for signs that anyone was around. There were a few lights on in rooms around the complex, but they were either bathroom lights with frosted glass or rooms with the blinds drawn. In the distance, dogs barked, and the rare car passed on the main street a hundred yards to Jericho's right.

It wouldn't get any better than that. He put on his thin leather driving gloves, stepped out of the shadows, raised the hood on his sweatshirt, and walked straight for the stairs to Nadia's apartment. He didn't run. He didn't skulk. He just acted as if he belonged there, not wanting to raise any suspicion if someone happened to spot him.

The single overhead light illuminating the upper breezeway lit the space enough to keep Jericho from tripping over anything. Still, he had to turn on his penlight and hold it between his teeth to unlock Nadia's door. Luckily, he defeated the simple lock in under a minute, limiting his exposure and his risk of being caught.

He stepped inside, using his penlight to find his way. If it weren't for the knocked-over lamp from the side table, the end of the couch shoved out of place, and the fingerprint powder on various surfaces, you'd never know that a couple of nights before, a woman had been killed.

Nadia kept a tidy space, and he performed a quick search, looking for the identity papers he'd made for her. He checked all the usual places like dresser drawers and the nightstand. He also checked the not-so-usual places such as the freezer, cereal boxes, and possible hidden storage behind vents, the medicine cabinet, and the toilet tank.

Nothing.

Nadia's sheets had already been stripped from the bed. He lifted the top mattress even though any detective worth their pay would have already done it. He even got down on his hands and knees and checked under the bed.

He couldn't decide how he felt about not finding the fraudulent ID. If they weren't at the apartment, then who had them?

The police? Nadia's boyfriend? Had she hidden them somewhere off property where no one would likely find them?

Going to stand, something shiny flashed beneath the beam of his light. He stretched out on his stomach, reached under the bed, and pulled out the object. He sat back and his heels, holding the casino chip by the edges.

It was a fifty-dollar chip from the Butte. He'd recognize the red and gold brand anywhere. How many of those chips had passed through his hands over the years? He didn't know what the chip meant, but he carried it into the kitchen and put it in a Ziplock before stuffing it into the pocket of his sweatshirt.

He checked her spare room last. A small desk under the window and some boxes that she'd never unpacked. When he shined his light at an angle across the desk's surface, he saw the clean rectangular area in the middle surrounded by a fine layer of dust. He had to assume by that that the sheriff more than likely had her laptop.

He and Nadia had only conversed and texted over his burner sim card. A card that he'd immediately destroyed once he'd heard about Nadia's death. He couldn't take the chance that the sheriff would find out about his illegal activities. People's lives depended on him.

He left with the same silent stealth that he came with, the bagged chip in his pocket. As he hiked back to his truck, he wondered if the chip was hers?

Or was it the killer's?

He considered turning the gaming chip over to the authorities on the drive back to his cabin, but that would raise more questions than it would solve. Plus, the whole breaking and entering thing would be difficult to explain away.

And after the sheriff's department had cleared the scene, the department would be unlikely to use the chip in court since they wouldn't be able to establish a clear chain of evidence.

In the end, he decided to keep the discovery to himself. It could have absolutely nothing to do with the case.

Returning to the cabin undetected proved decidedly more difficult than leaving. He cut his lights before they swept the cabin. Though he could do little about the sound of his engine, he kept it at a low rumble as he drove up. At least he didn't have glasspack mufflers or a yappy dog at home to give him away.

He opened the front door, knowing the hinges would squeak, but there was little he could do about them.

In the kitchen, Cassie turned, the immediate question in her eyes. *Where have you been?*

In his head, he didn't hear her voice as shrill or accusatory, but he couldn't dismiss the disappointment in her eyes.

She turned away from him without a word and poured herself a glass of water. She had his Henley on, and by the way it skimmed the tops of her thighs, nothing else.

"Couldn't sleep. I went to clear my head." Lying had never been an issue for Jericho when it came to his job. This time though, the disappointment on Cassie's face only deepened as if she'd heard every word for the lie that it was.

Maybe his too-fast explanation made his lie unbelievable. She was a perceptive woman. He should have known she'd catch the lie. But telling the truth hadn't been a viable option.

He felt like a total shitbag for keeping the truth from her, especially after she'd shown him nothing but kindness and grace.

"At first, I thought you'd ditched me the way I had you," she said, "but pettiness doesn't seem like your style. And this is where you live, not a hotel room. You'd have to come back eventually."

"I'm sorry I left." Jericho meant every word. If it hadn't been critical to try and find Nadia's documents, no one would have been able to pry him from a bed with Cassie in it.

She offered him a sip of her water. He accepted, then set it on the counter. Stepping in closer, he pressed a kiss to her lips. He didn't take it any deeper. The kiss wasn't about sex. It was about wanting that connection.

He'd never been a particularly needy man, so he didn't quite understand his motivations.

"You ready to go back to bed?" He held his breath, waiting for her response, knowing that her getting dressed and walking out the door was a possibility.

She gripped the edge of the counter as if she needed that physical lock to keep her from reaching for him. "Can we make a pact? No more leaving without letting the other person know?"

Which implied there would be a *next time.* Jericho could get behind that. It would complicate his life, especially with the covert work that he did for abuse victims but something about Cassie made him run toward the complications instead of away.

"That no leaving in the middle of the night works both ways." He gave her a teasing, pointed look, trying to lighten the mood.

She held out her hand, and he shook it. He didn't release her hand, and she didn't pull away as he led her to his bedroom.

Stripping down to his boxers, he slipped into bed beside her, pulling her back to his chest. The semi he got with his groin nestled against her ass couldn't be helped, but they were both too damn tired to do anything about it.

He kissed her bare shoulder, and as his breathing evened out and sleep started pulling him under, Cassie said, "You get the one freebie. Don't lie to me again."

12

CASSIE DROVE OVER EVIE'S CATTLE GUARD AND PARKED BESIDE Jericho's truck. She took a moment to blow out a breath, accepting the inevitable—she wouldn't be able to avoid Jericho the way she'd hoped.

She'd planned on spending the day applying for jobs and trying to talk herself into telling Jericho that maybe it would be better if they didn't see each other. Being drawn to him didn't negate the feeling that something else was going on with him. Something worth lying to her about where he'd gone the night before.

She didn't need that kind of trouble in her life.

Deep down, something told her Jericho was fundamentally a good man if she could get to the bottom of what he had to hide. But the last thing she wanted was someone she needed to fix.

She didn't need a partner.

She sure as hell didn't need a project.

Experience with her father taught her that you couldn't help people who didn't want it. And whatever Jericho had going on, he obviously didn't want her involved.

What do you expect? You've known the guy only a matter of days, and you think he will trust you with everything in his life? You didn't trust him with all of your story. Don't hold him to a different standard.

Geneva walked up the dock to meet her dressed in her paramedic uniform, That-a-way nowhere around. With noon approaching, Cassie got out of her car, the flush of embarrassment rushing up her face.

"Thank you so much for doing this for Wyatt," Geneva said. "The plan had been for me to do some of this admin stuff, but with all the extra shifts I've had to take recently, I haven't been able to keep up."

"We both know why I'm here. You two are hiring me part-time because you feel sorry for me."

Geneva stuffed her hands into the pockets of her pants, her eyes red and irritated, probably from lack of sleep. "We don't feel sorry for you. You need work. We could use the help. Unfortunately, the guys are still working out of the kitchen, so it'll be cramped until they move into the new building. Which if you ask me, can't come soon enough."

"I almost turned you down."

"You're proud, but you're not *that* proud."

Cassie laughed. "Apparently not. I'm here. "

Geneva smiled, then it turned into a wide-mouthed yawn. Cassie eyed her friend, "Why aren't you asleep? I thought you had the overnight shift."

"I did, and I am. I just wanted to say 'hi' before I did."

Cassie had to hold herself back to keep from laughing in her best friend's face. "No. You wanted to find out about how last night went."

"All I got was a text saying you were heading to Jericho's place for dinner and that you would tell me about it later. Well, it's later. Spill."

Considering her reservations about pursuing anything

further with Jericho, Cassie downplayed the evening. If Geneva had any idea how Jericho made her feel, the orgasms that had rocked her, how comfortable she felt around him after such as short time, Geneva would read more into it than what was there.

"We had dinner. We had sex. Pretty great sex. But I'm thinking about tapping the brakes on whatever this is."

You hadn't been until he'd left in the middle of the night and didn't tell you where he'd gone.

Cassie knew he'd done more than 'clear his head.'

They fell into step beside each other and hit the top of the dock. Geneva stopped and said, "What did he do?"

"Nothing specific." Cassie didn't know why she'd left out the part about Jericho disappearing in the middle of the night. "He'd explained away his lack of presence on the internet as his attempt to keep his digital footprint to a minimum, which makes sense considering the line of work he's in. But there's something he's not telling me, and I don't know if I'm prepared to stick around long enough to find out what that is."

"You think he has skeletons in his basement?"

"He lives in a cabin up in the mountains. He doesn't have a basement."

Geneva pulled a face that was more of an eye roll than a real eye roll. "Secrets, then. And who doesn't have secrets?"

Her friend did have a point. The purpose of dating was to slowly get to know someone, not to expect someone to spill their deepest, darkest secrets on the first date. "You're right. And sadly, his secret isn't that he's bi."

"You did *not* ask him that."

"I did. But in all fairness, he's a *don't knock it until you try it* kind of guy, so maybe that MMF fantasy isn't too far-fetched."

"See? Give the guy a chance."

She didn't need another reason to dismiss her misgivings.

She needed more of a reason to stay away. But even as she thought that, she knew staying away might not be in the cards.

They stepped onto the houseboat. It swayed a bit, the mooring lines groaning as the boat shifted and tugged on the lines. She opened the deck's sliding glass doors and found Massey, Wyatt, and Jericho sitting at the table. They stopped their spirited discussion when she and Geneva stepped in.

Massey, per usual, had his nose in his laptop while Wyatt and Jericho had theirs closed in front of them. At the far end of the table from the guys sat an open laptop Cassie assumed was for her.

Wyatt stood and went over and gave her a hug and a platonic kiss on the cheek. "Thanks for agreeing to help us out. We're starting to get snowed in with case requests and need to develop a triage system of potential cases to take."

Cassie appreciated Wyatt making it sound like she was doing him a favor when he was the one helping her out. The backs of her eyes stung, and she blinked hard until the sensation cleared, fucking refusing to cry. The computer equivalent of filing would never be her dream job, but it would keep the roof over her head until she found something else, and spending more time with Geneva never hurt.

Or spending more time with Jericho. Maybe if you get to know him better when you aren't trying to get into his pants or bed, it might change your mind about him.

She sat down at the seat with the unoccupied computer and said hello to Massey and Jericho. Geneva gave Wyatt a quick kiss and excused herself to bed.

"Where's Gil?" Cassie asked.

"Baby appointment," Jericho said.

Wyatt added, "He and Tessa had an OB appointment in Alpine. Something about a routine ultrasound for the baby.

Their doctor was running way behind because of an emergency, so I gave him the day off."

"That was nice."

That's one of the things she loved about Geneva finding Wyatt. She couldn't have found a more genuine, thoughtful, and considerate guy. Though considering how rocky their relationship had started with Geneva trying to roofie him for what had seemed like a good reason at the time, it had taken a little miracle and a lot of trust for them to come out together on the other side.

See, just because things with Jericho may look a little sketchy, you might have to trust your instincts—the way Geneva trusted hers with Wyatt.

Or Cassie could be deluding herself because she damn well knew she wanted Jericho in her bed again.

"Well, I have complete confidence that Jericho could handle the work alone."

Jericho gave Wyatt one of those chin bobs in recognition of the compliment. "It was just a lot of legwork, running people down, seeing if they'd heard or seen anything unusual the night of Nadia's murder. Not a very productive morning, honestly."

Massey caught her eye. "The email we use for people to submit their cases is open on your laptop. I'll give you the logins to the other pertinent stuff when we're done here. Feel free to interrupt if you have any questions."

She sat and wiggled the mouse. The dark screen came to life. True to his word, she didn't have to log in to start work on the email account. Massey, Wyatt, and Jericho returned to whatever conversation they'd been in the middle of when she'd arrived. As she scrolled and scrolled through the emails, she felt it every time Jericho's eyes landed on her, no matter how briefly.

She tried to ignore it. They were at work, and they both had things to do, and she refused to repay Wyatt's kindness and generosity by making googlie eyes with his new hire. Especially since she still hadn't decided if she wanted to fuck him again or call the whole thing off.

Well, she knew she wanted to fuck him. That was something that didn't need deciding. Continuing to see him, did.

As the scrolling continued, her eyes almost crossed. She glanced up, waiting for a natural drop in the conversation for her to ask her question.

"All I'm saying," Massey said, "is that the DeadMoney bounty site is getting out of hand. I don't see why the Feds aren't taking this more seriously. I mean, I understand that the world would probably be a better place without most of those assholes on the list loose in the world to do more damage than they've already done, but pedophiles and murderers are not the only people on that list."

Cassie had heard Massey talk about the DeadMoney bounty site before. Whereas she felt that shitty people had shitty things happen to them and died like the rest of the people in the world, Massey had convinced himself that people were somehow using it as a way to order hits on these nasty people.

While she didn't sanction murder, she couldn't lie and say that she wasn't a little tickled that Quest could no longer infect the world with his vile words and unfounded conspiracy theories.

"Even if you're right," Jericho said, "I don't know what we can do about it. There have to be hundreds of people on that list."

"You've told the Feds about your theory, correct?" Wyatt stood and went to the coffee pot. Massey held up his tumbler, and Wyatt filled it for him, before getting a cup for himself. Jericho and Cassie waved him off.

"Yeah, but they won't take me seriously." Massey brooded on the other side of the table. "I even told them that DeadMoney's bounty for President Cawley keeps climbing."

"He's the president of the United States." Wyatt retook his seat. "I'm sure there are many people who would like to see him dead. You did what you could. We need to focus on our paying clients."

Massey grumbled, and Cassie used that moment to interrupt the conversation. "Speaking of paying clients. There has to be close to a thousand emails here."

"Nine hundred and sixty-seven at last count." Of course Massey would know that off the top of his head.

"That's what I'm worried about. I don't want to miss an important case."

"I trust you to do your best," Wyatt said. "Potential clients flooded our email after we got national coverage on the arms bust. There's no way we'll be able to help them all. All we can do is try to find the ones we have the most likelihood of making a difference. That's all we can do."

The rising apprehension in her chest ratcheted down a couple of notches. It still concerned her that she might miss something vital, but she'd do her best to get the highest priority cases in front of Wyatt and his investigators. "Okay. I'll see what I can do. It might take me a while."

"I never expected you to get it done in a day."

Massey's computer *ponged* with an incoming notification. "Oh, boy. Finn is sending in an update."

He silently read the alert and rubbed his hands together. With mild curiosity, Cassie kept one ear open for what had Massey so excited and went back to her task, prepared to leave the guys to their work. She started by going through the starred emails, which had probably been Geneva's first attempt at some sort of organization.

"What's Finn got?" Jericho asked. "You going to tell us, or you going to keep us guessing all day?"

"Finn says that the lady who lives across from Nadia's apartment got scared for her safety and installed one of those camera doorbells yesterday. Someone entered Nadia's apartment last night, and she got a video of it. Finn says it's grainy and that it would be a while before their computer guys get around to enhancing it. He wants me to see what I can do with it in the meantime."

Wyatt set his coffee cup down, and he and Jericho opened up their laptops to watch the video Finn had sent. "This could be a big break."

"Hang on a sec, and I'll share the video with everyone, and we'll see what we have." Despite some dexterity issues with his hands from his cerebral palsy, in his own way, Massey worked his keyboard the way a concert pianist worked the ivories.

Because Massey had Cassie's laptop connected to the network with the others, the video popped up on her screen as well. She went to 'X' out of the video when it started playing automatically. Instead of closing the video down, she expanded it to watch.

Two clips played, one after the other. One showing the shadowed person coming and one showing him leaving. The first one showed the back of what looked like a man wearing a hoodie. He wasn't in the frame long before he dropped to the ground out of sight.

"Looks like he's picking the lock," Wyatt said.

Jericho shifted and cleared his throat, his voice casual when he said, "They only have locks on the knobs on the outside. Inside, all the apartments had the keyless deadbolts."

Something in Jericho's voice made Cassie glance at him. She expected him to meet her gaze, but he studiously avoided looking in her direction. What was up with that? The video kept playing. Cassie watched Jericho watch the video.

"There." Massey stopped the video, ran it back, and paused it again. She knew that because Jericho's laptop angled her way enough for her to catch the movement of the frames but not see the images on them.

What *she* saw was the immediate stiffness in Jericho's posture before he willed himself to relax. All in all, it took no more than three seconds before Jericho returned to normal. With their noses in their video screens, neither Massey nor Wyatt noticed.

"This looks like the best frame," Massey said. "Still not good, but as he's leaving, we at least get a shadowed view of his profile."

Jericho leaned in closer to the screen. "That could be anybody."

Cassie glanced down at her computer and looked at the still frame on her seventeen-inch screen. The time stamp on the video read one-thirteen am. Yeah, between the graininess of the frame and the hoodie nearly obscuring the guy's face, it *could* be nearly anybody.

But Cassie knew different.

The timestamp.

The dark hoodie.

Jericho gone during that time to 'clear his head."

She stared at Jericho's profile, then compared it to the still frame again, the man's features obscured in the blurriness, but Cassie knew the truth...

The man in the photo was Jericho.

M*OTHERFUCKER.*

Jericho shifted in his seat, the muscle in his jaw working overtime to keep the string of curse words from spewing out of his mouth.

He vaguely remembered that the young woman in the apartment across from Nadia's had mentioned wanting to get a security camera. He just hadn't expected her to get one that fast.

Maybe if you'd been more careful, more focused on the vital task at hand than how quickly you could accomplish the job, slide beneath the sheets, and wrap your arms around a beautiful woman, you would have taken an extra fucking second and scanned your surroundings before bulldozing your way through the apartment door without much of a second thought.

Massey toggled back and forth a few frames before settling in on one. "In Finn's email, he said the department sent the video to Wyoming's Computer Forensic Lab. They're good, but according to a friend of mine, fast isn't in their vocabulary."

Facedown on the table, Jericho's phone buzzed with an incoming text, but he ignored it. His right cheek burned where Cassie's stare drilled into him. He kept his focus on Wyatt and Massey, afraid that if he glanced her way, she'd see the confirmation of the conclusion she'd come to. He didn't know how she could tell the photo was of him when Wyatt and Massey had no clue, but the fact he'd left in the middle of the night around the time that footage had been taken, didn't help his case any.

So much for starting a promising new relationship. This would certainly be the end of it.

Cassie took a breath, and he braced, waiting for her to tell the group what she knew about him, but instead, she said, "This is the killer?"

Without taking his focus off the grainy image, Wyatt said, "Possibly."

It said a lot about Wyatt that he didn't jump to conclusions.

"Who else do you think it could be?" Cassie's tone was at the same time skeptical and curious.

Why hadn't she told Wyatt what she suspected already? Jericho chanced a glance at her. She raised a brow at him as if expecting him to insert his own speculation. He split his attention between Massey and Wyatt, afraid anything he might say could make him seem suspect or guilty.

"Could be someone opportunistic." Massey's fingers clacked on his keyboard, his brow furrowed as he worked.

Jericho assumed Massey's singular focus had to do with setting up the image enhancement. How much longer did Jericho have before Massey found him out and Jericho had to explain himself? He considered coming clean right then and there. It would go a lot farther into his believability if he went to them instead of waiting for them to come to him.

But Jericho counted on the possibility that Massey wouldn't enhance the frame enough to identify him. Jericho didn't know where the neighbor had bought the security system, but the company had robbed her. The camera quality was criminally sub-par, which gave Jericho a frail, thin, unexpected thread of hope to hang on to.

"If Nadia is dead," Massey continued, "no one would be home. If someone found out about her murder, they could have come to rob her."

"It doesn't look like the guy took anything," Cassie said. "Unless he hid it under his hoodie."

Wyatt nodded, considering Cassie's assessment. "Jericho, why don't you head to the apartment complex this afternoon and see if anyone else has anything on this guy."

That hole that Cassie's eyes had almost lasered into the side of his face only heated further. He stood, ready to get out from under Cassie's direct scrutiny.

Or maybe he read more into the situation than was warranted. The paranoia could be getting to him. On the other hand, maybe he was getting too old to be living what felt like a double life where his chances of getting caught for forgery and going to prison weren't without merit.

But then what would these people do? Who would these people turn to when they had no place else to run?

That's why you keep doing this. But it's not going to continue without it costing you.

And that cost could be his freedom.

His phone buzzed again, but instead of looking at it, he shoved it into his front pocket.

"You need to take that?" Wyatt asked.

Cassie had returned to her computer, and Massey worked diligently on whatever program he had that might send the sheriff after Jericho.

"No," Jericho said, "it's nothing." The outright lie rolled over Wyatt. Why couldn't the lies do that with Cassie? What was it about her that made it easy for her to see right through him?

Jericho excused himself. As soon as he slammed his truck door, he answered the text from the newest woman needing his services. Earlier, he'd recognized the double buzz he'd set on his dual sim card phone, the one that meant he had a text from either his contact in Ohio, or a client. At least he'd have time after he got off work to get Rhonda's documents ready.

He headed back to the apartment complex per Wyatt's instructions. It would be a waste of time, but he needed to check that box before he could continue moving forward with his investigation into Nadia's death. After all, Nadia's killer remained at large, and he refused to go to jail before that asshole did.

As expected, the afternoon turned mostly into a bust investigative-wise. Except the apartment manager had finally agreed to let him see the original footage from the night of the murder from the camera pointing at the road leading into the complex.

The manager had refused to make a copy, so he sat there for hours going through the footage. To be thorough, he fast-forwarded through footage for the entire night and copied down license plate numbers of every vehicle that had driven in. It remained entirely plausible that Nadia's boyfriend had another car or had borrowed one from a friend.

Finn's people would have to run the plates, but hopefully, he'd pass the information back to Wyatt for Jericho to further investigate. All his work could be for nothing because the boyfriend could have parked off property the same way Jericho had and walked in.

He made a note to see if the bar would give him a copy of their footage from that night. Who knew. Maybe he'd get lucky.

Later that night, as he drove to meet up with his client, with a copy of the bar's security footage from the night of the murder, what he did know was that *he* wasn't going to get lucky that night. At least not when it came to Cassie.

She hadn't texted all day. The practical side of Jericho told him she wasn't the type of employee to be on her phone during working hours, and the realistic part of him knew that whatever he'd started with Cassie had already met an untimely death.

The concern that coiled in his chest like a cobra told him that he'd already grown more attached to Cassie than he had a right to. But who could blame him? Sure, she was beautiful, but more than her body attracted him. She had a quick intelligence, a daring side, a mischievous and fun side. And he loved how she kept him on his toes and kept him guessing.

He didn't want her to feel threatened—or... he didn't know what the hell she'd feel—if he contacted her after he suspected she knew what she did about him. He'd wait for her to make the first move. If she didn't contact him again outside of work, then he'd have his answer.

His newest client, Rhonda, requested only the bare minimum of identification changes. A driver's license. He'd tried to talk her into getting a social security card as well to make it easier for her to find work wherever she decided to go, but that would have taken time the woman didn't have.

In the outermost slots of a grocery store parking lot, he met with his new client, far from the reach of any cameras at the front of the store. The exchange took no more than a minute as the woman slid into the passenger seat of his truck. She had the same haunted eyes and paranoid demeanor he'd come to expect from his clients.

She couldn't have been older than her early twenties, and fuck did it piss him off that she had to go on the run because some jealous, violent piece of shit couldn't control his vicious tongue and keep his goddamn hands to himself.

In an envelope, she handed over his low, previously agreed-upon fee. He charged all of his clients on a sliding scale based on their ability to pay, though he never turned anyone away because they didn't have the funds. Sometimes it covered his expenses. Mostly, it didn't.

He opened the envelope in front of her, not because he needed to count the money to ensure she hadn't shorted him, but because he needed to make sure the photos she supplied him met the specifications for the driver's license. Unlike Nadia, she had enough means to travel to where she wanted to go, so Jericho didn't have any involvement with any of her escape plans beyond the driver's license.

"When will it be ready?" The woman scanned all the windows, keeping a close eye on her surroundings. Because it was dark, he kept the interior lights off in his truck because you could never be too careful.

The woman had dark hair cropped short. The gaps and uneven edges told him she'd done it herself. With the light shining in from the parking lot light a few cars over, he noticed she had a splotch of hair dye on her skin. And even with the console between them, he could practically hear her heart fluttering in her chest.

"Tomorrow night. I'll meet you behind Cruisers. It's that biker bar on the outskirts of town." He didn't want to take the chance of meeting her at the same place twice in a row. Extra caution paid dividends.

"You can't get it to me any sooner?"

He would have to get it done that night for him to deliver it after work the next day. If he woke up early, he could meet her before work, even if Murdock was in the complete opposite direction as the Yates ranch. So much for getting a good night's sleep. But he would sleep better knowing she was safe. "How about tomorrow morning. Does six a.m. work?"

The woman's knee jackhammered, and tears sprung to her eyes. She looked like a terrified little girl, and his heart threatened to melt into a useless pile of goo.

"Any sooner? I just—I just don't know when he's going to be back. He's out of town until the day after tomorrow, but he's come home sooner before thinking he'd catch me with another man. I can't get rid of this guy. Why the hell does he think I'd want another one?"

Jericho wanted to hug her and tell her that everything would be all right, but he didn't want to scare her, and after what had happened to Nadia, he couldn't bring himself to say those words. All he could do was work his ass off to get the driver's license to her in time.

"How about later tonight?" He'd already had several nights in a row without much sleep. What was another? "I don't know when. I'll have to contact you when I'm done. Sometimes they can take longer depending on if I have any issues."

The relief on her face made the backs of his eyes sting. She buried her face in her hands, and her shoulders shook. He laid what he hoped would be a reassuring hand on her shoulder and gave it a gentle squeeze before releasing it. It took a minute before she raised her head, her cheeks a wet blotchy mess. He dug a fast food napkin from his center console and handed it to her.

Her chin trembled. "I don't know how to thank you."

"Pack your bags while you wait for me and promise you'll leave right after we meet. Don't go back home for anything. You got me?" When she nodded, he added, "You getting out of town safely is thanks enough."

She jumped out of his truck, and he waited in the parking lot until she'd made it safely back to her car. He kept a vigilant eye on her until she'd pulled into traffic, watching for anyone following her car and hoping like hell that he didn't read a story in the morning about her death.

13

At nearly eleven that night, Cassie lay in her bed when she should have been asleep. Between job hunting, doing work on the side for Wyatt, and the emotional whirlwind that had been the past few days, exhaustion gnawed at her bones, but sleep just laughed at her and turned away.

She climbed out of bed, stepped into a pair of sweatpants, and rescued Jericho's Henley from the dryer. She'd hated washing it, but after wearing the shirt non-stop for what felt like two solid days, it had practically walked to the washer on its own and jumped in.

Sticking her head in the fridge, she shoved aside the pizza box with the lone petrified slice and took out the block of cheese. Then she tossed it back in. She didn't need food. She needed answers.

Like what the fuck had Jericho been doing breaking into Nadia's apartment?

He wasn't a killer. Somehow she knew that in her bones and on a cellular level—but what was his connection to the dead woman?

And why had he kept it a secret?

She drafted a text to Jericho, then deleted it. That wasn't the kind of question you asked over text. It was the kind of hard question you asked in person, no matter how uncomfortable it made you.

The next thing she knew, she had her keys in her hand and had padded out to her car barefoot, not caring about the time or that her feet were bare. If she didn't do this now, she didn't know when she'd have the chance or the courage to ask again. She didn't want to confront him at work because she figured he had a good reason he hadn't yet told Wyatt.

Her headlights sliced through the night as she turned onto the road and headed for the mountain.

Why do you care so much? Why do you have to know?

Was it because she felt a connection to this man beyond the hot sex? Or, if she were honest with herself, did her need to know stem from her necessity to be so wrong about another man?

Her father had never deserved her unwavering trust, did Jericho?

Three or four times on her drive to Jericho's, she almost came to her senses and turned around. Each time, she pressed on. The last time she'd driven up the mountain road, there had been little traffic. This time, she got stuck in a small line of cars behind an RV whose engine couldn't handle the steeper inclines. On a windy, two-lane road without a passing lane for miles, she settled in for the slow drive up the mountain.

As she approached the long driveway to Jericho's cabin, she spotted headlights at the head of the drive. The truck pulled out into the opposite lane, heading down the mountain in the other direction.

Jericho passed no more than four feet from her, the dash lights highlighting his face. He never looked her way.

Where the hell was he going that late at night? Did he have a hot date? Or did he have more nefarious plans? She whipped into his drive, made a three-point turn, and followed him into town.

He turned right when the mountain road dead-ended into Caribou Canyon Road, which led to Murdock. There had been three cars between them before he made the turn and only one after. She didn't think he'd spot her following him. After all, he had no reason to suspect she'd be behind him.

She lost the cover car two blocks from where Jericho turned into Cruisers' parking lot, a biker bar on the outskirts of Murdock. She nearly turned around and went back home, except instead of parking in front with the other bikes and trucks, Jericho pulled around to the back.

Making the block, Cassie cut her lights and parked in front of someone's house a block away, her view of Jericho and the back of the bar clear. He sat in his truck in the near pitch black, nothing more than a shadow with no glow from his interior lights or even his phone. Five minutes passed. Ten. Fifteen.

Another car pulled up. Jericho exited his vehicle. The car's window rolled down and Jericho handed something to the woman. She took it and gave Jericho a brief hug. The rest of the conversation ended less than a minute later. Jericho watched as the woman drove away.

When he turned to leave, he surveyed the area around him, his gaze drifting over Cassie in her parked car. But instead of heading to his truck, he turned and headed straight toward her.

Fuck.

In a panic, she started the car, knowing he'd spotted her, but before she made a fool of herself and burned rubber, she killed her engine and rolled her window down. What was the point in running? She'd see him at Wyatt's in the morning.

Jericho walked directly toward her, which shouldn't have

come as a surprise since he didn't strike her as someone who'd avoid a confrontation if one were warranted.

And considering she'd crossed a line, she had the confrontation coming.

On high alert, Jericho scrutinized the area as he approached. She should have known he wouldn't be an easy person to tail. He leaned his forearms on the sill of her open window, his gaze raking up her body, the hint of recognition in his eyes when he realized that she still had on his shirt.

With effort, she stifled that part of her brain that wanted to tell him that at least she'd washed it, but she could tell by the annoyed expression on his face that the shirt was the least of his worries.

"What are you doing here?" His words didn't convey the exasperation clearly written in the lines on his forehead.

"I was going to ask you the same thing."

"It's not what you think."

Cassie's sarcastic laugh bubbled up from deep within. "And what do you think I think it is?"

He opened his mouth to answer, then closed it again, his eyes narrowing in thought. "You're not jealous."

"Why would I be jealous? We slept together one time."

Some of his annoyance abated, and a sliver of humor slipped in. "Technically, twice."

"We never made any commitments to each other. I don't have a right to tell you who you can or can't see." Before he could respond, she added. "A courtesy I expect goes both ways."

"Naturally."

She blew out a breath. His total lack of He-Man misplaced jealousy refreshing.

He leaned in farther, his voice gruff as gravel when he said, "Until we come to an understanding."

First, they'd have to get past what the hell he was up to

before they made any sort of promises or commitments to each other, that's *if* he were even interested in anything beyond the pure physical.

She waited him out. She hadn't followed Jericho because she wanted to hash out the parameters of their relationship. Cassie had followed him to find answers.

"But you're not here for that," he correctly surmised.

"No."

"Then why are you surveilling me?"

"I think you know the answer to that."

Straightening, Jericho stood at her window. Would he leave her there with all of her questions unanswered? Or would he trust her and bring her into his world?

When he leaned in again, the resignation rang clear in his voice. "Follow me."

He didn't give her a chance to ask any more questions. He just turned on his heel and headed toward his truck. Cassie didn't have to follow. Starting her car, she contemplated going home and going to bed. Was what Jericho did in his free time any of her business?

Anxiety tightened in her belly. A distant cousin of fear. Not of Jericho, but of what he'd tell her.

But that anxiety didn't keep her from turning on her lights and slipping in behind Jericho as he passed, the answers more important than thoughts of sleep or safety.

---

*W*HAT THE FUCK ARE YOU DOING?

A valid question that Jericho had no answer to as he pulled in front of his cabin. He didn't have to wait long before Cassie rolled up beside him on the gravel drive. She opened her car door but didn't get out.

He stepped over to see what the issue was and found her trying to find a comfortable place to set her bare feet on the sharp gravel.

"Where are your shoes?" If the worry about what she would say or do when she found out the truth about him hadn't eaten away at his stomach lining, he would have laughed. Who drove around in the middle of the night barefoot?

And in fuzzy pajama bottoms.

And your shirt.

She stood and hobbled out of the way of the door's swing. He caught her as she stepped on a sharp rock and her leg buckled. "Ow. *Fuck*. My shoes are at home."

At that rate, it would take her until morning to make her way inside. The conversation they were about to have would already take a while. If he ever had hopes of getting a few hours' sleep before having to head back to work, then he'd have to speed up her progress.

Because he figured she'd refuse if he offered help, he picked her up and carried her up the steps, and deposited her next to the door.

"You didn't have to do that," she said.

"You're welcome."

He hesitated with his key in the door, uncertain if he was doing the right thing in letting her into his cabin.

Into his life.

"Why aren't you opening the door?"

He unlocked the door and pocketed his key, leaning a shoulder against the door instead of opening it. "I'm not sure I'm ready for your opinion of me to change."

Strands of hair framed her face. She raised one of her skeptical brows. "Which opinion are you worried about changing? The one where I think that you're a decent guy with a bit of baggage, or the one where I think you have a penchant for burgling the houses of dead people?"

How about the one where you find out I'm committing a felony?

The calm that settled over her as he internally debated allowing her inside helped him make his decision. Everything he knew about Cassie so far told him she was a reasonable person who didn't leap to conclusions. Maybe she'd hang around long enough to let him explain.

"If it makes you feel any better, that was the first time I've ever broken into a dead person's home."

Cassie gave him one of those, *I guess so* shrugs. "Marginally. You going to let me in, or should I wait out here while you shove all your skeletons back into your closet?"

He chuckled at that. Stepping toward her, his need to pull her into his arms and kiss her flooded through him. He stopped short, half-expecting her to step away, but she didn't.

Cupping the back of her neck, he ducked his head and kissed her. She smelled like fresh laundry, and he couldn't help the thrill that went through him, knowing that she still liked wearing his shirt. A little thing, but it would make opening that cabin door a tiny bit easier.

The way her breath caught and she leaned into the kiss didn't hurt either.

With his hand on the doorknob, he said, "Will you give me a chance to explain?"

She dragged her tongue along her lower lip as if tasting him on her lips. The unconscious motion didn't help the semi he now sported. "I'm here, aren't I?"

The breath he held slipped past his lips, his semi retreated as the reality hit that he was about to tell someone about his extracurricular activities. He had to trust that doing so wouldn't land him in jail.

Turning the knob, he held the door open, and she preceded

him into the cabin. Normally, he was methodical about cleaning up his forgery operation each time he finished, being sure to hide everything in the space under the false bottom he'd made in the cabinet beneath the sink, but he knew Rhonda had been anxious to get out of town as soon as she could and with Nadia's death still haunting him, he hadn't wanted her to wait a second longer.

In his haste, he'd left all the lights on. He had his laptop, his ID blanks, his magnetic bar encoder, and his laminator on the kitchen table. Everything he needed to fake the ID. Cassie picked up the ziplock of blanks and ran a finger over the laminator, snatching her finger back and sticking it into her mouth when she landed on a hot part.

Reaching over, he turned off the laminator and took hold of her wrist, examining the patch of red on the pad of her finger. He ran it under the cold water in the sink. "You okay?"

She didn't answer. She pulled her finger out of the water and dried it on her pajama bottoms. "What is all this? You asked me to let you explain. So, explain."

"That woman tonight was a client of mine." He waved a hand, indicating all the equipment on the table. "These are the tools of my trade."

He held out a chair for her, and she sat instead of running. An encouraging sign. Lowering himself into the chair beside her, he took her hands, wanting or needing that connection, unprepared to lose her yet. Though, deep down, he knew there'd be no path forward for them without being upfront with her. Wishful thinking on his part that it could have gone any other way than it had. The forgeries weren't something he could have hidden forever.

And for the first time in a long time, he wanted something more permanent with a woman.

Here went nothing.

"I'm a forger. I make passports, driver's licenses, birth certificates, social security cards. If you need it for identification, I make it."

She picked up one of the ID blanks and pressed a button on the magnetizer that encoded the person's required information onto the magnetic strip on the back of the driver's license. The neutral look in her eye when she glanced up at him gave him an inkling of hope.

No judgment hung in her eyes, just an openness that told him she'd hear him out before making any kind of decision about them.

Or report him to the authorities.

"Why?"

"The short story—because it's late—is that I help abuse victims escape their abusers when they've run out of other options." To go deeper into his why would require a lot more time, and preferably a bottle of scotch.

"For money?"

"Sometimes. I spend far more on quality supplies, and bus tickets, and sometimes evens hotel rooms ever to make a profit. But yeah, for money."

"And if you get caught?"

"Probably going to prison." He didn't add that technically, she could be considered an accessory. Fuck. He hadn't thought about that. That alone should make him cut their budding relationship short, but he sure as hell didn't want to. Did that make him an asshole?

With a flinch and a nod, she took that information in. Instead of berating him, she simply said, "You're a hero."

He laughed. "I'm no hero."

"To these people you are."

"They're the real heroes. These people are saving them

selves. Their children. Sometimes leaving everyone and everything they know behind. That's not easy."

"I can't imagine that it would be. Why are you willing to risk telling me all this?"

The quadrillion dollar question. Without wanting to sound too invested in the two of them too soon...

Face it. If you're willing to tell her this—when you've never *told anyone in your personal life about it—then you're already way too invested. What if she stands up and reaches for her phone to call the cops? What are you going to do then, Einstein?*

Call a lawyer.

But for once, he willingly took that chance because Cassie seemed like someone worth the gamble. And if truth be told, he was fucking tired of going it alone.

"It's important that you know because *you're* important to me."

"We had sex once. I didn't know my girly bits had the kind of Marvel Comic superpower to make men fall at my feet."

"Jesus Christ." Jericho barked out a laugh, the tension in his chest easing a fraction. "You slay me."

"All kidding aside—" Cassie stopped mid-sentence, a hand slapping over her mouth, and her eyes went big as a harvest moon. "Nadia... she was one of your clients."

It wasn't a far leap, but Cassie jumped it with aplomb and grace. A knot between his shoulders loosened. He should have been worried that Cassie knew about his connection to Nadia, but like with the forgery stuff, his gut told him that she'd keep his secret safe.

Jericho nodded because an unexpected lump clogged his throat thinking about what that bastard had done to a vibrant young woman.

"You have to tell Wyatt."

Fuck. So much for keeping his secret. "You know I can't do that."

"It's going to come out. Give Massey a day. Maybe two. And he'll have that photo cleared up enough that they'll recognize you. Maybe not by the general public, but you can bet that sweet ass that Massey, Gil, and Wyatt will know. Hell, I knew, and the photo was blurry as fuck."

"Or I could quit."

"What? And go on the run? You didn't kill her."

"But I did forge her identification papers."

"Can anyone prove that?"

Jericho stood and paced in front of the table. He had no fucking clue where Nadia's identification papers were. They sure as hell weren't at her apartment. And if Nadia's boyfriend had taken them, the guy might have been smart enough to get rid of them. The only thing Jericho had to concern himself with was explaining away his breaking into Nadia's apartment.

He braced his hands on the table and let his head drop between his shoulders. Could he really get away with telling a partial truth without the rest coming back on him?

Cassie sat in the chair with her heels on the edge of the seat, her arms wrapped around her knees, and that maddeningly sexy brow raised at him as if she knew she was right and she was waiting for his pea-brain to catch up. "Wyatt's likely to fire my ass."

"Give Wyatt a chance. If you explain why you were at Nadia's apartment, then—Why *were* you there?"

"There had been no report about recovering the false IDs from the newspaper or Finn. I had to make sure that if she'd hid them in the apartment, that someone wouldn't come later and find them and maybe have them lead back to me. I'd prefer not to go to jail."

"Yeah, well, for a guy who is jail avoidant, you seem to keep doing things that could send you there."

She couldn't understand his drive to help these people, and he didn't have it in him to drop that emotional bombshell on her. A budding relationship could only withstand so much.

That's if she ever wants to see you again. Frankly, you're lucky she's not calling the sheriff.

Cassie stood and tied a knot in his shirt as she eased toward him, the soft, fuzzy pajama bottoms riding criminally low on her hips. With considerable effort, he dragged his eyes from the divot near her hip. It hadn't been a move meant to seduce, but it had that effect on him just the same.

She leaned that hip against the table, and he steered his thoughts back on track.

"That night at the casino," she said. "It was Nadia's murder that had you so torn up."

"It—" How could he explain the arctic blast that had blown through his system? The dump of useless adrenaline that buzzed around in his veins with nowhere to go? The immediate flashback to himself as a kid stumbling onto his mother's lifeless body?

He put his hand to his chest, still able to feel the bruising on his heart from that brutal blow. He settled on a version of the truth. "It's happened to other people I know who also try to help. But *I'd* never lost a client before."

14

Cassie held out her arms, and Jericho walked into them, his hug so tight it made it hard for her to breathe, but she didn't break it. She gripped onto him, not letting go until he did.

She had no doubt Jericho needed to come clean to Wyatt about why he'd broken into Nadia's apartment. A calculated risk, but Wyatt had been known to break a few rules on occasion. And while the end didn't always justify the means, surely this case had exception graffitied all over it in bright, bold, eye-catching colors.

Taking his hand, she tugged him toward the bedroom. He resisted when he realized where they were headed. "Where are we going?"

Laughing, Cassie said, "You know, I've never had this much trouble getting a guy into bed with me before."

He closed the gap between them and cupped her face. "You know it's not because I don't want to go. It's just—"

Jericho's brow scrunched, and the worry lines on his forehead told the story of the internal conflict warring within. "I don't want you getting mixed up in all of this. It could all go wrong. If you leave now, we can pretend this conversation never happened. That you didn't see all my equipment laying out on my kitchen table, that I'd never told you what I did."

"Too late for that. I'm not ashamed of you for what you do. I'm fucking proud. If that puts me on the wrong side of the law, then I can live with that."

He shook his head. "You don't—"

She shut him up with a kiss and put a finger on his lips when she pulled away. If he got that full sentence out, she'd have to slap the sense into him. "Don't say it. I've worked dispatch for years. I have friends who live and breathe law enforcement. Don't you fucking dare tell me I don't know what I'm doing. You got me?"

Her voice had risen with her indignation, but it only made Jericho's grin wider and sexy enough to set her panties ablaze— if she'd been wearing any.

"Got it."

"And tomorrow morning, we'll head into work and tell Wyatt together. Unless you'd rather do it by yourself. Either way, I'm on your side."

He hugged her again, tucking her under his chin, his heart beating a steady rhythm beneath her ear. She'd rarely noticed a man's heartbeat before, but something about *this* one spoke to her. It seeped into her, steadying her own.

She might have told Jericho she supported him, but she'd be naive to think she couldn't be facing some serious accessory charges if Wyatt didn't respond the way she hoped.

"That means the world. And yeah, if you want to be there, I could use all the support I can get."

This time when he extricated himself from the hug, he led her into his bedroom. One look at the bed with the rumpled sheets and soft, fluffy pillows, and her eyes started to close on their own. She went into the bathroom, brushed her teeth with the spare toothbrush she'd used before, raked her fingers through her hair, and crawled into bed without even bothering to shower or wash her face.

Jericho followed a few minutes behind and cut the bathroom lights. She curled into him the moment he laid on his back. The tension in his body remained as he absently rubbed her back and stared up at the ceiling.

She threw a leg over his thigh. "Try to get some sleep. Tomorrow won't be as bad as you think. I promise."

He pressed a kiss to the top of her head, his whisper gruff when he said, "I fucking hope not."

The entire drive into work the next morning, Cassie had second thoughts about the advice she'd given Jericho to tell Wyatt about the break-in, and by extension, Jericho's forgery operation.

She and Geneva had been best friends since high school, and she'd gotten to know Wyatt well over the past year, but as much as she thought that Wyatt would protect Jericho as well as he could, a niggling part of her couldn't deny the potential for things to go sideways.

That thought had kept her up most of the night, and it must have kept Jericho up as well because the bags under his eyes that morning could have held enough clothes for a month-long trek into the mountains.

Jericho had already arrived by the time Cassie had gone home, showered, and drove to work. He sat on the tailgate of his truck, scratching the middle of That-a-way's forehead.

Cassie parked and came around the back of the truck. Small flies sat in clumps on the cow's back, and Cassie had to bat away a few flying around her face. "Looks like you have a new friend."

"She's a good listener."

"What did she think of our plan?"

By the sour, dyspeptic scowl on his face, if he'd told her that he'd changed his mind at the last minute, she'd have no problem believing him. "I'm pretty sure she thinks I lost all sense, but she's intelligent enough to keep her opinions to herself if only to keep the scratches coming."

"Smart girl." She eyed Jericho. "Does that mean what I think it means? Are you coming clean?"

WITH HARDLY A WINK OF SLEEP ALL NIGHT, AND EVEN AFTER drinking a thermos full of coffee on the way into work that morning, every cell in Jericho's body felt like it had mutinied. He struggled with its need to shut down every second. He'd managed and fought serious lack of sleep before, but it had been a hell of a long time ago, and he didn't bounce back from that kind of sleep deprivation the way his younger self used to.

He wanted more time to think about what he wanted to do, but Cassie had been right. He needed to get ahead of this before Massey did his magic on the photo, and Jericho had to extricate himself from a much bigger hole. He might have another day. Two if he were extremely lucky, but this wasn't the kind of thing that you counted on luck to get you through.

"Yeah. I'm telling Wyatt everything. I should have said something yesterday, but I'd hoped I'd figure out a way around it."

"If you can't go around, you've got to go through." Cassie put her hand on That-a-way's shoulder and gently guided her out of the way so he could get clear of her horns and jump down. She started walking toward the houseboat.

"Wyatt came by a few minutes ago. We're working in the new building now. He and Massey got computers up and running last night and assembled some of the furniture."

She fell into step beside him. The newly finished official office of Steele-Wolfe Security sat a hundred yards behind Massey's barn, partially shielded by a hill. With its metal construction, it looked like the hay barns he'd driven by on his way to work. Only instead of having hay, this building supposedly had training facilities with offices above.

"How did Wyatt seem when you saw him?"

"Acted normal, as far as I could tell."

She slipped her hand into his, their fingers loosely locked. "That's good. Then Massey hasn't refined that photo enough to recognize you yet. We can still get ahead of this."

"*We?*"

She stopped walking, and he did as well. "God, you're fucking stubborn. I said I'd be there for you. I didn't mean just until things got a little rough."

He started walking again, the relief making it easier to breathe. "I don't deserve you."

"Everyone deserves support. You're no different. And if you open your mouth and try to argue with me, we're going to have a fight on our hands."

Jericho laughed. "You think you can take me?"

"I hear Wyatt installed sparring mats. I'd be happy to let you have your best shot."

"You're not even kidding, are you?"

"I used to date a cop. First and last time I'll ever do that. But he did teach me a few things."

The parking lot had not been laid yet. They navigated the ruts to get to the people-door entrance at the front of the building.

Next to the people door with the small covered porch large enough for a few chairs to sit down in after work, have a beer and watch the sunset, Wyatt had installed two large roll-up doors. Jericho had yet to see inside the training facility, but if he still had a job at the end of the day, he'd have to check it out. And maybe have that spar Cassie was itching for.

They wiped their feet on a new mat in front of the door. He

almost felt bad for dirtying it up, though that was why it was there. The door opened up into a windowed entry area with an elevator, a set of stairs, and a wheelchair-accessible door leading into the training area.

They took the stairs to the second floor, the morning sun streaming through the windows. Along the wall facing away from the road sat a short bank of offices, each with a window overlooking the main open area and the view of the mountains beyond, giving the area a spacious feeling.

The main area had a kitchenette currently without the refrigerator or microwave installed, but you could bet your sweet ass the extra-large coffee maker had already been set up, and from the aroma in the space, it had already brewed its first pot.

Through the corner office's interior window, they saw Wyatt taking a call. Cassie and Jericho headed over for a much-needed jolt of caffeine. They each poured themselves a cup, using the stash of new mugs on the counter.

Cassie boosted herself onto the counter because the table and chairs for the kitchen area were still stacked and wrapped in plastic off to the side.

Jericho stood beside her, leaning against the counter, the caffeine starting to stir in his veins. His fingers drummed on the counter where he'd curled them, but that probably had more to do with what he had to tell his new boss than the rocket fuel Massey called coffee.

The elevator whirred and pinged, and Massey stepped out using his cuffed crutches. He had his backpack strapped to his back. He came up short when he saw Jericho and Cassie in the kitchen. Massey looked down the building at Wyatt's office before stepping up to the coffee pot.

"You talk to Wyatt yet?" Massey asked Jericho. The way Massey wouldn't meet Jericho's eyes made the drumming stop and his stomach drop back to the first floor. Did they know? Or was it the paranoia talking?

Without waiting for a response, Massey said to Cassie, "I set your laptop up at the conference table. I'm not sure when the rest of the office furniture is showing up. If that doesn't work for you—"

"It's fine," Cassie said. "I'll work anywhere."

One of the offices looked large enough to be a conference room. At the opposite end of the main space sat a nearly diamond-shaped smart conference table that could easily seat ten people. Two on each of the edges, and one on either end.

Instead of one large screen on the wall, multiple screens hung from the ceiling, allowing anyone from any seat position to see a shared screen without straining their necks.

Massey screwed the lid onto his tumbler of coffee. With his crutches, he had his hands full.

"Would you like help with that?" Jericho asked.

Massey smiled, but it was one of those sympathetic, *poor bastard* smiles that did nothing to alleviate Jericho's anxiety. "Sure, that would be great."

They made their way over to the conference table, the top clear of any computing equipment, but then Massey pressed a button on the edge, and a recessed laptop popped up. He pulled out the full-sized keyboard tray from under the table.

"That's slick," Cassie said. "Do I get one?"

Massey gestured to the table, the cuffed crutch lifting with his arm. "Take any seat except the one at the head and the one with the clips for my crutches."

"Sweet." Cassie picked a spot on the second half of the diamond, while Massey and Jericho set up across from each other on the first, near Wyatt's chair at the head of the table.

Even though the last thing Jericho could concentrate on was looking through the copy of the security footage the bar had given him, he pressed the button on the edge of the table in front of him and a laptop popped up for him to use as well.

In Wyatt's office, his phone receiver landed in the cradle with a clatter that made Jericho jump. Massey scrunched his nose and only made the briefest eye contact. Cassie gave Jericho an encouraging little nod that he took to mean, *you've got this.*

At best, Jericho thought he had a one-way ticket to the unemployment office. The worst... he wouldn't let himself think too much about that.

Wyatt strode out of his office and headed straight for the coffee pot. When he'd finished filling his cup, he turned around. "What the fuck, Saint?"

So, they were back to last names. Not an encouraging sign.

Jericho didn't insult Wyatt's intelligence by acting innocent.

Massey clicked a couple of keys on the keyboard, and Jericho's face popped up on the overhead screens. He had to give Massey props. His photo enhancement skills were on point. Wyatt started walking their way, and before Jericho could respond, Gil walked through the door.

"Morning boys, we ready to catch a ki—" Gil stopped as he took in the heavy mood. "Who died?"

No one answered. Jericho wasn't dead yet, but he felt the breeze from the buzzards circling overhead.

"What's going—" Gil plopped into the chair beside Massey. Jericho occupied the chair across from him. Jericho's eyes went to the screen above him. His gaze dropped to Jericho, his eyes unwavering, his arms crossing over his chest when he said, "That's going to be fun to explain."

With a methodical, measured motion, Wyatt took his seat at the head of the conference table. "I'd like to know why I just fucking lied to Finn about Massey not finishing the photo enhancement yet."

Jericho released the pent-up breath through his nose, not

wanting to convey the epic relief riding the waves of adrenaline through his system. If Wyatt had lied, then it meant he'd been willing to hear Jericho out before firing his ass.

Cassie stood, and Wyatt turned his attention to her. "You can use the computer in my office if you'd rather."

Moving closer, she claimed the seat next to Jericho. "I'm staying."

Jericho nodded his agreement, and Wyatt sat back, an open if not somewhat skeptical expression on his face.

He hated to put his forgery operation in jeopardy, but he didn't see where he had much choice. If he walked out that door without a satisfactory explanation, all it would take is one call, and you could bet your ass the Feds would have him picked up before he could get fifty miles from town.

Cassie's knee knocked into his, and he appreciated her lending him her support. Jericho blew out a lungful of air and told everyone at the table everything that he'd confessed to Cassie the night before.

"How long have you been doing this?" Wyatt's first question wasn't what Jericho had expected.

"Five years or so now. Off and on. More *on* now, it seems."

Gil appraised him over the tops of steepled fingers. "About the time you left the force."

"More or less."

"Why?"

The one question Jericho didn't want to answer. It was a part of his fucked up childhood he preferred to keep to himself. Though he didn't see where he had much of a choice. "Because I couldn't save my mother. But I can help save others."

Cassie swallowed her gasp, and Gil nodded as if it made perfect sense.

"Finn needs to be looped in on this." Whatever Wyatt

thought about Jericho's motivation, his words held no space for ambiguity.

Jericho scrubbed his hands over his face. "You gotta do what you gotta do, boss."

Wyatt turned to Massey. "How long do you think it'll take the computer forensic lab to get that photo cleared up?"

"A little longer than it took me, but we have their backlog as an advantage. Considering this photo wouldn't be their top priority after Quest's murder, we could have a few days. A week or so even. However, Finn's going to expect us to have the answer much sooner. He wouldn't have given it to us otherwise."

Wyatt pulled out his cell phone, switched it to the speaker, and dialed Finn's number.

Jericho had no problem hearing Finn pick up, his greeting a rough and harried, "Finn."

"It's Wolfe. I've got something we need to discuss in person. Can you stop by sometime?"

In Finn's silence, Jericho heard traffic noise as if Wyatt had caught him on the street. "Today is out. The governor is on my ass, and it's all hands on deck running down the flood of tips. I might be able to swing by sometime tomorrow afternoon."

It didn't matter that it was a Saturday. When you had a case you needed to work on, you worked it. That went for Finn as well as everyone at Steele-Wolfe.

Wyatt winced. A day and a half was a long time waiting and hoping the computer forensic guys were equally as snowed as Finn. But Jericho appreciated Wyatt's willingness to wait for the in-person conversation.

Wyatt hung up with the sigh of a man who saw how this fiasco had the possibility of dragging his fledgling company to the ground.

"What do you want me to do in the meantime?" Jericho asked.

"I'd suggest you find something Finn can use that will make up for the forgery and breaking and entering charges he's going to want to slap on you."

Gil's laugh came out rueful. "This is *By the Book* Finn we're talking about. I've worked with this man. He doesn't have a bendable bone in his body. Titanium is less rigid."

Was Jericho fucked? "What are you saying?"

"That if I were you, I'd be getting my affairs in order in case he has you arrested."

15

THE DAY WORE ON. CASSIE SLOWLY WORKED HER WAY THROUGH Wyatt's vast *Potential Cases* email folder. She'd taken time out to pick up lunch for her, Jericho, and Massey because she was the only person not working on the murder investigation.

Wyatt had gone out with Gil to track down a few of the more promising tips that had dribbled into the sheriff's department that Finn had forwarded to them. She had no clue what Massey had been working so diligently on, but it required an incredible amount of coffee and caffeine, apparently.

If Massey cut himself, he'd bleed black.

Jericho ate his sandwich at his desk, having changed from coffee to the soft drink she'd brought him with lunch.

He slurped on his straw, and he set the nearly empty cup down. "Holy fuck, I think I might have found something."

Cassie glanced up.

Massey didn't. "Share it on the screens."

It took a few fumbles, missteps, and Massey telling Jericho how to share the video to all the screens. Cassie accepted the share instead of looking up and stared at the frozen video on her laptop screen.

"This is from the back parking lot of the bar I told you guys about. Watch this."

He hit play, and Cassie watched as a man exited from the rear door of the bar. The timestamp read, ten-twenty, p.m.

"Keep an eye on him," Jericho said.

The man walked past the vehicles in the parking lot. He flipped up the hood on his hoodie before disappearing off the bottom of the screen. From the camera's overhead perspective above the door, Cassie had difficulty judging the man's height. He didn't appear to be over six feet, but she wouldn't bet the case on that.

The time elapsed, and Jericho fast-forwarded the footage. Several customers came and went, their movements quick and jerky in fast forward mode. Then Jericho stopped the tape, about twenty minutes after the man in question had left the bar. "Here he comes."

"Oh, hello," Massey said. The man reappeared at the same location on the screen.

A woman left the bar and weaved her way to her car. The man didn't glance up, but he slipped into a late model truck that seemed similar to the description Nadia's neighbors had given Jericho and Gil. The woman turned her lights on and backed out of her parking slot, her headlights painting the truck in question.

Jericho paused the video. "There, do you see it?"

"Play it again," Massey said.

Jericho looped about five seconds of the video, and on the second replay, Cassie caught it. "You can almost read his license plate."

Massey's keys clacked. "Send that to me, Saint, and I'll have it cleaned up within the hour."

After Jericho had updated Wyatt, he had little else to do. He spent a lot of his time staring over Massey's shoulder. Massey had sent him to refresh his coffee for him a couple of times. Cassie got the impression it was more to give Massey some breathing room than the need for additional caffeine.

"Got it," Massey said at last.

Jericho rushed over from the kitchen, forgetting Massey's coffee in his excitement. Massey sent the image to the screens, but Jericho still looked over Massey's shoulder as if afraid it wouldn't confirm the same thing that Massey's screen did. If nothing else, Massey had the patience of a *real* saint.

"Fire that off to Finn," Jericho said. "They can run the plates and find out who this guy is."

"It could be nothing," Cassie said. "The guy could have gone to the bushes to take a piss before he left."

"For twenty minutes?" Jericho clung to the possibility that this was Nadia's estranged boyfriend. "It only took me about five minutes to walk to Nadia's apartment from the parking lot. Five minutes there, five minutes back. That still leaves ten minutes for him to get inside and strangle her."

"That's a pretty tight timeline." The doubt in Massey's voice doused Jericho's enthusiasm.

"Just send it. We can let Finn's people worry about proving out the timeline."

Jericho started pacing, and Cassie stood and snagged his hand. She liked that he didn't shake her off, especially with Massey in the room. He pulled her in for a hug, the tension leaching from his body.

"Do you think that'll be enough to get Finn on your side?" Cassie asked.

Jericho kissed her on the temple and let her go. "I sure as hell hope so."

ONE THING CASSIE LOVED ABOUT SEX WAS ITS ABILITY TO SHUT HER mind off, tune out the rest of the world and shrink it down to just the two of them. Or three, but hey, that wasn't on the table at the moment.

But Cassie was... on the table, that is.

Naked.

Jericho stalked toward her in all of his raw, naked glory. By the heated look in his eyes, the wide pupils, that devilish, rakish grin on his face, the hard cock between his thighs, he wasn't thinking about anything else than the pleasure they could bring to each other.

Hooking his hands on her hips, he stepped between her legs and dug a condom out of his wallet that he'd conveniently laid on the corner of the table after cleaning up the dinner dishes. She didn't think she'd ever be able to eat dinner at his table again without her panties getting soaked, but what was life without risk?

He rolled the condom on, but even though she hooked her ankles behind him and snugged him closer, he didn't shove inside her.

He leaned in. The feverishness in his little bites and nips and licks hadn't been there the other times they'd been together.

Neither one of them addressed it, but in no way could he not have noticed it as well.

Maybe because this could be your last time. If Finn isn't willing to bend a few rules—

She laughed in her head at her internal monologue. It wouldn't be *bending* a few *rules*. Finn would have to *break* a few *laws*.

Jericho flicked his tongue over her nipple, and she dropped the worry and the fear. She wouldn't let those thoughts strip this moment from them.

Her head fell back, and she held him closer, the sensations

curling her toes and sending salvos of friendly fire directly to her core. He reached down, sliding his thumb through her slick, thick heat. She unlocked her ankles and leaned back on her elbows, giving him full, unfettered access.

"Holy hell," he groaned, scooting her ass to the edge of the table and going down to his knees.

The breath Cassie sucked in caught in her throat as Jericho's lips landed on her inner thigh. The anticipation of where he'd go next tingled in her veins and made her heart kick at her sternum. If this man didn't put his tongue on her soon, she'd—

That expectant breath rushed out, her thighs clamping around his head. His self-satisfied chuckle rumbled through her lady bits. Her hand landed on the back of his head, directing him to her clit where she wanted him the most.

He sucked and nibbled on the bundle of nerves as she bucked up into him. Then he slipped two fingers inside her, and between his talented mouth and his fingers fucking her, she came hard.

She laid back, the delicious shivers and shakes rolling through her body. While she'd never turn down an orgasm, it wasn't nearly enough. She wanted all that he had to offer.

And deep down—if she were honest with herself—she wanted even more.

He wrapped her legs around his waist, pulled her into his arms, and stepped away from the table.

She kissed him, loving the way she tasted on his tongue. "Where are we going?"

"To bed," he said as he carried her toward the bedroom. "As much as I'd love to fuck you on the table, I'm renting, and I don't want to have to explain to them how we broke their table."

He laid her on the bed, the heat still in his eyes, but also a reverence, a fascination he'd never be able to deny.

Did he want more the same way she did?

Following her down to the bed, he covered her body with his, his hard cock nestled against her. He ground into her. His slow, languorous kisses and the way he nuzzled her neck made her heart ache. She'd never felt cherished and loved before, but she imagined this was what it felt like.

She couldn't wait any longer to take him inside her. Reaching for his cock, she guided him into place. Jericho's long slow slide inside made her back arch, and her head fall back.

"*Mmpfh.*" His guttural groan when he'd buried himself to his balls had her reaching for his ass, encouraging him.

"You're going to have to give me a minute." His words held a pleading edge as sharp as a sword's honed edge.

Jericho's harsh pants warmed her neck, and she loved the way she had him on the brink of losing control. She tightened around him, making it better and deliciously worse at the same time.

His body tensed, and his forehead dropped to her shoulder. "Fuck, baby."

But she didn't want his tight control. She needed his complete surrender.

"Don't fight it," she whispered in his ear. "Chase it."

Raising his head, he gazed down at her, his eyes half-glazed as he started to move inside her. She'd never been able to look a man in the eyes while they had sex, but Cassie couldn't look away. His heart, his compassion, his vulnerability filled her in places she had no clue had been empty.

He pushed to his knees, his hands beside her head, her breasts bouncing, the headboard thumping against the wall, but neither one of them cared. There was no one around to hear them.

As he drove them closer and closer to the brink, their breathing faltering and his pace picked up. She slid a hand down her body, hunting for that second release building and building inside her.

"That's it, baby." Jericho's words came out in short huffs and pants, the cords in his neck straining with his impending release.

Her thumb grazed over her clit, and that was all that it took to send her over the edge. She clenched around him, and a moment later, he cried out, stiffening above her.

His thrusts slowed as he came back to himself, bracing on his arms. "You feel so good. I don't want to pull out."

She wrapped her arms around him, both of them slick with sweat. "I wish we could stay like this. Shut out the rest of the world and not let it back in."

"Agreed." With one last kiss, he pulled out and rolled off the bed, his hand outstretched to help her to her feet. He engulfed her in his arms. "I would like nothing better."

He led her to the shower. Did he mean that, or was that just the sex talking?"

MASSEY ROLLED INTO THE OFFICE THE NEXT MORNING LATE, whistling to himself and using his wheelchair instead of his crutches.

Cassie glanced up from her computer screen. "You seem mighty chipper."

Despite the guillotine hanging over Jericho's head, he'd almost come into the office whistling as well, but having connected sex with an amazing woman tended to do that to a man.

"Got a lunch date today." Massey wheeled straight for the pot, which surprised no one.

"You okay?" Wyatt asked as he came out of his office, a pointed look at Massey's wheelchair.

Up to that point, Jericho had only seen Massey use his crutches.

"The spasms were extra bitchy all night." With an aggrieved expression on his face, Massey added, "But I'm fine, *Mother*."

Wyatt flipped him off, and Massey grinned.

Wyatt headed to the wall between the conference table and the kitchenette with a box cutter in his hand. He started slicing through one of the desk boxes that needed assembling. "Who's the lucky lady for your lunch date?"

"Well, it's not a *date*, date." The smile didn't slip from Massey's face. "It's with Isaac."

"Awh," Cassie said. "He's—"

"Just a friend," Massey reminded her.

Beside Jericho, Gil grunted, the corners of his lips turning down as he stared across the room at Massey. Massey glanced up as he wheeled his way toward the table. Gil stood and pushed Massey's desk chair out of the way to accommodate his wheelchair.

"What's the matter with you?" Massey asked, eyeing Gil and setting the brake on his chair. "You act like I'd said I had a date with your sister."

"You know Issac likes you, right?"

"You don't know that." Massey brushed Gil off and opened the laptop compartment.

"He used to be my partner and my handler when I worked deep undercover. I know what I'm talking about. If you want to lead a gay guy on, do it with some other man. Someone who's not my friend."

Massey's eyes narrowed, and the hardness that came to his face was the closest thing Jericho had seen to anger since he'd met the affable Massey. "Gay and straight men can be friends without it leading anywhere."

"Don't you think I fucking know—" Gil pulled himself up short, ran a hand down his face. When he spoke again, he'd moderated his tone, but the concern in his voice hadn't abated. "I just don't want you leading him on. I don't want to see him get hurt."

"It's just lunch."

Whatever else Gil wanted to say, he swallowed down. He abandoned the report he'd been working on and went over to help Wyatt with the furniture while he cooled off.

Massey's phone pinged, and the smile returned to his face when he saw who the text was from, though he glanced once at Gil before replying.

Powering up his laptop, Massey looked over Jericho's shoulder at Wyatt when he said to everyone, "Did you hear that Christian Novak got killed last night in Milan."

"Who's Christian Novak?" Cassie asked.

That name sounded familiar to Jericho as well. "Isn't he that director who can't keep his hands off the kid actors?"

"*Allegedly.*" Massey laid the sarcasm on so thick it could have insulated a bomb shelter from a nuclear blast.

"That's him," Wyatt said.

Gil helped Wyatt lift the desktop out of the box. "Let me guess. You think this is another one of the DeadMoney hits."

"That bet paid out a bunch CoinIt when the guy got iced. They did the world a favor if you asked me. Gunned him down in the streets, the same MO as Quest."

"From Murdock to Milan," Jericho said. "That's a long way."

"For the two-hundred-thousand-pound payout, the guy could have afforded a first-class hop across the pond."

"You seriously think a guy is going around collecting on

these DeadMoney bets by killing people?" Jericho didn't bother hiding his skepticism.

"Yeah," Massey somehow said it without sounding like someone who had an organized closet full of tin foil hats. "Except I think there is more than one person out there making their money that way, but those low-level hits are flying under the radar. But Quest and Novak, I'd bet were killed by the same guy."

"Playing devil's advocate here," Gil said, "Is anyone upset about two exceptionally shitty people not being around to spread hate and harm others?"

"What about if this thing takes off and it isn't just the assholes anymore who are getting killed?" Jericho added.

"Or governments overthrown." Massey pointed out. "President Crawley's betting pool is slowly rising, along with other world leaders. It's an emerging problem, and I don't understand why the Secret Service isn't paying it any more attention."

"I take it they haven't responded to your tips?" Wyatt pulled out the instruction sheet for the desk, groaned in frustration, then balled it up and tossed it over his shoulder.

"I'm pretty sure I'm in the Fed's frequent flier file, and they roll their eyes and delete my emails when they get any communications from me. They're not going to take me seriously, not when there are other, more credible threats out there. Even Finn elevating it up his chain of command at the FBI hasn't brought my concerns to the attention of anyone willing to order a closer investigation. I just hope this trend isn't going the way I think it will."

Wyatt's phone rang, and he leaned on the desk leg in his hand and answered. "Wolfe." He listened to the person on the other end of the line before adding, "We're in the new building behind the barn. Come on up."

Returning the desk leg to the box, Wyatt said, "Finn's here."

All eyes turned to Jericho, and it took everything he had to keep his heart rate steady and not gulp audibly. Had the state boys cleaned up that image way faster than they'd anticipated? Had Finn come to arrest him? "I thought he couldn't stop by until sometime this afternoon."

As if Wyatt had guessed what Jericho had been thinking, Wyatt said, "I don't think you should be reading anything into him getting here sooner. He could have had a break in his schedule, and it worked out better to come now."

The assurance did little to keep Jericho's pits from growing damp. Maybe he should open a window before he broke out into a cold sweat and Finn realized he had something to hide.

Correction... something to confess.

Fuck.

This is going to suck worse than a big bag of donkey dicks.

Jericho went to refill his mug even though he didn't want any more coffee. With the way his stomach twisted, the liquid had nowhere to go except back up the way it came.

But he had to have something to keep his hands occupied while he waited on Finn to arrive.

Cassie followed him to the kitchen, and the rest of the team settled around the table, giving them some space. "I want to tell you it's going to be okay, but—"

She must not have known how to finish that sentence because she shrugged and offered one of those tight-lipped sympathetic smiles.

Before he could respond, a ding sounded, indicating that someone had come through the door downstairs. Jericho kissed her on the forehead. "Thanks."

A few seconds later, Finn entered the office, his expensive suit less rumpled than it had been when they'd seen him right after Quest's murder. Maybe he'd had a chance to catch up on his sleep or at least go home and change his clothes.

Jericho and Cassie returned to the table, and after greetings all around, Finn took a seat next to the one Cassie had been using, giving Finn a good view of everyone on Wyatt's end of the table.

Jericho eyed the door. He wouldn't make a run for it, no matter how tempting.

The stoic expression on Finn's face revealed nothing, and Jericho fought the urge to fidget when he sat.

"We've had some developments," Finn finally said. "From that license plate you sent over yesterday."

Jericho perked up, but before Finn could continue, the elevator whirred, and Geneva came out of the elevator with a bunch of boxes on a rolling cart.

"Oh, hey. Hi, Finn. I didn't realize you were here." Wyatt got up and dragged the cart over by the rest of the furniture boxes.

Finn stood and greeted her with a kiss on the cheek. "Only stopped by for a quick update." He turned to the rest of them and said, "We found Nadia's boyfriend."

That got everyone's attention.

Wyatt and Finn retook their seats, and Geneva joined them at the table.

"Did they arrest him?" Jericho asked. As much as he wanted to get that asshole for what he'd done to Nadia, a small part of him got his hopes up that with an arrest, the detectives would care less about clearing up that security footage photo of him.

Cassie glanced over at Jericho, and he could tell she'd thought the same thing.

"No." Finn didn't sugarcoat it. "We brought him in for questioning but don't have strong enough evidence yet to arrest him. And his current girlfriend gave him an alibi."

"His name is Jordan Prince." Finn pulled out his phone, tapped a few buttons, and said to Massey. "I just emailed you a photo of his driver's license."

"Got it." Massey's computer pinged with the incoming email. After a couple of mouse clicks, he said, "Loading it up on the overhead screens now."

Cassie gasped as the image appeared. Jericho didn't know who he'd expected to see on the screen, but it wasn't the man Cassie had folded to at the Butte.

"You recognize him?" Geneva asked Cassie.

"I played poker against him the night Jericho and I met."

"Which night was that?" Finn pulled his pocket notebook and pen out, ready to take notes.

They were getting dangerously close to the time that Jericho would have to make his disclosure to Finn. His stomach cartwheeled as he found his voice. It might cost him his freedom in the long run, but it might be worth it if it brought Nadia's killer to justice.

"Wednesday night," Jericho said. "The night after the murder. He was with another woman. He didn't seem like a man who'd killed his girlfriend less than twenty-four hours before."

Gil's dark, humorless chuckle reverberated around the room. "Celebrating being free of Nadia and the responsibilities of a new kid?" Everyone grew quiet for a moment. As an expectant father, that news had to hit Gil extra hard. "*The motherfucker.*"

Finn rolled his pen over his knuckles. "Did you notice any obvious bruising or scratch marks on him?"

There hadn't been anything that had caught Jericho's eye. Then again, after a few drinks, he hadn't been exactly expecting to be running into the one man he wanted to get his hands on the most. "I didn't notice anything, but Cassie was closer."

All eyes turned to Cassie, who seemed unusually quiet. "I didn't see anything. He was just this regular guy. I used to think that if I was ever around anyone who could do something that evil, I'd have some sort of gut reaction. I mean, I sat across from him for hours and had no clue."

"Don't beat yourself up," Gil said. "No one would expect you to. I've spent enough time undercover with some really bad people who had done some shady and fucked up things. The thing about most of those people is that if I hadn't known they'd done those things, I never would have thought them capable as well. People can be good about hiding who they really are."

Massey had gone back to typing, half-listening in that way that he had when he couldn't keep from diving into his internet research or a problem in real-time.

Wyatt had been sitting there taking it all in, his assessing gaze occasionally landing on Jericho as if deciding when would be the best time to break the news to Finn about Jericho's involvement with Nadia. "What did Prince say in the interview?"

"I wasn't there," Finn said. "Nothing helpful. Sargent Howell indicated he didn't seem too torn up about the fact that his ex-girlfriend had been murdered, and Prince seemed to think that since they'd broken up more than a month or so before that, he shouldn't have much of a reaction to the news. They were over. He implied that he'd moved on."

"Bullshit," Jericho said, unable to keep quiet any longer. "That motherfucker couldn't stand the idea of Nadia dumping him. He tried everything he could to get her back, and when that didn't work, he tried intimidation, manipulation, and nearly full-on stalking."

Finn had one brow raised, his body language remained relaxed, but the intensity in his assessing gaze told Jericho that his outburst would cost him. Sweat pricked out on his upper lip as he waited for what Finn would say next.

Finn skimmed the other faces at the table and sat forward. "What aren't you guys telling me?"

Wyatt opened his mouth to speak, but Jericho was the one with something to hide. He had to own up to it.

Jericho rubbed his wrist. He could already feel Finn's cuffs locked around them. "Before her murder, and before coming to work for Wyatt," Jericho made a point of including the additional information about Wyatt at the last second because he didn't want Finn to think that Wyatt had been privy to Jericho's... *deception* wasn't quite the right word, more like an omission. "Nadia Bates had been a client of mine."

A muscle in Finn's clean-shaven jaw clenched. If he'd had his pen in his hand, it probably would have snapped. "Now would be a great time to laugh and tell me you're joking."

"No joke."

Finn's eyes went to Wyatt. Jericho gave his new boss bonus points for not throwing Jericho under the bus and reversing over the top of him by telling Finn he hadn't known about that tidbit of information from the start.

Instead, Wyatt said, "It's a complication we're working through."

Finn shook his head as if he could shake off the bad news delivered to him.

"There's more," Jericho said. He couldn't let the truth come out in drips and drabs, like a death by a thousand tiny cuts. He didn't want Finn braced for something bad to come out of Jericho's mouth every time he spoke. "And it isn't going to make things any better, I'm afraid."

16

Before Jericho could tell Finn about his forgery operation, Cassie put her hand on his leg under the table, giving him some moral support as he told his story to Finn about how he'd come to be involved with Nadia.

Each word out of Jericho's mouth seemed to deepen Finn's complexion shade upon shade. Though Cassie had to hand it to Finn, not counting a few clarifying questions, he let Jericho speak uninterrupted. Beneath the table, Jericho reached for her hand and twined their fingers.

Jericho's grip tightened when he went on to tell Finn about what the state boys would find if they were ever able to render the still shot from the security footage of him coming out of Nadia's apartment.

When Jericho finished talking, Cassie imagined the silence in the room was the thundering quiet that echoes for miles that hikers heard in the aftermath of a roaring, rolling avalanche.

Finn pinched the bridge of his nose, and Cassie couldn't breathe, waiting to hear his response. She squeezed Jericho's hand. She was so fucking proud of him for facing this head-on, knowing the truth could cost him his freedom.

When Finn met Jericho's eyes, he said, "This is a problem. One that I can't ignore. You know that, right?"

Jericho nodded, then cleared his throat, his voice cool and calm when he said, "I know."

Releasing her hand, Jericho stood, the tips of his fingers braced on the tabletop as if he needed them to keep him upright. "If you need to take me in now, I understand."

Jericho wouldn't look at Cassie, and he'd probably be the kind of asshole that wouldn't want her to visit him in jail if Finn took him into custody.

Finn motioned with his hand. "Sit down. I've got more important things to do right now than haul you in. I can't bury this. And ultimately, it will be up to the DA if they want to pursue charges, but I trust that when the time comes, you'll do the right thing and come in when we need you to."

If Cassie had been sitting any farther away, she wouldn't have heard Jericho release his pent-up breath. She wasn't any kind of empath, but the relief that slammed into her with a cataclysmic force had to be more than just her own. Jericho may have avoided trouble in the short term, but his uncertain future for him, for *them*, already knotted the muscles in the back of her neck.

"You have my word." The solemnity in Jericho's voice made it impossible not to believe him.

What Jericho had done was against the law, no doubt, but it had been with the best of intentions, and she found it impossible to fault him for that. Especially considering what he'd lived through as a child. He was so fucking strong.

"Where does this leave us," Wyatt asked. "Are we off the case?"

"I want this guy." Even as stoic as Cassie knew Finn to be, she sensed that deep down, emotions hit him hard, which probably made him such an effective FBI agent. A cool heat simmered beneath the simple spoken words. "Now that we know who this guy is, I don't want to take a chance of losing him before any evidence can catch up with him. With him admitting to being Nadia's ex, if his prints are found at her apartment, even a mediocre defense attorney won't have a problem explaining them away to a jury."

"You want us to sit on him." Gil had been quiet through Jericho's retelling, seeming to take it all in stride. But there ran a tight undercurrent to his words, and Cassie couldn't tell what part of the situation he had a problem with.

"I do." Finn's phone chirped. He read the message and stood. "I have to go. If this guy tries to skip town, I need to know about it."

"We're on it." Wyatt stood as well. "I'll walk you out."

Jericho slumped in his seat as the two men turned to leave, their conversation cut off as they entered the stairwell.

"That was pleasant," Massey said as he rolled into the kitchen and got himself a refill. He held up the pot. "Anyone else?"

There came a round of 'no thanks.' Cassie didn't need any more caffeine coursing through her system when the near-miss with Finn and Jericho already had her nerves frayed worse than cheap rope. While Finn might not have hauled Jericho in today, Finn had made it abundantly clear that Jericho was far from in the clear.

But Jericho had done the right thing.

"I'm proud of you," Cassie said, for whatever it was worth.

"That took a lot of guts." Despite his words and by the pinched expression on his face, Gil had other things he wanted to say to Jericho but held back.

Jericho must have sensed it as well because he said, "If you have something to say to me, come right out and tell me." He turned and included Massey in the comment. "You, too, Mass. If there's a problem, if you don't feel comfortable working with me, if you want to cuss me out, now's the time to do it. It's just us."

Gil glanced at Cassie, and Jericho added, "Whatever you have to say to me, you can say in front of her. There are no more secrets."

Massey rolled back to the table, and instead of burying his face into his computer screen, he waited to hear what Gil had to say.

"Why the fuck didn't you tell me about this? After what we'd been through together, you didn't think you could trust me?" Gil wasn't the kind of man who wore his emotions on a bright, ruffled sleeve but the flash of real hurt in his eyes told Cassie that Jericho's silence about his involvement with Nadia had cut him deep.

Jericho took the verbal slap, took what Gil had said, and answered the only way he could. "I should have."

"Damn right. This is a small firm. We have to have each other's backs. What you do or don't do affects everyone else on the team. We have to trust that if any one of us has a problem, we can take it to the team and find a way to work it out. You're with us now, and we stick together."

"It won't happen again." The tips of Jericho's lips curled up, and it looked like a battle to keep the smile down. Under the table, he reached for her hand and squeezed it. From what he'd told her, he'd been working alone for a while. It must feel great to be a part of the team, to know that these good people had his back.

"You have anything to add?" Jericho asked Massey.

"Can I see your forgery setup?"

"You're serious." The staid smile on Jericho's face turned into a full-sized grin.

"Yeah, I—"

"Absolutely not." The door to the stairwell slammed behind

Wyatt. He pointed to Jericho and Gil. "I want you two to come up with a schedule for the three of us to surveille this asshole." Then he turned to Massey. "And I want you to find a way to watch this guy's online activity. I want every link he clicks, every porn site he visits. I want to know everything."

"I can take shifts," Cassie offered. Four sets of man eyes turned toward her. "Don't give me that look. I can sit in a car and watch a guy just as easily as the three of you. And if watching this guy is going to last more than a few days, you're going to need more people helping. You know I'm right."

"What the lady said." Massey reached across the table, and they bumped fists.

Wyatt crossed his arms over his chest. "You want in on this, too?"

"Hell, yeah. I'm more than just a pretty face." Massey batted his eyelashes, and Wyatt barked out a laugh. "And with my white panel van, I'll look like any other utility vehicle on the street."

"Okay," Wyatt said in that way that said he wasn't going to argue with his people that were trying to make life easier. "And just so we're clear, Saint, what you did for those victims was the right thing. We all know it. *Finn* knows it. It's just a shame that the law doesn't know it as well."

Jericho swallowed hard before he nodded and said, "Thank you."

"All right, everyone, let's get to work. We've got a bad guy we need to make sure pays for what he's done."

JERICHO ROLLED UP TO HIS CABIN AS THE SUN ROSE, THE EARLY morning air cool and crisp on his skin. He couldn't help the smile that crossed his face when he saw Cassie's car in his driveway. These past few weeks working nearly nothing but surveillance on Prince had started taking its toll on all of them without a resolution in sight.

However, finding Cassie at the cabin, knowing she lay tucked up in his bed, made his morning. It still shocked the hell out of him that he hadn't scared her away yet, but damn if he didn't feel like the luckiest son of a bitch in the world either.

Quietly, he stepped into the cabin, shucking his boots at the door and stripping down to his boxers on his way to the bedroom. He needed a shower, but Cassie would be up soon for work, and he didn't want to miss the few precious moments he had left not snuggling under the covers with her.

She stirred when he crawled into bed, and she looked so damn delectable with her hair all tussled and the pillowcase lines on her cheeks. She rolled over, curled up against his chest, and threw a lazy leg over his hips.

He kissed her forehead, and she mumbled in that deep, sleep-thickened voice of hers, "How was your night?"

"Same as always. Prince was at his girlfriend's for the night by the time I relieved Massey. He stayed put all night. Completely uneventful."

What he didn't say was how he'd received a text from another woman who needed his services, and he'd tentatively agreed to help. There had to be something in between telling someone no and going to jail for helping, but for the life of him, he didn't know what that was. He couldn't sit by and do nothing and wait to read about another woman's death in the news.

Beside him, Cassie stiffened, then raised on one elbow and gazed down at him. The compassion and understanding in her features instantly made his throat tight. "Another woman texted you, didn't they?"

He couldn't lie. "Yes."

"We going to help?"

He rolled them so that he was on top and settled between her legs. "You are the most amazing person I've ever met. Do you know that?"

Jericho already knew that he'd fallen hard and fast for her. Deep down, he knew those feelings had grown way beyond crush and infatuation into a whole new territory that terrified Jericho.

He wasn't afraid to love, but he knew that she could completely tear his world apart if she decided she didn't feel the same. It made him extra cautious about expressing his feelings, afraid it was too soon and that he'd scare her off.

But to acknowledge to himself that he was falling in love with her, he could allow that much.

"Right back at you, babe."

He ducked his head for a quick kiss, but she wrapped her arms around his neck and her legs around his thighs, pulling him in tighter and pulling him under her spell. She reached between them and slid her hand beneath the waistband of his underwear, and took hold of him with confident hands. She would make them late for work, but he couldn't find any fucks to give.

Without breaking the kiss, he managed to shuck his underwear. She'd gone to bed naked, making it easier to slide inside her. Her warmth and wetness surrounded him, and it stole his breath.

Cassie grabbed his ass, holding him deep inside her. She bit her lower lip as her eyes fluttered closed. Her breathless groan echoed his own. "I love it when you're inside me."

She started moving beneath him, and with the tight grip her body had on his dick, he found it nearly impossible to breathe. She felt so damn good. And the way she moaned and cried out and egged him on, meeting him thrust for thrust, it drove him toward that knife's edge at warp speed.

He knew that she was close when she reached a hand down to her clit and bucked up against him. She came apart in his arms, and it had to be the most beautiful sight he'd ever seen the way she'd given herself over to him and their shared pleasure. He'd forever move heaven, earth, and all the cosmos if it meant keeping Cassie in his life.

Fire balled at the base of his spine, and as he came into her warm, welcoming heat, into her body, into her being, he realized way too late that he hadn't used a condom.

"Shit," he said as he tried to pull out. "I forgot the condom. I'm sorry, I—"

She held him tighter as he tried to pull away in panic. "I know. It'll be okay. It's done. Can we not just lay here a moment and deal with the consequences when we get up?"

"*Mmmm...*" He peppered her face and neck with the gentlest butterfly kisses and let the stress of his realization fade into the background as he enjoyed having Cassie in his arms, her warm breath and her sweat-kissed body wrapped around him.

He reveled in the aftershocks zipping through her body as she clamped down around his softening dick. His breath caught, but the moan slipped up the back of his throat, causing her to giggle.

"I've got you right where I want you, Saint."

"You wrapped around my dick feels anything but saintly, but making love to you is exceptionally divine." He wanted to slap himself for the 'making love' comment. For all he knew, this was only casual sex to her. He waited for her to stiffen at the slip-up. When she didn't, he rolled to his side and took her with him.

The movement caused him to slip out, and she grumbled her displeasure. "I suppose you're going to say that we have to get up now and get ready for work."

She traced a lazy thumb over his nipple. He grabbed her hand before she made him hard again, and they both called out at work. Probably not the best idea since he didn't need to do anything else to land on Wyatt's bad side.

"Unfortunately."

"You joining me in the shower?"

If only they had that kind of time. "I'd better not. You hop in. I'll start the coffee."

By the time he wandered back into the bathroom, Cassie stood at the sink in nothing but a towel as she brushed her teeth and dried her hair. He set her mug of coffee in front of her and quickly showered.

She handed him a towel as he stepped out. Her appreciative and equally hungry gaze at his junk didn't help. But he had to talk to her about the no condom thing. It wasn't something two responsible adults could ignore.

He wet the toothpaste on his brush and stuck it in his mouth. He raised his voice because Cassie had gone into the bedroom. "About the no condom thing…"

By the time he'd finished brushing, she'd come back into the bathroom fully dressed. The fact that over the past few weeks, she'd gradually moved much of her wardrobe over to his place pleased him more than a little.

She raked her fingers through her hair. Even with her face free of makeup, he couldn't quite read her expression. "Yeah, about that. I—I can't have kids. If you're worried about me getting pregnant, it's not something you have to concern yourself with."

"Can't as in no possible way, or can't in the way that you've been told you can't, but there's a small chance that you can?"

"Can't as in I had to have a hysterectomy in my early twenties."

"I'm sorry," Jericho said.

"It's not something I can change. But even before then, I'd never felt like I had to carry a child to be a mom. When and if the time comes, I'll foster or adopt. I would love any child the same. If that's a problem—"

Having his father's genes die with him had always seemed like the best gift he could give the world. "It's not a problem."

Cassie held his gaze as if needing to see the truth in his words there.

"Aren't we getting ahead of ourselves, though?" she asked.

The flush rushed up her cheeks, and she looked away, busying herself with cleaning up her stuff from the counter and putting it all away, pointedly avoiding his gaze when she'd held it so strongly only moments before. Did she think what they were playing at was a game? Did she not feel what he felt, did she not know the light she'd brought to his life, the calm, the joy?

Taking hold of her wrist, he stopped her from cleaning and turned her to him, stepping closer and trapping her against the counter so she couldn't avoid him.

"Are we, though?" he asked. "When I walked into that bar on one of the worst days of my life, I never expected it would ultimately turn into one of the best as well."

"This seems crazy fast."

Jericho almost held back, but he decided that he had to take a chance to get what he wanted. If she wasn't on the same page or didn't want the same thing, maybe he needed to know that now before losing even more of his heart to her. "Fast, yes, but fast doesn't mean it's wrong or won't work. I've been in enough relationships to know what doesn't work for me. But this. Me and you. It clicks. It *works*."

"So far, it works for me, too."

"What about Finn? About my forgery activity. If I get arrested—"

"Then we'll deal with that when the time comes."

"Does this mean we're exclusive?"

"If we are, does that mean I have to give up my dream of an MMF three-way someday?"

"Not if I'm one of those 'M's.'"

She'd never been with a man that her fantasy didn't threaten. She grinned up at him and sealed the deal with a scorching kiss that would make him think about her for the rest of the day, even though they'd likely be only a few feet apart at the office. "Exclusive with the MMF asteric then."

She pulled her phone out of her back pocket and scrolled to her pinned medical records. "My last STI screening. All negative."

He hardly glanced at her screen. "Mine, too. I can show you before we head in." From the other room, his phone pinged. "That's someone from work. We'd better get a move on before we both get fired."

Gathering his phone as he threw on some clothes, Jericho glanced at his screen and said, "Massey said he has something on Prince. He's going to show us when we get there."

Cassie followed Jericho to the office in her car. With them all taking shifts watching Prince, it made sense for them to take separate vehicles. Her body practically vibrated on the ride in. She couldn't tell if it was because of the jet fuel coffee Jericho had brewed, her excitement over what Massey had dug up, their scorching quickie that morning that still had her lady bits all abuzz, or, if for the first time, the thought of taking her relationship to the next level didn't tangle her tummy into knots.

Was this what a healthy relationship felt like?

With the new parking area poured, they didn't have to walk over from the dock. The building's double doors were rolled up, and the grunts and slap of bare skin drifted through the training area. She and Jericho walked in as Massey came out of the elevator on his crutches.

"Oh, hey," Massey said as he headed for the source of all the grunts and the occasional cuss. "I was just going to see if I could stop them before they did permanent damage to each other."

They followed Massey past the full set of weights and punching bags, the climbing wall, and the treadmills to the set of sparring mats where Gil and Wyatt were grappling.

"You two finished? Or do we need to hold the meeting out here?"

Gil released Wyatt from some hold that had him twisted into a knot, his face bright red. "Yeah, I think we're done."

"Until next time," Wyatt said as he rolled to his feet. He picked up a white towel off a nearby bench and tossed one to Gil.

They dried the sweat from their faces and bare chests enough that they could put their shirts on. Cassie glanced around. "Who's watching Prince?"

"No one," Wyatt said.

Before she or Jericho could add a *what the hell?* to that, Massey clarified, "We don't have to watch him anymore. Not when we know exactly where he's going to be next week."

Jericho glanced from Massey to Wyatt. "What are you talking about?"

"Come upstairs," Massey said, "and I'll show you."

The five of them piled into the elevator. It was a squeeze, but they all fit. In the couple weeks since they'd moved into the building, the other offices and the rooms with the overnight accommodations had been furnished for those times when the guys would invariably need to pull all-nighters or live at the facility while working an intense case. But even though there was enough room for them all to work in their own space, the main conference table seemed to be where everyone preferred to work.

On the overhead screens, Massey displayed Prince's driver's license photo. Since Wyatt had hired Cassie to work on his potential cases, she took her usual spot at the far end of the table and got to work, keeping one curious ear out for what Massey had to say.

"Where is this bastard going to be?" Jericho asked an undercurrent of irritation in his voice that hadn't been there before. Probably because Jericho had gotten little sleep in the past few weeks, and that man had been the cause of it.

Massey clicked around with his mouse.

Jericho's exasperated, "No fucking way," had Cassie looking up from the email organization that currently threatened to give her a headache, and she'd only just started for the day.

Her eyes went from Jericho's incredulous expression to the screen up above. "What does Prince have to do with the Butte?"

"After finding out who this guy was, I found him online. He's not on social media, but I sent him a phishing email and gained access to his computer when he clicked on a link."

Gil raised a brow. "Access to his computer?"

"He hacked in," Wyatt said.

"And got access to all of his emails. Unfortunately, nothing that might tie him to Nadia's murder. But this…" Massey pointed up at the screen, "this may be the break we've been looking for. He entered the spring poker tournament at the Butte."

"How does that help us?" Gil asked. "Beyond knowing that's where he'll be for most of the week."

Holy hell. It was almost like a gift. "We can get close to him there."

Jericho slowly nodded as the ramifications of what Cassie said hit home. "We could. Maybe he'd leak information if we got him drunk enough or befriended him in some way."

"That was my thought as well." Wyatt made some notes on the pad of paper beside him. "We would need to put someone in the tournament, so they'd have a reason to be in the poker room with him."

Gil raised both of his hands. "Don't look at me. I lose at *Go Fish!* to Jack almost every time we play. I'm pretty sure Tessa's kid is a damn card shark."

"I can't keep a straight face," Massey said. "Everyone can tell when I'm lying."

Wyatt glanced around the table, clearly unimpressed with the dwindling possibilities. "I've played with the boys some, back when I was with the department. I've got almost a week to brush up. I could—"

"You can't learn to play poker at a tournament level in under a week," Jericho said before Cassie had the chance to. She'd been too busy trying not to roll her eyes or slap her palm to her forehead to respond quickly enough.

"Give me another option then," Wyatt fired back.

With the way the morning sun shone through the office windows into the main area, the color change in Jericho's complexion catching Cassie's attention. It was the kind of change that made her think that his hand would feel cold and clammy if she held it.

Even though she wasn't one of the guys, and even though Wyatt had hired her more because she needed a job than because he needed the help, she said, "I'll do it."

"No fucking way," Jericho and Wyatt said at the same time.

Gil and Massey kept their opinions to themselves. Still, Jericho felt confident that with Wyatt on his side that Cassie's volunteering to sign up for the tournament would be crushed within the time it took for her to spit the first words of her argument out.

Talking her out of her hasty and ill-advised decision wouldn't be easy. Cassie stood with that same stubborn, determined look on her face that he'd seen when she'd caught him taking the driver's license to Rhonda. "Hear me out, assholes."

Massey and Gil chuckled. As against her signing up for the tournament as Jericho was, he struggled to hide his smile. Wyatt crossed his arms but kept his mouth shut.

"I'm the only one at this table who has won multiple poker tournaments. Not only do I stand the best chance of staying at the table with Prince, but out of the five of us, I'm also the only one who's beat him at the game."

That she had a fair point didn't make swallowing those words down any easier. Wyatt scrubbed at his jaw as if he was considering what she was saying.

"Wyatt," Jericho implored. "She has zero training beyond her skills as a poker player. It could be very dangerous."

"I didn't exactly expect you guys to drop me off and drive back home. I mean, you all would be there. You know, for backup."

"She has a point," Massey said, stating the obvious that Jericho didn't care to acknowledge.

Jericho didn't care that he, Gil, Masscy, and Wyatt would be there to keep close tabs on the situation. He didn't want Cassie anywhere near someone who'd strangled a woman with his bare hands.

And she may be smart and resourceful, but she was no match for a guy like Prince.

"And," Cassie said, adding to her argument, "who else here could befriend his girlfriend and maybe get some information about him? Like maybe he wasn't with her the whole night of the murder the way she'd told the detectives she was. Do you think she's going to tell any of you guys?"

She didn't wait for them to respond. As she came around the table to stand in front of Wyatt, she said, "No. She's not. You know it. I know it. I'm you're best shot. Admit it."

Wyatt scrubbed a hand down his face, his eyes flicking to Jericho before he responded to Cassie. Jericho knew what Wyatt would say before he even said it. And despite the promise Jericho had made to himself that he wouldn't gamble, that he wouldn't put himself in a position again that might cause him to backslide into a habit that had nearly ruined him, he couldn't let her go into that poker room alone.

Jericho would have to accept that risk. He'd rather lose himself to the gambling than take a chance on Cassie's safety.

And if he thought about it, gambling for the job had to be different than gambling for himself, right?

Hoping he wouldn't regret tempting his gambling addiction, he said, "I want in that room, too. I can hold my own in poker."

The unasked question in Wyatt's eyes said, *Then why didn't you volunteer that information a few minutes before?*

Jericho didn't shrink back from the question in his boss's eyes. If Wyatt wanted to have words about it, he'd go there, but he already had a huge strike against him. He didn't need to reveal his gambling issues and give Wyatt another reason to fire him.

Wyatt sat back, breaking eye contact. "I'll have to run this scenario past Finn to get his okay. It may be a hard sell even if it's our best chance on getting movement on the case."

Massey's fingers started working his keyboard. The now-familiar clackity-clack sounded a hell of a lot like progress. "I'll see what we have to do to register for the tournament and make room reservations before they get booked out."

"Good idea," Wyatt said. "We can always cancel later if we don't get approval."

"How many rooms do we need?" Cassie asked.

"I'm going." Massey's chin tipped up as if he expected Wyatt to give him problems about it.

"You damn well better," Wyatt said. "I'm not paying you to sit around here on your ass."

Massey nodded. The small smile seemed hard to control.

Wyatt addressed Cassie. "Five rooms then."

"Cassie and I can share." Jericho would be in her room anyway, no need for Wyatt to pay for a room that no one needed. "If that's okay with Cassie."

"If you can keep from being an overprotective asshole, that's fine with me. If you can't, I'm going to need my own space."

"Tell him, sister." Massey reached a hand up, and Cassie gave him a high-five, never flinching at the faux glare look Jericho shot him. "What? She's a badass. She can take care of herself."

"*Thank you.*" Cassie's hand slapped Massey's, and they ended the solidarity lovefest with a fist bump.

A smart guy, Gil kept his comments to himself.

All Jericho had to do was figure out how to complete the tournament without doing something ill-advised and lose Cassie or doing anything even worse and losing himself.

CASSIE PACKED HER SECOND BAG IN THE BACK SEAT OF JERICHO'S truck. She couldn't tell if the butterflies in her belly were because of the tournament, because she wanted to prove herself to Wyatt for giving her a chance or for returning to the place where she'd met Jericho.

Or because she knew that attempting to find a way to catch Prince admitting to what he'd done to Nadia could be extremely dangerous.

Prince hadn't seemed like the kind of guy who could strangle someone with his bare hands when she'd been sitting across from him while playing poker. But one thing that working as a dispatcher had taught her was that people could surprise you.

For better *and* worse.

Jericho locked up the cabin, and they climbed into the truck. He drew his sunglasses to the end of his nose and eyed the two stuffed suitcases over his shoulder. "We're only going to be there, like, five days, tops. You have enough clothes to last a month."

"I'm not playing in the tournament in my lucky pair of underwear, jeans, and a sweatshirt for four days straight. I'm not going to catch Prince's attention that way."

He turned around and started his truck, the muscle at the corner of his jaw ticking so hard she thought he might be going into a seizure. But she knew the truth. He hated that she was going, but at least he'd managed to swallow his objections.

"I know it's been hard putting aside your objections to this. And I appreciate you not being a total dick about it."

His snort of a chuckle surprised her. "*Not being a total dick* implies that I was somewhat of a dick."

"That thing a few days ago when you sneaked into Wyatt's office and tried to convince him to call the whole thing off qualifies as a bit of a dick move in my book."

The red crept up his neck. He didn't bother denying it. "You heard that then."

"The conversation did get a bit heated. The office has good sound dampening, but not *that* good."

They pulled out onto the main road. They'd already packed up the surveillance equipment they thought they'd need and piled it into the back of Massey's van the night before so they wouldn't have to meet at the office before making the hours-long drive to the Butte.

He held out his hand over the center console, and she linked her fingers with his. He squeezed her hand and said, "You've only just come into my life. I don't want to take the chance that anything will happen to you."

She took that in. At the same time that it gave her the warm fuzzies inside, it sparked that same protectiveness in her for him. It wasn't like this case wasn't without its risks for all of them. That's what happened when you lo—you had people you cared about.

You were about to say loved, *weren't you?*

Do you? Love him?

Knowing that she cared about Jericho wasn't the same thing as loving him. There was a whole lot of space in between. Yet despite his overprotectiveness, he'd proven to be caring, compassionate, and driven to do the right thing. To risk his freedom to catch Nadia's killer spoke volumes in her dog-eared book. But even with all that, there was something that he was hiding other than the forgery business.

Something he hadn't disclosed.

She didn't know how she knew, but she did.

And since she hadn't run after he'd told her about his forgeries, how terrible was the thing that he *wasn't* telling her.

You know a relationship isn't a deposition, right? He isn't obligated to tell you every deep, dark secret he has. Everyone has the right to some privacy, even in a relationship.

Still, it made her wonder.

And it made her wary.

But even then, she couldn't shut down her growing feelings for him. It would be like trying to hold back a flood with nothing but a little red bucket.

"This goes both ways. You know that, right?" Cassie glanced over. At least the ticking muscle in his jaw had gone away. "What about something happening to you? You don't think I'm worried about you doing something that'll get you shot or killed? Especially if you're trying to protect me. I couldn't live with that."

He kissed the back of her hand. "Trust me to do my job without getting killed."

"Only if you trust me to do the same."

Only the first half of a frustrated groan slipped out before he wrangled it under control. They drove the two-lane road through the twists, turns, ups, and downs. Her ears popped, and she had to close her eyes on a tight turn with a steep drop off and no guard rail.

"What you're forgetting is that I'm trained for this. You're not."

"I have bruises all over my body from all the self-defense work the three of you made me do this past week. I had to bring heavy-duty concealer. I don't want anyone thinking you're beating me if they see me in something more revealing than jeans and a T-shirt. At this point, I could probably take on the MMA welterweights by myself and win."

"The training doesn't count when it devolves into you pulling my clothes off and seducing me."

"*You* took your clothes off."

"Only because you played dirty and wrapped those sweet lips of yours around my dick and took me deep. What was I supposed to do?" The fake scowl pulled down his brows and tugged upward on one corner of his mouth. She had to laugh. "We're just lucky no one came downstairs and caught us."

"I'll bet we aren't the first ones to use those mats for some sweaty sex, at least not if I know Geneva the way I do."

"Yeah, but I'm sure it wasn't during office hours."

Jericho's deep chuckle warmed her heart and other, more intimate parts of her anatomy. If they didn't already have a specific time they were supposed to meet everyone at the Butte, then she would have made him pull off the road and do something about the buzz in her pants and the visible hard-on in his.

As it was, all the extra packing she'd had to do had them running late, and they didn't have any time to spare. Pity. Who didn't enjoy good road head?

The mountains turned to foothills and the foothills into plains as they drove closer to the reservation. When they pulled into the parking lot of the Butte, they couldn't find Massey's van anywhere. After checking in and getting all the keys to the rooms, the guys still hadn't arrived. Jericho pulled out his phone and called Wyatt to check on them.

She and Jericho stood in the shade under the covered breezeway at the front of the casino, the cool wind blowing Cassie's hair around her face. The call connected, and Jericho put the call on speaker so they could both hear.

"Everything okay?" Jericho asked Wyatt.

"A little hold up this morning. Gil was on the way to the

office to meet us when Tessa had to call an ambulance. Pre-eclampsia, the doctors think. She's doing okay, but she'll probably have to go on bed rest for the remainder of the pregnancy. Gil went to meet her at the hospital. We had to wait for his replacement."

Beside her, Jericho visibly relaxed. He'd already been concerned that the team was so small. Losing Gil would have made him even more paranoid and protective.

Knowing you couldn't pick up the kind of people with Wyatt, Gil, and Jericho's expertise off every street corner, Cassie asked, "Who did you find?"

"Boomer Wilcox," Wyatt said. "I don't think you've met him yet, Saint. He doesn't have a police background, but he's a former Marine, and you couldn't ask for a better man to have your back."

"I'll take your word for it. In the meantime, we're going to unload our stuff and have a look around. Hopefully, we can get a bead on this guy before you get here."

Cassie heard some fumbling around, and a horn honk on the other end of the phone before Wyatt came back on the line. "Right before we left, Massey was finally able to tap into the location services on Prince's phone. As of an hour ago, Prince had made it to the casino. And—"

Massey interrupted Wyatt, and after a short exchange, Wyatt said into the phone. "And according to Prince's girlfriend's post on social media not ten minutes ago, they're at the craps tables."

With Jericho still on the phone, Cassie started pulling him into the casino. She wanted to meet the kind of woman who visited casinos with a killer.

PRINCE'S GIRLFRIEND WAS NOTHING LIKE CASSIE HAD IMAGINED.

Not some hard woman with no feeling, more like this year's rodeo queen fresh off the farm with her flashy pink over-sized belt buckle, her ironed jeans, and long-sleeved rhinestoned cowgirl shirt. The only thing she was missing was the felt cowboy hat.

That first time when the girl had sat behind Prince at the poker table, Cassie hadn't paid the girl much attention.

She approached the craps table where the dice were making their way around the table to Prince. She cashed in some of Finn's seed money for chips. With it being a little past noon, the table wasn't full. Cassie found a place to stand across from Prince and his girlfriend. Tonni, Finn had said her name was.

Cassie placed her bet as Prince picked up the dice. After his first throw, Cassie and Prince both let their bets ride. Jericho stood back, a little behind her, watching. He hadn't gotten any chips for himself. He'd given some excuse about wanting the opportunity to watch for any signs that Prince may have come with people of his own, or any other dangers they need to be aware of. It was vague, though he'd said enough of the right things to be both plausible and a lie at the same time.

But Cassie would worry about that later. Prince rolled again, and the table cheered him on, the dealer stacking up chips all around the table.

Tonni bounced on the balls of her feet and clapped her hands. "Oh my God," she said, drawing the word God out into three long syllables. "This is so much fun."

She grabbed Prince's shoulder in her excitement as he went to roll again, knocking his arm. The dice rolled across the table, the first die landing on 'one' the other bounced off the wall, teetered on an edge before it also landed on 'one.' Snake eyes.

A loud groan went around the table. Prince turned and barked at her. "Damn it. Did you see what you made me do?"

The smile fell from Tonni's face as the tears sprang to her eyes. She put a hand on his arm. "I didn't mean—"

He shook her off as the dealer collected chips. "What the fuck. You just cost me a thousand bucks, do you know that?"

"Hey, man," a young guy at the end of the table said. He had the breadth and build of a rugby player. "It wasn't her fault."

Prince's rebuttal was lost on Cassie because Tonni glanced up at Cassie as Tonni's tears started falling. She swiped them away as fast as they fell. She mumbled something about going to the bathroom, but Prince was too angry and engrossed in the table's next roll of the dice to notice.

Cassie watched Tonni go, a perfect opportunity slipping away if she didn't follow.

She fake giggled and gave Jericho her remaining chips. "Nature calls."

She ignored the *what the fuck?* look Jericho shot her. After all, it wasn't like she was running off to meet Prince by himself. Tonni probably couldn't hurt a fly without breaking a nail.

Somewhere behind the slot machines, Cassie lost sight of her target. She hurried into the restroom, expecting to find Tonni crying in one of the stalls, but she only found an employee texting on her phone.

The restroom was located by the cashier booth, down a short hall that led outside—the same double doors her father used to sneak her through. She remembered there had always been scattered cigarette butts littering the ground from the employees taking their smoke breaks.

Taking a chance that she'd get locked out and have to walk around the casino and hotel complex to get back in, she pushed through the door, holding it open when one of the dealers snubbed out his cigarette and caught the door before it closed.

She found Tonni behind the door, leaning against the adobe

walls. The tears rolled down her cheeks uncontrolled, her hands shaking so badly she couldn't light her cigarette.

"Here, let me help." Cassie reached for the woman's cigarette and lighter. It had been years since Cassie had smoked, but she lit the cigarette and took a long drag before handing it over.

Tonni dried the tears and sucked in a lungful of smoke. She coughed and sputtered as if it were her first time but seemed determined to smoke it anyway. She held out the pack to Cassie, and she took one for herself.

Cassie lit it, took another drag, and dropped her hand to her side, content to let it burn down to the butt. "Are you okay?"

"I-I'm fine."

On that side of the building, there was nothing more than a small parking lot for the employees, and a wide drive allowed the supply trucks to resupply the casino. Beyond that, there was nothing much to look at. Dirt and scrub grass bumped into the back of a gas station about a quarter of a mile away.

With the sun high and the building blocking the breeze, sweat broke out on Cassie's neck.

She leaned against the wall, and Tonni said, "I remember you. You're that lady from the poker game a month or so ago."

No point in denying it. "I am."

"Jordy was mad that night after you won. It kind of scared me."

"I didn't win. I folded."

"But you had the winning hand. To him, that was all that mattered. And now you're here, and ever since he saw your name on the players' list, he's been acting weird."

"Weird how?"

"Just..." She made a vague motion with the hand holding the cigarette. She brought the cigarette to her mouth and took a small puff, the cough not nearly as pronounced that time. "He's in a bad mood all of a sudden. We had a great drive down, and I almost told him my news but wanted to wait for dinner tonight, but now... now I'm not sure I should tell him. At least not yet."

Sweat beaded on Tonni's forehead, and she unsnapped the little white pearl snaps on the cuffs of her sleeves and pushed them up while Cassie pretended not to notice the patchwork of old and new bruises running up both arms, much like Cassie's own.

At least Cassie had been bruised by men teaching her how to protect herself and not by an abusive asshole.

"You could tell me." Cassie tried to sound casual, but she wasn't sure she quite pulled it off.

Tonni scanned the bruising on Cassie's bare arms that her T-shirt sleeves couldn't hide before meeting Cassie's eyes. "I'd better not. I shouldn't even be talking to you. Jordy doesn't like it when I talk to strangers." Her eyes drifted to Cassie's bruises again. "You know how it is."

No. No, Cassie didn't. Not firsthand, at least. She counted herself lucky in that regard. The abusers tended to stay away from her. Probably because after working dispatch and being around cops, and even dating one and hearing all the domestic violence stories, she could spot the red flags from five miles out.

And while her father had been far from perfect, he'd never been physical with her.

"Sure," Cassie said, playing into the domestic abuse cards Tonni had dealt her and knowing that a real man didn't treat his woman the way Prince treated Tonni. "But Jericho is only looking out for me, you know? He's protective. He's jealous. But that's how I know that he loves me, right? I mean, when he gets mad, he doesn't mean to take it out on me. And he's so sweet when he apologizes. He brings me flowers and takes me out to nice restaurants."

"Jordy doesn't take me to the nice restaurants, but he does the dishes. And this one time, he made me breakfast in bed."

The queasiness churning in Cassie's stomach had nothing to do with her smoking and everything to do with Tonni not even knowing Prince was abusing her. Tonni thought it was normal.

"Awh," Cassie said, not knowing what else to say. And still, she had a morbid curiosity about what Tonni had planned on telling Prince. She thought she had a good idea what that was, and that only made her stomach pitch and roll even more. "Was it good news? Maybe it would cheer him up and put him in a good mood."

The sweetest smile came to Tonni's lips, her free hand drifting to her flat belly. "Maybe you're right."

The light came back to her Tonni's, and Cassie saw all of this young woman's hopes and dreams tied up in her little secret. Cassie assumed Prince was the father but couldn't be certain.

"How long have you two been together?" Even though Cassie didn't like where this conversation was headed, she couldn't let this opportunity to ask Tonni questions pass her by. She only hoped that Jericho stayed away long enough for her to get some useful information from her.

"Tonight is our sixth month anniversary." She touched her belly again. Whether consciously or subconsciously, Cassie couldn't tell. "That's why I wanted to surprise him at dinner with the news."

Six months?

Prince had been dating Tonni at the same time he'd been with Nadia. Maybe that was why Nadia had finally broken things off with him, not only because of the verbal and physical abuse but because she'd found out that he'd been cheating on her.

And maybe, Prince decided that he preferred not to be tied down by a kid.

A true prince, indeed.

18

Jericho extracted himself from the craps table when Prince lost the rest of his money. Jericho followed him at a distance through the casino, wanting to ensure that Prince didn't run into Cassie without Jericho knowing. From the man's demeanor, he'd recognized him and Cassie from the last time they were at the casino.

Prince clocking them made Jericho work even harder not to be noticed while he followed him. At least enough people milled around all the tables and slot machines that he could somewhat blend into the crowd.

After Wyatt texted that they'd finally arrived, Jericho passed the word onto Cassie and asked her location. The crew was heading up to their rooms, and Jericho and Cassie would meet them there.

He passed the info on to Cassie and waited for her under the *Winner, Winner* sign, where he had a decent bead on Prince. And while he didn't feel like he had to have an eye on Prince 24/7 the way they had in the beginning, he wouldn't trust him alone with Cassie.

Half of a double exit door down a short hall opened, the

bright early afternoon light flashing Jericho's retinas. Out of the stars in his vision, Tonni came through the door. Prince grabbed her arm and hauled her off like an errant toddler.

That Cassie stepped through less than a minute later didn't come as a surprise. The prominent worry lines on her face made his deepen as well.

"How did it go?" Jericho asked as he took her hand as they headed for his truck to get their luggage.

She glanced over her shoulder, but Prince and Tonni were long gone by then. "Okay, I guess. Good enough to confirm that Prince is a piece of shit, not that we didn't already know that."

Retracing their steps to the elevator, they stepped inside when the doors opened. They had the elevator to themselves, and he pulled Cassie to him, his finger skimming the furrow between her brows. "That bad?"

"Worse, I think." The elevator dinged, stopping on their floor. "I'll tell you all about it when we meet with everyone."

Jericho didn't press. He didn't want her to have to repeat herself. She looked shook up enough as it was.

She stopped outside Wyatt's door and turned to Jericho. "Just because I feel compassion for Tonni doesn't mean I can't do what Wyatt expects from me. They're not mutually exclusive."

He stopped her from knocking, not wanting to let that comment go without responding. "I never thought you couldn't, Cass. Do I feel protective of you? Yes. And considering we're dealing with a man who strangled a woman with his bare hands, I think rightfully so. Do I think that you can't do your job because of that? No. My job is to make sure that you can do your job in the safest way possible. I'd do the same for any one of the guys on the team."

Some of the tension left her shoulders, and she flashed him a hint of that sexy smile that always did a number on his ability to think coherently.

"Really? So you would share a room with one bed with Wyatt or Gil or Massey to keep them safe?"

"A room, yes. A bed… sharing a bed with you has nothing to do with your safety and everything to do with me wanting to wake up with you in my arms."

Down the hall, the elevator dinged, and Massey rolled out, a self-satisfied smile on his face that only brightened when he saw them.

He held up his fist to them. "Don't leave me hanging."

Cassie bumped his fist, and Jericho did as well. "What are we celebrating?"

Massey flashed his key over the card reader and punched the wheelchair access button. "I scored access into the casino's security room."

The door opened, and he and Cassie followed Massey inside. Massey had booked a wheelchair-accessible suite for him and Wyatt to share. They each had their own room and a large living space for them all to meet up. Plus, the bigger room made it much easier for Massey to maneuver if he preferred to use his wheelchair over his crutches.

The near floor-to-ceiling window faced the distant mountains. Wyatt sat in a club chair, his laptop open on the coffee table. A man came out of the kitchen with three full coffee mugs.

"Oh, hey." The man set one of the mugs on a side table with easy access for Massey's chair. He offered Wyatt one of the other mugs before setting his down.

"Boomer!" Cassie went over, and he gave her a bear hug that pulled her off her feet.

Boomer kissed her cheek and let her go. "Haven't seen you in a while."

"The job hunt has been keeping me busy. And now, with this temp thing with Wyatt, I haven't had a chance to come by the Lazy S." She turned toward Jericho and made the introductions.

They shook, and Jericho said, "I've heard a lot of good things about you. Glad you could join the team."

"Same," Boomer said. He had a disarming smile. From the stories Cassie had told him about Boomer on the drive over that morning, about him helping to take down a drug cartel that had nearly cost him his life, Jericho didn't think Brian "Boomer" Wilcox was a man anyone should underestimate. And if they did, it would be at their own peril.

Wyatt closed his laptop and glanced up. "Do you two have an update for us?"

"Yeah," Cassie said as she walked around Massey and took a seat on the couch by the sliding glass door. "Though I don't think it'll come as a surprise to anyone."

Jericho made a detour to the kitchen and got coffee for him and Cassie before taking the open seat beside her.

"I had an interesting conversation with his girlfriend, Tonni." Cassie told them about the bruising on the woman's arms. About Cassie's suspicion about the pregnancy. About her fear for Tonni's safety, if she told Prince, about it.

"I think we forged a bit of a bond." Cassie made a gesture at the bruises on her arms. "She thinks Jericho is like Prince. I think if I can befriend her, we might be able to get her on our side. If it comes down to it, she might be the one who can get the closest to Prince and get a confession out of him."

"It's bold," Boomer said, taking the remaining club chair next to Wyatt. "I like it."

"Or, she may tell Prince everything if we're not careful," Wyatt said.

As much as Jericho feared what would happen if Prince found out Cassie was prepping Tonni to turn against him, he saw the value in pursuing that avenue. "I think we have to come at this from more than one angle. But if I'm honest, this is the one I think would have the most likelihood of succeeding. Tonni gave the detectives an alibi for Prince, but with a little luck, she could help blow this thing wide open."

"Do you have enough equipment for everybody?" Wyatt asked Massey.

Massey gave Wyatt a withering look. "I've got enough wires and recording devices to go around. Don't worry."

"Do you think we can get ears in Prince's room?"

"We'd have to find it first," Massey said. "But that shouldn't be too big of a problem unless Finn won't allow it."

Boomer sat back, and the light shining in from the balcony bounced off the titanium prosthetic on his right leg. "Wyatt said you have a clone of Prince's phone?"

Massey twisted in his chair and pulled a phone out of the small backpack he had hanging off the back of his chair. He slid it across the coffee table to Boomer. "Every call, every text, every Google search. Every porn site. It's all there."

"It won't be admissible in court," Wyatt said. "But it can help us nonetheless."

Boomer picked up the phone. "With the SmartLock key system that the hotel is using, does that mean we can use this thing to enter his room?"

"Fuck." Massey reached across, and Boomer handed over the phone. "Why didn't I think of that?" He pressed a few buttons on the phone. "Looks like he declined that option at check-in. But I'll see if there's a way to activate it without him seeing the notification."

Massey's personal phone pinged, and he glanced up from the incoming message and smiled. "That's Peggy from security. She says she can take me on a tour of the security control room now."

"Do not sleep with her," Wyatt admonished as Massey pivoted and started rolling away.

"I promise I won't." Massey grinned at his boss over his shoulder. "At least not while we're working. When the case is over, all bets are off."

Wyatt shook his head at Massey's retreating back as Massey punched the wheelchair access button for the door and rolled out of the room. "I wish I'd had all that luck with women when I was his age. I'd like to know his secret."

"His secret is he's charming and sincere, and he doesn't pretend to be anyone but himself. It's refreshing," Cassie said. "And a total turn-on."

"It took me too fucking long to learn that shit," Boomer added. "Way too long. Luckily, Sidney waited around for me to figure myself out.

Wyatt chuckled. "Same with Geneva. She gave me just enough time to come to my senses and pull my head out of my ass."

Jericho didn't add to the banter. Instead, he stared out the window, the corners of his mouth turned down in contemplation. Would he ever reveal that part of him that he was hiding from Cassie? Or would it forever be this mystery between them?

And while she didn't think that people had to reveal every deep and dark secret to the person they're involved with, whatever he was hiding had him holding her at a distance. As if he couldn't fully give her his heart without spilling the truth.

Is that what you want? His heart?

Yeah. It was. For a woman who'd only wanted an anonymous hookup with no connection, and no strings, she'd fallen for a man with secrets and enough entanglements to make a string ball that reached the moon. And if she were truthful with herself, when she was with Jericho, she had no desire to cut any of them and set herself free.

Was that love? Wanting to be with someone and willing to accept them with all their faults and baggage?

Because if that were the case… she loved him. *Oh, fuck.* Did that change everything? Or nothing at all?

When this was all over, she'd tell him how she felt. They may be exclusive, but that didn't mean he felt the same. Hell, it might make him run. But if that was the case, it was better to know that now instead of months later when she'd invested more of herself.

"*Cassie.*" Jericho said her name as if he'd been trying to get her attention for a bit. She mentally shook off the feels and clicked back into the conversation going on around her.

"Sorry. What was that?"

Boomer stood as if he were leaving. "We're going to go downstairs and see if we can get eyes on Prince."

From the kitchenette, Wyatt added, "And we're going to get you and Jericho wired up, just in case you have any interaction with them. From here on out, we need to make sure everything is recorded."

She and Jericho got off the couch. "When do you want to meet back here?"

Wyatt rinsed out the coffee mugs. "Thirty minutes?"

"Works for me," Boomer said, "but I don't have to get too pretty."

"Thirty minutes, then." Cassie planned on changing into something more revealing and add a bit of makeup. Though she didn't want to look as if she were trying too hard to get Prince's attention, even if that was exactly what she intended to do.

She and Jericho were ready with five minutes to spare. She

wore a form-fitting skirt that hit her mid-thigh and paired it with four-inch, arch-killing pumps and an off-the-shoulder shirt.

Jericho followed her to the door of their room and put a staying hand on her arm. She turned around. "Hey."

He stepped closer, backing her against the door, one forearm pressed against the door, trapping her though there was nowhere else she'd rather be. "Hey, yourself."

He traced the back of his knuckles down her cheek and pressed his lips to hers. That one precious touch transmitted all of his concerns, fears, and affection. In his eyes, she saw all the things that he wanted to say swirling around in them, but they didn't have the time, and they both knew it.

"Is this the part where you tell me to be careful?"

"No. This is the part where I tell you I love you. *And* be careful."

Wait. What?

Cassie blinked. Her heart stumbled, then raced ahead. It was all her mind could do to catch up.

"Shit. Sorry." He ducked his head for a moment, not out of embarrassment, it seemed, but so that he could gather his thoughts. He met her steady gaze, no red blush covering his cheeks. "That wasn't the right time for that. But I don't want to take it back."

Those same words crouched on the tip of her tongue, ready to take that leap, but the words hesitated. What was the point in saying those words if she didn't know if she could stay? Not yet. Not when he still felt he had things he had to hide.

"I don't want you to take them back. They're mine now."

That arresting, endearing, sexy-as-fuck shy smile spread across his face, and if they had more than a couple of minutes before they had to meet in Wyatt's room, she'd let her body tell him what her words couldn't.

She pulled him into a kiss that made her heart zing and her

lungs crave air, giving him more than she took. When she finally let him go, she said, "We've got this."

She'd meant the job they were about to go on, but in a way, she meant their relationship as well. They had it in them to make it work.

If they could find a way to be open and honest.

He reached behind her and opened the door. They walked across the hall to Wyatt's room and let themselves in with an extra key. Boomer had already returned, and Wyatt had cleaned up as well. The men were in dressier jeans and button-down shirts. It made what she wore stand out less.

Jericho stepped over to the open briefcase on the frosted glass dining table and picked up the pendant. The gold chain dangled from his fingers, and he whistled. "Nice."

"I'm assuming that's for me." Cassie joined him and turned around, allowing Jericho to clasp it around her neck.

"It's your microphone." Wyatt handed Jericho and Boomer earpieces and kept one for himself.

Cassie stepped over to the full-length mirror in the entry hall and picked up the pendant nestled above her cleavage. It looked like an emerald held in an ornate gold cage. She turned it around and around but couldn't tell it was anything other than a piece of jewelry. "This is next-level James Bond shit."

Wyatt placed the earpiece in his ear. "You can thank Finn for all of this."

"I guess that means he was able to get the approval for this by his chain of command," Boomer said, a little impressed.

Wyatt pocketed his wallet and phone. "They were impressed with the results of our last case and were willing to give us the tools we needed to help get this asshole."

"Equipment, but no support?" Boomer asked.

"Nadia's murder isn't the Feds jurisdiction," Wyatt said. "Technically, they couldn't send in any people to help unless the sheriff asks for it, which he hasn't. But Finn managed to pull enough strings to at least get us these. As well as the recording equipment."

Wyatt slipped the recording device into the front pocket of his jeans, and it didn't look any more suspicious than a phone.

The butterflies swarming in Cassie's belly turned into a flock of pterodactyl. They were going to do this, and she'd been the crazy one to convince them to bring her along.

Fending off her second thoughts, she refused to back down now. Taking a deep breath, she pushed down on her misgivings and focused on the positives. They had their sights set on bringing a killer to justice, and best of all, Jericho loved her.

19

Jericho kept a proprietary hand on the small of Cassie's back as the four of them took the elevator down to the bar. A part of him freaking the fuck out over his verbal slip-up in their hotel room and the fact that she hadn't said those three little words back to him. While the other part of him focused on the task at hand.

He blew out a silent breath and knew that he had to put all of his concerns about fucking up his relationship with Cassie aside for the time being.

Wyatt's phone pinged, and he glanced at it as he switched his phone to silent. "That was Massey. He's still in the security room. Peggy is showing him around the extra security set-up they have for the tournament tomorrow. He doesn't know when he'll finish."

"We shouldn't need him for this," Boomer said. "I've heard about these earpieces. They've got a pretty good range. As long as we keep Cassie close enough, we shouldn't have any problems with the technology."

Jericho huffed out a laugh with a little *you're fucking right* thrown in. "Like we're going to allow her out of our sight for one second."

Cutting her eyes at him, Cassie said, "I don't want to be alone with this guy. Ever. So don't worry. I'm not letting you guys out of my sight either."

With a twist of his head, Jericho popped the vertebrae in his neck, feeling moderately placated. He trusted Cassie. What he didn't trust was her tendency to go off half-cocked. And while she might fully believe that she'd keep him or one of the guys in sight now, he wouldn't put it past her to forget all of that if she saw an opportunity to get the information they needed. Much in the way she'd ditched him at the craps table to follow Tonni outside.

As the day had given way to early evening, the crowd at the Butte picked up. They had to step around people blocking the walkway, mesmerized by all the lights and decor or simply trying to figure out where they wanted to go. More people meant they wouldn't stick out as readily if they hung out in the bar for a while.

The hostess showed them to a four-top table in the bar near a wall as Wyatt had requested. When they reached their table, the hostess placed the drinks menu on the table and said, "Kelly will be your waitress. She'll be by shortly to take your order."

"Thank you," Cassie said.

Jericho, Wyatt, and Boomer jockeyed for the best view of the bar that also put their backs to the wall.

"Oh no, you don't." Cassie moved to the seat with the most unobstructed view of the room and plopped down in the chair, her skirt riding up her thigh as she crossed her legs. Jericho had to glance away before he said *fuck all this,* and took her hand and dragged her back up to their room. "If the three of you sit on this side of the table, you'll look like the ex-cops and operators that you are. And no matter how crowded this bar is, you'll be made a mile away."

Wyatt took the next best seat because he was signing their paychecks. Jericho sat across from Wyatt beside Cassie, which left Boomer with his back to almost everybody, his grumbled *motherfucker,* the only indication of his irritation.

Cassie grinned at his discomfort. "One night with your back to the crowd isn't going to kill you. You know that, right?"

Boomer opened the drinks menu even though none of them were drinking that night. "Tell that to the overactive imagination of my adrenal glands. Every fucking hair on my fucking body is standing at attention." He pointed to the bead of sweat on his forehead. "And I'm starting to sweat."

Wyatt assessed Boomer with a calm and compassionate eye, then stood. "Sit here."

"I'm not taking your fucking seat. And fuck you for thinking I fucking—"

"Take the damn chair. I can tell by all the f-bombs that you're uncomfortable. I need you at your best, so sit your ass over here or head back up to the room and let us handle this ourselves."

Boomer stood toe to toe with Wyatt. "You're a fucking asshole."

A slow grin spread over Wyatt's face. "I know."

They both resettled in their new seats, and almost instantly, the tension visibly vanished, and Boomer muttered a quiet, "Thanks."

Wyatt clapped him on the shoulder. "Sure thing."

"Sorry," Cassie said. "I didn't mean—"

Boomer offered her a banal smile. "It's fine. I know you didn't mean—"

"My, my, my, my, my, my. What do we have here?" A curvy waitress walked over. She had long black hair in a bun on top of her head, the undersides dyed all the colors of the rainbow. Her name tag said Kelly K. She'd been their bartender the night he and Cassie had met.

"It's you two," she said to him and Cassie.

"We're back," Cassie said.

Stuffing her pen behind her ear and the notepad into the apron, Kelly snagged an empty chair from the table behind them and pulled it up. She muscled her way between Boomer and Wyatt. "Nothing better than being wedged between two beefcakes."

Boomer laughed. "We're all taken."

"He and I are happily married," Wyatt added with a finger waving between him and Boomer.

"Oh, honey," Kelly said with a salacious, unapologetic smile, "I don't want to keep you. I promise I'll give you back when we're done. Better yet, invite your women or your men along. I'm pretty sure I'd like your taste in people. The more, the merrier."

Kelly put her fist out for Cassie to bump. "Am I right?"

"Truth." After bumping fists, Cassie reached a hand under the table and squeezed Jericho's thigh.

He didn't know if he'd ever be ready to share Cassie with another person, but he'd known early on that Cassie was open to a little extra fun, and he didn't want to be the one to stifle that. After all, a supportive partner helped make all the things possible, not police and judge and take away their partner's fantasies.

Jericho couldn't sit there and worry that exploring a degree of openness in their relationship would lead to him losing her when the reality was, being in a closed relationship had never prevented someone from falling for someone else.

He had to trust that she loved him. Even if she hadn't been able to say the words, she'd shown it in all that she gave him. And he had to trust that she'd tell him how she felt when it felt right for her.

He tuned back in. Kelly let out an appreciative whistle as she squeezed Wyatt and Boomer's biceps. "What I wouldn't give to have those biceps wrapped around my—"

"*Kelly*," the floor manager passed by their table. "Stop hitting on the guests and take their order already."

Kelly's salacious smile turned into a pout as she stood and pulled her notepad from her apron pocket. "I guess if I can't take either one of you, I can at least take your order."

Cassie squeezed Jericho's leg, this time to get his attention as Wyatt and Boomer placed their order. He followed her line of sight and saw Prince wandered in and sit on a stool at the far end of the bar, Tonni nowhere around.

She leaned in and said, "Play along."

He didn't have time to ask her what she had in mind before she stood abruptly, her chair clattering on the floor behind her. The buzz in the bar came to a momentary halt. Cassie projected her voice so that the cooks in the kitchen could probably hear. "You want to sleep with her, don't you?"

Jericho's jaw dropped, and Kelly's eyes went wide and momentarily hopeful. Before Jericho could think of something to say, Cassie continued her tirade. Pulling her room key out of her clutch purse, she tossed it on the table in Kelly's direction. "Fine. Take the damn key if you want it. I won't be needing it."

Cassie stormed away from the table, heading straight for the bar.

Jericho stood because it felt like something he should do. "Cass, it's not like that, I—"

Boomer caught his arm before he could go after her as he held back his smile and utter respect for Cassie. Catching on quick, Boomer said, "Let her go, man. She'll come crawling back to you. Just you watch."

Around the bar, the conversations started up again once everyone realized the drama had passed. Jericho reclaimed his seat and glanced up at a now pale Kelly.

She leaned over, resting a hand on the table between Wyatt and Boomer, her voice barely a whisper when she said, "I didn't mean to cause a problem. I was just trying to have a little fun." She glanced between Wyatt and Boomer and added, "Mostly," as if she didn't want to take all possibility of a hookup off the table.

"And really," she mumbled so that only they could hear, "I mostly meant these two hunks here. But if you want to come to, I wouldn't kick you out of my room."

Boomer laughed, and Wyatt couldn't contain his grin.

Jericho didn't know how to respond to that. "Um… thanks?"

"Sorry about your girlfriend," Kelly put a finger on the keycard and inched it toward herself. "Should I take this and…?"

"No." They all said at the same time.

She dropped her hand and started backing away. "Okay. I'll just get those drinks now."

She'd forgotten to take Jericho's order, but he didn't stop her from leaving. He had other things to worry about, with Prince making his way around the bar toward Cassie.

CASSIE PLACED HER DRINK ORDER WITH THE BARTENDER, intending to use it for a prop instead of for drinking, but between the buzz in her belly and the predatory focus in Prince's eyes, she swallowed a mouthful to settle her nerves.

With his body, he shouldered his way by a smaller man and took the recently vacated seat beside her. The way she'd angled her body away from the bar, she had Jericho, Boomer, and Wyatt in almost her direct line of sight. Wyatt looked watchful. Boomer had an amused tilt to his lips as if he couldn't wait to see where she took this opportunity. And Jericho… well, she had difficulty reading his schooled expression, though if she had to guess, she would say it hit somewhere between pride and *what the fuck are you doing?*

She'd focus on the proud part and let him figure out the rest along with her because the truth was, she had no fucking idea what the hell she was doing. She just knew that nothing with Prince would happen with Jericho attached to her hip.

Prince glanced behind her at her table of men, then said, "Problems in paradise?"

"We're fine."

"Doesn't look like that to me. If you want my advice—"

"I didn't ask for it." She laughed on the inside, though it held a hint of her dark humor. What better person to take relation-ship advice from than a man who'd strangled his girlfriend?

"All I'm saying is if your man doesn't treat you with respect, he doesn't deserve you."

Coming from any other man, she would have agreed, but coming from a murderer, his hubris was priceless. "And I suppose I deserve someone like you?"

Prince chuckled. His eyes crinkled with his smile as he gave a practiced shy shrug and poured on the charm. She could see why someone might fall for him in the beginning. He could play the nice guy when it suited him.

Too bad it was all an act.

He lowered his voice, forcing her to lean in to hear him and make sure the mic picked up everything. "Can I buy you a drink?"

Her drink sat in front of her, untouched except for the first fortifying sip she'd taken. "I have one." It felt a little like deja vu having this same conversation in the bar where it had all started with Jericho. The big difference here was that she could trust Jericho with her life. "But I can buy you one."

Over Prince's shoulder, Jericho's lips flattened as he crossed his arms over his chest. Good thing Prince had his attention on her and not the men she'd arrived with.

Prince grinned, his gaze narrowing as if he knew he had his prey in his sights, and all he had to do was blend in and creep a little closer before he pounced and sunk his claws into her tender flesh.

He raised a hand to the bartender, and Cassie pushed a twenty across the glossy bar top and told the woman to keep the change from Prince's beer.

When the bartender went to take another order, Prince said, "Are you always that generous?" From the shift in his tone, they weren't talking about tipping anymore.

"Depends." She steeled herself from glancing over at Jericho. It wouldn't do any good to watch the emotions play across his face. As much as Jericho believed he had a poker face, it didn't seem to work where she was concerned. "What did you have in mind?"

A chair scraped on the polished concrete, and Wyatt's hand landed on Jericho's arm to keep him in his seat. And here they'd been worried that *she'd* be the one who'd be a problem for the investigation. If Wyatt didn't keep Jericho calm, he could blow the whole thing before they got any useful information.

Prince ran a finger from her elbow to her wrist. "Why don't we go up to my room, and I can show you."

Cassie took another one of those fortifying sips as she considered her options. She had no intention of going inside Prince's room. On the other hand, they didn't know where his room was, which was vital information they could use. She could always make an excuse at his door and leave.

"What about your girlfriend?" Cassie asked.

"She's not my girlfriend. You don't need to worry about her."

Not his girlfriend? Only the mother of his unborn child. I wonder what Tonni would have to say about that.

"She's not?"

"No." Even though she knew Prince was lying, he sounded convincing. "We have an understanding."

Yeah, Cassie wouldn't bet her life on that.

He downed his beer in three long swallows and held out his hand to her. She glanced at it before making her decision. Over Prince's shoulder, Jericho shook his head emphatically. But they needed this. She knew it, and as much as the guys didn't like it, they knew it, too.

Leaving her drink on the bar, Cassie took his hand, his skin cold and damp from his frosted mug. As they walked toward the elevator, she realized they hadn't come up with a covert word for her to let the guys know she needed help. But it was too late for that now. While she had a good chance of lifting his key card out of his back pocket, they still needed to know which room it belonged to.

If she wanted to help the investigation, she had to go through with it. She pressed the elevator button and glanced behind her as the two of them waited for the car to arrive. Jericho headed for one set of staircases as Boomer hurried to the other. Wyatt held back, his attention on a slot machine, but Cassie had no doubt he'd stay there in case she came back down that way.

The elevator arrived, and they stepped inside. She raised her hand to the panel. "What floor?"

She hoped that the microphone reception would be good enough that Wyatt could relay her words to Jericho and Boomer before she disappeared behind the doors.

"Seventeen."

"Seventeen it is." She pressed the button, knowing that Boomer and Jericho were probably cussing her right then as they sprinted up seventeen flights of stairs.

Her stomach sunk, and it had nothing to do with the

elevator racing upward. What if Prince forced her into his room before anyone saw which room they'd gone into.

She hesitated when the elevator doors opened, but Prince's hand at the small of her back had her stepping forward. He turned right down the long hall. The carpet was clean but dated. The casino's renovations hadn't made it up that high on the hotel floors yet.

Cassie tried to slow her steps, giving the guys as much time to catch up as she could, but they seemed to make it to Prince's door, room 1750, in no time.

"You know," Cassie said as they made it to his room. "Maybe this wasn't such a good idea. My boyfriend—"

Prince flashed his key card in front of the reader and held the door open for her. "Forget about that guy. You're with me now."

She took a step back, glancing over her shoulder, half expecting—or was that hoping?—that Jericho would burst through the stairwell door and shove Prince aside. But no one came through the door. And as much as she hated it, she was on her own.

Behind her, the elevator dinged, and they both turned. As the polished steel doors slid open, Wyatt didn't step through the door, but Tonni did. The relief that coursed through Cassie felt like the glow of a spring sun after a hard winter storm.

"Fuck," Prince muttered under his breath as Tonni approached. The smile on her face faltered as she recognized Cassie.

She dropped the armload of shopping bags at her feet. "What's going on?"

"I was just leaving," Cassie said, not wanting to miss her opportunity to escape.

"Jordy, what is she doing at our room?" The confusion

shifted to anger as the red flush ran up her face, the realization of what had been about to happen settling in.

"She's just a friend." Prince tried to placate her.

Tonni was having none of it. She shoved into Cassie, knocking her into Prince, not enough of a surprise that she didn't have her wits about her, and take advantage of the body contact to slip Prince's keycard out of his back pocket and palm it.

"I thought you were my friend," Tonni said to her. The anguish on her sweet face made Cassie's heart hurt, and Cassie meant it when she said, "I am."

Tonni rolled her eyes and laid into Prince. Cassie hadn't expected Tonni to have enough nerve to stand up to Prince. Cassie used the distraction to slip into the stairwell two doors down, expecting with every step for Prince to realize his keycard had gone missing and to come after her.

JERICHO SPRINTED UP THE STAIRS, THE LOWER ACCESS DOOR slamming closed behind him as he ran. He took the steps two at a time, but his legs felt like one of those dreams where you were running through molasses and getting nowhere fast. Turn after turn, floor after floor, he went, his heart violently colliding with his sternum with every beat.

His air came in gulping breaths that seemed beyond his control. If she weren't in the hallway when he got there, he would kick in every door until he found her.

Then he'd kill her.

Not really, but man... his heart couldn't take that kind of stress knowing who she was with and not being able to get to her if she were in trouble. And no matter how good she'd improved with their defense training back at Wyatt's facility, the reality was, Prince could overpower her if he were determined enough.

Jericho counted the floors as he ran. Even though they had the numbers labeled on each floor, his mind needed something else to focus on to keep his near sheer panic at bay.

"Mother fucker," Boomer groused in Jericho's ear, his harsh

panting matching Jericho's. "Why the fuck couldn't this asshole be on the second floor?"

Wyatt piped in. "Stop being a baby. I've run more floors in less time."

Jericho wanted to laugh. He'd only known Boomer a very short time, but he pegged Boomer for the type of guy who'd find someone busting his balls motivating.

By the fifteenth floor, Jericho had to take the steps one at a time to keep up his brutal pace. When he hit the seventeenth floor, he wanted to rip open the door and drag Cassie into the stairwell and say *fuck it* to the case. Instead, he put his back to the wall—his chest heaving, his calves, thighs, and lungs burning—and peeked through the door's narrow window.

He saw movement a couple of doors down, but he couldn't tell if it were them because of the bad angle. He palmed the doorknob and twisted. Opening the door a crack, he heard a woman's dismayed voice. "I thought you were my friend."

"I am," Cassie said.

Jericho heard the pleading in Cassie's voice as if she didn't want to lose the tenuous connection she'd made with Tonni, but being found in the hall with Prince outside his room didn't look innocent.

Was this the first time Tonni had caught Prince out, or did she already have an inkling that she couldn't trust him?

Tonni started yelling at Prince. Jericho hadn't expected her to stand up to him that way. Had Tonni reached her limit? He hoped like hell that didn't push Prince over the edge.

Jericho didn't have time to think about that because as Tonni and Prince argued, Cassie came into full view as she hurried toward him. He moved behind the door, so he wouldn't be seen if Prince glanced her way as she opened it.

Jericho expected to hear Prince's heavy footsteps rushing down the hall after her, but they never came.

As soon as the door closed behind her, Jericho grabbed her arm. She stifled her scream as he peered through the narrow glass. "They're in the room."

"I've got her," Jericho said, his voice uncharacteristically thick as he updated Wyatt and Boomer. Cassie's ass-chewing would have to wait until he had the breath to spare, which would be sometime after his heart climbed out of his throat.

He ushered her down the stairs, wanting to get at least a few flights down to get some distance between them and Prince in case the guy changed his mind and decided to go after her.

A couple of floors down, he backed her into a corner by the fire extinguisher.

Jericho slumped a shoulder against the wall beside him, his breaths still coming hard and heavy from the sprint upstairs. He pulled her into his arms and wrapped her up so tight he felt her heart pound against his.

"I'm sorry," Cassie said. "I didn't mean to worry you."

"You didn't worry me. You scared the ever-loving fuck out of me. Don't ever do that again. You got me?"

Instead of the argument he'd expected, she said, "Yeah. I get it."

The smile that came to her lips next made his stressed heart slip a beat. She held up her hand. "But I got this."

He pulled the keycard from her hand. "You picked his room key?"

That saucy grin he loved so much grew. "I did."

"What if he'd caught you?"

"He didn't."

"But what if he had?" That time he didn't manage to keep the exasperation out of his voice, and if he were being honest with himself, some aggravation crept in as well.

The satisfaction drained from her face, and he hated that he'd stolen that from her. "Just... don't do that again."

"Or what?"

Jericho couldn't understand how she could have that sexy tease in her tone after narrowly escaping being alone in Prince's room with him. He tried to push aside the fear that had the adrenaline still swirling through his system, making his hands shake and his heart continue racing.

And why did her bravery, boldness, and brashness also make him hard as hell? A feral growl escaped the back of his throat. "Or else I'll—"

"Did he just fucking growl?" Boomer asked.

Wyatt chuckled. "Hot mic, Saint."

Wyatt's and Boomer's words echoed in Jericho's ear. And the calculating, mischievous grin on Cassie's face didn't do anything to alleviate the problem below his belt.

"To be fair—" Cassie started.

Jericho shut her up with a kiss, knowing by that damn glint in her eye that he didn't want Wyatt or Boomer hearing what would come out of her mouth next.

He broke the kiss that left her more breathless than the run-in with Prince had. Pressing a finger to her lips, he said, "Hold that thought."

Taking her hand, he opened the door and took her to the elevators. From there, they went to their floor, meeting up with Wyatt and Boomer already in Wyatt's suite.

Boomer had sweat stains under his arms, the front of his shirt damp from the exertion, his limp more pronounced as he grabbed bottles of water for everyone out of the fridge.

"Thanks," Jericho said as he sat on the couch beside Cassie, twisted off the top, and handed it to her to share. He would have preferred something stronger, but that would have to wait until they'd closed the case.

Cassie dropped Prince's keycard on the coffee table. Boomer

gulped down the last of his water. Leaning forward, he gave Cassie a fist bump. "Nice work."

The suite's door opened, and Massey wheeled in. "What the hell was that all about?"

He pushed his chair to the coffee table and set his brake. "You could have told me your plans." He sounded put out as if Wyatt didn't consider him a part of the team. "I had to watch it all on the security screens."

Wyatt eyed Cassie. "Yeah, well, Cassie's going up to Prince's room wasn't exactly in the plans."

"Look, I know I deviated from the plan, but we've got Prince's room number and a key to his room. That's got to come in handy at some point."

Massey harrumphed, but he couldn't hide the veiled pride.

"It's a helpless feeling watching it all go down on the screens and not being able to help direct the operation. Suffice it to say, the Butte security team now knows what we're doing here."

Massey eyed Wyatt as if expecting a clap back. It never came. "I know you wanted to keep this as quiet as we could, but as soon as I asked her to follow your progress upstairs, Peggy caught on pretty quick."

"No," Wyatt said. "You did the right thing. Knowing you had our backs in case things went sideways makes up for the need to keep our investigation quiet. I just have concerns that—"

As if anticipating what Wyatt had been about to say, Massey quickly added, "Peggy gave me her word that what happened in the booth, stays in the booth. Along with vouching for the professionalism of her crew. If anyone else finds out the real reason we're here, it won't come from security."

Wyatt gave Massey a brief nod. "Sounds like we're good then. Does she think we're law enforcement?"

"She didn't explicitly ask, and I didn't clarify for the record.

We need her and her team's cooperation, so I left it at that. If you want me to set the—"

"Only if it's absolutely necessary. Finn's chain of command bought off on the operation, but her believing we're law enforcement avoids a complicated explanation."

Things started winding down. He and Cassie needed to get some sleep before the tournament the next day. Not that he would be getting any real sleep that night, not with what could have happened still at the forefront in his mind. Plus, the added stress of not knowing what would happen when he gambled again would make sleep elusive.

Jericho felt fairly confident he'd be fine.

Maybe, or maybe it'll be like that first hit of heroin after being sober for years.

Did he have the strength to walk away from it again?

Jericho stood. "If that's all. I think we'll call it a night."

Boomer glanced at his watch and grimaced at the time. "What time do you need to be down there tomorrow?"

"Seven-thirty for the player's breakfast," Cassie said. "The tournament doesn't start until eight-thirty, though.

"We should get in line early for the gallery seats," Boomer advised, referring to the roped-off seating area inside the poker room for spectators to watch the action live. "I poked my head in. The seating is very limited."

Everyone handed over their surveillance equipment to Wyatt to charge overnight. To Jericho and Cassie, Wyatt said, "Stop by before breakfast and pick up your equipment."

Because Jericho was in the tournament, neither he nor Cassie would have an earpiece. They couldn't risk someone discovering it and kicking them out thinking they were trying to cheat. It would kill Jericho not to listen in on her mic while playing, but it was more important he stayed in the tournament room.

They all said their goodnights, and Jericho helped Cassie to her feet, wanting a chance to get her alone and make sure she was as okay as she pretended to be.

Cassie closed their door and slumped back against it as Jericho continued into the room. They didn't have a huge suite like Wyatt and Massey's, but they had their own stocked mini-fridge and a seating area with a pullout couch across from a desk.

They didn't need much. They would only be in the room to sleep.

She kicked her heels off and left them where they fell. The aftermath of her adrenaline dump left her body sluggish and unwilling to follow her brain's simple commands.

Jericho popped his head around the corner. The curious tilt of his lips told her that his frustration with her had dissipated.

Good thing because she didn't have the strength or the mental capacity to defend her actions.

Now that she wasn't caught up in the moment, she questioned the stupidity of what she'd done. Yeah, they had a room number and a key to Prince's room, but when she thought about what could have happened if he'd forced her into his room—

"Hey, hey, hey." Jericho stepped down the hall, his warm hands cupping her face, tipping her head up so he could look at her. "Why all the tears?"

She hadn't realized she'd been crying until he swiped the wetness from her cheeks with his thumbs. He pulled her into his arms, and he held on as tight as she did.

He didn't demand a response to the question she didn't have the answer to. He just let her breathe. Finally, she dried her eyes, and Jericho picked her up with one arm behind her back and one under her knees. She didn't protest. It felt too nice to be cared for.

He stood her beside the bed and helped her out of her clothes. The slow, tender kisses he planted on her neck and collarbone made her knees go weak even though he wasn't trying to turn her on, just let her know that he loved her.

She wanted to say those three little words, to let him know what was in her heart.

Still... she held back.

He stripped her down to her panties and gave her one of his T-shirts to wear. She'd brought pajamas in case she wanted them, but his butter-soft shirt smelled like him, which made it even better.

Pulling back the comforter, he tucked her into bed. She could tell he had more he wanted to say about the little stunt she'd pulled, but he kept it to himself. They both knew it had been a boneheaded move that luckily hadn't cost them anything.

Or her everything.

He pressed a kiss to her forehead and clicked off the bedside lamp. The remaining light coming from the hall cast his face in shadows.

"Sleep tight," he said. "We have a big day tomorrow."

Jericho turned to walk away.

"Wait," she propped herself up on a shaky elbow. "Did you want to play a few hands of poker to warm you up for tomorrow? You haven't played in a long time and—"

He gently pushed her back onto the bed.

A good thing because it would have been embarrassing to have her arm give way and flop back onto the mattress.

He hesitated before answering. His voice tight and clipped when he said, "I'm good."

And there it was, that sense that he held something important back, the same something that kept her from giving all of herself to him.

"You know you can tell me anything, right?" Cassie said, hoping to knock a brick or two loose so he'd let her in.

She caught a flash of that same sad smile she'd seen before, then he schooled his expression and kissed her again. "Go to sleep, Cass. You need the rest."

He needed the rest as well, but that didn't stop him from staying up. At one point in the night, she rolled over, only to find him sitting in the chair in the dark, stray light from the billboard outside filtering through the cracks in the curtains, highlighting the apprehension in his features.

She patted the bed next to her. "Come to bed."

He came back to himself and stood, dropping his pants and coming to bed in his underwear. She curled up against his chest, and as sleep pulled her under, she vowed that once they'd concluded their investigation into Prince, she'd find out what Jericho had to hide.

THEY WOKE EARLY TO GET READY FOR THE TOURNAMENT breakfast. Jericho had bags under his eyes, and while he didn't take his foul mood out on her, all his responses were monosyllabic even as he guzzled a pot of coffee before they headed over to Wyatt's room to get the microphone necklace.

They walked into the breakfast room together. Prince was already there sans Tonni, but that didn't mean anything since it was a players-only breakfast. However, that didn't stop Cassie from hoping that Tonni had come to her senses after seeing her at Prince's room.

Then Cassie's stomach flipped. Would Tonni have gone through with her plans to tell Prince about the pregnancy?

And what if he hadn't taken the pregnancy news any better than he had when Nadia had told him about their baby?

Then again, even if Tonni had told him, surely Prince wouldn't be thickheaded enough to do anything to Tonni at the casino where there were cameras everywhere.

She wouldn't be able to stop worrying until she knew for sure that Tonni was okay. She worked her way through the buffet line, earning herself a couple of irritated side-eyes as she settled behind Prince at the scrambled eggs.

Prince caught sight of her and grunted. "It's you."

"Yeah. Sorry about yesterday." She scooped watery eggs onto her plate and helped herself to some of the sliced fruit that looked more appetizing. "I hope your girlfriend wasn't mad."

"She's not my girlfriend. And it was nothing I couldn't handle."

Which only made her worry more for Tonni's well-being.

"Will she be watching you play from the gallery?"

"She's supposed to be in line now."

He glanced around the room until he found Jericho sitting at one of the tables, working another cup of coffee like it was his job. "He's still here."

"He's in the tournament. Why wouldn't he be?"

Prince shrugged and helped himself to enough bacon and sausage to clog every coronary artery in a ten-block radius. "Thought you two were on the outs."

"It's complicated," Cassie replied, keeping it vague since they hadn't come up with a cover story about where their fake relationship was in the aftermath of their little public spat. But she also didn't want to let the idea go that she might be available.

Prince picked up silverware and napkins, and she did the same. "What did he think about you leaving the bar with me?"

He had a glint in his eye as if he enjoyed the idea of making Jericho jealous. Cassie went with the truth. "He wasn't a fan. But I'm my own person. I can do what I want, and no one is going to stop me." She bumped his shoulder conspiratorially and leaned in, lowering her voice. "You know what I mean."

He threw his head back and laughed. She would have thought a laugh from such an evil man would have made goosebumps run up her spine or remind her of every evil character in every B movie ever made. But it didn't. It sounded normal, which Cassie found even more disturbing.

They parted ways, and Cassie met up with Jericho at the table and started picking at her breakfast. "You're not going to eat?"

"Tournament jitters," Jericho admitted.

"So you decided to drown them with coffee jitters?"

"Seemed like a good idea at the time." He held both hands around the nearly empty mug. His eyes followed Prince, who'd retreated to the other side of the room. "You two looked cozy."

"Jealous?"

"Of him? No." He left Prince to his devices and met Cassie's eyes. "Wary. Worried."

"Of me, or him?"

"A little bit of both."

She appreciated that he owned it. That he didn't deny his concerns or try to justify them. And the last thing they needed to do before they went into that tournament room was to get into all the reasons why what she'd done the night before had been ill-advised.

Yeah, she got it. Lesson learned. Time to move forward.

Jericho's expression shifted and softened, and instead of the concern and stress, the love he'd professed shone in his eyes. Not heat and lust and eros. But something so true, so sweet, so sentimental, that it made her heart want to break right open and let those three little words tumble out of her mouth.

But this wasn't the time or the place.

The tournament director announced that the breakfast would be closing down and reminded the players when they needed to be seated at the table and ready to play.

Jericho picked up Cassie's dirty plate and his empty coffee cup. "Come on. Let's show them what you're made of."

Holding Cassie's hand, they walked out of the breakfast room and went looking for the rest of their group.

"Do you think they found Tonni?" Cassie asked. "Prince said she was supposed to be waiting in line. But he could have said that even if he'd done something to her. I mean, it's not like he'd just tell me over the steaming pile of biscuits that Tonni was more trouble than she was worth, and he'd decided to do something about it the way he had with Nadia. Then again, if he had done something, then wouldn't he have made some excuse as for why she wasn't there and not—"

Jericho yanked her hand and pulled her into a vacant service hall. She finally stopped talking as he pressed her against the wall, boxing her in with his body. "Take a breath, babe."

"We don't have time, we need—"

"What we don't have time for is for you to get all wound up before the tournament. Now, do what I asked and take a breath."

She rolled her eyes, and he wanted to kiss that insolent expression off her face. She took a quick breath in and out. Cassie's raised eyebrow said, *Are you happy, now?*

Jericho chuckled, which only seemed to confuse her. "God, I love you." He pinched her chin between his thumb and forefinger and made her look at him. The defiance that blazed in her eyes almost had him saying fuck it to the tournament and taking her hand and dragging her back to their room. "Take a real one this time."

Her eyes darted to the gambling floor, but instead of trying to make her escape, she slumped against the wall. Closing her eyes, she drew in a long, deep breath then blew it out again. The tension in her body eased. When she opened them again, calm, rational Cassie had replaced frantic Cassie.

"We're going to find her and make sure she's okay. Don't doubt that."

"Okay." She took another deep breath, this one unprompted. "Let's go find everybody."

They made their way across the red and gold carpet toward the newly renovated tournament room only to find the line for the gallery snaking around the corner.

They scanned the line but didn't see Tonni anywhere.

Cassie's fingers tightened in his hand as she leaned in and whispered. "I don't see her."

They turned the corner. Jericho spotted Wyatt and Boomer in line. Boomer saved their place in line while Wyatt left and met them by a bank of empty slot machines.

"Have you seen Tonni," Cassie asked Wyatt.

"No, should I have?"

Cassie fell back a step. "Wait, you didn't hear me talking to Prince? He said Tonni was in line for the gallery. I thought you guys would pick up on that and check and make sure she was in line. No one has seen her since she walked into their room after finding me there."

"All we heard was you talking to Jericho about—" Wyatt cut himself off as Massey approached them on his crutches.

Jericho caught himself before the groan escaped. He knew Cassie had a mic, but he'd forgotten all about that when he'd pulled her into the hall and told her he loved her. Boomer would probably give him hell for that. Not because they had a problem with his involvement with Cassie, but just because he could.

Boomer had to know damn well what it was like to fall for a strong-minded woman, and he probably thought it was hilarious as hell to watch Jericho tip head over heels.

Out of breath and with beads of sweat forming at his hairline, Massey walked up, taking one of the seats for the slot machines to rest.

"What's going on?" Wyatt asked.

"I was coming to tell you that we're having technical issues. Well, not us," he amended. "The casino."

Jericho stiffened. "What do you mean?"

"The wifi is all messed up. Keeps dropping. They've got people working on it now, but I have no idea when it'll be more reliable."

Cassie clutched the hidden mic in the pendant around her neck. "But I thought the mic has Bluetooth."

"It does," Massey said. "When it's within range. If it goes out of range, it automatically switches to wifi. That's why I came down here. We need to make sure one of us is in the gallery and close to Cassie in case the wifi goes down."

Jericho understood that losing the wifi could be a problem, but Cassie wouldn't be in the room alone. "It's not like I'm not going to be in the room with her. If there's a problem, I can handle it."

Massey gave him a look but waited for Wyatt to say the obvious. "Unless you get eliminated from the tournament. Then she's on her own."

"I'm not going to be eliminated." He hadn't even considered that a possibility, but he had to face the reality that just because he didn't want it to happen didn't make it so. And when you were dealing with a game that had an element of luck, he, of all people, knew you could never be certain that you would win and keep winning.

Wyatt glanced at the line behind them. "We're too far back. There's no way any of us are getting in. We should have been in line sooner. I didn't realize it would have such a large draw."

Getting to his feet, Massey said, "One of us will get in. I have an idea. Wait here. I'll be back."

He didn't wait around to explain, which was fine. They all trusted him to accomplish what he said he would. In line, Boomer held his arms out to his sides as if to say, *what are we doing here?* Wyatt held up a finger, telling him to hold on.

The three of them waited there for Massey to return. On the overhead speakers, they announced that the player seating had started. He and Cassie didn't have much time before the organizers closed the doors on them, but he'd be damned if he went in that room without any idea what constituted the team's plan B.

They stood there, trying not to look too conspicuous as they watched the elevator for Massey's return. They checked their watches and tapped their toes. Cassie's grip made his fingers go numb. At this rate, he wouldn't have enough dexterity in his fingers not to fumble his cards.

The final call for player seating came over the speakers as an usher opened the door to allow the eager spectators to file in.

"We have to go," Cassie said. "We need to be in there."

But that didn't keep Jericho from dragging his feet.

"There he is," Wyatt said.

The three of them met Massey halfway as he wheeled himself over from the elevator. A grin spread across Wyatt's face a second before it hit Jericho, what Massey planned to do.

"You're going to use the handicapped seating, aren't you?" Cassie said.

The grin on Massey's face spread. "I only saw one guy in a wheelchair. They're bound to have more than one spot for us."

Wyatt reached into his pocket without prompting and handed Massey the discreet recording device tied to Cassie's necklace. He made a quick check before stuffing it into his front pocket.

Massey turned to Jericho and Cassie and said, "You kids go on in. We've got your back."

Cassie tugged on Jericho's hand, not giving him any time for any clarification. They jogged toward the player doors, Cassie calling out to the usher to hold the door as they started closing them.

They made it inside. Most of the other players had already found their seats. They handed their player cards over to the usher, who escorted them to their seats at separate tables. All up, the room held fifteen tables of eight players each. It was a shootout tournament, meaning that the players stayed at the table until there was a winner. The winners of those tables would play in the final game. Normally, these were single-elimination tournaments, but the double-elimination element gave Jericho a chance to stay in the game if worse came to worse.

He just hoped like hell it didn't come to that.

The spectators filed in one by one with no sign of Massey or Tonni. Cassie sat across from Prince at the same table. Her color had drained from her face. Her attention focused on the door watching for Tonni to walk in. Cassie's nearly palpable concern made Jericho fear that Cassie wouldn't be able to focus on the game if the woman never showed.

The ushers went to close the doors as they cut off the line of people entering the gallery. She shot Jericho a look, and he made a discreet patting motion with his hand urging her to stay put even though a part of him would not be disappointed if their cover were blown. There were already too many things he didn't like about this operation, the least of which being that Cassie would be in danger until either Prince landed behind bars or they were back home where there were plenty of people around to protect her.

A knock sounded at the door, and the usher cracked it open, then stepped back to open it fully.

"Thank you. Excuse me. Pardon me." Massey's voice carried as he and his wheelchair rolled through the door. His hands sat in his lap, so someone must have been pushing his chair, which was unusual since Massey preferred to push it himself.

Massey glanced from Jericho to Cassie, his smile as bright as a searchlight as Tonni came into view, pushing his chair.

Cassie did a double-take, the color rushing back into her face. Prince glanced behind him but didn't seem to care that his girlfriend had arrived. Not when he had Cassie sitting straight across from him.

Tonni and Massey settled into the handicapped seating in the front, middle of the gallery. With Massey's little thumbs-up, Jericho settled in at his table. At least now, if the wifi went out, the Bluetooth connection from Cassie's mic would reach the recorder Massey carried. Not that Jericho expected Prince to confess to murder in between bets, but they wanted to make sure they had all the possibilities covered.

After a couple of announcements, the dealers filed in and broke open the cards. As they prepared to deal, Jericho glanced around his table at his competition. His table consisted of all men except for a grizzled woman old enough to be his great-grandmother. She had rheumy, watery eyes that she dabbed with a tissue. But he didn't let that fool him. She had a shrewdness to her gaze that put him on notice.

The rest of the table was a mix of men of different ages and weights. There were the guys with the hoodies up over their heads, guys with dark sunglasses, and that one loud guy that used his affability to dupe others into thinking he wasn't a threat.

Jericho had seen all the types before. You didn't play as many hands of poker as he had and not come across the vast variety of players out there.

The dealer started cutting the deck, and with the flutter of cards, Jericho's stomach settled somewhere around his knees. He wiped his hands down his thighs. Was he going to go through with this? Was he going to risk his recovery for a case?

He scooted his chair back, but one look at Cassie and Massey, who were counting on him, and one glance at a man who deserved to spend the rest of eternity and beyond behind bars, Jericho knew he'd willingly take that risk.

He'd come into the room afraid to lose and be dismissed from the tournament, leaving Cassie in there alone with Prince. But as the cards landed in front of him, that old familiar dump of adrenaline flooded his system. As the nerves settled, as the slide of the cards in his hand made him feel like he'd come home, the distinct scent of a new deck of cards wafting up, it no longer terrified him he'd lose the game.

It terrified him that he'd lose himself.

And if he lost himself... he'd lose Cassie as well.

2 2

____

THEY ENDED THE DAY WITH ROOM SERVICE IN WYATT AND Massey's room, refusing the dining table to favor the more comfortable seating in the den area and setting the food out along the generously sized coffee table.

Massey sat in one corner of the couch, his burger and onion rings on a plate in his lap. Cassie sat beside him, with Jericho on the other side.

Boomer pulled up one of the club chairs and took the cover off his steak and potato. Wyatt came into the den last with an armload of beers and passed them around, saving the soft drink for Boomer since he didn't drink. They had no plan to get drunk, but a single beer after such a long-ass day would go down smooth.

Cassie had so many questions. She swallowed her bite of chicken sandwich and turned to Massey and asked, "Okay, spill. How did you manage to have Tonni push you into the gallery?"

Massey laughed. "She came running out of the elevator as the gallery doors started closing. Not sure I believe her, but she said she overslept, and she was petrified what Prince might think if she didn't show up. *That*, I do believe. And according to the casino's ADA guidelines, I'm allowed an attendant if needed. I chose her."

"She didn't question that?" Wyatt asked around a bite of his Philly Cheesesteak.

"I told her we'd be helping each other out. She was so relieved to be getting in. She didn't seem to care about why."

"Did you make friends?" Boomer asked as if he didn't already know the answer to that question.

Massey feigned indignation. "You think I've lost my touch?"

Boomer shrugged and popped a bite of potato into his mouth. "Wrapping women around your finger is a perishable skill. With the time you've been spending with Issac outside of work, I would have thought—"

"I don't know what Gil told you, but we're just friends," Massey cut in. "Nothing more."

"We didn't see you guys all day," Cassie said to Boomer and Wyatt. "You hanging out by the pool?" She knew that would get a rise out of them and laughed at the way Wyatt playfully cut his eyes to her.

"I introduced myself to Peggy in security," Wyatt said, "And thanks to Massey greasing the skids for me, she was more than happy to let me sit in the security booth all day. They had a bunch of cameras on the tournament. I had eyes on pretty much everything."

"I sat in the overflow room," Boomer said. "They had the video feed on a short delay, but it had a good showing of everyone's hands at the tables."

"Speaking of poker hands," Wyatt said. He glanced at Jericho, who seemed up in his head. He hadn't paid any attention to the conversation.

Cassie nudged him with her arm. "Hey, Wyatt's talking to you."

Jericho glanced up from the plate of food he'd barely

touched. "What was that?"

"What happened in there?"

"I kept losing." The gruff irritation dripped off each word like a caustic fluid. "What did it look like I was doing?"

"But the idea is to win and stay in the room." Boomer's joking tone was lost on Jericho.

"What the fuck do you think I was trying to do? You think you can do better?"

Boomer raised his hands. "Dude. You know I didn't mean it that way. There's a reason I'm watching and not playing."

The muscle in the corner of Jericho's jaw tightened, and he needed to take one of those deep breaths that he'd insisted that Cassie take earlier that morning, but she didn't think he'd appreciate the reminder. He stared out the sliding glass door leading to the balcony. This wasn't Vegas, so the sounds of the strip didn't leach through the glass, but the reflected lights from the massive sign out front sparkled in the glass.

"Sorry," Jericho grumbled to Boomer. Then to the group said, "But I'm still in the game and the room, even if I'm at the losers' table tomorrow. I plan on taking full advantage of the fact that it's a double-elimination tournament. Tomorrow is going to be better. I won't let you down."

Massey yawned and glanced down at his phone when it pinged. "That's Tonni. We're going to meet in the morning, so I can help her get into the gallery again."

Wyatt started gathering up the empty plates to put outside the door. "And Prince is okay with that?"

"I guess. He saw her sitting with me. I don't imagine he sees me as a threat of stealing his woman."

"The guy doesn't know you too well." Boomer gave Massey's shoulder a playful shove. "He's got Elk Creek's own Casanova sitting next to his woman. Peggy in security is going to have to get in line if he's not careful."

"I'm not sleeping with anyone." Massey raised his hands in exasperation. "Why won't anyone believe me?"

Wyatt walked by with the precarious stack of plates. "Because we know you." He stopped at the door. "Can someone open this for me?"

Cassie hopped up and nudged Jericho, who was still lost to the conversation. "We're coming. We need to get to bed anyway and get ready for tomorrow."

Everyone said their goodnights, and she took Jericho's hand and led him to the door. She helped Wyatt set the dishes in the hall before sticking her keycard in her lock and pushing Jericho through it first.

When the door closed behind her, she took his hand and pulled him toward her. He came back to her, physically *and* mentally. "There you are."

"Sorry." He propped a shoulder against the wall. "I'm not sure where my head is at."

"You just need some sleep. It's been a long day, and you didn't get hardly any rest last night."

He brushed the back of his hand down her cheek. "Have I told you yet how brilliantly you played today?"

"No. But I'm not in there to win. I'm in there because Prince is in there. Plus, I had cleavage on my side."

He didn't laugh the way she'd hoped he would. What was going on with him? This wasn't the Jericho Saint she'd come to know and love. Yes, *love.* She could admit it if only to herself.

But that was part of it, wasn't it? Her hesitancy to give him her whole heart had everything to do with what he had going on in his head that he refused to share. What was he hiding? What was he afraid of?

"Do you ever wonder if this is going to work? I mean, what are we doing here? He's not going to confess over a pile of chips and a shitty hand." Jericho glanced down at her. "What? Why the perturbed face?"

"Now I know you need sleep if this is putting you into some sort of existential crisis," she said.

"No existential crisis. I'm just not convinced this is the right way to go, is all."

"Since when?"

He dropped her hand and stepped away instead of answering her. She didn't bother convincing him that she thought their best bet moving forward was to get to Tonni. She was the one who'd alibied Prince for the time of the murder. If anyone cracked, it would be her.

Cassie didn't know what was bothering Jericho, but she knew that mentally he wasn't in a place to talk about the case. He sat on the bed, one leg on either side of the corner, his thoughts already turned inward again. Beside the bed, she stepped out of her shoes and started unbuttoning her blouse. "I'm grabbing a shower. Want to join me?"

She expected a sly grin and for him to strip naked in less time than it took her to finish the last couple of buttons.

Instead, he stood and went to the dresser, stripping off his watch and kicking off his shoes, in no hurry to join her. He wouldn't look at her when he said, "You go ahead."

It was as if he knew that if he looked at her naked, he wouldn't be able to keep from taking her up on her offer, and that was the last thing that he wanted.

He braced his hands on the dresser and hung his head. Cassie eased over, putting her arm around his shoulder. Whatever he had going on concerned more than just the tournament. Or the case. "Would you talk to me?"

He took that deep breath that he'd needed back in Wyatt's room, then straightened. Her hand fell from his shoulder at the starkness on his face. "There's nothing to talk about."

She wanted to call him out on his bullshit. She wanted to shout that she was there for him, that he could tell her anything. But...

Sometimes she wondered if that were true.

She already knew about his illegal forgery activities. What could be so bad that he couldn't tell her what was going on in his head?

Taking a step back, she finished undressing. It felt a lot farther than a step. It felt like a mile. It felt like a chasm.

Jericho must have felt it, too, because he finally met her eyes and said, "You know I love you."

Cassie swallowed hard. He hadn't said it with the usual spark in his eyes that promised a lifetime. "I know."

He nodded once as if he'd dismissed her. She backed away, her heart battering her ribs worse than it had when she'd been standing in front of Prince's door. Because of the stark way he said those words, she knew her heart was in grave danger.

In the bathroom, she started the shower, turning the temperature up to scalding as she stepped in, needing to feel something to compensate for the way her heart beat with a hollow numbness.

Maybe he just needs some sleep. The case is stressful. Things will be better in the morning.

Even as she tried to convince herself of that, she knew it was a lie.

Jericho sat in the upholstered chair in the corner of the room. He had his head in his hands, listening to the shower running. If he were a smart man, he'd climb in behind her and pull her against his chest, hold on tight, and never let her go.

But that was the fantasy talking. That wasn't real life. Not really.

He stood. As exhausted as he was, he couldn't sit still any longer. He stepped back into his shoes and went into the bathroom, pulling back the shower curtain. She had her back to him as she washed her hair. Sudsy water sluiced down her back, over the rise of her ass, before falling and swirling the drain. He ignored the blood that rushed toward his groin.

She turned and caught him staring, her face red as the steam billowed out. It had to be from the heat, not from crying. A tentative, hopeful smile came to her lips. "Change your mind?"

"I'm going to go clear my head."

"Want company?"

"No." She winced, and he knew his answer had come out too fast and harsh. "Get some sleep. I won't be gone long."

She didn't reply. She only nodded. He left the room before he could change his mind.

He barely felt the chill of the night air as he walked around the casino, his mind going back to the tournament. He couldn't remember a time when he'd played so poorly. The stakes were high, but he'd played in games where the stakes had been higher.

He'd played in games where he'd risked it all. *Won it all.* Only to come home to an empty house, his wife gone. He hadn't *won* anything. He'd lost everything.

The same way he'd lose Cassie.

But that didn't stop him from finding himself in front of a poker table at midnight with a pile of chips. That familiar buzz of adrenaline coursed through his system as the waitress brought him drinks. In the background, the slot machines chimed.

Why, after so long away, did sitting in front of a poker table feel like coming home?

He should go upstairs and go to bed before he did any more

damage, but after the way he'd played that day, he needed the practice more than he needed the sleep.

At least that's what he tried to convince himself.

He didn't know what time it was when he bought chips for the third time. He'd left his watch and phone in his room, and like any good casino, the Butte had no clocks on the wall. He wobbled as he stood and stretched, not sure if it was the exhaustion or the booze making him unsteady.

If he were smart, he'd call it a night.

And he would.

Right after he won his money back.

The next thing he knew, a hand shook his shoulder. "Hey, buddy. You can't sleep here." The man had one of those carpet sweepers in his hand that didn't make any noise.

Jericho straightened in his chair, his neck and back stiff from being slumped over the poker table. The group of guys he'd been playing with was gone as well as the dealer. A placard in the middle of the table said *closed.*

Jericho stood, the chair falling back and banging on the floor. A line of people filed into the room where the players had their breakfast the morning before. "Hey, man. What time is it?"

The man stopped mid sweep and glanced at his phone. "Seven-thirty."

"AM?"

The man chuckled. "Yes. AM. As in morning."

"*Fuuuuuck.*" Jericho ran a hand down his face as he stumbled to the bank of elevators. His head swam, his mouth felt like the desert, and every muscle in his body wanted to mutiny. His stomach threatened to stage a revolt though he had nothing in it to throw up.

He'd need a shower and a couple of pots of coffee before he felt as good as death warmed over.

That's if Cassie didn't kill him first.

Cassie heard the fumbling at her door and opened it to a disheveled Jericho. "Where the fuck have you been? We should have been down for breakfast ten minutes ago."

"Go on down." Jericho pushed by her. The stench of alcohol and body odor made her hold her breath as he passed. "I'm going to catch a quick shower."

She closed the door and followed him into the room. "Why are you doing this?"

He pulled his undershirt over his head and turned. The microphone around her neck caught his eye, and he brushed a finger over it, his voice hardly a whisper when he said, "What did you tell Wyatt when you went to get this?"

"That you were getting ready."

Jericho grunted as if that had been the last thing he'd expected.

"What did you think I told him?" Her whispers matched his own though he doubted anyone had started listening yet. "That you were gone all night? That you haven't had hardly any sleep in two days? That you probably have no business going back into that tournament room today, much less be on the case?"

"I'm fine."

"Yeah. You might want to check yourself in the mirror. You look exhausted and hungover. Or are you still drunk?"

"I'm not drunk," he managed to say without slurring, so Cassie didn't argue the point.

She stepped closer to him, and to her surprise, he held his arms out to her. She wrapped her arms around his neck. His arms went around her waist, and he buried his face into her neck.

"I want to help," she said. "*Please*, let me help."

He broke the embrace and held her at arm's length. "You can't help. Not with this."

"If you change your mind—"

"I won't." His expression softened, contrasting with the harshness of his words. A sliver of the Jericho she knew made an appearance. He kissed her on the forehead, then planted the sweetest, gentlest, most fleeting kiss on her lips. "But I appreciate you asking."

There he is. There's your Jericho. Not this shell of the man who'd inhabited his body for the past eight hours.

He looked her up and down. She was dressed and ready for another day of play. She still needed food... and coffee to make up for the restless sleep she'd gotten. At one point in the night, she'd woken to find his side of the bed empty and had called his cell to check on him only to have it ring in the room.

She'd contemplated going and looking for him and dragging him back to bed, but she'd trusted that whatever he'd been dealing with, he knew best what he'd needed. Clearly, she'd been wrong about that.

"Go. I'll catch up," he insisted.

Cassie smothered the urge to mother him, the same way she'd had with her father, and she hated it. Hated that Jericho had put her in that position. Hated that she wanted to do it anyway.

But she'd learned her lessons the hard way. Pushing, pulling, cajoling, begging, wouldn't get her... *them,* anywhere.

"Yeah, sure." She turned to leave with that same twisty, twirly knot in her belly she'd had as a teen when she'd leave her father at the tables, sitting with a dwindling stack of chips in front of him.

After a light breakfast, the food weighed like a ship's anchor in her belly. She spotted Wyatt, Boomer, and Massey by themselves over by a roped-off area of closed roulette tables and joined them.

"Where's Jericho?" Boomer was quick to ask.

Feigning nonchalance, she said, "He should be down any minute."

Tell them. Tell them he should be pulled from the case. Tell them.

She opened her mouth to voice her concerns, only to see a well-put-together Jericho step out of the elevator like he hadn't shown up to their room this morning with more brown liquor in his veins than red blood cells.

Wyatt waved Jericho over.

Jericho laid his hand on the small of her back and pressed a kiss to her cheek. "We about ready?"

He looked better. So much better. Even if his encouraging smile didn't reach his eyes.

"What dump truck ran you over?" Massey asked.

Wyatt gave Massey a quelling look, his gaze assessing as he took Jericho in. Jericho had circles under his eyes still, but he miraculously didn't reek of alcohol or look like he'd fall asleep on his feet.

"You good to go?" Wyatt asked. There was a whole conversation the two men had within a tension-filled clash of eyes.

"Why wouldn't I be?" Jericho pulled off the *I don't have a clue what you are talking about* expression with practiced aplomb, and Wyatt let it drop.

Jericho cut his gaze to Boomer.

"Don't look at me, buddy," Boomer said. "I didn't say anything."

Because they had a few minutes before the tournament resumed, Cassie wanted to talk to them about changing the immediate focus of the case. "Whatever it is we're doing here, I think we need to focus our efforts on Tonni."

"In what way?" Wyatt asked. That was one of the things she loved about her boss. He was always ready to listen to his team.

"If we can get to her, we can get to Prince. She's his alibi. Nothing is changing without that changing. She had to know he was gone the night of the murder if he was ever even at her place. I'm sure in her mind, Prince could never do what the police have accused him of. But that's what happens when you're in a relationship." She aimed her next comment at Jericho. "Sometimes you're too blinded by the feelings to see the truth." She returned her attention to the group. "Maybe if Tonni understood the kind of guy Prince is, she'd rethink her story."

Massey's attention ping-ponged between Cassie and Jericho as if he were watching a wicked tennis match. "You two okay?"

"Fine," Jericho said.

"Never better," Cassie added at the same time.

"Liars," Boomer muttered under his breath.

Wyatt glared at Boomer and Massey. "Not helping."

Massey and Boomer shut up and waited for Cassie to continue.

"I don't think that she'll listen to me alone. Not after finding me at the door to her hotel room with her boyfriend. She'll think I want him for myself." Cassie almost shuddered at the thought. Jericho may not be perfect. He may have some demons that he was fighting, but she never doubted for one second that he was a good man. "But maybe with the recording we have of Prince saying he and Tonni aren't serious, and if I bring Massey with me, if we tell her the truth about what happened to Nadia, maybe then she'll reconsider."

"You're friends with Tonni?" Wyatt asked Massey.

"I did get her into the gallery. And we sat all day together, even on the breaks. We're not friends, but we're friendly. And I think with her, it could be the right approach."

Wyatt plucked at his bottom lip, the cogs visibly churning in his head. "You're going to tell her who we are?"

"I don't see any other way." Cassie glanced at the faces of her team. At the heads slowly nodding in agreement.

"I like it." Boomer said.

Jericho grunted, but she knew that he wouldn't like anything that had to do with her being alone with anyone involved in the case. But she wouldn't be alone with Prince. And Massey would be with her.

The announcement came over the speakers for the players to be seated in the tournament room, and Wyatt said, "We'll discuss this further at dinner."

"I've gotta go," Massey said, "I'm supposed to be meeting Tonni by the gallery doors.

They broke apart, and Jericho walked with Cassie back to the tournament room, taking her hand in his. She stopped right outside the door and turned to him, her voice to his ear so only he could hear. "I don't know what is going on with you, but I do know that whatever it is, we can get through it if you'd only let me in."

She pulled back, and he winked at her. The quarter-smile on his face didn't reassure her. "You're going to kill it in there, and I'm going to be there to back you up every second of the way."

As soon as Jericho sat in his chair, as soon as the dealer dealt the cards, as soon as he made his first bet, everything faded. The worry that he'd lose Cassie, the fact that they were there to trap a killer, the fact that he could feel himself tumbling into that hellscape of his gambling addiction. Everything.

Despite his exhaustion, the game fueled him. With the alcohol burning away, his thoughts cleared, his playing improved. Especially as compared to the night before.

By the end of the day, he'd managed to hang on by the skin of his teeth.

One more day of play remained, but all that Jericho cared about was that he'd held on long enough that he hadn't left Cassie in that tournament room without him there for backup.

That's not the only thing you cared about. What about that last hand when you thought that you could win? Not just the hand, but the whole damn tournament? You expect anyone to believe that at that moment, Cassie was anywhere in your head?

"We going to dinner or what?" Cassie asked.

Jericho sat back from the poker table. She pulled out a chair across the table from him. Most of the other players had already filed out of the room, and the dealers and cleaning people were working hard to get things set up for the final day of play.

At his very limit, and starting to feel loopy with the effects of running on limited sleep for so long, he sucked in a lungful of air and looked at her, *really* looked at her.

She'd finger-combed her hair, the loose strands framing her face. Whatever makeup she'd put on that morning had long ago worn off. She had the faintest hint of bags and bruising under her eyes and the most empathetic soft smile on her face. It touched her eyes, and it tugged at his heart.

Fuck. He didn't deserve her.

But that didn't keep him from wanting her.

No, *needing* her.

"Yeah. I'm ready."

Hand in hand, they walked to the Butte's restaurant to find it packed after the tournament. They'd be lucky to be seated within the next hour. All Jericho wanted was to go back to his room and sleep for the next week, but they still had work to do.

In the far corner of the bar, Wyatt, Boomer, and Massey had saved room for them at a four-top table, a pitcher of cold beer in the center of the table.

Condensation formed rivulets and ran down the sides. Wyatt poured them both a beer as they walked up, the IPA forming a thick foam at the top. Normally, Jericho would be down, but the thought of one more drop of alcohol entering his system made his stomach threaten to shrivel up and run off.

But if he refused a glass, they'd be asking questions he didn't want to have to answer.

With only one available chair, he let Cassie take it and leaned a shoulder against the wall. His stomach growled despite the beer in his hand and the heady scent of hops assaulting his nose. "Can we order food in the bar?"

"They're coming over with menus," Boomer said. "I don't care what they have. At this point, I'll eat anything that doesn't still have a heartbeat."

"Same," Massey said. Then he reached up and punched Jericho in the arm. "Way to hang in there today."

Jericho shook his head. "I'm ready for it to be over, no lie."

"Oooh, Oooh." Cassie tapped Massey with the back of her hand, but she had everyone's attention.

Because the bar was more crowded than a bookie in the middle of March Madness, it took a minute for them to see what had caught her attention. Between all the people milling around, talking, drinking, eating, and laughing, Jericho watched Tonni leave her table and head to the ladies' room.

Cassie turned back to the team. "I'm going to go talk to her. Wait here."

They didn't have much choice, considering they weren't allowed in the ladies' room.

"We haven't even discussed what we're going to do," Jericho groused, already seeing this encounter going to shit, and he hadn't even gotten his menu yet.

"She's only going to see if Tonni is willing to talk," Wyatt said. "Right, Cassie?"

Boomer's chuckle rankled Jericho's already frazzled nerves. "Yeah. I'm sure that's all she's going to do." He didn't sound like he believed his words any more than Jericho did.

"It's going to be fine," Cassie said. "I'm just going to feel her out. She may not even be willing to talk to us."

Cassie headed for the back hallway. Jericho took her vacant seat, wondering what kind of trouble she was about to get herself into.

2 4

Cassie strode into the women's restroom, expecting Tonni to lash out at her. For such a crowded bar, there was only one other person in there reapplying her lipstick. Cassie still had her necklace on, so the guys might be able to hear her if she got into any trouble. Not that she expected Tonni to throw hands or anything.

Tonni came out of a stall, and she washed her hands, meeting Cassie's eyes in the mirror. "Oh. It's you."

Cassie asked, "Can we talk?"

"That sounds ominous." The woman beside Tonni interjected as she packed away her lipstick. "Do you need me to stay, honey?"

Tonni offered her a smile. Cassie assumed it was meant to let the woman know that everything was okay, but anyone could see by the tight lines around Tonni's mouth and the furrow between her brows that things were *far* from okay. "No. But thank you."

The woman eyed Cassie for a moment before picking up her purse and walking out with one last glance back.

Cassie took a step or two closer, but not too close. She didn't want Tonni feeling cornered. "That was nice of her."

"What do you want? I don't even know why I agreed to this. You were at the door to my room with my boyfriend. You were going to go in there with him, you—"

Okay. So, no to the small talk.

"I wasn't going in there. I know that's what it looked like, but..." How could she explain?

The door slammed open, and two women rushed in. One had her hand clutched over her mouth as she shoved into the first open stall. She dropped to her knees. The retching came first, then the smell. Tonni's nose wrinkled, and Cassie lost her appetite.

"Is there somewhere else we can talk?" Cassie asked.

Tonni glanced at the woman who seemed to be tossing up everything she'd eaten in the past decade, then back to Cassie as if staying and talking in the bathroom was her safest option.

"I'll bring Massey with me. Name the place and the time. It's important."

"What? How... how do you know Massey?"

"I'll explain it all to you then."

The sick woman continued retching, already at the dry heaving stage of stomach-content exorcism. Her friend held her hair back. Cassie thought about taking Tonni to either her room or Wyatt's but didn't think Tonni would go to some stranger's room, and she didn't blame her for that. If the situation were reversed, no way would she do it. Cassie was asking a lot of Tonni already, and she knew it.

After a long, smelly pause, Tonni relented. "We could go to my room."

"What about—"

"I don't expect him back for a while."

If Cassie had an earpiece, all she would have heard was

Jericho muttering curses in her ear. Yay for small favors. With Prince off property and Massey accompanying her, she felt the danger level was acceptable and certainly a lot lower than a lot of the questionable things she'd done in her life.

"I'll go get Massey and meet you up there if that's okay."

"Will you leave Jordy and me alone after that?"

"I will. Promise." She hoped it was one she could keep because she didn't think they had a plan C if this didn't work.

She left first to find that Massey had already extracted himself from the crowd around their table. Jericho crossed his arms over his chest, a vein now prominent at his temple. If the bar lights weren't so dim, she'd probably be able to see the flush of anger on his cheeks.

"You don't have to do this," Jericho said as soon as she made it to the table.

Before she could answer, Wyatt said, "It's an acceptable risk. We can keep a watch out for Prince returning and give them a warning as soon as he arrives."

"There aren't enough of us to watch all the entrances." Jericho wasn't going to give up without a fight.

"We'll put Boomer in the security booth. They have a camera at every entrance. We'll know as soon as he enters the building. Sooner if we spot his truck pull up."

Jericho grumbled, then relented. Cassie saw the toll it took on him. She wanted to pull him in for a hug, but he'd probably lock his arms around her waist and not let her leave. And she didn't want to keep Tonni waiting.

To Massey, Jericho said, "You have your earpiece?"

Massey tapped his ear, giving Jericho a look that said, *You know I do.*

They all stood, and when the waitress came by, Wyatt pulled out his credit card to close out their tab. Jericho took Cassie's hand and pulled her in close enough to whisper in her ear. By his tone and tenor, his "Be careful" came out sounding like an *I love you.*

She squeezed his hand. "Count on it."

Cassie and Massey rode up the elevator in silence. He pulled out his tablet and powered it on. The elevator dinged, and they stepped out onto Tonni's floor.

"What's the tablet for," Cassie asked.

"I have that recording on here of the conversation you had with Prince at the bar. The one where he insisted that he and Tonni weren't serious. Maybe that will soften her up to what else we have to say."

"Good idea." At Tonni's door, she asked, "You still have the recorder on you, right?"

"Yes. I'm also sending the feed to my computer, as long as the wifi holds out. Why?"

"I just wanted to make sure. With the wifi problems the casino has been having, I didn't want to have to trust it for our recordings."

She knocked. They waited. She knocked again. She put her ear to the door, but she couldn't hear any movement inside. Straightening, she said, "I don't think she's there. We should have followed her up here. There's no telling where she ran off to."

Massey rolled closer and knocked harder. "Come on, Tonni. We just want to talk. Just give us a minute. After that, if you want us to leave, we will."

Massey shrugged. "I don't know what else we can do other than camp out at her door. Without knowing when Prince will be back, I don't think that's a good idea."

The bolt flipped on the door's interior, and Tonni opened the door. "He's not coming back anytime soon. He told me not to wait up for him."

Cassie didn't want to pepper her with twenty questions, but

there weren't a whole lot of places nearby where Prince could have gone. Did he make them? Had he disappeared and left Tonni hanging while he had the chance? "Where did he go?"

Tonni glanced down the long hall toward the elevators as if she expected him to pop up out of nowhere. "He didn't say."

Massey edged his chair closer. "Can we come in? We just want to talk."

Even though she'd already agreed to speak with them, the way her gaze kept bouncing around the hall made Cassie fear she'd change her mind.

Finally, Tonni took a step back and held the door open, careful to put the security latch in place when she locked it behind her. What was she afraid of more? That Prince would come back or that he'd come back and find the three of them together?

Tonni led them inside. The sliding door to the balcony stood open, the curtains fluttering in the mild breeze. They had a basic room. Bathroom by the door. King-sized bed with a TV on the wall opposite. Massey couldn't push much past the hallway with all their clothes and the broken lamp on the floor.

Mumbling an apology, Tonni started picking up the scattered clothes.

"What happened here?" Cassie kept her voice soft and soothing. Something she'd use on an injured baby deer she feared would startle.

"I tripped," Tonni said as she stepped over the lamp with a handful of lacy underwear in her hand.

"You tripped on a bedside lamp?" Though it seemed Massey tried, he hadn't managed to keep the incredulity out of his tone.

Tonni raised her chin, the arms she'd crossed over her chest more defiant than self-protective.

"*Tonni*." Cassie's gentle, *you can tell me the truth* tone brought tears to Tonni's eyes, and she swiped them away as fast as they fell. Tonni's eyes went to the shopping bags in the corner of the room, the colorful streamers and banner torn and stomped into the carpet. A hand fell to her abdomen.

"You told him, didn't you?" Cassie asked.

Tonni's knees gave out, and the end of the bed caught her. The tears started falling again. This time she didn't bother wiping them away. "This morning." She gestured to the mess. "He didn't take it the way I thought he would."

Cassie replaced the lamp in its rightful spot and brought the chair over from the corner. She hated that Prince had taken the news out on the room, but maybe it would work in their favor. Maybe what they had to say would be more believable in light of what had happened.

"But you guys didn't come here to talk about that." Tonni made a motion with her hand as if waving away the evidence of Prince's temper tantrum. "Why are we here?"

"*This* is why we are here." At Tonni's confusion, Cassie said, "Prince isn't the man you think he is. Or think he was."

Leaning back on her hands, Tonni glanced between the two of them before settling on Massey as if she expected only he would tell her the truth. "Who are you guys? Are you two cops?"

If Tonni had that thought in her mind, maybe she'd been thinking more about the alibi she'd given Prince in the light of his outburst.

"Why do you think we're cops?" Massey asked instead of answering her question.

"Because this isn't normal. None of this is normal."

With a short nod from Massey, Cassie told her the truth. "We're not the police. Not exactly."

"What the hell does that mean?"

"It means that they sent us. To watch Prince," Massey said. "We're investigators."

Tonni jumped to her feet and started pacing the room. "I don't know what you're talking about."

"I think you do." Tired of mincing words and afraid Tonni might kick them out if they didn't get to the point, Cassie said, "It's about the night of Nadia Bate's murder."

Tonni stilled. "Jordy told me not to talk to anyone about that night."

"Why do you think that is, Tonni? Why?"

"No. No, no, no." Tonni pointed to the door. "I want you two out."

Cassie stood and raised her hands in surrender. "Okay. We'll leave, but let us play you one thing before we do. Deal?"

Tonni nodded, but probably only because it was the path of least resistance.

Massey cued up the recording of Cassie at the bar with Prince and hit play. As the words played out, as Tonni listened to him repeat again and again that he and Tonni weren't serious, that she wasn't his girlfriend, that there was nothing between them, the bed caught Tonni again. Only this time, the tears in her eyes looked less like hurt and more like anger, resolve, and determination.

Her chin came up again, and Cassie started loving this woman's defiant streak. "What do you want to know?"

Jericho leaned against a pillar near the front entrance to the Butte, trying not to look conspicuous. Hard to do when you were just standing there, letting a pillar hold you up. But he was afraid that if he sat for half a second that he'd fall asleep. He still might fall asleep. At least the fear of Prince walking in without warning kept him from completely nodding off.

Wyatt stood somewhere near the rear doors, out of Jericho's direct line of sight.

"Anything," Jericho asked for the umpteenth time.

"Negative," Wyatt popped off a second before Boomer up in the security booth said the same. They didn't elaborate. None was needed. And they didn't want to tie up the comms since they were listening in on what was going on with Cassie and Massey.

Somewhere behind Jericho, a large crowd of people had gathered around a craps table. The floor erupted with laughs, cheers, and a lot of clapping. He could barely hear what Cassie, Tonni, and Massey were saying. He just hoped like hell that Massey was managing to record it all to give to Finn.

He scanned the front entrance when the door opened. A small group of women walked through the door with no sign of Prince. He let his gaze drift over to the poker tables on the other side of the room. God, he couldn't wait for them to get out of Tonni's room.

Why? So you can play a hand or two. Or all fucking night?

No. So Cassie would no longer be in danger.

And then you can play without worry.

Jericho grunted to himself, unwilling to acknowledge the accuracy of the thoughts. Because if he acknowledged them, it would show how incredibly far he'd fallen in what felt like a microsecond in his life. How could it feel as if he'd landed back to square one? Back to the night that he'd come home from the casino to find that his ex-wife had moved out and moved on without a second glance.

It had nearly broken him. And the pisser of it was, he didn't know if he had the strength to walk away again.

He should never have agreed to the tournament. He should have told Wyatt the truth and found another way.

Too late now.

"Heads up," Boomer said. "I've got a truck pulling into the parking lot that matches Prince's truck.

With the earpiece, Massey would have heard Boomer's warning as well. Tonni had agreed to talk, but they needed more time. If Prince headed straight to the room, they would have risked everything.

He waited for Massey to say *Copy.* Or anything to let them know that he'd heard Boomer, but he didn't reply. Then Jericho realized that he no longer heard the feed from Cassie's microphone.

"Massey. Prince has been spotted. Do you copy?"

Nothing.

"Boomer. Wyatt. I lost contact with Massey do—"

Jericho glanced down at his phone screen. The wifi indicator had disappeared. Had the wifi fucking shit itself again? He called out to Boomer, Wyatt, and Massey several more times before knowing he was on his own. The crowd behind him at the craps table only grew larger and louder. Even if he yelled across the huge gaming room to Wyatt, no way he'd be heard.

And as much as he wanted to meet up with Wyatt to establish some sort of contact, it would require him to leave his post. With the front entrance being the most likely place for Prince to enter, he wasn't willing to give up his position.

The front doors slid open, and Prince swept in with a small mixed crowd of men and women. He didn't make a beeline for the elevators, so the rapid *rat-a-tat-tat* of Jericho's heart decreased to less deafening levels behind his eardrums. The way his heart pounded, even if the wifi came back on, he wouldn't hear anything beyond the tinny roar of blood in his head.

Jericho followed Prince deeper into the casino at a distance, headed away from Wyatt and any sort of backup. He just hoped like hell that Boomer could track them on the security monitors. Passing a security guard, he almost asked for help. He now regretted their decision to keep their business secret from the casino security. Sure, Peggy and her team in the security booth knew what they were up to, but it would take too long to explain himself to security personnel and risked losing Prince.

He kept checking in with his team but got no response, and Cassie's necklace feed still didn't fill his ear. He had no clue if they'd finished or if they were in danger.

As he approached the raucous craps table, a roll must have hit big because the crowd exploded with cheers. They hugged and shoved, and a large older woman collided with him. The force nearly tumbled him. He reached out to keep them both from falling, but she still took him to his knees. Someone stepped back, and like a comedy of errors, Jericho's low position caught the man at the back of the knee. The man's arms windmilled, and he tumbled them all to the ground.

A foot landed on Jericho's ankle and pain shot through it. He lost precious moments extricating himself from the pile of arms and legs and torsos. He didn't apologize. He just shoved to his feet and half-hobbled, half-ran in the direction he'd last seen Prince heading.

Motherfucker.

In the aisle between the roulette wheels and the high dollar slots, Jericho spun around. Prince had vanished.

"I lost him." Jericho automatically said.

Wyatt responded in his ear, the transmission garbled, when he said, "Repeat."

"Repeat," Jericho said as he spun and sprinted for the bank of elevators. "I lost him."

"WHAT YOU'RE SAYING," CASSIE SAID, WANTING TO MAKE SURE SHE got Tonni's story right, "is that Prince—I mean Jordan—was with you the night of Nadia's murder. But not all night?"

"I can't be positive." Red rimmed Tonni's eyes, and the damp tissue in her hand had been mangled well past any semblance of usefulness. "We went to bed together. But we'd had a few drinks at dinner, and I took a sleeping pill. When I woke up, he was there. But he could have left in the middle of the night, and I would never have known."

Massey made a small rolling motion to Cassie with his hand, urging her to hurry it up. Unease crept up Cassie's spine with little tendrils that stuck to her skin like leeches. Whatever was going on couldn't be good.

"But how could he kill that woman and just crawl into bed with me like nothing happened?"

"Because he doesn't have a soul," Massey quipped.

Cassie's eye roll said, *Not helpful* even if it were the truth.

"The next morning, did he tell you to lie for him?"

Tonni's gaze dropped to her hands, and her already choked voice thickened. She sniffed back the tears. "He said that it was nothing. That Nadia was jealous and was just trying to make trouble for him. At first, the cops didn't tell me she was dead."

"What about later. When you found out that she was?"

"I was afraid to change my story, and Jordy didn't seem capable. How can someone wrap their hands around another person's neck until the life drains out of them? How could anyone be so cold? How could Jor—"

The lock on the door beeped, and the lever turned. Cassie jumped to her feet, and Tonni swallowed a scream as the door slammed against the security latch. Prince pounded on the door. "Open the fucking door."

Massey must have been trying to contact the guys because he talked directly into the hidden microphone on his collar. He shook his head at Cassie. A loud thud came at the door. It shook in the frame. The latch held, but it wouldn't last.

"I can't reach anyone. Use the hotel phone. Call security," Massey ordered Tonni. "Boomer would have seen Prince come in. I'm sure help is coming." His tone lacked all confidence, and his expression didn't contradict that.

Cassie went for the biggest weapon in the room, the lamp, tearing off the lampshade and wielding it over her shoulder like a club. Massey turned his wheelchair sideways. Prince would have to go over the top of him to get to her or Tonni.

"Open the door!" Prince must have come at the door with his booted foot because the jamb cracked where the latch attached to the frame.

Bam!Bam!Bam!Bam!Bam!

The jamb shattered, and the door slammed against the wall. Prince stumbled into the room, a plastic shopping bag still in his tight fist. Tonni screamed again as she tried to dial the phone. Prince roared at the sight of Massey and Cassie in his room. It didn't take more than a second for him to connect the dots.

"What did you tell them?" He stormed down the hall, yelling

at Tonni, Massey, and his wheelchair barrier no match for Prince's unhinged rage.

"What did you tell them?" Prince shouted as he blindly went for Tonni. With one hand, he took hold of the armrest on Massey's chair and toppled him with ease. With the other, he fended off the lamp as Cassie swung at his head.

Cassie might as well have been beating Prince with a pool noodle for all the good it did her. Then with one quick motion, Prince stripped the lamp from her hand and sent it flying out the sliding glass door, out of reach. Tonni frantically dialed the front desk, but Cassie couldn't be sure it had connected before Prince ripped the phone out of the wall and bashed it against the side of Tonni's temple.

Tonni crashed to the floor without even a groan as if Prince had flipped her 'off' switch. Massey worked to right himself, the wheelchair blocking his way. He tried to crawl over it, but Cassie couldn't stop to help him. Prince dove at Tonni, his hands going around her throat as he yelled over and over, "What did you tell them? What did you tell them?"

Cassie pounded on Prince's back, but Prince barely seemed to notice. As a lost resort, she jumped on his back and wrapped her arm around his neck, trying her best to get a chokehold.

Out of the corner of her eye, she noticed Massey coming over, using the wall and then the bed to support himself. By bracing on the bed, he had enough leg strength to kick at the side of Prince's knee. The man didn't go down, but the pain had him stumbling back.

Prince lost his chokehold on Tonni, while Cassie maintained her own.

Time slowed. What felt like minutes of fighting, in reality, could probably only account for a short run of seconds. But when you hung on to a hundred and eighty pounds of enraged man and muscle, time dragged on.

Her arms and legs grew tired as she stuck to him like industrial-grade Velcro, knowing that if he were capable of killing the person he supposedly loved, he'd have zero qualms killing her or Massey.

She thought she heard Jericho call out her name. It had to be wishful thinking. Prince slammed her back against the wall, trying to dislodge her. Her head hit. Stars bloomed. Her grip around Prince's neck loosened a fraction.

"Hold on!" Massey yelled to her as he dove for Prince's legs, sending Prince reeling as he pulled free of Massey's grip and struggled to regain his balance.

Prince stumbled out the open sliding door, the balcony railing hitting Cassie in the back of her thighs as she and Prince nearly toppled over the railing.

"*Cassie!*" That time she did hear Jericho call her name, and it wasn't her imagination or wishful thinking.

Help was coming.

Jericho was coming.

She just hoped like hell that he wasn't too late.

JERICHO DIDN'T KNOW WHAT HAPPENED TO HIS HEART. THE whooshing behind his ears vanished the second he realized that Prince was in the wind. He spun on his heel and wheeled around so fast as he headed for the bank of elevators that he must have left his heart in his wake.

"Repeat." Wyatt's calm voice echoed in his head. The wifi must have kicked back on.

"I lost Prince. I'm heading up to his room from the main elevators." The goal wasn't to find Prince. He didn't have to find Prince. He just had to find Cassie and Massey safe.

"Found him." Boomer's even tone followed Wyatt's as Jericho

punched the Up button a hundred times in quick succession. "He just came out of the elevator on his floor. I'm on the way. Peggy is sending security."

"On the way," Wyatt reported.

Security wouldn't do a whole hell of a lot of good when they'd be minutes behind when they were playing a game of seconds. The doors dinged, and Jericho stepped in, blocking the door and smashing the button for the seventeenth floor. He didn't even have to tell the handful of people to take the next car. His formidable expression must have said it all.

The ride up was terminally slow. His heart must have caught up and hitched a ride in the elevator because the roaring in his ears returned, and the rapid, frantic kick against sternum felt hard enough to fracture cartilage and bone. He dug his fingers into the doors' seam, prepared to pry the doors open when he reached Prince's floor.

As soon as the doors opened, he heard Prince roar, "What did you tell them!"

The carpet couldn't muffle the pounding of Jericho's feet as he sprinted down the hall. He heard thuds. Someone cried out. His legs couldn't go fast enough. He felt like that nonathletic kid on the playground, knowing he wasn't fast enough to outrun the bullies.

He clocked the shattered doorjamb twenty yards away. He called out to Cassie again, but he only heard the thuds, grunts, and thumps of a hard-fought struggle.

At the door, he went through shoulder first, not knowing what to expect, but from the sounds coming from inside, he couldn't spare the time for caution. He called out to Cassie again, not expecting a response, as much as needing her to know that he was coming.

In a fraction of a second, he took in the room. Massey's wheelchair lay on its side, blocking the hall. A lampshade on the bed, a gouge in the far wall where the base must have hit. The sliding glass door wide open, and... *holy fuck*, Cassie wrapped around Prince's back, Massey using the railing for balance as he did his best to fight Prince and keep him from stripping Cassie's grip from around his torso.

Jericho leaped over the wheelchair, catching sight of Tonni slumped on the floor. He couldn't tell if she were alive or dead. At the moment, between being inside the hotel room and out on the balcony, he could only watch as Cassie's grip slipped from around Prince's neck, the beat red color of Prince's face returning to pink.

Cassie screamed as her arms flailed and pin-wheeled, her weight leaning backward, her legs pinned precariously between the railing and Prince's body. The rest of her dangled seventeen stories above concrete and asphalt.

Free from Cassie's grip, Prince took a solid punch to the gut from Massey, his rage fueling his fight. Prince lost no more than a breath before he launched himself at Jericho as he rushed through the door.

Jericho heard Cassie scream again, her feet flipping up and over the railing as Prince's shoulder connected with Jericho's stomach, knocking them both into the sliding glass doors. The safety glass shattered and pebbled beneath them as they landed in the room.

Cassie!

Was she alive?

His brain couldn't even wrap its synapses around the idea that she was dead.

With the amount of fury-induced adrenaline coursing through Jericho's body, he ignored the pain in his abdomen and reached for the lamp base.

He swung.

The *crack* of the lamp base clocking Prince in the head shot through the room, sounding like an over-the-wall, walk-off home run to win the World Series. A sound that would echo in Jericho's head for the rest of his life.

Prince crumpled. Jericho shoved the man off him, not caring if he'd just killed the man.

"*Saint!*" Massey hollered.

Jericho scrambled over the sea of pebbled glass. On the balcony, Massey lay flat on his stomach, his face jammed up against the railing's uprights, his complexion almost purple from the strain.

Massey grunted. "I can't hold on."

Jericho dove in beside Massey, shooting his arm over the side, his hand clamping down over Cassie's wrist. *Holy fuck.*

"I've got her," Jericho said, even as Massey's grip slipped and Jericho took Cassie's full weight on his arm. Jericho's shoulder screamed with the shear strain.

Massey panted beside him, his strength sapped. From Jericho's and Cassie's position, they couldn't see each other. Their only connection was his tenuous hold on her wrist. Massey rolled out of his way, and Jericho stuck his other arm through. "Grab onto my other hand."

Motherfucker. The pressure on his shoulder increased exponentially with each passing second. Sweat started to slick his hand. He couldn't hold on much longer. The arm she dangled from swung with her effort to grab his other hand.

"I—I can't."

Cold, naked fear skittered up Jericho's spine at the unmitigated terror in her voice.

"You have to." There was no other way, but he refused to say those words out loud.

He almost made a promise to the man upstairs. A promise that if He saved Cassie, Jericho would never set foot in another casino for as long as he lived.

But he couldn't gamble her precious life on a promise he might be incapable of keeping.

He wanted to tell her to hurry. He wanted to tell her that he was losing his grip. That he loved her one last time. The words wouldn't come. And they'd only panic her further. Jericho gritted his teeth, his hand cramping, his arm threatening to separate from his shoulder.

Massey repositioned and managed to grab Cassie's forearm below Jericho's hand, relieving some of the strain. Jericho's eyes closed with relief. Then Cassie's free hand locked onto his other wrist. When he opened his eyes again, he stared into Massey's. The silent *thank you* passing between them.

Behind him, Jericho heard a commotion and braced for another assault from Prince. He must not have killed the bastard after all.

But the expected blows never came. Instead, Wyatt laid out beside him and grabbed one of Cassie's arms.

"About fucking time you got here," Jericho ground out, his relief so immense he almost couldn't get the words past the boulder lodged in his throat.

"Shut the fuck up and pull," Wyatt groused.

I can't popped into Jericho's head, but he refused to let the words escape. He gritted his teeth and used every bit of strength he had left to help pull Cassie up. His breaths came hot and fast, every muscle nearing its breaking point. Sweat sluiced off his body with the effort.

Inch by excruciatingly inch, they pulled Cassie up. Boomer arrived at some point, anchoring the toes of his shoes beneath the bottom rail and reaching over. The top of her head appeared first, then those green eyes that could drill straight through the bullshit in his head to his beat and battered soul.

"Hey, stranger," she said, a saucy, exhausted, turn to her lips.

He worked his way to his knees as they pulled her up. He couldn't have spoken even if he had the words.

"I've got her," Boomer said as the toe of one of her shoes touched the balcony. "You can let go now."

But he couldn't. His head knew she'd reached safety, but try telling that to his over-taxed body. Massey had to pry Jericho's hands from around Cassie's wrists so that Boomer and Wyatt could finish helping her over the railing.

As soon as her feet hit the ground on the balcony side of the railing, she dropped to her knees, nearly toppling them over. Jericho's eyes skimmed over the controlled chaos that was Prince's hotel room. Hotel security had Prince in handcuffs, and someone helped Tonni to the bed, her hand to her head.

He wrapped his arms around Cassie and held on as tight as he could, which wasn't nearly as tight as he wanted. He felt the moisture on his face as the tears came unbidden. She shook in his arms, sobbing and her breath hitching. Wyatt, Massey, and Boomer returned inside, giving them a spec of privacy. When her crying slowed, she swiped at her eyes and tried to sit up.

He rearranged her so that she sat crossways on his lap. He took her face in his hands, his brows furrowing when he said, "Don't—"

She put a finger to his lips to shut him up. "If this is where you say 'Don't you ever do that again,' don't worry. Wyatt's getting my resignation as soon as we get back. At least for any fieldwork."

"Thank fuck for that." He let his head fall back to rest on the railing as what little remained of his strength drained away. He brushed a kiss over her lips and pulled away, brushing the stray strands of hair from her face. "Are you okay?"

"I'm not sure yet." Before he could start patting her down and insisting Wyatt track down a paramedic, she added, "Physically, I've only got bumps and bruises, scrapes and scratches. But in here…" She pointed to her heart and then to her head. "I think I'm going to have a few long-lasting scars."

She held his gaze, a head full of questions swirling around in her skull. She only voiced one of them. "How about you?"

He didn't want to tell her how she'd scared a decade off his life or that it would probably be years before she could leave his sight without him breaking out into a panic and a cold sweat. But he didn't want to put that burden on her. He'd deal with his issues in his own way.

Which means you're not going to deal with it at all. You're going to bury your feelings so deep that not even those mammoth earth-borers could ever excavate them.

He couldn't argue with that. After all, it had worked for him all of his life. Why change now?

"I've been better, but this," he said as he snugged her tighter against him, "this is helping."

"Get your fucking hands off me," Prince grumbled as two of the reservation's finest took hold of Prince and escorted him out of the room.

An Indigenous woman with long black hair gave orders to several security people in the room as the tribal police escorted Prince away to await the arrival of officers from the BIA. She had a radio in her hand and gave the person on the other end directions. Jericho assumed the woman was Peggy, the head of security that Massey had been talking about.

She glanced around the destroyed room, her gaze hitting on Boomer and then finally Wyatt. "Epic cluster fuck."

Wyatt had the decency to look chagrined. "Yeah. Sorry about that."

But they all knew that despite the mess, a dangerous man would hopefully be off the streets forever. Jericho appreciated that he wouldn't have to break the news to Finn that the government owed the Butte a little cash for all the damage.

A couple of paramedics helped Tonni out of the room, and then it was only the five of them and Peggy remaining. The arresting officers had told them to expect detectives to arrive any minute. No doubt they'd all be spending the next couple of hours answering questions for the police.

Moving inside, Jericho sat Cassie on the bed. Her body shook with the adrenaline still coursing through her veins. Wyatt found a spare blanket in the closet and wrapped her up in it while Jericho ran down the hall and met the other dispatched pair of paramedics as they came off the elevator, filling them in on what Cassie had been through as they walked back to the room.

When the paramedics came into the room, Cassie rolled her eyes. "I'm fine. I don't know why they didn't send you back before you got here."

"Then we'll be in and out in a few minutes." The paramedics weren't easily discouraged, even though they could tell she wasn't in a medical crisis. The taller paramedic set down her medical bag and knelt in front of Cassie as she started her evaluation.

Wyatt, Boomer, and Peggy talked in hushed tones on the balcony, giving Cassie a semblance of privacy for her examination. On the right side of the bed, Massey's wheelchair had been shoved out of the way. Jericho spun around. Where the hell was Massey?

Cassie had reluctantly cooperated with the paramedics, so he tuned them out and searched the room for his friend. It wasn't a large room. He found Massey sitting on the floor in the small space between the dresser and the wall next to the sliding glass door.

He had his head resting on his upturned knees. His arms wrapped tightly around them.

"Hey, man. You hanging in there?" Jericho kept his voice low to not call attention to Massey. The last thing the man needed was a million eyes on him as he tried to hold himself together.

After Massey swiped a hand over his ruddy, tear-streaked cheeks, Jericho squatted in front of him. Massey looked up at him and said, "I couldn't hold on." The skin around his eyes reddened again as fresh tears welled. "One more second and—"

"You held on as long as you had to," Jericho said. "That's all that matters. If it weren't for you—"

Jericho's voice broke, and all the two men could do was stare at each other. He hoped Massey could see the undying gratitude in his heart. It wasn't deep down. It lay at the surface, bubbling over, defying any containment. When Jericho finally found his voice again, he said, "I owe you."

"I don't want anything. Except maybe my chair."

"Sorry." Jericho jumped up and wrestled the wheelchair from where it had become wedged between the bed and the wall and brought it over to Massey. "Want a hand?"

Massey nodded, holding up his shaky, non-dominant hand, the one that hadn't had all the strain on it from catching Cassie's fall. They locked wrists, and even with that small tug, Jericho's shoulder and back muscles strained. He'd be lucky if he'd be able to lift his arm enough the next day to scratch his ass.

When he got Massey to his feet, Jericho wrapped him in a hug, then held him at arm's length. "I fucking love you, you beautiful man." He grabbed Massey's cheeks and planted a loud smacking kiss on his lips that had the others in the room laughing.

"Stop," Massey said, his grin wide. "You're going to make Cassie jealous."

Jericho laughed. "*Jealous.* Hah. It'll probably give her ideas."

One of the paramedics coughed to cover an indiscreet chuckle. Jericho held the chair while Massey sat and got settled.

Boomer came in from the balcony with Wyatt and Peggy trailing behind. "*Probably*, my ass."

Cassie playfully cut him a look but didn't bother correcting anybody on their assumptions.

"Right," the paramedic said. "I think you're good to go. But be sure to get checked out if anything changes."

Cassie offered up a polite smile. "Thanks."

The paramedics packed up their gear and left. Peggy turned to all of them. "I need to turn this room over to the police. Why don't you go to your rooms, and I'll have my people send the detectives up as soon as they arrive."

"We'll be in my room." Wyatt gave her his room number and glanced around at everybody. Since no one contradicted him, they stuck with that plan.

That plan was as good as any.

On legs made of noodles, Cassie stood, wobbled, then caught herself.

Jericho held onto her elbow until she'd steadied herself. "Want me to carry you?"

Cassie shook her head, a soft, sweet smile on her face. "I think you've done enough for me today." She reached out and squeezed Massey's shoulder. "Both of you have."

They waved at the security guard that Peggy had posted outside of Prince's room, unhurried on the long, quiet walk back to Wyatt's, all of them lost in their own thoughts.

Back at Wyatt's room, he ordered room service and made a large pot of coffee. They were going to need it to get through the next couple of hours with the police.

Cassie and Jericho took the couch, but the other three could have joined them because Jericho wasn't satisfied with having Cassie right next to him. He had to have her in his lap, her head resting on his shoulder as he traced circles at the small of her back.

Wyatt excused himself from the group and went out onto the balcony to fill Finn in on what had happened. She'd much rather have been the person dangling seventeen stories high than be the one to have to make *that* call.

Boomer played waiter and brought them all their coffees. He put hers in her hand and didn't let go until she looked up at him. "Way to hold on like a boss."

He held up his fist, and she gave it a bump with a laugh. "It seemed like the thing to do at the time."

"Now, if you'll excuse me, I think I'll give Sidney a call before she gets wind of this on the news and freaks the fuck out." Boomer headed into Wyatt's bedroom to make the call.

Massey blew on his coffee before taking a sip, his eyes never leaving Cassie as if he couldn't believe what he saw. "You really okay?"

She almost gave him the pat answer of *I'm fine*. But... she wasn't.

She didn't know what she was.

"I'm alive. Thanks to you." She prided herself for getting that bit out without choking up or bursting into tears. "But I don't know how I am."

Jericho stiffened. She almost changed what she'd been about to say to spare him the truth. But she didn't want to hide anything from him or the team. She trusted them with her life. She could trust them with her emotions as well.

"Numb isn't the right word," she said, trying to explain something she had difficulty finding the words for. "Maybe immune or inoculated is better. I grew up with an unpredictable father and learned not to complain. That even as bad as things were, even as young as I was, I somehow knew that things could get a whole lot worse."

She paused to take a breath, almost afraid to put a voice to what was in her head. She didn't want anyone thinking there was something really, *really* wrong with her. Jericho continued to rub circles on her skin, switching from her lower back to the hand he had on her lower thigh.

"Today... as I hung there, I realized that was *it*. *That's* the worst. My life didn't flash before my eyes. I didn't think about all the regrets in my life. I just... I just had this calm come over me, and I thought, they're going to save me. And if they don't, for a fraction of a second, it's going to hurt like hell."

A breath ripped from Jericho's chest, and Massey's eyes widened, his color turning the same shade of white as premium Italian marble.

"But I survived. I survived the worst. And I don't think anything can be better than that."

A knock came at the door, and she peeled herself from Jericho's grip and answered it. Stepping back, she let room service in. The detectives had ridden up on their heels, and she let them in as well.

Wyatt ended his call. They each took their meal, and the detectives split them up to get everyone's story down. By the time they'd finished, all Cassie wanted to do was curl up in bed with Jericho beside her and show him exactly how much she appreciated what he'd done for her.

The detectives would probably have more questions, but they collected everyone's contact information and would get in touch if they needed to. Wyatt was unusually quiet as he showed the detectives out of the room. He plopped back into his chair and picked at a couple of his cold fries.

"What did Finn have to say." Boomer rubbed his hands together as if expecting something bad in a good way.

Finn didn't seem like the kind of guy who would be excited to get the news that Wyatt had to deliver. But on the plus side, they got Prince off the street before he could hurt anyone else, and with the attempted murder charges the BIA would likely slap on him, he'd be in jail until Finn could finish his investigation into Nadia's death.

"Finn…" Wyatt shook his head. "Finn took it better than I thought he would, considering this was only supposed to be close surveillance. He's pleased with the outcome, but he's going to want a full debrief as soon as we get back."

Massey's phone pinged at the same time Wyatt said, "Anyone want a drink?"

Massey glanced at the message, a sly smile crossing his face. "That's Peggy. She sent me her room number." He stuffed his phone back into his pocket and rolled backward. "I'll take a rain check on that drink."

"You said you weren't going to sleep with her," Boomer said, an *atta boy* smile on his face.

"I said I wasn't going to sleep with her while we're on the case. We're done, so…"

"*Massey.*" Wyatt's tone held both a warning and a hint of indulgence.

Massey grinned and turned toward the door. Over his shoulder, he said, "Don't wait up for me, *Dad.*"

"I think I'm headed to bed." Boomer said.

Wyatt glanced between Jericho and Cassie, and she squeezed Jericho's hand, not wanting to put off getting Jericho naked another second. "I think we have other plans as well."

They all said their goodnights, and she and Jericho walked across the hall to their room. He closed the door and threw the lock. Turning to her, he said, "Strip."

"What do you have in mind, sexy."

"You. In a warm bath."

She tried to hide her disappointment. She wanted to get her hands on him. Wanted to feel his skin against hers. Wanted to feel every synapse she had fire as she came beneath him.

But his idea wasn't so bad either.

In a matter of minutes, he'd drawn her a bath, making bubbles with a generous amount of shampoo. He tossed his clothes aside and climbed in behind her. It was a very tight fit, but she leaned back against his chest. He brushed her hair off the side of her face and planted a kiss on her damp skin, his gentleness enough to have her distant emotions come roaring back.

He wrapped his arms around her and held her together as she fell apart.

FEELING DRAINED AND LOVED AND SEEN AND THOROUGHLY SPENT, Cassie crawled into bed. Jericho held the covers up for her. He tucked the top edge under her chin and planted a chaste kiss on her forehead.

She couldn't remember the last time she'd been tucked into bed—if there had been a time that she'd ever been. No lie, she could get used to it.

Only Jericho's gentle sweetness was not what her body—or the rest of her—craved.

At first, she worried that he'd sit up all night in the corner chair the way he'd done the previous night. Then he lifted the covers and slid into bed behind her.

With an arm around her middle, he tugged her closer until her ass seated against his groin. Almost immediately, he went rock hard—even after all of his sleepless nights, the long, exhausting days. And—oh, yeah—that whole part where one of them almost died.

He shifted away.

Cassie grunted her disapproval and turned her head to eye him. "Where did you go?"

"I'm still here." His arm tightened around her waist, his chest still pressed against her back, and his foot still locked between hers.

She wanted more.

Rolling to her back, she kissed him. "I want this." She reached down and wrapped her hand around his hard cock. "And I want this."

He hissed in a breath, his eyes fluttering closed for a moment before focusing on her again. "Maybe this isn't such a good time. You—"

She cut his words off with a kiss before he could remind her of something she'd *never* forget. "What better time than now? What better reason than because I'm alive and I want to?"

He rolled on top of her, bracing himself above her even though his shoulder strength had to be shot. His naughty grin summoned a bevy of bees to her belly.

Could she ever get enough of this kind, generous man?

Jericho had a way of looking at her—the way that he was looking at her now—not like she was the only thing that mattered to him but that she was what made everything else in the world worth caring about.

He kissed her, his tongue diving into her mouth, quick and playful, making the shitty day fall away. She didn't want somber lovemaking. She wanted a life-affirming fuck.

Her fingers fisted into his hair. He worked his way down her body—from the sexy words he whispered into her ear, the open mouth kisses down her sternum, the licking, sucking, and teasing of her sensitive nipples, to the quick dip of his tongue into her navel.

The covers fell away as he settled between her legs and hitched her thighs over his shoulders. The little nips he made on her inner thighs had her hips thrusting upwards. She had other plans for that mischievous mouth, and he needed to get on with it before he drove her mad.

"Don't be a tease," she grumbled, her exasperation building.

His deep, throaty chuckle sent a luscious chill up her spine. She opened her mouth to complain again, but his tongue licked a long line through her wet folds, a low moan escaping her throat on a huff of hot breath.

He pulled back just enough and said, "I love the way you taste."

She glanced down at him, and she knew she'd never get tired of the view of him between her thighs, his pupils blown, the hungry desire naked in his eyes. She watched him watch her, his tongue tracing and tasting and teasing until her head fell back and her eyes closed.

He chuckled again, the warmth in the sound surrounding her.

All her senses concentrated on that one point where their bodies joined as he sipped and savored. She ground up against him, loving his mouth on her, but needing more.

Always more with this man.

She pulled him up, that sexy, arrogant smile dropping when their pelvises aligned.

"Fuck, you feel good." The words fell from his lips, and he moved with her, his mouth capturing hers. She loved smelling herself on him, loved how it made him taste. Loved the sounds that they made together.

Reaching down, she took him in her hand, slicking the copious amounts of pre-cum leaking onto her abdomen up and down his length. He deepened the kiss, rutting into her hand.

"I want you. Now." She planted her feet on the mattress and tilted her hips, lining him up at her entrance, waiting for him to break the kiss and meet her eyes. "You ready?"

"For you? Always."

She released him, and he sunk into her body, his face dropping to the crook of her shoulder as he shuddered and breathed her in. He buried himself to his balls, bracing his weight on his forearms. Cupping his ass, she pulled him even deeper, locking her ankles behind him.

The cords in his neck strained as he pulled out nearly to the tip, her climax already closer to the surface than she'd expected. Maybe it was the near-death experience that made all her nerves raw and super sensitive.

Or maybe it was the man above her.

A man who had literally saved her life.

And a man who made her want to believe in fairy tales. In happily-ever-after.

They raced toward the edge together, the sensations igniting her nerves, their breath hot, their bodies slicked, their hearts pounding. He'd already proved to her that he'd catch her if she fell, so she let herself go.

No holding back.

She gave him all she had.

A few hard strokes later, he came, her name on his lips as he filled her with his heat.

He held her tight as he came down from his climax and peppered her skin with tender kisses. When he pulled back a fraction to look at her, the love shined brighter than a star going supernova. She saw it all in his eyes. The way he cherished her. The way she lit up his world. Against her chest, his heart beat with hers.

Those three little words popped into her head. She'd never said them to a man before, and the enormity of what she wanted to say choked her up. "I—"

She closed her eyes and cleared her throat. When she opened them again, the bright expectation in his eyes had her choking up again. This man deserved to hear those words.

He deserved to hear the truth.

"I—" The fucking words wouldn't come.

For the briefest of seconds, the disappointment flashed on his face before he schooled his expression.

He kissed the tip of her nose. "I know. You don't have to say it."

What should have been a relief only made her feel worse. His cock softened. He rolled off her and out of bed and returned from the bathroom with a warm washcloth.

After cleaning up with a warm washcloth, he crawled into bed behind her, cradling her against his chest. Her body sated, the adrenaline long wrung out of her body, Cassie's eyes drifted closed. She would have thought that after the day she'd had, she'd never fall asleep again.

But she was wrong.

She'd tell Jericho in the morning that she loved him and prove to them both that she wasn't as fundamentally broken as she seemed. "Tomorrow," she mumbled.

Kissing that spot between her shoulder blades, he whispered back as sleep dragged her under, "Tomorrow, then."

So why did he sound so empty?

***

Jericho waited until Cassie had fallen into a deep sleep before quietly extricating himself from beneath the covers. Despite his utter exhaustion, he wouldn't be able to sleep tonight, or probably any other night, after what had happened.

You almost lost her.

He'd never forget the way the slick sweat had built on his skin or the slow, gradual slip of her wrist through his grip.

And the thought of her falling that fatally far...

He paced the room. Needing to move. Needing air.

Needing... *Fuck.*

Dressing in the dark, Jericho slipped on his shoes, pocketed his wallet and room key. At the door, he ditched the last shreds of his self-respect.

The whole way down to the casino, he told himself he could turn around anytime he wanted to, that just because he went to the ground floor didn't mean he had to gamble. He could do any number of things, like take a walk outside, get a drink at the bar, people watch. The possibilities loomed limitlessly.

And he wasn't fooling anyone, much less himself.

At a poker table, he traded cash for a stack of chips. He'd only play a few hands. Just enough for his mind to wind down and the physical fatigue to catch up and make him want to check out for an indeterminate number of hours.

Leaning on the edge of the table, the muscles in his forearms ached, and his shoulders wanted to mutiny and find another man who wouldn't abuse them the way he had.

But he would heal in no time, and the only scars he'd have from the day were the mental ones. For now, he'd try to bury himself in a game and let the world and all the Jordan Princes in it fall away. If only for an hour or so.

Later—though Jericho didn't know how much later because he'd forgotten his phone and hadn't asked anyone for the time— Jericho returned to the poker table after a quick run to the restroom. The booze buzz he'd carefully maintained since the waitress had found him had cleared the day's earlier nightmare from his head enough for him to concentrate on the game.

Money-wise, he was down a few hundred dollars. Not much. Fortunes could change in the span of a hand. He stuck with it, even if the man sitting beside him had to nudge his arm once or twice when he nodded off to tell him it was his turn to go.

Jericho rubbed his eyes and ordered another drink since the good buzz he had going on had started to wear off. His chips continued to dwindle, but the guy across the table had developed a tic in his right eye. Jericho knew the guy had bluffed, and the woman at the end of the table couldn't stop her nose from running.

It would be nearly impossible for anyone to beat the hand he had. He doubled down on his bet.

"What are you doing here?" Cassie's voice came from over his left shoulder. He couldn't immediately decipher the tone. Worry? Contempt? Disgust? Regret? Disappointment?

He did a double-take when he realized she'd come downstairs in a pair of pajamas and bare feet.

"Uh, oh," the man beside him said, unable—or not trying—to hide his chuckle. "Did you sneak out without telling the little missus where you were going?"

The guy with the eye twitch laughed. "*Busted.*"

Okay, so maybe he'd snuck out to come downstairs, but it wasn't what they were thinking. They had no idea what they'd been through a few hours before.

Cassie ignored the players as she stepped up to the table, her hair a riot from the sex they'd shared and her obvious restless sleep.

This isn't the real me.

Then why are you sitting here when you should have been laying in bed beside her and holding her tight. This *is you.* This *is exactly what you were afraid of.*

The real you.

"Are you okay, kid?" the dealer asked her. He looked like he wanted to drop all the cards, wrap her up into his arms, and protect her from the world's evils.

Protect her from *him.*

The player across from Jericho had the decency to lay his cards face down on the table and stand. The others followed suit, stepping over to a closed table a few yards away. Far enough to give them a semblance of privacy, but close enough to keep their eyes on the cards and chips.

Cassie blinked up at the dealer as if seeing him for the first time. *"Jimmy."* Tears filled her eyes, but being a stubborn woman, she refused to let them fall. At least not in front of Jericho. Not now. "No. I'm not okay."

The dealer palmed his radio handset. "Do you need me to call security?"

Her chin went up, and she regained some of her lost color. "I just need a minute. This won't take long."

The last sentence had a finality to it that made Jericho's heart stall in his chest, hitting a complete standstill. He put a finger to the pulse point on his neck. Its galloping rhythm defied the sudden death in his chest.

Jericho watched the silent exchange that passed between the dealer and Cassie. If Jericho's heart had still been beating in his chest, the sympathy in the dealer's face would have nearly shattered it. The dealer took a couple of symbolic steps back, but they all knew he couldn't abandon the table.

Jericho stood when she rested a hip against the poker table and turned to him. He took her hands in his, but she shook them off. "Is this it? Is this what you've been hiding? That you have a gambling problem?"

His eyes fell to the table. He couldn't deny what she'd seen. "Yes."

At some point, while the emotions flit across her face—at what his gambling meant to them. At what it meant to her—his heart started beating again, this sickly, erratic beat that made him lightheaded and words nearly impossible to speak.

"I lived through this with my fa—" Cassie cut herself off, her eyes closing as she composed herself. "You didn't think this was something I needed to know?"

He didn't have anything but lame excuses, so he didn't offer one. There *was* no excuse. He'd known that then. He knew that now. And he gambled on the idea that she'd never have a reason to find out.

And it all went to show that it doesn't pay to gamble. The odds are always stacked against the player.

He cleared his throat a couple of times before he got one short sentence out. "I should have told you."

A dark, gritty, sarcastic laugh ripped up the back of her throat. "Ya think?"

She raised her hands in defeat and let them fall by her side as she took a step back. "I love you, Jericho Saint, but this," she waved her hand in the general direction of the poker table, "I can't do this."

He must not have schooled the devastation on his face because she added, "I was waiting for the right time to tell you how I felt. I guess that time has passed."

To hear her say she loved him in the same sentence as saying things were over fractured a piece of him that he hadn't known had been so fragile. All the fragmented bits lay on the ground at his feet, too sharp and dangerous to pick up lest they lacerate the rest of him.

She turned to go. He snagged her hand and gave it a gentle squeeze to encourage her to look him in the eye. "Ask me. Ask me, and I'll leave the table right now."

He thought that he'd make her smile or at least see hope spark in her eyes, but any spark of hope that might have remained snuffed out, the frown on her face and the furrow between her eyes deepening. "I don't need you to leave the table for me. I need you to leave the table for *you*. And if you can't see the difference, then I really do think we're done."

Letting her hand slip through his, cut him like a katana.

"I'm sorry," he said as she turned and retreated, the words sounding as lame and insufficient outside his head as they had inside his head.

She stopped and swiped a hand over her face before glancing at him over her shoulder. "Yeah. Me, too."

Jericho turned away because he couldn't watch her leave. He sank into his chair, his head in his hands as everyone returned to the table to resume the game.

He folded and watched the game continue in front of his eyes, not knowing what to think, do, or say. A numbness settled over him that even the chirps and chitters of the slot machines couldn't break.

He could have lost her that night because of an evil man.

Instead, *he* was the reason he'd lost her.

The guy with the twitchy eye tossed a chip at him to get his attention. The man bobbed his chin in the direction of the front entrance. "I hope you've got a ride home because your girl's leaving."

Jericho turned around in time to see the double doors *woosh* open, and Cassie stride through, still dressed in her pajamas. At least she wore a pair of shoes this time.

"You should go after her," another one of the players said.

"I don't want to make it worse," Jericho grumbled. They needed to mind their own fucking business, even if they might have a valid point.

"She's leaving," Twitchy eye said. "How can you make it worse?"

Fuck it. Jericho started shoving the rest of his chips toward the dealer, giving them to him as a tip.

The dealer held a hand up. "I don't want your money. I want you to make this right. And if you can't do that, you need to let her go."

"I don't think I have any say in that. I think she's already gone." And Jericho didn't mean just in the physical sense.

"Listen to me." The dealer had that avuncular quality to him that made you feel like he was on your side while at the same time giving you the ass-kicking that you rightly deserved. "That girl needs someone to fight for her. Someone to fight to stay in her life. She needs to know she's the priority, not the afterthought."

It wasn't that Jericho disagreed.

It was just that if his previous life were any indication, he was much better at fucking things up than fixing them.

Cassie pulled up to Geneva's dock in Jericho's truck. The sun had risen, and if you were going by the warmth, the clear skies, and the twittering of the birds, you wouldn't have any clue how crappy of a day it was already.

She didn't even know why she'd driven there instead of straight to Jericho's cabin to grab all her things, except that she didn't think she could do that without completely breaking down, and she refused to do that over a man who'd hidden something so vital from her for so long.

He hid it because he knew you would end it once you found out. All you did was prove him right.

Maybe. But she had herself to protect.

She climbed out of Jericho's truck, her legs stiff from the ride, her eyes gritty, her lids puffy, her cheeks red and fucking damp again.

Fuck, fuck, fuck.

She leaned against the side of Jericho's truck, and That-a-way ambled over, her lips green with grassy slobber. She didn't even care that the cow slimed her fuzzy pajamas when she nosed Cassie's leg looking for alfalfa cubes.

Cassie's hand fell to the swirl in the middle of the cow's forehead, scrunching her fingers through the short hair. "I told him I loved him and left. How fucked up is that?"

That-a-way eyed her with those big, soft, brown eyes and gave Cassie a slow blink before breaking eye contact. Yeah, Cassie could hardly look at herself either.

Heaving herself off the truck, Cassie schlepped down the dock toward the houseboat, the rear door sliding open and Geneva stepping out before she even made it to the back deck. One look at Geneva's face, and Cassie knew Wyatt had given Geneva a heads-up.

"Wyatt called you, didn't he?"

"Yeah."

Geneva pulled Cassie in for an all-encompassing hug when she boarded. Taking a half-step back, Geneva brushed the ratty tangle of hair from Cassie's forehead. There was a reason why the gas station attendant had side-eyed her and asked if Cassie needed help when she'd stopped for gas.

"What did Wyatt tell you?" Cassie let Geneva lead her to the cushioned bench at the stern.

Geneva held up a finger. "Hold that thought."

She disappeared for a few minutes and returned with glasses of orange juice and a half-empty bottle of champagne that had lost much of its fizz, but it was alcohol, so Cassie didn't turn it down. She snuggled into the corner of the bench and held a square cushion to her chest.

Geneva poured herself a drink and took a sip before starting where they'd left off. "Wyatt didn't tell me much. Just to watch out for you. That you and Jericho..." She let the rest of the sentence drop as if not knowing what else to say about that. "And Wyatt called me last night as well. You know... after—"

"After the Prince thing." Cassie filled in.

"*After the Prince thing?*" Geneva's voice rose like a well-trained opera singer. "You could have *died.*"

"Yeah." A derisive huff clawed its way out of her throat. "I lived long enough to find out that falling in love doesn't automatically mean you get that happily ever after. Sometimes it just means you're in for another heartbreak."

Geneva opened her mouth and then closed it. Cassie had known her long enough to know that Geneva was dying to find out more about the whole falling in love with Jericho part. Instead of asking about that, she narrowed her eyes. "Tell me what the bastard did."

If Jericho had been standing in front of Geneva, Cassie knew Geneva would have gone for the jugular. "He's not a bastard."

That those words had fallen from Cassie's lips in his defense surprised her as much as it looked like it had surprised Geneva.

"You escaped the hotel in the wee morning hours in Jericho's truck, leaving him to hitch a ride back with the guys." Pursing her lips, Geneva took another sip of her flat mimosa. "So, I'll be the judge of that. Spill."

Cassie spilled. It didn't take long. Geneva knew about her estranged relationship with her late father. Had known the damage that relationship had done to her and how hard it had been to cut off contact with him for her mental health and well-being.

Geneva didn't interrupt. She let Cassie say everything she wanted to say. By the time Cassie finished, That-a-way had come down the dock and laid on the blanket in a patch of sun, chewing her cud. The water lay still and flat except for the small ripples from fish flitting at the surface as they fed off water bugs.

With every vehicle that passed, Cassie glanced over her shoulder, afraid that the men would show up. She wanted to be out of there long before Jericho arrived. She was in no mood for any kind of confrontation. However, she shouldn't have been concerned. She had to have been hours ahead of them.

Geneva refilled Cassie's glass, going heavier on the champagne. Cassie didn't stop her. With an excess of care, as if she were gathering her thoughts and constructing what she wanted to say, Geneva set the now-empty champagne bottle an the deck at her feet. "Jericho isn't your father."

"I know that," Cassie shot back, not managing to keep the defensiveness out of her voice.

Geneva leaned in as if Cassie were hard of hearing. "I don't think you heard me. Jericho is *not* your father."

"You said that."

"Because you listened to my words, but you aren't hearing what I'm saying."

"Fine. Explain it to me then, with diagrams and lots of arrows, like I'm a kindergartner trying to understand advanced grammatical sentence structure because clearly, I'm not getting it."

"Jericho isn't selfish. He isn't self-centered. He's put his very freedom at risk to help people he doesn't even know escape from horrible situations. And he did that at a real personal and financial risk to himself. Your father only cared about himself and what others could do for him. He put your safety at risk on multiple occasions when you were a kid because it was all about the gambling. Then he gaslighted you on what you experienced and made you feel like you should have been grateful for the scraps that he'd thrown your way. Fuck that man, and fuck him for screwing with your head and making you think that every man with a history of gambling issues is just like him."

"You're saying I should give Jericho another chance."

Geneva shook her head. "All I'm saying is to forget all the shitty lessons your father inadvertently taught you and listen to what Jericho has to say. You said you loved him, right?"

"That wasn't the plan."

"That's not what I asked." For all of Geneva's good qualities, Cassie sometimes found it a problem that Geneva could use her ability to stay on topic against her.

"Yes. I love him." She almost threw in an *Are you satisfied?* But by the sly grin on Geneva's face, she was, indeed, satisfied by Cassie's reluctant answer.

"I'm not going to say that he deserves a second chance. I'm saying that the least you could do is hear him out."

"I don't know what he can say that could change my mind."

"Me neither. But for both of your sakes, it's at least worth a conversation."

Cassie shrugged and nodded simultaneously, not able to quite put her finger on the point of her ambivalence.

Geneva scooted closer and took her hand. "You almost died last night. If Massey and Jericho hadn't been there, you would have. I would have thought that that would have been the scariest thing ever to experience. But looking at your face, it isn't. What are you really afraid of, Cass?"

The calcified rock in Cassie's throat threatened to rip through her esophagus when she cleared it. "That I'm right about him, and you're wrong. That it will prove what my mother had always told me. That giving your heart away is for suckers."

"You don't believe that."

"I don't want to." Cassie slid down farther on the bench, having a hard time staying awake any longer. From the traumatic night with Prince to the revelation about Jericho, to the heavily leaded mimosas that Geneva had poured, all she wanted was a bed and to wake up in a world where she hadn't almost died, and her boyfriend was who she'd thought he was from the start.

"Come on," Geneva said, taking her hand and helping Cassie

to her feet. "I'm putting you to bed. Take the forward birth. The guest bed is already made."

Cassie enveloped Geneva in a hug. "Thanks for listening."

Geneva hugged her even tighter. "Thank you for being too stubborn to let go. I don't know what I would have done without my best friend."

A cold shiver colonized Cassie's spine. The feel of Jericho's hands slipping through hers as she dangled high above the ground would be a sensation she'd never forget. Or those quiet words he'd whispered, so low that she didn't even know if he knew that he'd said them. *Don't let go. Don't let go. Don't let go.*

Cassie snuggled into the forward birth with the hatch open to let in the mild breeze. If Jericho hadn't been willing to let go easily, then maybe she shouldn't either.

"If I'd known you were a fucking idiot, I never would have hired you in the first place." Wyatt's words hit Jericho the second he'd opened the sliding door to Massey's van after tossing his and Cassie's bags through the rear doors. She hadn't even stayed long enough to pack her things and take them with her.

Jericho climbed into the seat and slammed the door. Wyatt turned in the front passenger seat. For once, Massey and Boomer kept their sarcastic, unhelpful comments to themselves.

Jericho's hackles raised. "Having a gambling problem doesn't make you an idiot."

"No. It doesn't," Wyatt said. "I wasn't talking about that."

Massey pulled out of the parking lot and onto the road that would take them home. Jericho's stomach rolled, a combination of knowing he'd utterly fucked up, his tenuous status between drunk and hungover, and sitting in the back seat where he still to this day got car sick.

Turning toward the front, Wyatt added, "But not disclosing you had a problem when we started the case does."

"I didn't have a choice. If we wanted to—"

"There's always a choice. And there are always other options to any plan. Putting your recovery at risk like that was a bone-headed move. Our work is sometimes dangerous. I need to trust my people to advocate for what's best for them in any given situation. Not stay silent, gut it out, and hope for the best. If you want to remain on my team, you'd best remember that."

Despite the warning, Jericho's stomach settled a fraction. So, he wasn't fired, then.

"And if Cassie quits because of you..." Massey said from the driver's seat, letting the rest of his threat go unspoken. His tone lacked some of the menace that Wyatt's had, but Jericho got his point anyway.

"I won't let her quit."

Boomer chuckled beside him. "The same way you didn't let her walk out of your life."

"She's not out of my life."

Boomer shook his head. "Keep telling yourself that."

If Boomer had been sitting in front of him, Jericho would have kicked the back of Boomer's seat. He didn't need the man saying the exact thing that he'd been saying over and over in his head from the moment she'd walked away. And the hell of it was, Jericho couldn't blame her at all.

Massey set the cruise control and met Jericho's eyes in the rearview mirror. "You have to find a way to make this right. Even if that means you let her go."

Jericho didn't answer. For the entire drive back, he couldn't get Massey's words out of his head. As much as he loved Cassie and wanted her, *needed* her, would she be better off without him?

They rolled over the cattle guard into Massey's ranch and pulled up next to Jericho's truck. As soon as the automatic locks released, Jericho bolted from the van. On the drive home, Wyatt had received a text from Geneva telling him that Cassie had shown up at the boat. Even after that long, sleepless drive, he didn't know what he wanted to say to Cassie, only that he needed to talk to her.

Geneva met Jericho on the dock before he even made it to the houseboat.

"Where is she?"

While making a keep-it-down motion with her hand, Geneva said, "She's finally sleeping."

Jericho took a step back and sucked in a calming breath to prevent himself from brushing past Geneva to go looking for her. Even in his current mental state, he knew that barging into her room while she got some much-needed rest wasn't the right thing to do. He needed to put Cassie's wants above his own.

"How was she?"

Geneva's expression softened, but it didn't lessen the brutal blow of her words. "About as good as you'd expect after the man she loves turned out not to be the person she thought he was."

"I never lied to her," Jericho said, the defensiveness roaring back.

"A lie of omission is still a lie."

Geneva didn't have to tell him what he already knew. He scrubbed a hand over the back of his neck and leveled his gaze on hers. "I love her. I never meant to hurt her."

He caught a flash of Geneva's sympathetic smile as the sound of tires crunching gravel came to him. He knew without turning around that Finn had arrived. "Will you tell her I stopped by?"

"I'll let her know."

Hours later, after going through the debrief, Finn had been called out into the field. Wyatt walked Jericho back toward the parked vehicles. Jericho stood in the empty spot where his truck had been. Turning to Wyatt, he said, "I'm going to need a ride home."

An empty one, no doubt.

IT WAS FRIDAY NIGHT, AND MORE THAN TWO WEEKS HAD PASSED since they'd come home from the casino. Jericho still hadn't heard a word from Cassie. He would have worried more about her, but her car had been parked in front of Steele-Wolfe's Security's building each morning when he got there, and it was there when he left at the end of the day.

He caught flashes of her through the window in the closed office door as she moved around one of the offices. She'd chosen to do her work there with the blinds closed instead of sitting out at the big table with the rest of the team as they did preliminary workups on potential upcoming cases.

Gil returned, but since doctors put Tessa on bed rest for the remainder of the pregnancy, he'd been on kid shuttle duty, getting his step-son Jack to and from school each day and dropping Jack off with Massey's grandmother Evie to watch while Gil finished work.

Jericho closed out of the site they used for their deep background checks, not quite sure how Steele-Wolfe had gained access to that kind of data, but he'd let Wyatt worry about the legality of it.

"You leaving already?" Gil asked as he glanced up from his computer screen and rubbed his eyes with a thumb and forefinger.

Jericho glanced at his watch even though he knew the exact time.

Time to get Cassie back.

It was past time for that, but that wasn't why he had to leave.

He'd been giving her space, but he didn't know how much longer he could stay away.

"I've got a thing," Jericho said, being intentionally vague.

Massey didn't bother looking up. Jericho had gotten used to having full conversations with Massey and never seeing his face. "You've had two things this week already. And three last week."

"You going to tattle to the teacher on me?" He didn't put any real heat behind the words. He got his work done. If Wyatt had a problem with him leaving an hour early a few days a week, he hadn't said anything about it yet.

Wyatt spent much of his working day in his office, drumming up business and taking a lot of calls that would have disturbed the rest of them while they worked.

"Wyatt has a window that overlooks the parking lot," Massey said. "He already knows when you leave."

Jericho pulled his keys out of his drawer, twirled them around a finger, and caught them in his grip. He had nothing to add to the conversation, so he didn't. He knew Gil and Massey had to be curious where he went when he left early, but he didn't answer to them. Only Wyatt. And Wyatt hadn't asked.

He would answer to Cassie, too, if she were talking to him.

He hadn't even made it halfway to the stairs before Gil called out to him. "Hey, Saint."

Jericho stopped, his shoulders sagging. Without turning around, he asked, "Yeah?"

"You know, we're here... if you want to talk."

That said a lot, coming from a man who himself didn't talk much unless he had to. Jericho turned and met Gil's gaze and then Massey's, and even though he had no intention of taking them up on it, he said, "Thanks, I appreciate that."

When he turned to leave, they let him go.

Cassie sat at the far end of the bar at The Eagle, a quite small-town bar, trying not to be noticed as she drank away another shitty week. Her phone pinged, and she almost didn't click on the email from her old boss at the Bison County Sheriff's office, but she did because she didn't have a life.

Sure, Geneva kept inviting her to dinners with Wyatt or lunches with her sister, but she knew a pity invite when she got one.

Pity invite? She's your best friend.

Okay, so Geneva had only been trying to take her mind off *he whose name shall not be mentioned.*

Though, really, she couldn't stop thinking about Jericho. He haunted her dreams. His voice traveled through the noise-dampened walls at work. His laughter resonated through her open window when he took his lunch and ate it outside. Though as the days wore on, he laughed less and less.

Wynn, the owner and one of the bartenders at The Eagle, came to check on her during a lull. "You need another?"

She'd reduced her Shirley Temple to nothing more than a

few hapless chunks of chewed ice chips and the dregs of the watered-down ginger ale and grenadine. "Sure. Thanks."

She picked up the maraschino cherry stem and nibbled on the end as she opened and read her email. In short, her boss wanted her back. The new hire had decided dispatch wasn't for them. Not everyone was made for that kind of job.

Question was, did she want her old job back?

She enjoyed what she did for Wyatt, and while fieldwork may not be her desired field, a keyboard warrior had their place on the team as well. If Wyatt was willing to keep her on.

And if she could get over the whole Jericho thing.

Which would be a whole hell of a lot easier to do if she didn't love the man.

But if she stayed with Steele-Wolfe, she couldn't spend the rest of her work hours hiding out in one of the offices. She enjoyed being in the mix.

She tied the cherry stem into a knot and made lines in her damp cocktail napkin with her fingernail. If she decided she wanted to stay, she'd have to pull her big girl panties on, sit down with Jericho, and find a way to work in the same building without all the hiding and the awkwardness.

He's the one who's been an adult about this. He's willing to talk to you. He wants to talk to you. You're the one making it awkward for yourself and everyone else.

Her next one-night stand would definitely be that. One night. No turning it into something that it was never meant to be.

Your next one-night stand? You'll have to stop dreaming about Jericho before you do that.

Or she could fake it until she made it. What was that saying? The best way to get over someone was to get under someone else? Maybe she needed—

Wynn set her fresh drink down in front of her as the man

and his date beside her left. It gave her more breathing room but left her more exposed.

Someone sat down next to her. She ignored them and pretended to be engrossed in her phone when in reality, the letters in front of her jumbled together until they were nothing more than a mass of nonsensical lines and squiggles.

The guy leaned in and asked, "Can I buy you a drink?"

Jericho.

Her palms broke out into a cold sweat, and the lump in her throat went down about as easy as a Fear Factor food challenge. She managed a mangled, "I have one."

He laughed, but it didn't have that same tenor it had the first time. "Fair enough."

The deja vu rolled through her, and she didn't know if she were up for playing this game a second time. That Jericho had remembered their exchange at the Butte word for word, quieted the riot of voices in her head telling her to shut this down. She didn't need to get hurt again.

Before she could decide what to do, she heard herself say, "But I'm not opposed to a little conversation, if that's what you're looking for."

The shy, devastating smile he sent her warmed the center of her chest, and she couldn't help the fraction of a return smile when he said, "I'd like that. What's your name?"

Were they really going back there?

Maybe *there* had been a better place. She could pretend, just as well as the next person.

She looked him up and down, and for a moment, her heart forgot it was broken and just allowed herself to enjoy what it felt like to have someone look at her with nothing but love in their eyes.

Reaching up, she peeled the name tag off the front of his shirt, the white kind with the blue lettering that said *Hello, my name is:* with his name scrawled beneath in thick black sharpie.

She folded it on itself and slid it under her napkin. Out of sight, out of mind. "Are names really necessary?"

His grin lit his face and made crinkles at the corners of his eyes. "No. Not at all."

He shifted in his seat, his thigh brushing against hers. Whatever had been her next line tumbled out of her brain. That one touch brought back everything she'd missed the past couple of weeks, and she hated sitting eight inches from him and feeling as if the Mariana Trench kept them apart.

Their eyes met, and in that next moment, the Groundhog Day vibe vanished. And it was just the two of them. Here. Now. In a crowded little country bar somewhere in Wyoming. Someone bumped into Jericho, and her shoulder brushed his.

"I missed you," they both said at the same time.

He cradled the back of her head and planted a kiss on her temple. She hated that it left her wanting more.

So much more.

"You know, I had a woman recently tell me that she loved me."

"Oh, she did, did she?"

"Yeah. And then I fucked everything up. And when I say I fucked things up, I mean that it takes *real* skill to fuck things up as badly as I did. Like *superhuman* skill. A true talent."

She had to break eye contact. The naked vulnerability in his eyes nearly drowned her.

Cassie rubbed the condensation on her glass, her emotions a wild vortex that should be setting off public warning sirens in the neighboring three states. She knew all about second chances. She'd given her father a million of them over the years, and he'd never ceased to disappoint her.

But as she braved another look at Jericho, as his love reached out to comfort her, as she took in his sincere eyes and his mop of messy hair, the words Geneva had told her that morning came rushing back to her—*Jericho isn't your father.*

In her head, she had always known that, but with her heart battered and limping along, it was taking it a little longer to catch up. Maybe it was time for her to give Jericho a chance to prove that to her. Because the hell of it was, when she'd said she loved him, she'd meant it.

"Look, Cass. I'm not asking you for a second chance. I'm just asking for you to hear me out."

"Okay." The response came quicker than she'd expected. If Jericho hadn't been leaning in, he wouldn't have heard her over the chatter of the people and the beat and twang of the jukebox.

He slipped his fingers between hers. "You want to go some-place where we can talk?"

Jericho squeezed Cassie's hand, waiting to see if she'd agree to leave the bar and talk. It was a lot to ask, but her not having Wynn throw him out when he'd first sat down had given Jericho newfound hope that they might be able to work through some of their problems and perhaps he'd regain some of her trust.

Cassie's quick nod was all the affirmation he needed. He slipped cash under her glass. "You going to finish that?"

She shook her head, and he picked it up. He hadn't come here with any intention of drinking, but a couple of swallows of liquid courage might do him some good. He tossed back the rest of her drink and sputtered, managing to swallow it down without spitting it out.

The adorable, got-ya smile on Cassie's face made his colossal mistake worth it.

"What the fuck was that?" Jericho asked as he led her out of the bar.

Cassie's snorted and couldn't hold the laughter in any longer. "A Shirley Temple."

"That doesn't even have alcohol in it."

"I came here to be alone. Not to drink."

They headed for his truck, though he had no destination in mind. It was just a relief to get away from all the noise. "Let me get this straight. You went to a crowded bar on a Friday night to be alone and not drink. Couldn't you have done that at home?"

"I got tired of staring at my four walls."

Fuck if that didn't speak directly to him. He knew exactly how many logs made up each wall. He knew all the places where the chinking had developed cracks between the logs that the owner would need to repair before the next winter. And he already had enough hardwood chopped and stored to last him two winters, and it wasn't even summer yet.

At his truck, he said, "Do you want to go to my place to talk? Or we could go to yours."

When she hesitated, he quickly added, "Or we can talk here." She brightened at that possibility, and he got an idea.

Unlocking his truck, he pulled out an old blanket that he'd meant to give to Wyatt as an extra to put on the end of the dock for That-a-way. She followed him around to the back of the truck. He dropped the tailgate and laid the blanket out in the bed. "How's this?"

"This is good."

With hands on her hips, he handed her up into the truck bed and followed her in. They settled down, the flat ridges pressing into their backs as they stared up at the stars. They were far enough on the outskirts of Murdock that the light pollution didn't obliterate all of them.

"How did you know where I was?" Cassie asked. Her question held no accusation, and he refused to start this conversation with a lie or insult her intelligence by suggesting that he'd happened to run into her.

"Wyatt can track the work phones." He raised a hand when she opened her mouth. "And before you ask, yes, he tracks everyone's phone when they are on, not only yours."

"I'm not on a case."

When he simply raised his eyebrow at her, she *harrumphed*. He wanted to lean in and kiss that pout off her face but didn't think she would welcome it. She rolled to her side to face him, her head resting in her upturned palm. "Where do you go when you leave work early?"

Her office didn't face the parking lot, but she would have had access to the security camera feed and would have seen him coming and going if she'd been interested. Which apparently she had been. The knowledge that she'd cared enough to at least check on him boosted his confidence. Perhaps he hadn't completely killed their relationship.

He took a deep breath and then blew it out. It wasn't like he hadn't planned on telling her. It was that he hadn't planned on leading with that. "Therapy."

At least now, he could say the word without inwardly cringing, even though he knew there was nothing wrong with getting the help he needed. Despite his not wanting it, some of his father's legacy still lived within him, and one of those being believing that seeking help of any kind was an inherent weakness.

A fault.

It wasn't. And his father's shitty beliefs wouldn't make it any farther in Jericho's family tree. Nope. That kind of Neanderthal thinking ended with him.

"Good for you."

"And I'm meeting with a local gamblers anonymous group.

Before, when I'd quit, I did it myself. I stayed away, but I never fixed the root of the problem. I want to fix that, and I'm willing to do the work to try to make that happen. They taught me that I'd used gambling as an unhealthy coping mechanism."

She didn't say anything else as if waiting to hear more. And though he knew the next words would be hard to say, he had to put them out there. He pushed himself up and sat cross-legged. She did the same. He took her hands in his, brushing his thumbs over her knuckles.

"I love you, Cassie. That's never going to change. But this work I'm doing on me, I'm doing it whether or not you're with me. Because if I don't do this work, I'll continue to make the same mistakes over and over again. I don't want to live like that."

She swiped at a tear which made the next thing he had to say even harder.

"If you need to not be around me for this, I get it. If this, if *us*, needs to end now, I won't like it, but I'll understand. I'm not asking for a second chance. All I'm asking is for you to leave the door open a crack. I can't promise I'll be perfect. All I can promise is that I'll give therapy, and you, everything I have."

The silence played out for a long time. People came and went from the bar. The occasional car drove by on the nearby road, their lights sweeping across the bed of the truck, highlighting the streaks of moisture on her cheeks.

He wiped them away with his thumbs and cupped her face. "I'm sorry." The words came from deep down, from a part of him that until only recently had rarely seen the surface. "I'm so very, very sorry."

Jericho leaned in, stopping a breath away from her lips, giving her the chance to pull away. Instead, she held onto the back of his neck and pulled him in, brushing her lips against his. They both sighed into the kiss, the pent-up tension leaving their bodies.

She pulled away before either of them could take the kiss deeper. He didn't want to get back into her pants. He wanted back into her heart.

"Geneva pointed out to me once that you're not my father. And though I knew it was true, those words stuck with me. I couldn't see it then. But I see it now."

That had to be good, right? Jericho didn't interrupt. He wanted to hear everything she had to say.

"I see you, now. And you're trying. They say the first step is admitting that you have a problem. My father never even made it to that step. Even when we had to go to the food bank to have enough to eat until he got his next paycheck, the answer had never been to fix his problem. The answer had always been finding the next poker game."

The deep, shuddering breath she took had the backs of his eyes stinging with moisture. "You're not the only one who has to learn to do things differently. I need to learn not to paint every man with my father's brush. There are happily-ever-afters out there, and I want to see if this could be ours." She leaned in, and this time when she kissed him, his heart took notice, and his dick did, too. "I love you, Jericho Saint."

He laughed, those five words a soothing balm to his soul. "Those words sound even better when you're not shouting them at me."

Cassie snorted out a laugh. Jericho lifted her into his lap and held her tight. If they could stay like that for the rest of their lives wrapped up in each other, it would be a hell of a way to go.

"CAN YOU COME IN HERE, A MINUTE? I NEED YOUR HELP," CASSIE said as she shimmied into the big red bow and adjusted it around her bare ass as she laid down on Jericho's bed.

"Be there in a sec."

Cassie dropped her head to the comforter when he didn't appear right away. What the hell was taking him so long? Wyatt had generously given them the morning off to get the rest of Cassie's stuff moved into Jericho's cabin since the renters she'd leased her condo to planned to move in the next day.

Some might have said that two months into their reconciliation was too soon to make any commitments, but they didn't know Jericho the way she did. They didn't see the hard work he'd put into himself. The hard, emotional work he continued to put in.

That said a lot.

And though she didn't live with blinders on, she loved him enough to give him the benefit of any lingering doubt.

He tackled each day determined to prove his commitment to his recovery and the both of them.

"You coming?" she called out again, injecting a petulant pout into her tone.

"I'm coming. I'm coming." Jericho got louder the closer he came. "Don't get your panties in a tw—"

"I'm not wearing any panties." Cassie grinned up at him as he stopped short in the doorway. The cutoff gray sweatpants he wore did nothing to hide his growing erection.

He pounced on top of her, crushing the big red bow between them. He nibbled her neck. She laughed as his whiskers tickled her skin. Grinding up against her, he growled in her ear. "What's this for?"

"House warming gift."

"Fuck." Jericho wrapped his arms around her torso and breathed her in. "You always know exactly what to get me."

He dry humped against her, his hard length settling into the crack of her ass. He shucked his shorts and tore the ribbon away, sinking his teeth into one of her round cheeks before rolling her on her side.

"We don't have time," he said. "We have one more load to bring over before we head back to work."

She reached down and wrapped her hands around his cock. She didn't play fair, and it was one of the things she knew he loved about her. His eyes fluttered closed as one of his free hands ghosted over hers.

"We can stop by on the way home from work and get the last load." She stroked his entire length skimming her thumb through the bead of pre-cum gathering at the tip. "Yours is the only load I'm interested in right now."

He choked on a laugh with her downward stroke. "I fucking love your dirty mind. I—"

From the kitchen, one of their work cell phones rang.

"Ignore it." Cassie doubled down on the onslaught and raked

her tongue across one of his flat nipples. "We have to be there after lunch anyway."

Another work phone rang. Now both of their work phones were going off.

Jericho pushed himself off the bed with a grunt and a sexually frustrated sigh and went searching for the phones. She knew that Massey had to be behind that sneaky maneuver.

Jericho walked back into the bedroom, the phone to his ear, his dick already deflated, with a shade of color knocked off his complexion. She pushed herself up and sat on the edge of the bed, the torn ribbon mocking her from the floor.

"What?" she mouthed.

"Yeah, I'm on the way." Jericho ended the call and leaned against the door jamb as if he didn't trust his knees to support him. "Wyatt wants me to come in. He's expecting Finn in thirty."

Which didn't even give them enough time to shower. "What for?"

"My guess? It's about my forgery case that Finn brought to the district attorney."

"I'm going with you." Cassie dug a clean pair of underwear out of one of the boxes.

"You don't have to go."

"You're fucking kidding me, right? You're not alone. I'm here. And I'm going."

Before she could turn back to her haphazardly packed box of clothes, Jericho caught her arm and drew her up against him. "I didn't mean it that way." After a beat, he added, "Thank you. And I really would like it if you came."

He didn't say what they both feared most, but she put the words to it. "Do you think he's there to arrest you?"

Jericho tightened his arms around her, his heart hitting her sternum with each kicking beat. "We knew from the start that an arrest was always possible. Finn didn't sugarcoat that."

"Yeah, but it's been so long since we'd heard anything that I thought—"

He put a little space between them and cupped her face. "You thought they'd forgotten about it?"

"Well, not forgotten, but…" She didn't know what she'd thought. "I'd just hoped it wouldn't come to this."

FINN HAD ALREADY GONE UPSTAIRS TO THE OFFICE BY THE TIME Jericho and Cassie arrived. Each trudging step Jericho took closer to the stairs felt like one less free step he had left. Cassie's hand clenched his, the tips of his fingers tingled, starved for blood.

It should have come as a relief when he opened the door at the top of the stairs when there wasn't a handful of armed men there to arrest him, though Finn knew Jericho well enough that if he were being arrested, he'd go peacefully.

"Finn," Jericho said, nodding to the impeccably dressed man.

Finn's crazy hours right after Quest had been gunned down had gone back to their more normal crazy even though the killer hadn't been captured. The Feds had brought in a new team dedicated to tracking the guy down, and Finn returned to commanding the local joint task force.

Finn returned Jericho's greeting with a curt nod, his face giving nothing away. Maybe Finn should have played in the poker tournament.

"Have a seat," Wyatt said as he held the back of a chair for Jericho.

Gil sat at one end of the big table, taking Cassie's spot after she'd defected to one of the offices. He hadn't given it back even after she'd turned down the dispatch job to stay at Steele-Wolfe.

Massey sat in his usual spot, trying to look busy. Jericho couldn't hear the clatter of Massey's mechanical keyboard, so he knew Massey was faking it.

Finn took Wyatt's usual seat at the end of the table opposite Gil while Wyatt held up the wall behind Massey.

"Want us to leave?" Gil asked?

Finn glanced at Jericho, deferring to him.

"You can stay."

"Damn right we're staying," Massey muttered, cutting a glance Gil's way. "If this is going to be our last chance to say our goodbyes, then—"

"No one is saying goodbye." Finn worked the barrel of a fountain pen that probably cost more than Massey's favorite computer.

Cassie sank into the chair beside Jericho. The little gasp she gave traveled around the now ultra-quiet room. They needed to get more sound dampening on the walls if sound traveled that easily in there.

Jericho sat back as he shifted their joined hands to his thigh, his grip now tighter than Cassie's as he waited for Finn to explain.

"After further review, and in light of your contribution to the Prince case and other mitigating factors, the district attorney has declined to press charges in your case."

"What does that mean?" Cassie asked.

Wyatt stepped up to the table. "It means that Jericho is in the clear."

"For now." Finn leveled his gaze at Jericho. Despite how well Finn dressed, he had an edge that told Jericho not to push his luck. "As long as you keep your nose clean. The DA is holding onto your file, just in case."

"Then he's going to be holding onto it until he retires," Jericho said.

Finn stood. "Let's hope so."

Jericho didn't tell Finn that he hadn't stopped helping people. But he'd found a different way to do it, and the non-profit he and Cassie were in the process of starting would go a long way to helping the vulnerable people in their community. His contact in Ohio hadn't been too happy to hear that Jericho had gone out of the forgery business, but he'd rather deal with Jerome's disappointment than a six by eight cell.

The door to the stairwell opened, and a curvy Latina woman walked in wearing the black tactical pants a lot of the LEOs wore, her black T-shirt tight across her ample chest.

Finn frowned as he and the woman locked eyes.

"What are you doing here?" they both said at the same time with the same accusation.

A smile toyed at the corners of Massey's lips as he watched the heated exchange.

Finn sliced Wyatt with a look full of accusation.

"She called me," Wyatt said.

"Hey, Soto," Gil gave her a nod.

"Hey, Brant," she countered, not taking her eyes off Finn.

If Gil and Finn both knew her, Jericho assumed she had to have ties to the task force in some way.

Gil started to stand. "I think maybe we should leave now."

"Oh, no," Massey said, low enough for only those at the table to hear. "We're definitely not leaving now.

That same cutting gaze Finn had focused on Wyatt sliced the woman's way. "Why did you call him?"

"To get his brownie recipe. Why the fuck do you think I did?"

Enough sexual tension bounced off the walls to power a nuclear sub. If Finn and Soto weren't banging, they needed to.

"Well, this isn't awkward," Massey said, this time loud enough for everyone to hear.

"You're not working for him," Finn said.

Soto came closer, and it was then that Jericho noticed her limp. "You don't have a say in this, Finn."

Jericho glanced at Cassie, her eyebrows up around her hairline as she watched the exchange. All Jericho felt was the relief that he'd be sleeping in his own bed that night.

"I'm your boss," Finn said.

"Oh, snap." Massey ducked his head behind his computer screen when Wyatt flicked an eraser at him to shut him up. Wyatt wasn't the kind of boss to get between his employees on personal matters, and he seemed content not to change that philosophy when it came to Finn and Soto.

"I'm on medical leave."

"Still your boss."

"Until I turn in my resignation."

That knocked Finn back a step. His voice losing some of its confidence when he said, "You'd never leave the task force."

Soto stepped up to him, her black ponytail swinging. The top of her head came up to the middle of his chest as she stared up at him. "I dare you to give me a reason to stay."

Why did Jericho suddenly feel like Soto wasn't talking about the task force anymore?

Beside him, Cassie held her breath, and Massey's eyes darted between Finn and Soto, waiting to see who'd break the staring contest first. Jericho had to give it to Soto. She didn't wither under Finn's uncompromising, authoritative gaze.

Finn glanced away and took a step back.

"Yeah," Soto said, "That's what I thought."

"I've got to get going," Finn said as if he and Soto hadn't almost thrown fists. Or fucked. He gave Wyatt and the rest of them a nod and turned on his heel to leave.

"Asshole," Soto muttered.

"I heard that," Finn said as he approached the stairwell.

"You were supposed to," Soto called after him.

"Why don't we take this into my office." Wyatt waved his hand at the rest of the table. "You all call it an early day."

Gil jumped out of his seat and headed for the parking lot before the words had left Wyatt's mouth. Massey closed the top of his laptop with great reluctance.

"Whatever you say, boss." Jericho stood and pulled Cassie to her feet, making it to the door at the top of the stairs as the door at the bottom swung closed behind Gil and Finn.

At his truck, Jericho opened the passenger door, Cassie's attention on Finn's ass as he climbed into his car and drove away. Jericho closed the truck door before she could get in and caged her against it, the salacious smile on her face giving him an instant hard-on.

He was almost afraid to ask. Afraid... but in a good way. "What dirty thoughts are swirling around up there?"

"Do you think Finn would be up for a threesome?"

Jericho threw back his head and laughed. He captured her mouth in a kiss that left them both breathless. "I doubt it. But we can always ask."

With that sexy, saucy grin she gifted him, Jericho would be up for anything she threw at him. For now, and hopefully, for many years to come.

He opened the truck door. "Now get in. I'm taking you home."

A LETTER TO MY READERS

Dear Reader,

Cassie may have gotten her man, but is Maria Soto destined to a life of unrequited love?

Or has Oscar Finn finally met his match?

Your next adventure starts here: **Sweet Justice** (Coming soon)

In the meantime, you can catch up on Finn and Soto's ups and downs in **Cowboy, Undone** and **Cowboy, Undercover.**

ADDED NOTE: After getting rights back for **Must Love Horses,** and **Hot on the Trail,** I changed their titles to better align with the rest of the series. Must Love Horse became *Cowboy, Untamed.* Hot on the Trail became *Cowboy, Undone.*

ROMANTIC SUSPENSE

Lazy S Ranch Series
Cowgirl, Unexpectedly (Book 1)
Cowboy, Untamed (Book 2)

(Previously published as Must Love Horses)
Cowboy, Undone (Book 3)
(Previously published as Hot on the Trail)
Cowboy, Undercover (Book 4)
Cowboy, Unbridled (Book 5)
Cowgirl, Unbroken (Book 6)
Lazy S Ranch Box Set (Books 1-3)
Lazy S Ranch Box Set (Books 4-6)

Wright's Island Series
Don't Look Back (Book 1)
In Her Defense (Book 2)

Steele-Wolfe Securities
Wyoming Confidential (Book 1)
Dealing With the Devil (Book 2)
Sweet Justice (Coming Soon)

CONTEMPORARY ROMANCE

Rockin' Rodeo Series
Luck of the Draw (Book 1)
Photo Chute (Book 2)
Reined In (Book 3)
Rockin' Rodeo Series Collection (Books 1-3)

MM ROMANCE

Black Stallion Studios Series
One Shot (Book 1)
Key Grip (Book 2)
Best Boy (Book 3)
Black Stallion Studios Box Set (Books 1-3)

Valley Boys
Art of Love (Book 1)
Flight of Fancy (Book 2)
Den of Thieves (Book 3)
The Valley Boys (Books 1-3)

ABOUT THE AUTHOR

Vicki Tharp makes her home on small acreage in south Texas with her husband and an embarrassing number of pets. When she isn't writing, you can usually find her on the back of her horse—avoiding anything that remotely resembles housework—smelling like fly spray and horse sweat.

Join my newsletter at: http://bit.ly/V-W-T
Join my street team and receive free Advance Reader Copies of my upcoming books at: http://bit.ly/S-W-S-T
You can find my website at: www.VickiTharp.com
I love to hear from readers. You can email me at vwtharp@VickiTharp.com

Or you can stalk me at:

facebook.com/VickiTharpAuthor
instagram.com/author_Vicki_Tharp
bookbub.com/authors/vicki-tharp
amazon.com/author/vicki_tharp
twitter.com/vwtharp